FATEFUL FLIES

DAPHNE

In fide vade.

OTHER BOOKS BY DAPHNE

THROUGH EBOLA TERRITORY

THE DAFTEST JOURNEY

Both are true accounts of travels across Africa in regions where roads were 'imaginary' and conditions unimaginable.

© Daphne Martin Heyring 2015

All rights reserved. No part of this publication may be reproduced, stored in a retrievable system, or transmitted, in any form or by any means, electronic, mechanical, photocopying, recording or otherwise, without the prior permission of the author.

This book is sold subject that it shall in no way of trade or otherwise be lent, resold, hired out, or otherwise circulated without the author's consent in any form, including the binding or cover, other than that in which it is published and without similar conditions being imposed on the subsequent publisher.

A WORD FROM MADDY

Dear Reader,

In Africa, during the 1970s and 80s, my son, Nick, and I survived some pretty hairy adventures when we sailed our dinghy on a vast inland sea near our home. We were lucky not to have been blown across the enormous lake to the territory of guerrillas so starved that they had become cannibals. That appalling fate did happen to people whom we knew. Our friends were never heard of again.

Daphne has used their sad experience and our escapades to write *Fateful Flies* which is set in 1986. She has taken liberties with geography, placing the drama in an imaginary African country called 'Kangalia'. The names of actual locations and of our family members (who really do exist) have been altered. Other characters in *Fateful Flies* are not supposed to resemble any known persons. The names of our dogs and boat have not been changed.

If you've read Daphne's book: *Through Ebola Territory*, which is a true and exciting story, you may spot several clues in *Fateful Flies* that give away the actual real-life identities of Nicholas, Maddy and Callum. There's a challenge for you!

In *Fateful Flies* you will enjoy reading about the teenagers' thrills and spills, capture and...
Well – whatever happened next? Read the story and find out.

Have fun.

Maddy

P.S. The cousins, who are the heroes of the story, use a smattering of foreign words. At the end of the book you'll find a helpful glossary interpreting those, and there is also an explanatory list of Sailing Terms. The Australian slang is explained in the text.

Fateful Flies Outline

A word from Maddy — page v

Part One Making it to Lake Kangi
Chapters 1 – 11   pages 1- 42

Part Two Baboon Bay
Chapters 12 – 16   pages 43 - 89

Part Three Enjoying the lake
Chapters 17 – 25   pages 90 - 167

Part Four Danger and Adventure
Chapters 26 – 57   pages 168 - 411

Part Five Delivery of the Killing Bottles
Chapters 58 – 59   pages 412 – 428

Glossary of Kangalian/ South African/ Latin/
 Greek/Middle Eastern words.   429
Sailing terms   430

MANY THANKS to...

My niece Tristin Sheen (née Heyring), of 'Whale Discoveries', for her super underwater photos of her daughter Dior. These are on pages 98 and 283. Thanks to Dior for being the model. Tristin is one of the heroines in *Fateful Flies*.

I'm deeply indebted to Mike and Verena Petzold for photos of *Frolic* on Lake Kangi, and for the trouble they took in getting those pics to me at short notice. (They're on pages x and 81.)

Of course it's best to start at the beginning to get the full 'feel' of the characters; but if you want to...

You can start reading this book in various places:
Chapter1, Chapter 12, Chapter 17, Chapter 26

If you start reading at Chapter 12 you need to know:

Ella Stanleigh and Carol Chorton are the oldest and youngest of five cousins who are in Kangalia to sail for a week on Lake Kangi, which is one of the huge inland seas in the Great Rift Valley of Africa. The other three are Nick Robertson, Gerald Stanleigh, and Kirstin Chorton.

Nick's home is in Kangalia but he goes to boarding school in Scotland. The Chortons live in Western Australia and go to day school. The Stanleigh parents are in Hong Kong, and their offspring, Ella and Gerald, go to college and school in England. Toby is Kirstin's and Carol's infant brother.

Unexpected complications nearly upset the plans but after a long, hot and stressful day the cousins manage to arrive by Land Rover at Baboon Bay where Nick's mother, Maddy, has arranged for them to stay overnight with the Sampson family.

Nothing has so far gone to plan so why should everything turn out hunky dory now?

It is a dark evening...

In Chapters 13 to 16 the cousins pass an interesting night on a beach in Baboon Bay. The next morning they rig the boats and set off.

If you start reading at Chapter 26 you will have skipped some interesting material.

**But if you *do* start reading at Chapter 26 then –
as well as the content of chapters 1-16 you'll need to know
the story between pages 90 and 167 which, in outline, is:**

The cousins rig up, cast off and have a great day sailing and swimming far out on the immensely deep lake. It all turns into hard labour as the wind drops. They spend the night on the beach at Colander Cove, which is in a game park. After Baboons steal all their bread, Nick and the Stanleighs sail off to try and buy replacements from a local village while Kirstin and Carol remain temporarily in Colander Cove. They plan to reunite to camp for the second night on Elephant Island.

The tail of a cyclone has hit the lake so dangerous winds make it very hazardous to emerge from Colander Cove. Nick and the Stanleighs struggle to achieve that. In the evening they then wait in vain, and with mounting anxiety, for their Australian cousins who fail to turn up. Have the girls been shipwrecked in the storm?

THE ILLUSTRATIONS ARE MUCH BETTER IN COLOUR

I digitised my old slides but the digital images had to be turned into black and white prints for the book.
This is a great pity as many of the photos are lovely in colour.

IF YOU WANT TO SEE SOME OF THE PICTURES IN COLOUR
go to the website
www.daphne.es
On the website menu click *Fateful Flies* and you'll get the colour pictures on your screen. It's really worth doing this.
On that website there are other stories that you can read and other pictures to be seen.

ABOUT THE AUTHOR

Daphne is well qualified to write about the Dark Continent. Her knowledge of and love for its fauna, flora, history and landscape is evident in her writing.

She was brought up in various parts of Africa and the Middle East where she and her family travelled widely, often camping in primitive locations.

After secondary education and university in England she returned to Africa as a teacher and university lecturer. Later she worked in Mallorca and still lives there.

This book reflects her experiences when she sailed her GP14 dinghy on one of the huge inland seas of the African Rift Valley where she and her son and friends spent time on islands so deserted that animals and birds, unafraid of humans, roamed between the campers' sleeping bags.

This book was written for:
Emma, Giles, Tristin, Bruce, Cerys and Toby
hoping that they will enjoy it and forgive any misinterpretations of their characters that may have crept in!

0. Frolic at 'sea' (− on Lake Kangi).

CHAPTER 1

Last breakfast in Hong Kong.

"Appalling!" exclaimed William Stanleigh from behind *The Hong Kong Post*.
"What's the matter?" asked his wife absently as she studied the toaster. "This thing's got a chunk of bread stuck in its innards!"
"Just listen to this, Alice – Disconnect before you start prodding. – It's about Lake Kangi – in Kangalia."
Alice forgot about her breakfast and showed interest. Her cousin, Maddy, lived in Kangalia with her husband Callum Robertson, and their son, Nick.
"Listen," repeated William, and started reading aloud a column that was headed 'GRISLY DEATHS'.
'Two months ago it was reported in this newspaper that the motorised yacht Ebony Girl, owned by British residents in Kangalia, had vanished during a cruise on Lake Kangi. It has now been revealed that on board with the disappeared British owners were the well-known philanthropists, Mr and Mrs Tang Wu, of Hong Kong... They have never been seen or heard of since...'
"Goodness!" interrupted Alice, shocked. "How dreadful! I wonder why Maddy never told us about this."
"Don't know." William shrugged his shoulders, and went on reading:
'Lake Kangi is one of the enormous expanses of fresh water on the volcanic floor of The Great Rift Valley of Eastern Africa...'
"We know about that."
"Yes, but wait till you hear the next bit.
'Our reporter has discovered that savage Bafando rebels are now using Ebony Girl. It is thought that one of the violent storms that can blow up in the Rift Valley must have swept the yacht across Lake Kangi to Bafandoland on the eastern shore, which is now held by fierce insurgents.

No sign can be traced of the owners of Ebony Girl or of their Chinese friends, who will be sadly missed by everyone in Hong Kong.'

"William!" exploded Alice. "Lake Kangi! That's where Ella and Gerald will be sailing next week! We have to stop them." In her agitation she impatiently pushed aside a colourful bowl of hibiscus blooms. Water sloshed about and splashed onto the tablecloth.

"Now calm down, Alice. Our kids won't be going anywhere near the eastern shore. They'll be footling about round Baboon Bay, in the southwest – and perfectly safe."

"We must change their end-of-holiday plans. Do you really want your daughter and son exposed to the hazards of being captured by ferocious ruffians?"

"My dear," ordered William kindly. "Stop flapping, and use your common sense. The rebels are in another country altogether – on the northeast side of Lake Kangi."

Alice didn't seem very convinced so William went on. "It's a huge inland sea and I'm certain Maddy will make sure the children don't venture far from the Kangalian side," William spoke soothingly and in view of Alice's worries, he refrained from reading out the last paragraph of the report. It said:

'Extreme food shortages in Bafandoland, the arid guerrilla-held country northeast of Lake Kangi, have become life-threatening. Not only has fighting despoiled the territory but failure of rain in recent years has aggravated the situation to the point that hundreds of people have died of starvation, and cannibalism has become accepted. It is feared that the four holiday-makers on the motor yacht may have been consumed by their desperately hungry captors.'

Alice's tumultuous thoughts were interrupted when Ella breezed in, and pecked her parents on their cheeks. She had finished a slice of pawpaw and was helping herself to a small portion of *congee* (a Chinese food) when her brother put in an extraordinary appearance.

"Good Heavens!" exclaimed William, lowering the paper abruptly, and staring at his son over his spectacles.

"Gerr!" exploded Ella. "That's the kimono I was going to give Aunt Maddy. Hand it back at once!"

"Thought I looked rather fetching in it," grinned the teenager doing a little swirl and striking an attitude. His sister couldn't help giggling. Overlong muscular arms and hairy legs extended comically from the dainty gown, which was strained round an athletic torso. Even William and Alice had quirks at the edges of their lips.

"Pooh, Nell!" said Gerald, "How can you eat that stinky porridgy stuff?"

"I *like* Hong Kong food, and we aren't going to get any more for another three and a half months... " She pointed through open French windows to the terrace where a tree, thick in white flowers, was growing in a large pot. "You can stick your nose in the frangipane if you want a different kind of smell."

"Go and brush your hair, Gerald," ordered Alice trying to sound firm. "Take that thing off and put it back in Eleanor's room."

"Well – if you insist," grinned her son pretending to disrobe, "but I've got nothing on underneath... "

When Gerr was back William asked sternly:

"Have you two got your suitcases properly organised? Remember that you won't be coming back home here to Hong Kong before you fly straight on from Nick's place to England for the autumn term.

"Yes, Dad," chorused two bored voices. They'd heard it before. So had Alice. She therefore expanded upon anxieties that seemed much more pressing to her: the dangers of Kangalia.

"Oh! Don't worry Mum," consoled Ella. "You know that neither of us has a clue how to sail. We won't be *able* to venture far from harbour."

"The others will teach us in two ticks," her brother assured her. "You wait and see."

"That's exactly what I'm afraid of," agreed his mother. "Nick is so much at home on the lake that he'll lead you astray."
"Well, I think it will be much more likely that our Chorton cousins will be teaching us to get up to mischief," said Nell slightly enviously. Kirstin and Carol Chorton, the dare-devil girls who lived in Perth, Western Australia, were adventure-prone.
"Good-oh!" said Gerald, and Alice winced.

The family from Perth was already in Kangalia. The parents, Ken, an entomologist and artist, and Elizabeth, a sculptor, were regular visitors to that African country, where they had business connections. They would be in the south collecting biological specimens while the five teenagers went to Lake Kangi with Maddy and the girls' infant brother, Tony. The Stanleigh pair were excited about their first trip to Africa. Alice, their mother, was worried stiff and, as it turned out, she had every reason to be anxious. The friends were about to have one of their most thrilling adventures yet.

1. Fishermen on Lake Kangi.

CHAPTER 2

Arrival in Kangalia. Ella's huge bag.

For many hours Ella and Gerald's flight was boringly routine; but things livened up after they changed onto a local airline at Aden. Only 30 minutes after take-off their 'plane developed engine trouble. Passengers panicked. Men wearing romantic robes and flowing head-dresses ran up and down the aisle. Women in black houbrahs tried to calm bawling children. The aircraft cabin reeked of fear as passengers who everyday ate garlic, onions, spices and beans perspired profusely, and desperately needed the toilets.

Juddering, the 'plane circled slowly back to Aden. There, after a sweaty, dreadfully tedious delay of many hours a different BAC 1-11 was provided, so the Stanleighs did not end up in the sea, or back in Yemen for the third time. They flew on, bouncing in air pockets above African highlands, and reached the Kangalian capital, Lawara, exhausted and filthy, but safely. As they touched down Ella grinned naughtily as she saw Gerald comb his hair.

"Looking forward to seeing Kirstin?" she teased.

Her brother went bright red and scowled but made no reply apart from a subdued growl.

What seemed like a whole battalion of relatives was waving from the balcony of the small airport building. Formalities were quickly behind them.

"What happened?" Maddy (Nick's mother) wanted to know.

"Why were you so much delayed?" asked Uncle Ken, Maddy's younger brother.

"Tell us all about it," ordered Ken's daughter, Kirstin.

"What an adventure!" That was Aunt Liz – Ken's wife – who was trying to restrain four-year-old Tony from jumping up and down with excitement. She didn't understand that the two Stanleighs had been through a very frightening experience. Nicky smiled and hoisted Ella's heavy luggage.

"This way. We've brought Uncle Ken's hired Kombi and

Mum's Land Rover so we'll all just about fit in, even including this mammoth suitcase of El's."

There followed a few enjoyable days of picnics and general sorting out. Then, full of plans to collect biological samples, Ken and Liz departed for Southern Kangalia clutching specimen jars and reference books. Standing among the others, and holding his sister Carol's hand, Tony waved off his parents rather tearfully but was comforted when his other sister, Kirstin, reminded him:

"Hey! You're going to spend a week with us and Auntie Maddy at the Sampsons' house right down on the lakeshore, remember? You and your pal Mark will have a great time building sand castles and watching monkeys in the trees. You can paint lovely pictures of us all sailing in two boats."

Later the friends were preparing a mountainous pile of goods for the journey to the lake. Surrounded by sailing clutter they were on a broad veranda whose roof gave welcome shade. In the sunlit garden, the tent which the boys were using as a bedroom could be seen at the corner of one of the terraces. Nick winked mischievously at Gerald. Trying not to grin, he said:

"The trouble with females is... "

Then he paused for effect — and got it. Three fair heads immediately turned towards him and three indignant mouths started to open defensively. Ella, Kirstin and Carol were prepared to give as good as they got. What was Nicky going to tease them about *this time*? But their provoking host, pretending he never had any intention of adding anything else, let the unfinished sentence hang tantalisingly in mid air,

Knowing that the girls were dying to hear the end of his annoying silence, Nicholas couldn't quite hide his smile as he went on calmly threading a mainsheet through a double pulley. In the expectant lull Gerald's smile was very similar to Nick's as he picked up a rudder intending to slip it into a padded bag. But Gerr had no sailing experience so he looked puzzled when the disobliging thing bent at the hinge and wouldn't co-operate at all! Carol had to help. {Despite Nick's comment, girls aren't *always* troublesome!}

The unusual hush stretched with the three 'victims' nearly bursting as they tried not to rise to Nicky's 'bait'. But the Australian sisters, couldn't contain their curiosity. At last Kirstin felt she'd explode if she didn't find out.

"So – you *shonky galah* (dubious idiot – but she didn't mean it literally) – what *is* the trouble with females, then?" she asked.

"Oh!" Her cousin airily implied that he had forgotten all about the matter; but relenting, he explained: "Well. Of course, it's just that they always have so much *takunda* (luggage)."

"Oy! Catapaulting Kangas! I like that!" exclaimed Kirstin acting outraged. She made as if to drop the heavy carton of provisions that she was carrying onto Nicky's bare toes. Carefully making sure that it would land a few centimetres *away* from his feet, she let go. Crash! Smiling beatifically, the boy jumped as if terrified. Then, with one foot he pushed that weighty box over the veranda's highly polished cement floor to join the heap of gear.

"I'll have you know that box isn't *my* stuff!" Kirstin's Australian twang was even more pronounced than usual. "It's part of the Commissariat. If *you* want to leave it behind and go without food for a week you're more than welcome to do so." She was about to add: "A spot of slimming won't do you any harm," but she remembered just in time that Nick was tall and slim, so instead she finished off:

"I, however, get hungry after a long day's sailing."

"Oh, you get hungry anytime, anywhere," said Gerald joining in the fun with a cheeky voice. Skilfully he dodged a half-hearted punch from Kirstin. She was grinning because she knew perfectly well that the boys were only fooling.

Most of the teasing had passed over young Carol's head. Now she looked thoughtfully at her sister.

"You do eat plenty, Kirsty," she announced calmly and factually, almost as if it actually mattered who ate the most. Caro was so serious that, although she joined in the bark of laughter from Ella and the boys, Kirstin was temporarily taken

aback by this apparent turncoat in the girls' ranks; but after a gulp, she retorted with what she thought would be the final clincher. Pointing her chin at her Robertson cousin she said:
"Well, we all know who will *really* eat most of the food, anyway."
"Yes, El of course," came the snap answer from Gerald. This ridiculous statement provoked another general burst of guffaws in which even his offended sister participated.

Poor Nell! The eldest of the bunch of six cousins, she ate virtually nothing yet despite all efforts to become sylphlike she remained comfortably plump. If the cousins were blown across the lake, starving guerrillas on the far side would have no trouble deciding which of the cousins to eat first! Luckily William Stanleigh had binned the copy of The Hong Kong Post with the devastating paragraph about hungry people in Bafandoland becoming cannibals, so nobody even thought about such a grisly subject. Little did they know that in about a week's time their comfortable ignorance would change.

"Ho! Ella doesn't eat even as much as my white mouse," said a squeaky voice. With devastating frankness it continued: "It's Gerr 'n Nick who eat a lot." Then, trying to make his point completely clear, Tony added in very wise tones: "Like hyenas, you know!"

He emerged from under an upturned cane chair where he had been playing at 'submarines' and solemnly nodded a tousled head at his two tall relatives. Everyone collapsed laughing. Of course the little chap was absolutely right. But the bigger boys couldn't let this cheek from their tiny cousin pass without a bit of horseplay.

"Traitor!" exclaimed Gerald and Nick together. They advanced upon Kirstin and Carol's young brother. Tony acted scared, and squealed in delight. Knowing that he was about to have a wonderful romp, he pretended to try to escape. One powerful arm caught his small, squirming body.
"What shall we do with him, Gerr?" asked Nicky holding the wriggling infant aloft.
"One day," said Gerald catching Tony's agitated feet, "you'll

be a great strong hungry man like Nicholas and me."
To the youngster's intense joy his big cousins vigorously bounced him on the soft waterbed that served as a veranda settee. The surface rippled about and the child yelled happily.

2. Sept '85:
Nick and 3-month-old Rana (a Rhodesian Ridgeback) on the veranda.
By late August '86, when the cousins were collecting their luggage right here, Nick and Rana had both grown tremendously, but Rana still skidded about comically on the shiny floor.
Just off the pic to the right is the waterbed on which Nick and Gerald bounced Tony.

3. Noodle, the only bat-eared Alsation -shaped 'Labrador' in the world

4. Frisky

Hearing the rumpus, three dogs arrived yelping and barking, eager to participate in any excitement. Frisky rushed from the garden. Small and alert she leapt nimbly onto the undulating waterbed adding an explosion of high-pitched "Yips" to the general mêlée. She bounced up as Tony fell, and subsided as the infant rose on his section of the settee. Joyous chaos!

Noodle and Rana, both large dogs, shot out of the house onto the veranda in a tangle of gold and buff. Ears and huge tails flipped everywhere as each struggled to get ahead. Noodle was older and cannier. Sidestepping as she burst out of the carpeted hall onto the highly polished concrete veranda, she spread her big paws ludicrously, yet effectively, and managed to avoid an undignified skid; but poor Rana was young, gawky, and inexperienced. Her long, uncoordinated legs slithered in four different directions till with a loud 'slap!' she landed on her tummy. Momentum kept her moving so, spread-eagled, wearing an expression of horrified amazement, she slid rapidly across the slippery floor. Still stretched out like a hairy hearthrug, she came to rest on the very brink of the steps down to the lawn, and lay there with the loose skin of her furry brows wrinkled up as if she found everything very perplexing. She didn't like it when everybody roared with laughter!

Noodle, now running in frenzied but very careful circles, bumped heavily into Ella who was still standing in the doorway clutching a large and bulging hold-all. The dog's impact projected Nell into the middle of her cousins and her big bag fell out of her arms like a load of lead. It was this huge bundle that had caught Nicky's eye and prompted his complaints about girls' luggage. Ella glared belligerently at her cousin.

"What does *takunda* mean anyway?" she demanded as the pandemonium died down a little. "You shouldn't use local words when there are people around who don't understand the language."

"I think it's a super word," said Kirstin chanting: "*Takunda! Takunda! Takunda!* It means 'Gear'... Junk! Junk! Junk!"

"Ha! Are you suggesting that my luggage is *junk*?" asked Ella dangerously. With a grunt because of the effort, she lifted her hold-all onto the growing heap of baggage. "The rest of us aren't as uncivilised as you boys! Some of us need essentials."

"I don't take a lot of stuff," put in Kirstin virtuously. "There's my *takunda*." She pointed to a very modest parcel well tied up within two plastic bags. *Her* clothes and painting things wouldn't get wet even if the boat capsized. She and Carol were old hands in a sailing dinghy. They had one of their own back home in Oz.

"Oh, but El always takes masses," revealed her ungallant brother. "I bet she's got dozens of love stories in that hold-all and millions of earrings, and ... "

"Ger-*ald*!" his sister's voice was ominous. "You... "

Her grinning brother tall, as she was short, lean as Nell was plump, and agile as she was not, slipped out of her way, leapt over the collection of parcels and danced round Tony's upturned submarine chairs.

"Yes, Eleanor dear?" he asked playfully, avoiding his sister with ease as, with a big smile on her face, she lunged playfully at her brother.

In a nearby tree an iridescent Lourie flashed crimson underwings. As if it was joining in the merriment, it cackled its raucous way up the scale in mocking laughter that ended on several harsh notes.

5. A glittering, purple-crested Lourie, (48cm long) spreads magnificent burgandy - coloured flight feathers as he prepares to fly off.

"No. But... " Nick did his best to be tactful. "It is a huge ... er... I mean... quite a *big* bag, Ella. Do you really need it all? We're not going on a Mediterranean cruise, you know."

Kirstin with feminine intuition, or maybe because she knew her cousin well, asked:

"How many cozies have you packed, Nell?"

"Well... er... I only put in three."

"There you are. What did I tell you?" crowed Gerald from the far side of the wide veranda. "If we each packed three bathers that would be fifteen of them – quite a sizable bundle – yes? You don't want to sink the boats with the weight of all your stuff – and *really* have to swim for it, do you, El?"

"Often the Kangalians go in fully clothed or else in the nude. So take your pick," Nick told them. "There'll be absolutely no one else where we're going, El. We don't mind in the least if you forget *all* your swimsuits at home."

There were sniggers all round.

"I think I won't come" meditated the plump girl in a threatening tone but they all knew that she didn't mean it. Eleanor was so good-natured that she never took offence and she wasn't really cross.

"That would make more room in the boats," agreed Nicky brutally. Carol however, factual as usual, was unintentionally soothing.

"But we won't get such good meals if you don't come, El. You know you're much the best camping cook amongst us all. When Nick cooks we get awful half-smoked fish with maggots in it. Ugh!" She shuddered at the memory.

"Worms are full of protein," growled the ex-caterer justifying his culinary mistakes of a year or so back.

"No! No, Nell. We really need you," Kirstin assured her eldest cousin. *She* had no intention of being chief cook herself.

"Come on," she urged, picking up the offending hold-all with an effort. "Let's see if we can sort this out together. You won't need any curlers, or make-up, you know – only anti sunburn cream. We're going into *the black stump* – the back of beyond. I'm sure there's a lot of stuff in here that you can leave behind and never miss."

The girls took a handle each and disappeared into the house closely followed by Rana who thought she'd detected a whiff of chocolate in Ella's huge bag.

CHAPTER 3

Packing Pythagoras.

"Right," said Nick when the two girls had vanished, "Let's check that we've got everything."
He sent Carol to fetch the pencil (which no one was ever supposed to remove!) from beside the telephone.
"Thanks," he said. "Now – Sails: Four for the G.P. – Yep. In that brown canvas bag, Gerr."
As Gerald picked up the bulky parcel Nicky pushed another bundle towards him. "Four more sails —for the Enterprise. O.K. – Two pairs of paddles... that's a pair for each boat... "
As Nick used the purloined pencil to tick off items on his list, his cousin carried them into the waiting Land Rover. Carol was sitting on the floor competently sorting out battens, bottle-screws, shackles and spare ropes. She stopped work to gaze up at her big cousin. He was so tall and handsome. He spotted her gawping and gently lifted her chin.
"Having a doze, Caro?" he asked. Her mouth closed and her eyes did a double take. Then, blushing, she got back to her sorting job. Nick was only three years older but she thought he seemed so grown up.
Carol was the youngest of the cousins apart from her little brother, who now arrived carrying a cotton sack held together with elastic straps.
"Saucepans," announced Tony importantly.
Nick's mother followed with another box of food.
"Have you packed the flares?" she asked.
"Yes. Two sets in the pocket of each life jacket: one white pack and one box of red flares.
"Good."
"Flares?" queried Gerr, excited by the thought. "What for?"
"In case you run into difficulties and need help, or if the boats get separated."
"The flares are for night times. We use smoke bombs in daylight because the flares don't show up enough, or for long

enough in strong sunlight," said Nick.

"Oh!"

"Weren't you there, Gerald, when I briefed you lot about the use of flares?" asked Maddy.

"I couldn't have been."

"Well, Nicky will have to explain details very carefully. I'm a bit rushed now. Haven't quite finished my own packing. Nick, make sure everybody knows how to set off a flare and learns the colour sequences for various messages."

"Yes. Sure."

Gerald imagined powerful fireworks or enormous sparklers. He half longed to be able to let off dozens and yet he hoped that an emergency, when they would need to use flares, would never arise. As she went back into the house Maddy remarked over her shoulder:

"And there's to be no letting them off accidentally-on-purpose. That's like crying 'Wolf'. You might get people rushing out to rescue you all for nothing. And apart from that – the smoke bombs and flares are difficult to get hold of in this country. So please be sensible with them."

"Aye! Aye! Admiral!" agreed Nick.

"Bailers," said Tony knowledgably picking up two plastic buckets and two unbreakable mugs. All had long cords for tying them to the boats. Bailing was Tony's speciality: a lovely, messy, splashy job that he thoroughly enjoyed.

"Good-oh. Put them over there next to Pythagoras. And – here, Tony! Take the two big, mopping-up sponges as well." The little fellow grabbed the strings that Nick was holding out and strutted over to the vehicle.

"Pythagoras?" queried Gerald.

"All our Land Rovers have had the same name," explained his cousin. "When I was a baby we had an ancient model that had no streamlining at all. It was all right angles, so my parents called him 'Pythagoras'. Besides – his number plate was 'BC 585' and that's about the year when the ancient mathematician was born. Since then every time we've changed the Land Rover we've kept the number plate.

We love him! He's taken us over some really rough tracks in the past."

Tony didn't know anything about the square on the hypotenuse, but neither did he need anyone to explain about the Land Rover's name. This might be the first taste of the Dark Continent for the Stanleigh pair but the Chortons made frequent visits to Kangalia so the little chap was familiar with such details. Enjoying the din of cups rattling about inside pails that were themselves bouncing noisily over rough ground he dragged the bailer buckets across the dirt drive towards Pythagoras. The big lumps of foam danced along behind the pails with Frisky in close attendance, snapping at the cavorting objects. Giving her high pitched "Yips!" of excitement she pranced in circles round the small boy and his fascinating load. Rana, who had abandoned Ella in disgust when the chocolate was hidden in a cupboard, lolloped seriously but vociferously at the rear of the procession.

Nicky watched till he was sure the bailers and sponges had reached their destination, *and* had been left there! With Tony you could never be sure... Lake Kangi storms were sometimes vicious so he knew that bailers could make the difference between sinking and surviving; but he couldn't foresee how vital they would be in three day's time as Kirstin and Carol battled desperately in a gale.

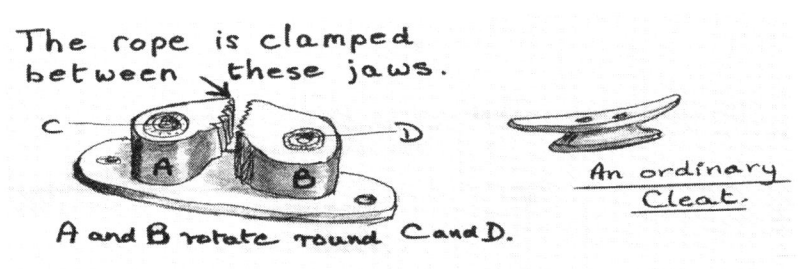

The rope is clamped between these jaws.

A and B rotate round C and D.

An ordinary Cleat.

One kind of Jamming Cleat

6. You can use a cleat instead of your hand to hold a rope.
The diagram shows 2 kinds of cleat for fastening the end of a halyard, sheet or any rope. A 'halyard' is a rope that, tied to the top of a sail, pulls it up. A 'sheet' is a rope that, tied to the sail's lower corner, pulls in the sail or lets it loose.

7. There are lots of Baobab trees in the Rift Valley. This one was pink.

CHAPTER 4

Disappointment.

Kirsty appeared with a small overnight bag wrapped in plastic.
"I think we're all set," she said. "Here's Ella's bundle."
Both boys looked at her with awe.
"*How* did you persuade my dear, demented sister to reduce her *takunda* so drastically?" Gerald gasped. "She usually travels with the whole caboose *including* the kitchen sink."
"Easy!" Kirstin assured him. "We just threw out all unnecessary things. Packed a small face towel instead of a huge double-sized bath robe, and… " Magnanimously she added: "Oh, but I did allow her two books. – Awful sloppy things."

Kirstin had every intention of dipping into Ella's love stories herself, but her scornful tone would never have led anyone to think so. In fact neither girl got the chance to so much as open either book, which ended up sopping wet, with pages glued together by lake water. In a swamped boat when struggling to survive a dreadful storm the last thing they thought of saving were Ella's romantic novels. However, all that was in the future, and just now they were packing.

"Where are the killing bottles?" Gerald wanted to know.
"*Killing bottles?*" Carol sounded horrified.
"Yes – you know – to kill the Lake Flies that we're going to catch for Uncle Ken – your dad." Gerr spoke happily and unfeelingly. But his young cousin didn't like the idea at all.
"Oh no! You mustn't call them that!" she said in a tight voice. "That's awful. In our house we call them Preserving Flasks."
"That's a good name," approved Nicky. "After all, the stuff inside the jars will kill the flies first but then it will preserve them. They mustn't go rotten before we can get them back for Uncle Ken to examine. Where are the containers, anyway?"

Kirsty, who had suddenly vanished, re-appeared looking surreptitious and cradling two enormous clip-topped flagons. Each was half full of a colourless liquid.

"Here," she said. "Dad gave them to me before he and Mum left. Nicky, he told me we mustn't let your mum see them!"

"Why?"

"Because he borrowed them out of her pantry without asking her."

Nick was laughing. "They *really are* preserving jars," he chortled. "They're her very, *very* precious Kilners for jams, and pickles, and potted fruit and so on. My goodness! She'll be awfully cross if we break them – or let them sink!"

"Do you always put your Dad's specimens in pickling pots?" asked Gerr, amazed. Used to a very correct and well-organised kitchen at home he was fascinated and rather horrified.

"Oh yes, of course. Unless something else comes in handier."

Gerald gaped, but pressed the point.

"Do you sometimes use the same containers for beetles and jelly fish or embryo sharks, or what-have-you... and then later for plums, peaches etc... ?"

"Well – yes – naturally. It just depends on what we need the jars for most."

Kirstin could think of nothing more ordinary than her family's use of kitchen items.

"Horrible!" said Gerr shuddering. "You and your arty family! Your mum and dad are so busy with their sculpture and painting and insects that I don't suppose they'd even notice if the specimens and the jams and pickles were all mixed up together in the same glassware!"

Carol considered this in her usual earnest way.

"They *might* notice," she decided. "The jam and stuff would spoil the specimens."

"But it hasn't happened yet. At any rate none of us noticed if it has!" twinkled Kirsty. "Come on. Let's get them hidden someplace where they won't smash."

"What's the stuff in the bottles?" asked Nicky.

"Gin," Kirstin told him matter-of-factly.

"Gin!" The boys were astonished.

"Yes. Well — formalin's so dangerous. Makes ghastly white fumes and blinds your eyes and chokes you... We always use gin for Dad's specimens."

"And I just happen to guess that your dad 'borrowed' the gin from my dad's booze cabinet," giggled Nick.

"But, of course," agreed Kirstin affably. "That's another reason not to let your mum see the Kilners. And the third reason is because Aunt Maddy thinks we shouldn't try to catch Lake Flies at all. She says it's much too dangerous."

"Well — Dad was only joking really," said Caro wisely. "We'll be sailing at about the time of full moon; and the Lake Flies are usually supposed to appear when the moon is new. Besides Dad knows we'll never manage to sail far enough north to get to the places where they hatch."

"We can have a jolly good bash to get there."

Nicky's voice was determined and his eye held a decided glint that boded ill for caution.

"Look!" said Carol. "A red-headed woodpecker on the jacaranda tree."

"I know. I seed him afore," Tony announced unexpectedly. "Aunt Maddy sez he's tapping for insets."

"Insects," corrected his sister automatically.

"Ha!" laughed Gerald. "The insects are inset into the bark! He's got a point."

"Yes. A pointed beak!"

The others groaned.

Tap. Tap. Tap... Tap. Tap. Tap...

They all watched the industrious little bird pecking his way round the branch, and jumped when Ella suddenly arrived and explosively dropped the final food box. She announced flatly:

"We can't go!"

"We can't go! What *do* you mean?"

"We can't go to the lake. We can't do our cruise." Nell sounded really fed up.

She'd been seriously doubtful about whether she actually wanted to spend a week sailing about in a small dinghy on a huge expanse of deep African water, sleeping on deserted beaches and hobnobbing with hippos and crocs... no doubt being seasick... getting horribly dirty... But now that it was all off she suddenly realised with surprise that she was very disappointed.

The others stared at her too puzzled and shocked for speech. Surely she wasn't hoaxing? Nell didn't joke about that sort of thing. Besides, it was late August – not April 1st... Her brother was the first to recover.

"Don't be daft, El. Of course we're going. We're absolutely ready and we're supposed to be off in... " He looked at the waterproof watch his godfather had given him in anticipation of the cruise. It had a compass and a light incorporated on the luminous face. "We'll be off in ten minutes from now."

Ella explained in the same flat tone that she had used before.

"Maddy can't drive us to the lake. Nick's Dad's secretary has just phoned from the office. Five business visitors are arriving this afternoon. Aunt has to collect them from the airport and also prepare a big dinner party for tonight. *And* she's got to put two of them up for a week. *And* one of them's bringing a wife so Aunt Maddy will have to take the wife sightseeing and look after her all the time that the business visitors are here. So... " Ella's voice trailed to a miserable halt. The list of calamities was too great. She stared unseeingly at a lovely russet hoopoe that was bustling about the lawn.

The stunned silence became, if possible, even thicker. "*BLOW* business visitors! *BOTHER* them!" exploded Nicholas stamping violently. He had had far too much experience of this sort of thing. "Why can't my flipping father warn us in advance? I mean – Mum could have taken us to the lake and dropped us there last week... Or even yesterday... He *must* have known the blimmin office visitors were coming! In nine days' time we're all leaving for next term in the U.K. – or in Oz. We can't delay the cruise."

"I expect he just forgot about out plans," said Ella who also knew Uncle Callum of old. The hoopoe raised a splendid ginger and black crest, and looked at her out of one brilliant eye with his head cocked sideways. Then he resumed the apparently urgent business of hunting for hidden larvae. He stabbed the lawn with his long needle-like beak.

Jab. Jab... Jab. Jab... Jab. Jab...

'Wish he'd attack the business visitors instead of the grass,' thought Nell as the hoopoe gave a particularly vicious poke. How would they spend the next week if they couldn't go sailing?

"BLOW! BLOW! BLOW! BLOW!" Gerr was almost beside himself with fury. His face was pale and his lips thin with anger.

"Puking Possums!" exclaimed Kirsty and Caro explosively. It was their most fearsome expletive and it just about summed up everybody's furious, baffled distress.

8. Hoopoe. (abour 28cm long). Eats insects, including larvae of Processional Caterpillars that attack pines.

"Certainly! In fact Puking Possums *squared*!" agreed Nell strongly and bitterly.

All their preparations... All their plans... All their happy anticipation... Tony looked wonderingly at his two sisters and three cousins. Evidently something terrible had happened. "Wailing wallabies!" he concluded dismally.

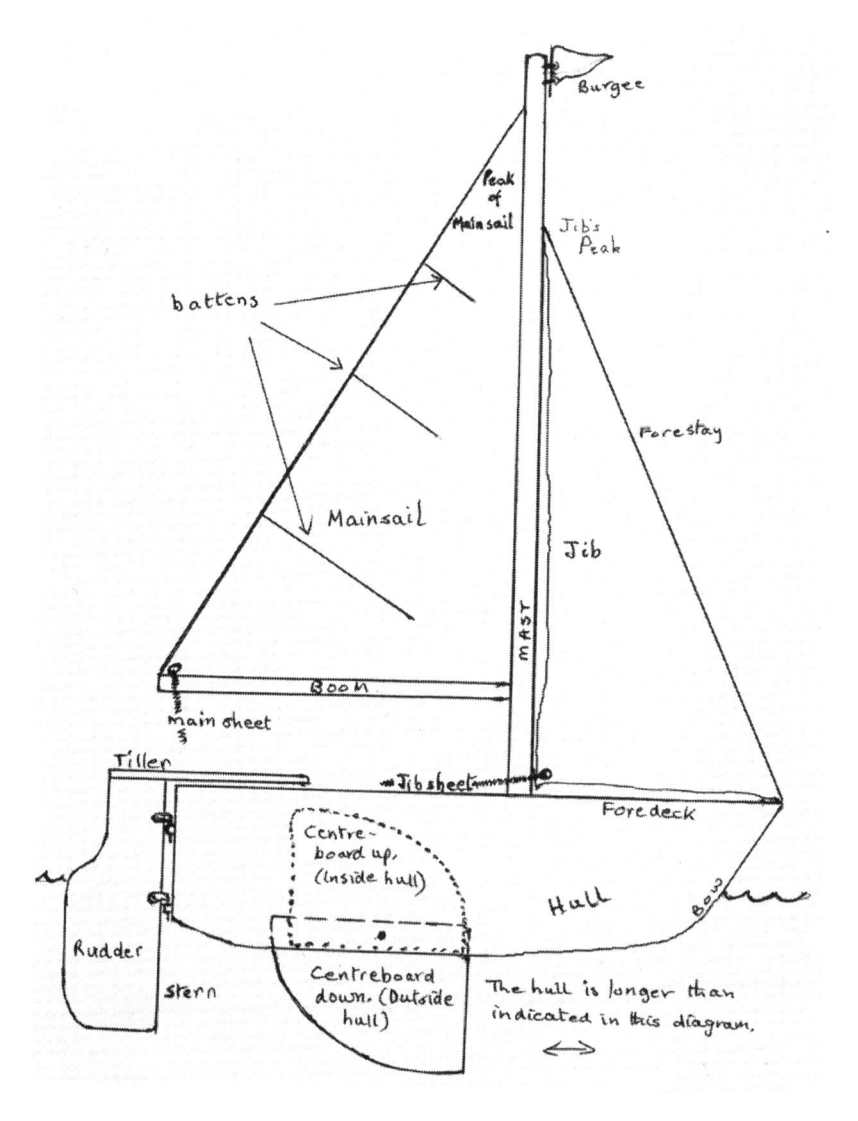

9. Diagrammatic side view of a dinghy with mast stepped on the foredeck. You can use this diagram for reference later - if necessary.

CHAPTER 5

Ella to the rescue?

Glumly they sat under the jacaranda. The immense tree was completely bare of leaves yet it was a glorious sight because of the incredible froth of indigo flowers that effervesced on all the boughs. The cousins' mood was even bluer than the blooms, and they didn't appreciate or even notice the beauty above their heads. The woodpecker still tapped busily. The hoopoe still hurried round stabbing the lawn as before. Theoretically the sun was still shining as brightly as it had ten minutes earlier. But for them the world had turned dark and depressing. Everything was dim and gloomy.

The dogs, catching their mood, lay silently with their noses on their paws. Gerald looked yet again at his new watch. 'If it hadn't been for stupid 'phone calls and even stupider business visitors,' he thought bitterly, 'we'd now be bouncing off down the road.' They'd be happily jammed in the Land Rover with Maddy at the wheel and Tony probably balanced on top of the luggage in the back.

Aunt had planned to spend an enjoyable week with the Sampsons at Baboon Bay, have a well-earned rest, do some sketching, and bring some variety to the lives of the small number of expatriates who formed the isolated Baboon Bay community. Tony would jump off the rocks and make sand castles with his friend Mark Sampson. Meanwhile the five older cousins would sail the lake exploring islands south of Baboon Bay and sleeping on beaches. They would all meet up for a couple of camping nights in the middle of the week.

Instead, here they were – desperately miserable. Obviously it would be advisable to remove their bundles from the Land Rover before the odious visitors arrived. But there was still time – several hours in fact – before that dire invasion; and no one had the heart to start unpacking. Joyous expectation had given place to dull despair.

"We could go by bus," suggested Carol optimistically.
"There aren't any coaches to Baboon Bay," mumbled Nick in a depressed voice. "Only local buses, and they take over nine hours... if they don't break down. They're extremely crowded with sweaty people, and horribly badly ventilated. I know. I've been on them."
"And the weather's awfully hot just now," put in Kirstin with a wealth of meaning in her tone.
"We can't possibly hitch," stated Gerr being practical for once. "There are far too many of us, and we've got far too much *takunda*. It just wouldn't work."
The others agreed and fell silent again.
"Train?" suggested Ella. Laughing mirthlessly, Nick confirmed their fears:
"There's only one short line in Kangalia and it doesn't go to Baboon Bay."

Dreariness deepened. Lackadaisically they watched a chameleon carefully cross the drive. Its slow progress and glum expression epitomised their despair.

10. Chameleon

At last Kirstin said desperately:
"We'll just *have* to go by bus. Maybe Maddy will drop us at the terminal at dawn tomorrow."
As no one had any other ideas they all trooped into the kitchen where hurried preparations for a four-course dinner for twelve people were in full swing.

Nick's mother, looking harassed, had flour on her nose but, sympathising with their frustration, she didn't order them brusquely out of her way. Patiently she listened to their request.
"Well. It's an idea," she temporised. "But I'm afraid I'll have to refuse permission."
"*Why*?"
"We won't mind the squash."
"We've got money to pay the fares."
Protests poured out of the five cousins.
"Now listen. The heat and the crush and the constant bumping and jarring will probably give you horrible headaches. Besides, I'm sure Alice wouldn't like the idea of Nell and Gerald travelling with goats and sheep and pigs and chickens, window frames, furniture, unwashed humanity, and goodness knows what else."
"It's not very nice when your neighbours are spitting chewed sugar cane remains all over the floor," added Nick.

Ella blenched. So did Gerr, but he swallowed hard and nearly said: "We needn't tell her." However, he thought better of that and stopped. He knew Aunt Maddy would never allow prevarication. Besides he could imagine his mother's reaction if she ever got to hear of such an episode, and he trembled. Dad, of course, wouldn't object. He'd been brought up in Africa himself. But Mum was different. Apart from now living in super-civilised conditions in Hong Kong, she hadn't been out of England much and was always so clean and beautiful. She just didn't understand dirt.

Strangely Ella wouldn't actually mind the jostling and the hoi paloi. She liked people. But Gerald couldn't deny that she probably would get the most painful headache. What a bore! But then… In all honesty Gerr had to admit that he hadn't felt too good himself that hot day last summer after the bus journey in Spain. And that had only been a fairly short trip.

"A lot of the road is under repair at the moment," Maddy went on studying the mutinous faces in front of her and wondering what she could suggest to replace the cruise on the lake.

"That means the traffic has to leave the tarmac – such as it is – it's in a shocking state these days – and take diversions on rough tracks through the wild. It's horribly dusty in the slow old bus with all the windows half-open: not open enough to cool the inside but gaping more than enough to admit *clouds* of dust all along the route. I shouldn't be a bit surprised if all of you didn't get bouts of nasty sinus trouble."

The list of miseries went on…

"The waterproof covers of your bundles are certain to get torn if you go by public transport. They'll be on the roof of the rackety old bus, and I expect one or two will bounce off and be lost for ever. It'd be no joke if a sleeping bag or some sailing equipment went missing."

"But it's our only way to get to the Baboon Bay!" wailed Kirsty. "Oh – If *only* I could drive! Tony, take your fingers out of the sugar basin!"

For a second Nick brightened. He said: "*I* can drive!" But then he remembered. "But I'm too young to have a licence. Bother it!"

He had learnt to drive at the age of twelve and his mother let him take over Pythagoras or her little Fiat whenever they were in the bush, or on big properties with private roads. She wanted him to be able to manage the cars in case he ever needed to do so in an emergency. But trundling round tea or tobacco estates was not the same as threading busy roads with Pythagoras stuffed full of a crowd of cousins and a mountain of luggage. Sinking deeper into despond, he didn't notice Ella taking a sharp breath. Gerald looked sideways, and then prodded her with a sharp elbow.

"El's got her driving licence," he announced proudly. "She passed her test first go last March. Mum and Dad gave her a yellow Beetle to celebrate. Remember? Now she drives to and from college every day – and to other places as well."

Yes. Now that he mentioned it, everyone did recall Nell's triumph. But his sister was looking scared.

"I couldn't possibly drive the Land Rover," she gasped. "It's so big! And heavy! And the roads and traffic here are so strange... so different from England... I mean... "

Maddy was gazing at her in a measuring sort of way.

"We-ell... " she murmured.

"You drove that jeep thing on the farm near Hastings last Easter," urged Gerald. "I bet Pythag is just as easy."

"Oh no! Oh gosh! " gulped his sister.

"Go on. I bet you can! Of course that handsome farmer chap isn't around to encourage you... You really liked him sitting beside you with his hand over yours on the gear stick... " added Gerr letting all sorts of cats out of bags. "You can make this an excuse to write to him to tell him how well you drove in Kangalia. What was his name? Richard... or Barry... or something. He'd love to hear from you."

Ella had gone bright puce but she said firmly.

"His name's Norman."

"There you are, then," Gerald wasn't abashed. "I knew it had something to do with William the Conqueror. Told you we were at Hastings." Everybody laughed. There was hope in the air.

Maddy made a quick decision.

"We'll see. Kirsty and Caro, go and cut flowers from the garden and arrange nice vases in the sitting room, hall and dining room – Oh! You know where – in the usual places. Throw out the old flowers.

Nick and Gerr, in the spare room, please make up the beds, put out clean towels and turn on the hot water heater. Vacuum the hall carpet. Rana and Noodle have just brought in a whole whirlwind of mouldy leaves."

She paused, then went on thinking things aloud.

"We'll have that banana and brandy pudding. Cook can get on with that by himself.

Eleanor, you and I will go out in the Land Rover now, this minute, and see if we can teach you how to cope. Tony! Leave that sugar alone! Go and help Kirsty and Caro, there's a good boy."

Stunned by her aunt's rapid thinking aloud and all the orders, but mostly by the prospect of the ordeal just ahead, Ella gasped, went very pale and then blushed bright red.

"I haven't got a Kangalian licence," she choked.

"That's all right. You're a visitor. You're allowed to use your British licence."

"Go it, El!" shouted Gerald thumping his sister on the back. She staggered. Much as she wanted to help she felt matters were getting out of hand. They didn't understand... How on earth would she be able to manage that huge vehicle?

"You'll be O.K." Nick assured her. "'Seasy! Heavy but easy. *I* can do it so I'm sure *you* can."

"Good old Mum!" he went on. "I'm sure you'll teach her fine! After all – look how you taught the dogs all sorts of things... "

Ella didn't quite appreciate the last sentence but the others were all too delighted to bother with details. Tony, not fully grasping the situation, understood that there was cause for jubilation and started a war dance giving shrieks of joy and exuberantly repeating "Wailing wallabies!" (happily this time) at the top of his voice. Rana, never one to be outdone in rumbustiousness, joined in heartily with dangerously waving tail, loud barks and great excited bounds.

"OUT!" shouted Aunt. "Out of this kitchen this *instant*!"

They all scattered. Maddy gave some high speed instructions to the cook, wiped her hands on her apron, rushed outside to Pythagoras, shot back inside to comb her hair and find the car keys, and hurried outside once again. All three dogs immediately leapt into the vehicle and sat on the front seat expecting an exciting expedition, or at least a trip to an interesting walk.

"Out! *Out!*" repeated Maddy. "We can't have you with us when a lesson is going on. Out, I say! *Out!* Frisky *you* haven't passed your test, so *move!*" Frisky, sitting in the driver's seat, pointed her long snout into the air and looked supercilious, ignoring orders. Next to her Noodle thumped her tail vigorously, pleading to be allowed to stay in the car. But they were swept off their high perch and down onto the drive. Then Nell and Maddy were off... or they would have been off if Ella had engaged the correct gear! Unfortunately the Land Rover started to grind its way *backwards* instead of forwards!

What started as a cheer turned into a groan.
"Never mind," Nick re-assured the others, "my Mum and I both made that same mistake when we started driving this particular vehicle – we did it *dozens* of times. First gear is dreadfully difficult to find on this Pythagoras. The reverse slot always seems to get in the way."

After a few more jerks and mis-starts, Ella crawled the Land Rover out of the gate and down the dirt lane towards the proper road. The others clapped and shouted. Gerald suddenly felt his hands hurting because he was holding his thumbs so hard.
"Well she didn't hit the gate post," said Kirstin as they all rushed off to do their allotted jobs. Would Ella get the hang of the vehicle well enough to drive them to the lake? It was a terribly long way and the road was awful.

Tony and the three dogs took themselves off suspiciously quietly and were temporarily forgotten. They were next seen (by Cook) looking very replete, all four sitting companionably round a well-licked plate. Earlier in the day there had been a splendid chocolate cake on that dish.

11. Taken in 1981. Nick, Kirstin and Carol with friends jumping into Lake Kangi off rocks near Baboon Bay. In 1986, when Fateful Flies happened, Tony was planning to jump off a nearby, lower rock.

CHAPTER 6

The horrors of the eastern shore.

Thirty-five minutes later Pythagoras rumbled in through the garden gate with a beaming Ella apparently in full command. Everyone rushed out to welcome the home-comers.
"Good old El!"
"Hurray for Aunt Mad!"
Catching the optimistic cheeriness Tony ran headlong onto the drive, clapping and shouting. Kirstin only just grabbed him in time to prevent a nasty accident.

Nell jammed on the brakes and the heavy vehicle shuddered to a stall. Frisky and Noodle jumped up at the doors to show that their delight was equal to anyone else's and Rana ran round yowling.
"Right. She'll do! Load up anything that's not yet packed," ordered Maddy.
There was a chorus of:
"Oh! Thank you!"
"Ripper!"
"Wow!" and
"Corker!"

As the doors were flung open the dogs leapt onto the front seats looking hopeful and happy. Their eyes glowed. Their tails thumped. The last bits of luggage were crammed into the back.
"Now come and have a quick snack," said Aunt Maddy. Make it snappy because you'll be leaving rather later than planned and you don't want to be driving after dark.
"Oh! What splendid flowers, you two. Is the spare room impeccable, boys? Good.
"Thank you – all of you."

When Maddy brought a platter of hot samoosas out of the microwave and lifted a huge jug of milk from the fridge, the cousins were aware of unusual earnestness in her voice. They looked enquiringly at her.

"Now listen, you lot." she said as she placed the dish on the dining room table. "I'm not at all happy about this Lake Fly project of yours."

"But why?" asked Gerald. "We promised Uncle Ken we'd bring him samples of the miniscule flies that hatch just under the surface of the water. He needs them for his research."

"The season's right. They emerge about this time of the year," added Kirstin.

"Catching them won't be difficult," Nicholas assured his mother erroneously. He wouldn't admit that collecting the insects would entail sailing into an asphyxiating fog of tiny flies. "The only awkward bit will be getting far enough north to reach their incubating areas."

"Unless the winds are exceptionally strong there's little chance of you getting there at all," agreed his mother. "But just think... "

"I never think. It's a mistake... " began Gerald facetiously but Ella stepped on his toe so he subsided.

They all tried to look serious and attentive when in fact their minds were on delicious hot, greasy samoosas. The original mound of small, scrummy, spicy triangles was rapidly dwindling to a hillock, and even that would soon be gone.

"The Lake Flies swirl out of the water and form an incredibly dense cloud," Aunt Maddy told them.

"Yes. We know," nodded Kirstin licking her fingers energetically. "It'll be so thick that we'll be able to swing a towel, or basket, or basin, or anything, through it and we'll collect thousands of the little beasties just with one sweep."

"Correct. Now if you sail into that cloud you could be suffocated. The boat and sails will be coated with literally millions of flies all stinking of fish and I doubt whether we would ever get rid of the smell. Once I drove through a swarm that had been blown over the shore and it took about a month of washing before I could get into the car without puking. And I couldn't have been in the fog of flies for more than a few seconds. I expect the gungy mess would ruin the sails for ever. But that's a very minor point compared with the desperately real danger. If I'd been there when you discussed the project with Ken I'd have stopped it." She paused briefly but went on: "Local fishermen paddle like mad to get away from Lake Flies as they burst out of the water's surface, and the men are sometimes killed if they can't escape from the spume of millions of little midges; and here are you actually planning to sail *towards* a cloud and capture some of them… "

"But such miniscule little creatures couldn't hurt a fly" said Caro and then blushed as she realised why the others had giggled.

"No. Of course, each one is harmless on its own. But the air gets so utterly full of insects that sometimes fishermen can't help breathing them in. Their lungs become all congested. They asphyxiate: coughing, spluttering and choking to death. I suppose you could call it 'drowning in Lake Flies'."

There was an appalled silence. What a dreadful way to die!

"So you see why I'm worried? I think it was very wrong of my silly brother to put the idea of collecting his wretched specimens into your heads."

"Well, to be honest," said Ella astutely, "I thought at the time that he had a twinkle in his eye, and I wondered why. I concluded it was the wrong season or something and there wouldn't be a single fly in sight."

"But in any case" put in Nick, "I don't believe he thinks we'll ever get anywhere near the hatching grounds. I suspected all along that he was just 'Giving us an objective'. You know how he loves to give people 'objectives,' Mum."

"Hm," sighed his mother.

"As if we *need* an – a –a – a whatsit – an objective!" snorted Gerald. "We're going for the sailing aren't we, and the camping, and the birds… and… and… things."

"Yes, of course. But still… well… I know you lot… How are you actually planning to catch the flies if you *do* manage to reach the correct part of the lake?"

Nicky neatly bit off a corner of his final samoosa and squeezed a liberal potation of lemon juice into the hole. He was extremely partial to the tasty speciality.

"We hadn't actually got that far in our schemes," he admitted. "But we understand your point, Mum. We'll be terribly sensible and horribly careful. That is *if* we manage to get anywhere near the right region."

"Yes. We will," echoed the others, and Tony accepting the last samoosa from Aunt Maddy, who did not yet know about the chocolate cake, also nodded solemnly.

"Hm," said Maddy again. "I don't like it. And the other thing is the actual location... "

"Oh. You mean it's too close to the Bafandoland border?" said Kirstin, who sometimes read the newspaper. She'd been wondering about this point herself, and had even discussed it with her sister, who now assured her aunt:

"We absolutely promise not to go anywhere near the border with Bafandoland. We'll keep most definitely *miles* from their shoreline. We really, *really* don't want to get mixed up in a terrorist war, thank you very much. We honestly and truly promise you. *Dinkum die.*"

Aunt smiled a trifle grimly.

"No! Indeed!" she said with great conviction. "Whatever else you do, stay on the Kangalian side of the lake. Keep away from the far coast at all costs. The last lot of people who got blown across have never been heard of or seen since."

"Gosh!" gasped Gerald. "Why not?"

"We don't know," shrugged Nick making a ghoulish face. "Probably got captured and tortured and eaten by the starving Africans in the other country."

"You wouldn't believe the state things have deteriorated into over there," his mother confirmed.

"Sadly they've had drought for years and years. Hence no crops. Because of political upheavals vicious bandits have rampaged around devastating the country. Roads and railways have been blown to bits so communities are completely isolated and left to fend for themselves. They can't get supplies of any kind. No seeds to plant food crops. No paraffin for lighting. No cooking oil. No spare parts for any machines; and, of course, no batteries, so they can't run radios to hear any news... They've cut down all the trees for fuel. Without trees the rains fail utterly and there're no roots to bind the soil, which therefore erodes in dreadful winds. The country has become a desert. The different little villages attack each other to grab whatever meagre items they can steal... and the terrorists prey on them all. It's a complete mess over there."

There was a shocked, sad silence.

"Perhaps we shouldn't go at all," suggested Ella in a small, depressed voice.

"No. No. If there was any danger of you drifting across we wouldn't dream of letting you go on this cruise," her aunt reassured her. "I just thought you ought to be made aware of the situation. So, for Heaven's sake, keep to *our* section of the lake."

"Oh yes. We will," the cousins assured her fervently.

Lots of people had, of course already told them to keep to the west side of the lake but the terrors of the eastern side had seemed remote, like someone else's nightmare. Now, with the possibility of being blown across to a desert full of hungry savages, the dangers suddenly came into horribly clear focus and loomed large, real and frightening. They were very quiet.

But depression and worry couldn't last long. They were soon winkling the dogs out of the Land Rover and climbing into it themselves. Ahead they had a long and difficult journey on rotten roads. Would Ella manage it?

12. One sketch on the next page shows the Land Rover keys. They were attached to a big piece of yellow oilskin which made it hard to lose them. But - no wonder Ella hid them in the Bolognese sauce! (Mentioned on pages 47, 76 and 426.)

The other sketch shows a burgee. You can see 2 of them flying on 2 masts in the pic on page x. Burgees are also referred to on page 79.

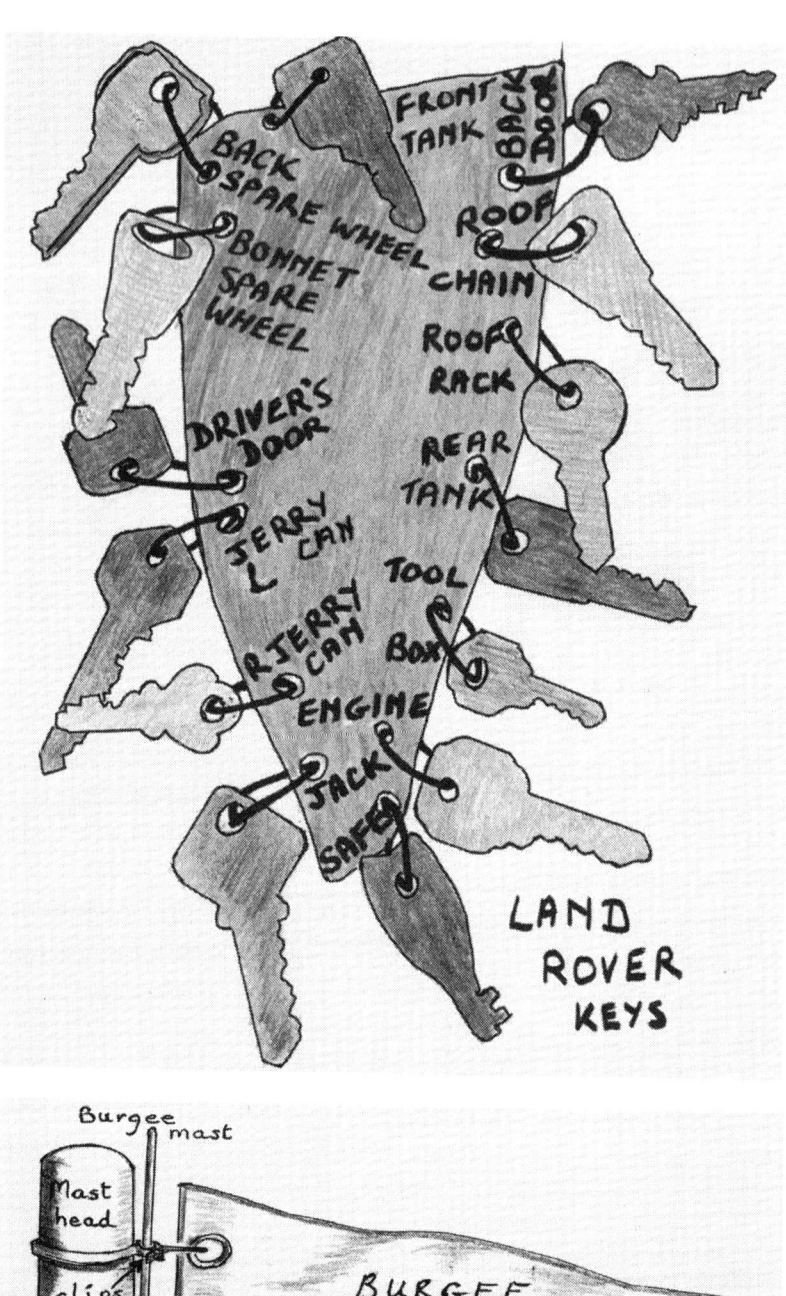

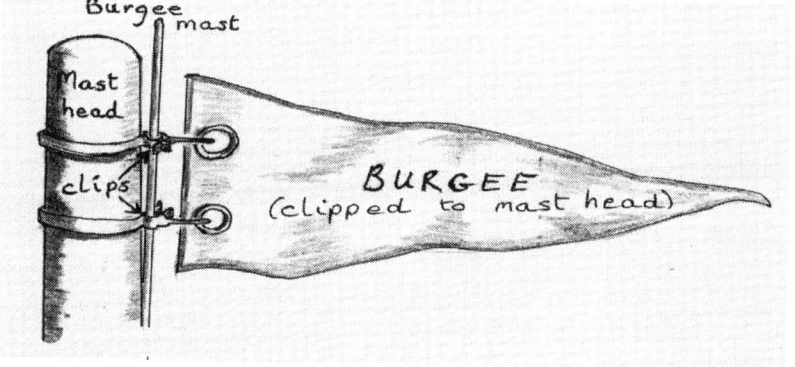

LAND ROVER KEYS

BURGEE (clipped to mast head)

CHAPTER 7

Leaving town.

They were all wedged in the Land Rover and ready to go; but Ella didn't switch on the engine. With a horrified expression she sat staring through the windscreen as if she had been turned to stone.
"Buck up, Nell. We want to be off!"
"We're already late starting."
"We want to get there before dark!"
"What're you waiting for, El?"
She shook her head.
"I'll never be able to turn in the drive."
"Well – Jolly well back out," advised Gerald cheerfully.
"Yes. Go on! Reverse gear is all too easy to find!" encouraged Nicky with a wicked chortle.
"No," Ella was adamant. "Not with all you hooligans with me."
So Aunt Maddy reversed out of the gate and pointed the car down the lane towards the tarmac road below.
"There you are," she said bracingly. "Don't forget to use mosquito coils. Remember to take your malaria pills. Give the Sampsons my love and say I'm sorry Tony and I won't be staying with them. The stew's in the cold box and… " Her instructions, messages and reminders never seemed to end.
"Yes!" "Yes!" "Yes!" They assured her impatiently – and promptly forgot what she had just told them. They were far too excited to take it all in, and anyway, she'd said it all before – lots of times."
Suddenly Maddy was *extra* serious.
"Now, Nell, remember. Take it easy and you'll be fine. And the rest of you, DO NOT tease her or annoy her. Your safety depends upon Eleanor."
They all promised faithfully. Maddy clambered out of the high vehicle and called out:
"Good luck! Have a lovely time," and tried to pick up Tony who was crying. He wanted to go with his sisters and cousins.

He was rather too big and sturdy now for Maddy to cuddle easily but she did her best.

"Give them a wave," she urged. "They'll be back next week." In her mind she prayed: 'I hope.'

"Come on. Let's go and wash your face."

"I want Kirstin," he sobbed. "I want Carol. I want to go to the lake."

"You can go another time – when you're bigger."

"But I'm a nexpert sailor. My Daddy sed so."

"Yes, I know. But, well, just for another year or two it's better if you don't go cruising unless there's a grown-up going as well."

To forestall further discussion she added:

"D'you know? This morning I made a lovely chocolate cake. Shall we go and look at it?"

Tony's complaints suddenly withered into a guilty silence. He allowed his aunt to lead him into the house.

"After you've had a nice sleep this afternoon we'll go down to the airport to collect the visitors. You enjoy seeing the 'planes, don't you?"

"Yes," said Tony doubtfully. He didn't want to go into the kitchen where sooner or later someone would notice that the cake had vanished.

Manfully he dried his eyes. His dirty fists left black smudges on his cheeks.

"Will they be or-right?" he asked acutely sensing Maddy's worries.

"I sincerely hope so." Her tone was so dire and abstracted that the infant was upset again. Suddenly he was as full of misgivings as his aunt was herself.

Maddy distracted the little fellow successfully but as the hectic day sped past she had difficulty overcoming premonitions of disaster. Her mind was constantly returning to the busy dirt road where a Land Rover was, she trusted, grinding is way to Baboon Bay. She wished that she could be sure that she had made a wise decision. She willed her son and his cousins to arrive safely; and regretted not having made them promise to telephone on arrival. She tried to get through to the Sampsons herself but was told by the operator that the lines were down, and had not been functioning for three days due to elephant damage.

"We think – it is possible – perhaps – telephones might be operating again – maybe – in two days time," the company representative told her. Aunt Maddy sighed. Well – there was nothing for it now but to hope for the best.

****

There was complete silence in Pythagoras as he bumped down the dusty lane between a double row of young jacarandas. Fallen blue flowers forming a dense carpet burst with high-pitched pops under Pythag's heavy, thickly-tracked tyres. Everyone was *willing* Ella not to stall the engine or to get stuck. It would have been difficult to involve the vehicle in any trouble on that short, unfrequented, though rutted, lane but their feelings were so wound up that logic had deserted them. A dislodged life jacket fell forward onto Nick's shoulder and he jumped with fright. Then, impatiently he pushed it back amongst its fellows.

They turned onto the tarmac road. It was a little-used dead end, which only served a few houses and they had it to themselves until they had rumbled past the clinic and stopped at the halt sign beside the church. Would Ella find first gear to start off again? She could almost hear the bated breath all round. With a tussle she engaged gear and released the clutch. Obediently Pythagoras began to move – backwards! Alas! The electric atmosphere had been too much for her.

Silence was suffocating as she tried again. Four pairs of eyes watched her every move. Four hearts beat wildly. Four brains tried to hypnotise her into getting it right. This time everything went well. Phew! Now they were in traffic. Kirstin noticed that Carol had four pairs of fingers crossed, and looking at her own hands, was surprised to find that her own fingers were twisted round each other in just the same way.

Deliberately she untwined them but feeling superstitious she nearly rewound them. Trying to look casual she crossed her legs instead. But it was no good. She didn't want to be the one to bring bad luck on the expedition so she twisted her fingers again. In fact she crossed her thumbs as well!

'At any rate,' Gerald was thinking, 'we're bigger than most of the other things on the road.' As if to contradict him a petrol tanker roared past, deafening them, puffing fumes everywhere, dwarfing the Land Rover, and making Gerr wonder why on earth, before they'd started, he'd jumped into the front seat beside Ella, and why none of the other three had disputed his occupation of that usually coveted place. Generally they fought for turns in the front.

Gradually – very – *very* gradually – the tension eased. No one had yet dared to speak but the atmosphere was definitely less prickly – until they came to one of the many roundabouts and had to slow down. However, Ella managed to dawdle without coming to a complete stop, and juddering somewhat, yet not quite stalling, they continued without having fists shaken at them. Yes. Roundabouts weren't so horrendous... El seemed to be able to cope with those; but there were a few fearful moments when she sped out in front of cars whose drivers showed by hooting that she should have waited her turn with more patience. However, there was a general feeling of a little more confidence in the car. Ella noticed the slight relaxation with relief and responded accordingly.

Traffic lights were the next major hazard. Perhaps it was as well that they met only one set before they escaped from the traumas of town. There was a communal groan as they had to stop. Ahead were a small van and a smart Mercedes.

"Get into first gear now," advised Nick.

"And sit on the clutch?" exclaimed Ella, shocked.

"Well – better wear out some of the clutch than start off in reverse and back all over the tiny Fiat behind us," remarked Kirstin brutally.

The novice driver was rattled. She engaged gear and tentatively raised her foot from the clutch pedal. Obedient as always, Pythagoras began to reverse. Nell gulped.

"Sorry!" she muttered, red in the face and sweating liberally. Gerald made an impatient movement. He was sure he could have done better, but as his experience of driving was limited to the Golf Club buggy, and some extremely hair-raising go-cart attempts there was no chance of his being able to justify his thoughts. He had over a year to wait before he could even try to pass his driving test.

The couple in the Fiat were talking so earnestly they never noticed the Land Rover's aborted movement in their direction. Ella again wrestled with the gear stick. After several moments, as she was just about to let out the clutch, Nick blurted out:

"Stop! That's reverse again."

His cousin almost sobbed. How she wished she had never agreed to try and drive this horrible vehicle!

"It's all right El," comforted Nicky with surprising gentleness. "That first gear's an absolute brute. You'll be OK once we're on the open road."

"*You* try!" groaned Nell.

Everyone stared at her with astonishment and consternation. Surely she wasn't going to give up already? Why, they hadn't even got out of town yet. But after a startled glance Nick caught her meaning and clambered into the central seat in the front. As he was already over 6ft tall and athletically built this was no easy feat; but he managed it somehow and the others grinned to see him squashed in with his knees up near his ears.

"Got your foot on the clutch?" he asked as he settled into the tiny middle seat.

"Um," affirmed Ella desperately.

The lights had changed. The head of the queue of cars was beginning to move. If she didn't get this wretched machine going forwards very soon the vehicles behind would start hooting impatiently. She held her breath while Nick fought the gear lever.

"There!" he said. Ultra gently Nell let out the clutch. Kirstin and Carol looked fearfully out of the back window; but with a small jerk and many sighs of relief they rolled forwards, gathered speed, and soon had left hated traffic lights behind.

Nick dug Gerald in the ribs with one hefty elbow so his cousin took the hint but didn't feel he could climb into the back.

"When you're brave enough to stop, Ella," he said, "I'll move. Nicholas is overflowing that tiny central seat so drastically that I think I might pop out of the door."

Later, when Gerr had transferred into the back with the Australians, Nick slid sideways out of the uncomfortable middle seat into Gerald's place and stayed in front. This seemed to give Ella confidence, so with no more adventures worth recording, they found themselves running gradually downhill and out of town. It was going to be an eventful trip.

CHAPTERS 8 to 11   Journey to the lake.

First on the high plateau they bumped along potholed, undulating roads. Then their steep, broken-up track wound a long way down to the bottom of the Rift Valley. It was hotter at this low altitude with houses and vegetation that were different. Sometimes swelteringly hot, and mostly excessively dusty, the drive was long and tiring; but it was packed with interesting experiences and enlivened by strange local sights.

They had to hand it to Ella. She dodged dogs and donkeys, avoided suicidal chickens, and threaded a market thronged with meandering people. She even managed to scrape past a witch doctor, dressed in leaves and a fierce mask, who tried to jump in front of the car.

However, as you are no doubt pining to reach the lake and start sailing, chapters 8 to 11, which detail the excitements of the trip, have been stored elsewhere. Just now the main thing is that Ella managed to get Pythagoras and his passengers to the lake intact.

CHAPTER 12

Settling in at Baboon Bay.

"What a sunset! D'you think the world's going to burn up?" asked Kirstin as they finally approached Baboon Bay. Her Australian twang was very noticeable because she was tired. Through a mammoth yawn Carol announced:
"I'm so sweaty, and we've been through so much dust that I've got a layer of caked mud all over me – like a buffalo."
"Yes," said Nick, scratching his back. "It's been a very itchy-making, long day. But we're almost at journey's end, now."
    The sky was a sheet of tremendous horizontal red and gold streaks against which, along hilltops, silhouettes of bush trees stood out like black lace fringes.
"The Baobabs look as if they're squirming in Hell," said Gerald.
    Then, at last, their destination appeared. It was a mysterious rectangular expanse of water in deep shadow between two long bluffs that pointed northeast. (*Map on page 106.*) All that could be seen of its surroundings were monstrous boulders and wild bush so to the two Stanleigh cousins who had never before been to this area, it seemed dark, deserted and savage.
"What are those far away pinpoints of light at the tip of the west arm of the bay?" asked Carol.
"Cooking fires of a fishing hamlet," replied Nick. "At this nearer end of the bay there are some homes, the Fisheries Research Depot, and a small shipyard, but they're hidden from us just now by the blackness of trees."
    The Land Rover suddenly rumbled through a scant collection of tatty-looking shops from which glimmered weak flickers of paraffin lamps.
"Behold the great metropolis of Baboon Bay," scoffed Kirstin. Carol giggled.
    As the glorious, fiery evening changed into sombre greyness, they found the third fork of the entire day.

Kangalia's system of dirt roads could hardly be described as 'complicated'!

"Left, Nell," murmured Nick.

Longing for the journey to end, Ella had found the trip stressful and everyone had worried constantly about whether she'd manage safely. They plunged into dark shade to follow the shoreline along the western bluff. They couldn't see the black water that was below them on their right.

"Gosh. I don't like this tunnel of weird trees," said Gerald with a shiver. "Their bare branches look like spooks' fingers stretching over us. They don't half make the place murky!"

Kirstin who was now sitting in the front, found a light switch but two bright beams cutting empty blackness ahead only seemed to emphasise the surrounding gloom. There was an exhausted silence in the car as everyone longed for the wearing drive to end. Again Carol yawned hugely.

They twisted, bumped and jolted between thick, wild vegetation.

"Turn right now. This is the Sampsons' drive," said Nicky at last. On an even rougher track the vehicle nosed its way carefully down a slope towards the lake.

"Jolly good! Park at the end somewhere."

Ella did as she was told, switched off the engine and pulled up the handbrake with a satisfying jerk. As she snapped off the headlights darkness crashed onto and into the car. For a moment they sat, stunned. Then:

"Phew!" exclaimed Nell with a huge sigh. "We made it!"

They clambered noisily out of the rattly vehicle exclaiming:

"Good on you, El!"

"Well done, Sis!"

"*Bonza!*"

"Gosh! Am I glad we're here!"

"It's too dark to see properly, and there're lots of creepers, but below us I think I can see the roof of the Sampson's place," said Kirstin peering down through shadowy branches.

"Strange!" said Gerald. "There isn't a light anywhere."

"Probably the electricity's failed," guessed Nick. "Often happens."
"Where's the Sampsons' car?" enquired the observant Carol.
"Maybe they're at the Club, or out to dinner," suggested her sister as, relieved to have space in which to stretch arms and legs, they wondered what to carry down to the house.
"Hm... " Nick had a nasty feeling in the pit of his stomach. Such total lack of even a glimmer filled him with foreboding.

Suddenly out of dismal shadows an even blacker, *enormous* shape loomed frighteningly beside them. It was strangely proportioned. Carol's keen eyes had noticed the terrifying object arriving but she'd been too shocked to even squeak a warning. The boys jumped and raised arms defensively. Kirstin gasped and stepped backwards. Nell was too shattered to react visibly but her heart seemed to squeeze itself into a tiny dehydrated lump of lichen-like matter. Only Nick, used to the ways of the country, was able to calm down reasonably quickly. Now, however, Carol pulled herself together.
"Are you the *bezan*?" she asked in a voice whose wobble indicated taut nerves.
"Who's using local words now?" quizzed Gerald, letting his fear escape in sarcasm.
"Yes," replied the dark lump. "Me. Watchman."
His bizarre shape was explained when he repositioned the knobby stick that he was carrying over his shoulder. A huge, rumpled blanket engulfed his head, shoulders and the massive weapon.
"We have come to visit Mr. and Mrs. Sampson," said Nick.
"Ah? Eh! Are not here!"
"Well, that's obvious. Where are they?"
"They have gone!"

Gerr snorted impatiently. Really it was like talking to a badly programmed computer! Nick persevered. He knew that little by little they would probably winkle out of the vast, blanket-wrapped man what was going on.
"To which place have they gone?"

"Yesterday. Morning time."

Kirstin giggled at the *bezan*'s answer, but Nell reprimanded her:

"You shouldn't laugh. He probably never had the chance to go to school, yet he can make himself understood in your language. You can't do the same in his."

In fact the poor fellow was a byword in the village for being slow-witted. The rest of his intelligent family and friends laughed cruelly at his bumbling motion and clumsy speech.

"To which place did they go?" repeated Nicholas patiently.

"Eh?"

"Will they come soon?"

"I do not know."

"Why have they gone?"

"Baby too sick. He go hospital in Matambata."

"Oh dear! I wonder what's wrong with Mark. It may be serious if they've headed all the way to Matambata."

"Why didn't they phone us? They knew we were coming."

"Lines probably not working. Often go on the blink. Elephants knock down the poles." Nick was cynical but accurate.

"Or maybe they left in a panic. Perhaps Mark's got appendicitis or been bitten by a rabid dog, or… "

Kirstin interrupted her sister's uncomfortably fertile imagination.

"They probably just forgot all about us."

"Ah well. They must have left a key for us," hoped Nick. "Bezan, you got key?"

"No key."

"Oh! I expect Cook will have it. I'll go and rout him out from the servants' quarters. Can anyone find a torch easily? My rucksack's well and truly buried and it's jolly pitchy black under these trees."

"I'll come with you," offered Gerald.

"What? Oh no. It's O.K. You don't have to — but thanks all the same. This gallant streak of lightning here will show me the way." Nick indicated the ultra-slow-moving watchman. Then he spoke to his cousins in general. "I suppose you'd better haul out the sleeping bags – and the supper – and anything else we'll be needing." In what Ella sarcastically thought was true male fashion he didn't bother himself with details.

"Thanks, Kirsty," he said as she handed him a headlamp. "Hey! It doesn't… "

"Oh! I forgot! Hang on. I'll put in the *thingos*." She was rummaging in her personal bundle. Torches were always carried empty so that they couldn't switch themselves on in a rucksack and rundown the batteries uselessly. Kirstin unearthed two AA batteries and slipped them into her torch.

"If it goes out you must bash it – like this." She demonstrated to get the gadget working. "There's a soft spring or a loose connection or something," she explained. Nick shook his head and grinned in the darkness.

'Typical Chorton!' he thought.

Weirdly silent, with a bear-like roll the huge watchman followed slowly and ponderously as Nick vanished down the brick steps into what seemed like unparalleled gloom. The tiny bobbing flicker of his light grew smaller and then vanished; and the other four were in pitch darkness again. After a few preliminary mistakes with wrong knobs, Nell found the switch for the light inside Pythagoras.

"We'll need to excavate sleeping bags, *esqui* (cool box) and individual bundles," murmured Kirsty.

"There," said Nell a little dubiously, her arms full. "I think that's all we need. Here're the keys, Gerald. Will you lock up?"

"Yes, ma'am," he replied thinking vengeful thoughts about bossy elder sisters. Taking the big yellow triangle of oilskin *(pic page 36.)* from his sister he jangled its trimming of 14 keys in a rebellious way but did as he had been asked. Slowly, but with ever growing confidence as their eyes became adapted to the funereal surroundings, they stumbled down towards the hump of greater obscurity that was the house.

Nick met them as they reached the kitchen door. A second exceptionally large, inky shape accompanied him. This one had four legs and he greeted them all ecstatically.

"This is Dizzy, the Sampsons' dog. The servants' quarters are empty and locked up. I expect the cook's gone on the binge and forgotten all about us. I bet he comes back with a hideous hangover tomorrow," added Nick with relish.

"So we can't get into the house!" Kirstin stated the obvious. "Caterwauling Kangas!"

"Oh!" The exclamation didn't express Nell's disappointment at all but it was as much as she felt capable of saying. She was totally deflated and had so much been looking forward to a warm bath and a soft bed!

"What shall we do?"

"We'll sleep on the beach," decided Nick. "Who's got the car keys? I'll get the saucepans if you like, while you people find a suitable place to spread the sleeping bags. Follow the path across the terrace. Steps at the end lead down to a strip of sand. Watch it! There are lots of rocks lying about to wreck your toes. Do we need anything else from the Land Rover?"

No one had any inspirations so he clambered up and the others clattered down. Dizzy, like an enormous black panther, padded after Nick, stepping on his flip-flops and pulling them off with annoying regularity.

"Dizzy!" admonished the boy on the twelfth step up. "That's the seventh time since the servants' quarters! If you do it again... " In the weak glimmer of Kirstin's headlight Dizzy panted happily and extended an extremely long and very pink tongue. He licked his new friend enthusiastically and plonked his huge paws on Nick's feet yet again.

"Oh, Dizzy! You so-and-so!" exclaimed the victim giving up the struggle. Warding off another dozen advances of the hound's soft black muzzle he took off his flip-flops and carried them.

The watchman, torn in his duties, hesitated and hovered. Should he follow the group of strangers going down the steps, or go after the youth who was heading upwards? Finally he plodded slowly towards the beach. It was easier going downhill! When he saw Kirstin and Gerald hunting for firewood while Nell and Carol unrolled sleeping bags, he obligingly found three suitable stones for the fireplace, and contributed a pleasing heap of fuel. Then, feeling proudly that he had done more than could have been expected of him, and conveniently never considering that perhaps he should have questioned the right of these strangers to sleep on his master's beach, he withdrew to the Sampsons' back porch. There he had long ago discovered an ornamental piece of petrified wood. Pulled into a corner out of the wind it made what he felt was a very acceptable seat. In a warm glow of self-satisfaction he extracted an old piece of newspaper from below a flowerpot and, with a pinch of tobacco taken from his dust-filled pocket, he rolled himself a mal-odorous cigarette.

'What if my brothers and sisters are all clever and have good jobs in the city.' he thought vaguely. 'I don't care. I like being able to sleep on the job!'

13. A just-lit mosquito coil.
The flame will go out and the coil will go on smouldering for hours, scaring off mozzies with its smoke.

Down at the beach the zephyr, that the *bezan* was avoiding, was welcome.

"Good thing there's a breeze," remarked Kirstin. "Otherwise I bet we'd be eaten alive by bities – what with all these trees and the nicely watered garden up there, and those reeds on the other side of this miniature bay..."

"Yes. We'd better get the coils out before we go to sleep, in case the wind drops during the night."

Nick and Gerald located the mosquito coils and set three going. They also placed one, together with a box of matches, beside the head of each sleeping bag.

"There you go," said Nick. "Self Service. Start your own coil burning if you wake and find yourself being gnawed to pieces. That is, of course, if it's mozzies that are chomping your bones. I don't think a coil would frighten off hyenas, jackals, leopards..."

Ella shrieked.

"You're not serious are you, Nick? We can't sleep out here if all those ravenous creatures will be prowling about."

"Nowhere else," replied her cousin shrugging dramatically.

"Dozens and dozens of them," Gerr assured his sister with a wicked laugh. "You won't get even half a wink of sleep because of all the growling and the sound of their paws padding around all night."

Although he spoke in jest, half carried away by his own make-believe, he shivered and flashed his torch all round. He saw only a pair of dozing Sacred Ibises with awesome scimitar-shaped bills. In daylight the birds would hunt fish and frogs.

14. Sacred Ibises.

"You can sleep in Pythagoras, if you like Nell. We can put the back seats down more or less flat, you know."

Eleanor looked up through dense blackness below thick trees, imagined scores of hungry eyes glaring at her, and decided to remain where she was – for the time being anyway. Carol shivered and crept a little closer to the fire where she was stirring a pre-cooked frozen stew, and trying to break it up into melt-able pieces. She wasn't cold but she was weary, and tired people are not usually extra brave.

Dizzy, his nose twitching appreciatively at the smells that were starting to emerge from the pot, inched closer and leant against her. The young cook found his presence comforting.

"Good old Dizzy," she said giving him a hug, and promptly got her face thoroughly 'washed' by the affectionate beast.

"Here, can someone fetch us some lake water?" suggested Kirstin, busy slicing bread. We'll need to boil it because we can't get into the house to fetch clean drinking stuff. Don't take it from the edge where the scum always collects off the waves."

"Can't we drink the lake without boiling it?" asked Gerald in surprise.

"Yes – elsewhere – whenever we're far from humanity," said Nick. "But although this is a very big bay it's also enclosed, with a lot of people living all round it.

What are you giggling about, Caro?"

"Gerr. Talking about boiling the lake. It would take a whopping huge saucepan." She chuckled again.

"Well, anyway, the water here's bound to be polluted to a certain extent."

"Better not take chances. But it's an awful bore to have to boil before drinking."

"We'll have tea or coffee. It won't be as bad as drinking just hot water," consoled Nell.

"Or cocoa," suggested Carol in a greedy voice.

"Oh yes. Cocoa," endorsed the boys.

"I say! I'm awfully sorry. We need the drinking chocolate, and rice, and powdered milk, and sugar and... "
"Oh! El-*la!*"
"Yes! Well... I forgot... We *all* forgot... Our minds weren't thinking about having to camp."
"We did bring the *esqui*," said Kirstin, but Nell went on:
"Yes; but that's only got frozen food and marge and fruit and things that will go off. The dry stuff's in the yellow carton. Gerald *dear!* – You know what a sweet little 'angel' you are..."
"Hmph!" snorted the six-foot-something 'little' angel staring at his diminutive older sister.
"Come on, Nick. Let's go. Now – think carefully, Nell. Is there *anything* else?" He looked round confrontationally. "Anything else *anybody* needs? Speak now or... "
"I don't think so," said Ella doubtfully. "Kirsty, Caro, Nick can you think of anything else?"
"Um... No... " came two replies.
"Bailer buckets," said Nicky. "I'm getting water in a saucepan but it will be much better to use the buckets because they're bigger and besides the pan will soon be in use."
"Hmph!" snorted the 'angel' again even more sardonically than before. Then, in a happier tone, he added:
"Look! The moon's just popped up above the hills on the east side of the bay. Good show! Now at least we'll be able to see the hyenas, and leopards and crocs before they eat us!"
    Ella squealed.
Suddenly, however, the world took on a different aspect. Rocks that had loomed forbiddingly now cheerfully reflected the moonlight. The rustling reeds no longer sounded menacing. The call of a night bird was lovely instead of spooky. Even the owl up the road saying "Hoo-Hoo... Hoo – Oo-oo" was recognisable and friendly.

    But would their little bay continue to be 'friendly' all night?

Chapter 13

The army alarm. 'Midnight' swim.

Up the steps again! Nick felt he would soon know each one by heart: the rise with a gap; the ridge where two bricks were particularly thick; the place where badly smoothed cement felt like the roots of a tree – or like writhing snakes; the very narrow step; the particularly high one; and those which were hardly there at all... He led the way in silence and Gerald followed.

Just as they were about to reach the car a horrifying, raucous yell – half shout, half shriek made their hairs stand on end. It was a decidedly aggressive human scream! The boys froze and instinctively turned back to back with fists raised, ready to fight whatever it was that was about to attack. The clump of heavy boots and the clatter of a rifle did nothing to reassure them. But inexplicably, next they heard the shout: "Friend!" followed by another clatter.

Nick collapsed onto a stone laughing, and Gerald looked startled. Had the fright driven his cousin mad?
"What on earth... ?" he began angrily to hide the nasty shock they'd both had. "Who, in the name of thunder, is screaming: 'Who goes there?' into the middle of the African bush night? For goodness sakes! What do they think they're up to?"
"Soldiers," chortled his cousin. "Didn't you see the gates of the army camp at the very end of the lane when we arrived? – Just before we turned right and drove down the Sampsons' drive?"
Gerald shook his head. "It was too dark to see anything," he justified himself.
"Just now the guard must have challenged somebody approaching the gate," said Nick. "You heard the person answering 'Friend'?"
"Whatever! It's totally stupid!" argued Gerr angrily. He hadn't liked that scare at all. "As if an enemy would say 'Foe' and warn the guard."

He jumped again as the terrible shriek echoed through the trees once more. "It's enough to make your blood run cold!"

After they had found the items they had been sent to collect, Gerald turned to his cousin.

"I say, Nick," he suggested mischievously, "Let's dump all this stuff for a while and roll up to the gate. We'll yell 'Friend' and see if we can get into the camp."

But Nick wouldn't co-operate.

"No," he said. "No. It's not worth landing ourselves in trouble and starting an international incident. There was an almighty fuss the time my mum had difficulties when she was windsurfing and landed on the army beach by mistake! Besides, the girls would never know why we hadn't come back. I don't suppose they'd mind if *you* didn't materialise," he teased, "but they *do* want the rice etc."

Water was boiling by the time the boys returned. Although the evening was balmy a hot cuppa was comforting and welcome.

"Tea now," said Ella firmly. "Cocoa later. You can have as much sugar as you like. We've got plenty and it will replace lost energy."

With the moon rising, the lake lapping gently at their feet, rice and stew making happy bubbling noises, life took on a more relaxed and an altogether jollier tone. They sat around sipping till Nell and Kirstin doled out four enormous helpings of supper and the usual tiny portion for Ella. After all that had disappeared Carol handed round bananas as Kirstin prepared cocoa and Nick boiled more water to pour into drinking bottles when it had cooled.

"Oh no! Not bananas!" groaned Gerald in disgust. "I hate them."

"Yes. Bananas," asserted Kirstin. "Apples are dreadfully expensive. They're imported."

"But why must we have bananas?"

"They're very nutritious but they don't keep. We've got bananas for today and tomorrow. It'll be apples, oranges, narchees and 2 pineapples from then on."

"You can mash them up with powdered milk – like Nick and me," suggested Carol squashing away cheerfully. "Bananas mixed with powdered milk are absolutely scrummy:"

"Pass the milk, please," groaned Gerald.

"You'll need lots of bananas if you're going to mash them." grinned Kirstin, adding to his misery. "Here's the bunch. Help yourself."

Gerr groaned artistically again. Then he said belligerently: "After this I'm going to swim!"

"What *now*? At this time of night?" gasped his sister.

"Yes. Why not?"

"Well – er – I don't know really. Except that it seems dangerous and of course, you've only just had your supper."

"Toffee to that! I won't go far; and the water's so warm, surely I won't get cramp."

"No! But the hippos might get *you!*" said Nicholas wickedly.

"Aw! Hippos! They wouldn't come as close as this to the house!" said Gerr. Less confidently he added: "Would they?"

"Don't they just! See that bush behind you?" Everyone started nervously and turned to gaze at the stunted shrub.

"Well, that was once a flourishing little tree. Unfortunately hippos found it and decided it was tasty. So now the hippo family keeps it pruned. The Sampsons are furious. But there's nothing they can do. At least the hippos also keep their lawn well mown."

"Nick! You're joking!"

"No. Honestly. I'm not. In the rainy season, when the ground's soft, there are often whopping great holes – hippo prints – all over the garden."

"We can't sleep here! Not if hippos are going to trample all over us! Do they eat flesh?"

"No. They're vegetarians. They graze. But they chomp up people who get in their way or disturb them – say – by sailing over them. They won't hurt us here. They may munch some of those reeds over there but they won't come into this tiny baylet where we are. The watchman told me they don't like it because it's so rocky. They prefer the smooth slipway and the sands on the further side of the garden. And they don't care for the retaining wall just here that holds the lawn above this beach. They like to amble upwards on a gentle slope, not rope themselves up to scale vertical stones."

His cousins were sceptically silent so Nick added:

"Look. If you're worried we'll pull the sleeping bags up against the wall. We'll definitely be safe there."

Carol was already almost asleep. All she wanted to do was to roll into her bag and close her eyes. As far as she was concerned hippos could come or stay away. She was beyond caring.

"I'm going to wash my teeth," she announced. "Who's hidden the boiled water?"

They pulled the sleeping bags up against the wall and re-disposed the mosquito coils and matches. Gerald had placed his bag beside Kirstin's so now she took the opportunity to move hers to the far side of the group. 'Gerr's O.K. as a cousin, and for sharing adventures with... ' she thought; but she was perfectly happy with Tim, her steady boyfriend back home in Oz, and she had no intention of encouraging Gerald's pretensions. By the time the others had sorted out torches and candles Carol was already dreaming happily.

"I say! It's only ten past eight," said Gerr admiring the luminous dial of his splendid new watch. "I feel as though it's at least midnight!"

"Let's have a midnight swim," said Kirstin. She, Nick, Gerald and Ella soaped and scrubbed. Then three of them wallowed round in shallow water but Ella rinsed at the water's edge. It was good to get rid of the sweat and grime of the day and to slip into clean long-sleeved shirts and jeans.

"We should, of course, have washed and changed earlier," meditated Nell as they enjoyed yet another cup of cocoa. It was amazing how dehydrated they all were.

"Yes," agreed Kirstin. "But somehow it was so murky dark that it wasn't inviting earlier on, was it? And I, for one, was too pooped anyway. Supper brought me alive again."

"Me too!" said Ella with feeling. "Ah well... at least now, with our longs on, we're protected against bities. Does anyone want some insect repellent to smear on face and ankles and hands?"

The boys declined. Kirstin smoothed some onto her sleeping sister and onto herself. Nell applied liberal doses to all exposed portions of her anatomy. She was determined not to let any anopheles mosquitoes come anywhere near her. She didn't want to develop malaria! Oh no, sirree!

"Put some on the seat of your trousers," advised Nicholas.

"What?" Was Nicky teasing her again?

"Well, the material there is stretched and mozzies can sting through it. Not just you, Ella, but on everyone."

"Oh!" Ella obeyed his advice.

Despite the brightness of the moon many stars were remarkably distinct. It was good to lie on the warm sand and look up into the heavens which seemed to be full of lights.

"Hey! A satellite!" exclaimed Gerald. "Gosh! Just look at that clear sky! Back in the UK we'd see nothing but clouds."

"No we wouldn't," corrected his sister. "Back there it'd be raining so we wouldn't be lying out on a beach like this anyway. Isn't the silence super?" she added with satisfaction. "Not a car. Not a radio or TV. Not an aeroplane..."

They watched Gerr's satellite, a tiny fleck of light, moving across the sky.

"I wish you hadn't told us about the hippos," yawned Kirstin, "or the other creatures... especially the hyenas and leopards."

"Oh yes, leopards especially" said Nicky evilly, knowing full well that there were scarcely any leopards left in this inhabited region. "They'll be after Dizzy here. They just love eating baboons and dogs, don't they Dizzy, old boy?" Dizzy, stretched out on the sand beside his visitors, his tummy full of leftover stew and rice, thumped his tail and raised a mini sandstorm.

"But they might decide on a change of diet — just for variety, you know, and sample humans," went on wicked Nick as they wriggled into their sleeping bags.

"I won't get a wink of sleep," groaned Ella, only half acknowledging that her cousin had been teasing as usual. She prodded her bundle of clothes into a better shape for her head. "I wish Kirsty had let me bring a pillow."

A strange yodel came from the far side of the hill. The nasty spine-chilling wail echoed round the bay. Nell shot up and sat stiffly staring all round.

"What's that *ghastly* sound?" she asked in a terrified voice. "It sounds like ghosts in pain!"

"Only a hyena," chuckled Kirstin.

"Oo-er," wavered Nell. "I feel sure we're going to have a very disturbed night."

It was too hot to shiver with cold but she quivered from fright, and trembling, she slipped cautiously back into her sleeping bag. Would she suffocate if she pulled the top of her sack over her head and closed the opening?

There was no comment from Nick. Ignoring more hyena howls, he was already snoring very softly.

When Gerald sat up suddenly a few moments later to see what had gone 'Plop!' in the little bay, he saw that hippos, civets, jackals, hyenas, genet cats, and even leopards had been forgotten, and all his companions were fast asleep.

'Good thing Nick didn't say anything about crocs,' he thought. 'Maybe he teased us about things that wouldn't come and kept very quiet about really possible dangers. I bet crocs revel in that patch of reeds. I wonder if that 'Plop' was a croc diving in... ' He struggled out of his bag and built up the fire. 'But it won't last long' he thought. 'Must try and keep it stoked all night.' Like most good intentions this one didn't get fulfilled.

Gerald looked dubiously round. The heap of fuel seemed dreadfully small but no ways was he going to brave the shadows to find more.

'Where're the boats that we're going to be sailing? Never thought of asking. We were all too busy to enquire about tomorrow. There's that noise again! I wonder... Good thing there's the watchman stomping round. He'll chase off hippos and hyenas and things... not crocs though... '

Gerald's nightmares   (pics: 15, 16, 17, 18.)

hyena after the dinner dishes

15. Hungry hyena

16. Croc about to explore the beach.

Leopard on the prowl

17. Leopard looks for a meal

Gerald's faith was misplaced. At the moment the *bezan* was of no more use than a sack of mealies. Slumped against the corner of the back porch, with his blanket tucked round gaunt shoulders, he was comfortable on his stump of petrified wood and was snoring fit to burst! A hyena would have had to start chewing his toes before he even stirred. He wouldn't wake till the morrow's sun was well risen and warming his eyelids. To expect him to spot – and moreover to repel! – marauders of any kind was nothing more than a pipe dream.

Gerald wriggled into his sack and squirmed around to adjust the shape of the sand on which he lay. Then, secure in his mirage of safety, he shut his eyes.

18. Marinading hippos

CHAPTER 14

Breakfast on the beach.

High in a Baobab on the hill behind the Sampsons' house a magnificent African Fish Eagle dipped his snowy poll and then tossed it arrogantly tail-wards. The jerk carried his head to the glowing russet of his back, and his beak flew open to emit a triple mewing cry that is so characteristic of African waters. Again and again he and his mate nodded and then jerked their heads to screech greetings to the world below. From their high vantage point they could tell that dawn was about to break. Similar calls replied faintly from across the bay as still more Fish Eagles picked up the announcement so that, together with echoes from cliffs and boulders, the whole bay seemed to be full of Fish Eagle hilarity.

In the pitchy pre-dawn Ella woke with a terrified jolt. There were hyenas cackling all round! Sweating with fright she half-opened her eyes and saw a huge, obscure, four-footed shape snuffling nearby. With a muffled scream she made herself small and cowered as far down inside her sleeping bag as she could. Horrified worries whizzed through her brain. Should she force herself to get up, and yell, to warn the others? Would the pack of hyenas lope off or would her cries make them attack? Oh! – Terrors! She could hear huge pads approaching and monster claws clicking on rocks... She couldn't bear to think! At any instant great, stinking, powerful jaws might close round someone's head, or hand... Something was sniffing her sack gustily. Nell was utterly petrified! A monstrous snout came nosing inside her sleeping bag. Hyenas *do* attack humans, especially if the people are asleep – or drunk... Ella knew that for a fact! And they have incredibly strong jaws. Jaws that easily crack open bones of even the strongest and biggest animals. Oh Heavens! How *awful*!

Suddenly she could stand it no longer! Without knowing what she did she shouted and frantically punched the muzzle. She sat up prepared to fight for life. Dizzy yelped and danced away from her!

Dizzy????... Ella looked about feverishly. No hyenas? And all that fiendish hyena cackling? She could hear nothing but cries of Fish Eagles. Sheepishly she checked all round. The other four were still peacefully cocooned.

"Wha's' matta?" asked Kirstin sleepily turning over and relapsing into slumber.

"Dreaming," admitted Nell. "Oh Dizzy! You and those horrid birds *did* give me *such* a fright!"

The dog advanced cautiously towards her. He had merely been investigating last night's unwashed supper saucepans and she had disturbed him with her scream. Then, as he had politely wandered over to see what she wanted, she had shouted and punched his nose. Really there was no understanding humans! However... he decided to forgive her. She seemed to be in a friendly mood now. He gave Nell one of his very best wet licks.

"Oh, you so-and-so!" scolded the still-shaky girl again. "You demon!"

She patted his strong black neck and tickled him behind the ears. The dog sighed happily and settled himself comfortably beside her. He would wait until this troublesome human had gone back to sleep before resuming his early morning stroll and the exciting inspection of promisingly dirty plates.

Hammerkops, standing solemnly on rocks or on moored boats, now started high-pitched metallic monosyllables, which was their unmelodious greeting to the morning. Their ridiculous sharp-beaked and elongated heads glinted like copper hammerheads. Suddenly all sorts of other birds were shouting about the dawn. Cormorants and darters "croaked", kingfishers twittered, weavers, warblers, bulbuls, wagtails, and many others piped, squeaked, chortled, chorused, sang and whistled. Ella didn't know the songsters' names.

19. Above: Hammerkop - about 50 cm from beak tip to end of tail.

<<20. Juvenile Cormorant. An agile swimmer. In this picture his long neck is fore-shortened by being bent backwards.

'What a racket!' thought Nell unappreciatively. 'How *can* the others sleep through it?' She put her fingers into her ears and resolutely shut her eyes, so it was not long before Dizzy was free to resume his saucepan investigations. A little later he would toddle off to rouse the night watchman from his noisy dreams. That was usually the conscientious dog's priority job each morning, but today he had other interesting matters to inspect first.

****

Some time later Kirstin lay admiring the pink and golden sky. The sun had not yet burst over the hills on the far side of the bay and the air was brisk – almost chilly.
'But not anywhere like as cold as it must be back home in Oz, just now," she thought. Her friends at home, south of Perth, would still be suffering winter's cold reality. Theoretically, of course, it was winter here too because the month was very late August and they were in the southern hemisphere – just.

But here, so much nearer to the equator than her home, the climate was much milder. Kirstin smiled. She liked this nice, warm, tropical type of 'winter'.

She wondered what had woken her. Some sort of noise, perhaps... But apart from the normal chatter of birds and the lapping of small waves on the beach all was quiet. In fact such sounds as there were just emphasised the utter tranquillity all round.

What time would it be in Perth now? Her watch said that here it was ten-to-six! So – at home it was – Gosh! It was almost 2pm. Soon her friends would be coming out of school and exercising their horses. She and Carol were missing a few weeks of lessons. Kirstin grinned about that! And then she frowned. 'Were Deanna and Penny looking after her pony and Carol's properly? How funny it had been that time when Nick had visited Oz and had fallen off his horse into the sea!'

Bell-like notes floating musically from across the bay brought her back to the present. Somewhere in the tiny shipyard, a long piece of metal was hanging from the branch of a thorn tree and someone was banging it with an iron pipe to tell the Baboon Bay inhabitants:
"It's six o'clock. Time to get moving." It was a calm, gentle sound, in keeping with the unspoilt surroundings.

Kirstin's peaceful ruminations were brusquely interrupted by several ear-splitting, reverberating CRASHES! and scampering noises – a repetition, she now realised, of the sounds that had woken her. Monkeys! On the Sampsons' corrugated metal roof! Kirstin sat up to watch them but the retaining wall, against which they had all slept, blocked her view. Hm! Monkeys! She'd better keep her eye on the expedition's food boxes. Sure enough, a few minutes later, a couple of furry black faces came peering over the wall.

"*Rock off!*" said Kirstin waving her arms.
She knew that it wouldn't do to encourage them although they were so sweet with their long white side-whiskers and cute little black fingers almost exactly like human hands. The vervets vanished but a large group was soon sneaking down

through trees towards the beach. They could smell biscuits, bread and fruit. Kirstin watched them running nimbly across the sand and rocks, then stopping short of the supper things and food boxes. The monkeys studied these unfamiliar objects prior to plucking up the courage to tear open containers and take bites out of anything edible or inedible.

21. Vervets

"Buzz off!" Kirstin repeated before the little creatures could start on this plan of action. Small faces turned enquiringly at her. Their round eyes, glinting like carnelians, stared a little crossly at this interruption. One of the males stood as tall as he could on his hind legs, using his tail to make a tripod support. He glared at Kirstin. Another did a few pogo jumps with all four legs stretched very stiffly and straight. His rough cries were silenced by Dizzy who came bounding down the hill, scattering monkeys in all directions. This was his second task that he revelled in every morning.

Panting with pleasure he came to Kirstin waving his enormous tail in huge ecstatic sweeps.

"Good work, eh?" he seemed to say with a wide smile. "Dratted monkeys! Never manage to catch one no matter how hard I try!" With a "WOOF!" he was gone again, chasing the vervets round the garden, standing non-plussed as they clattered over the roof, and leaping ineffectually at them as they sat chattering at him from trees.

Gerald, who had received one of Dizzy's massive paws in his tummy, sat up with a groan.

"What on earth... ?"

"Dizzy," explained Kirstin.

"Oh, Dizzy!" said Gerr, preparing to go back to sleep.

"Oh no, you don't," bullied Kirstin. "Time to get up and wash the supper things." Her cousin groaned even more artistically. 'How can I possibly admire this harridan?' he thought. 'But I do. I wish she liked me just a little bit.'

Although properly awake by now he buried himself in his sleeping bag. But Kirstin was out of hers and shaking him.

"Come on," she urged. "Come and help wash up – or get the fire going if you like."

"No. That's my job," yawned Nick who had also been woken by Dizzy's precipitous departure, and who did not enjoy washing up. He crawled out of his bag, unzipped and opened it then draped it over a bush to air.

"Ugh!" he said, stretching, and scratching his head till his hair was all on end. "Ugh!"

"Yes," agreed Gerald meditatively studying the expanse of tummy that showed between his cousin's top and bottom garments.

"I agree!" Gerr grinned. "'Ugh' is a pretty good description of yourself, I should say!" Smiling broadly and hastily whisking up his sack he retreated from Nick's vicinity and spread his own opened sleeping bag on a distant bush. Nicky watched Gerr's rapid departure with a grin that mirrored the other boy's. He yawned again, then called sweetly after Gerald.

"'Ugh' yourself! Amazing, isn't it, how everyone always remarks how similar we look!" He mimicked one of his grandmother's French friends:

"Zose boys are zo zactly like eech ozzer! Zee eyes! Zose zo dark eyes! Zose boys are zo luckee."

"Bigheaded rather, I'd say," remarked Kirstin dryly, but she was smiling. She handed Gerald a pile of dirty plates.

"Come on, Gerr."

When she smiled at him in that particular way poor Gerald simply couldn't refuse.

Taking cutlery, crockery and saucepans down to the lake edge, they started operations, using the sand as Vim. Tiny fish wiggled up in great numbers to sample the bits that were being scraped off into the water. Behind them Nicky stirred the embers of last night's fire and blew skilfully till a handful of dry leaves burst into bright yellow flames. Carefully he fed twigs into the blaze and soon a presentable fire was ready between the three stones. They could now boil water and cook eggs and bacon. Ella and Carol slept on.

"If I knew where the tea towels were I could help you," said Nick provocatively, but looked round for the tea towels as he spoke.

"As we've nearly finished... However – we don't like to disappoint you... You'll find an extra towel in the saucepan sack." Kirstin was apparently without sympathy. Leaving the boys to finish drying she went to shake her sister and cousin.

"Come on, you two," she said, "or you'll miss the boat."

"Where *are* the boats?" asked Caro rubbing her eyes as she sat up.

"In the Fisheries' yard. We got special permission to leave them there just this once."

"What are they called?" That was Gerald.

"My G.P.'s called *Frolic*."

"Oh, yes. I remember," said Carol. She and Kirstin had sailed in *Frolic* before, on previous visits to Kangalia.
"And the Enterprise?"
"I don't know. My Mum fixed up the loan of her while I was away at school in Scotland."
"Jolly decent of her owners to lend her."
"I'll say. I wouldn't lend *Frolic* to *anyone*."
"We wouldn't lend our boat either," agreed the Australian pair.

Breakfast took an awful long time and was enjoyed to the full. They wouldn't get bacon again till their return. It would go bad without a fridge so there was no point taking any with them.
"Give Dizzy the rinds," said Carol as they finished eating and started packing up.

"What shall we do with this Bolognese sauce?" interrupted Ella. "It's still frozen – well – almost. Chunks of it are still solid. Aunt Maddy said we should leave it in the Sampsons' freezer. It's for supper on the night that we get back here."
Everyone looked doubtful.
"We can't do that because we can't get into the house." Kirstin had the knack of stating the obvious.
"Take it with us," suggested Gerald, "and have it tonight."
"No. We've got frozen curry for tonight. Or at least, it's half frozen at the moment," said Kirstin. "That *esqui* and the cold blocks are very efficient, but we can't take them in the boats. The curry and Bolognese will both have melted by tonight and be warm even before we start cooking."
"They'd never keep till the following night."
"Oh. Well – we'd better eat it now!"

But not even the boys could face Spaghetti Bolognese, or even the sauce on its own, at half past seven in the morning, and after a whacking great breakfast. The watchman had vanished so they couldn't give him the food.
"Perhaps the Fisheries have got a freezer we could use."
"Um. Good idea! Let's hope so."

After a swim they slogged everything up the hill to the Land Rover.

"Hey! You mustn't come!" said Nick to Dizzy who was gathering himself together for a jump into the high vehicle. "You must stay to guard the house, old boy."

"D'you think anyone is looking after him while the Sampsons' are away?" That was kind-hearted Carol. "Who's feeding him d'you think?"

"I'm certain they've made arrangements Nick comforted her.

"He wasn't at all ravenous last night – or even this morning, come to that," said Nell. "I expect the cook and the gardener come in to give him his dinner."

"Hm," said Carol.

"Sure to. Stay Dizzy! Stay!" Nick ordered hopefully as they prepared to drive away. Dizzy, however, being a dog of character, had ideas of his own...

22. Pied Kingfishers
With frenziedly beating wings they hover above the water on the lookout for small fish.

CHAPTER 15

Getting rigged up. Shed Keys. Cane Rat. Wiston.

Thank goodness there was a turning circle at the end of the Sampsons' drive! Ella didn't have to back round tricky curves to reach the lane. Gerald couldn't resist a mischievous wave towards the sentry at the gate of the Army Camp and, to his amazement he received a cheery waggle of a rifle in reply. The guard outside the Fisheries Depot was less friendly.

"But it is a holiday!" he grumbled, eyeing Dizzy askance. Running along animal tracks on the lakeshore the clever dog had arrived as quickly as the vehicle. Now he panted proudly, grinning from ear to ear, and obviously eager to show his friends round.

"There is nobody here," added the man as if that clinched matters. He wanted advice on how to deal with the situation.

The cousins had forgotten about the Bank Holiday. However, after much argument and discussion, the gateman's scruples were overcome. He allowed Pythagoras to rumble down a slope into the gravel yard where several boats were lying. Other small craft were tied to the wharf.

"What a lovely smell of tar!" exclaimed Gerr.

"And, thank goodness – no stink of fish," added Ella. "In fact no fish anywhere in sight. Good! I can't stand their goggle eyes when they're dead!"

"Look at that huge squiffy thing over there." Carol pointed to a venerable, clinker-built cabin cruiser that resembled Noah's ark. Beyond hope of repair, it had been abandoned.

"With the long grass poking up all round, it looks like a broody hen on her nest!"

"There they are!" said Kirstin with satisfaction.

The two Stanleighs gazed perplexed. They had been expecting to see a couple of neat little boats, bobbing about ready to be loaded up and sailed away. Instead, onshore, under a Baobab, were two scruffy tarpaulins pegged to the ground in many places and stretched over asymmetrical objects that seemed to have two wheels apiece. The covers were thick with dust, dried leaves and desiccated flowers that had dropped from surrounding trees.

"Well – Let's get at them, then!" urged Nicky.
"Hang on a bit," begged Ella. "Where shall I park Pythagoras?"
"Take him down to the beach, Nell," said Nick. "We'll be putting the boats in there so we'll be needing the gear as close to the water as possible."

The tarpaulins were unpegged, rolled up and put in a bulky heap outside the office window. It was filthy work. What seemed like platoons of geckos, spiders and insects scuttled out of the folds and scurried off to safety. Gerald shrieked and leapt out of the way of a speeding scorpion.
"I hope the Fisheries men don't go and use our stuff," said Kirstin. "I mean – there're so many mountains of their junk and gear lying around. They could easily get confused."
"We'll leave a big notice on our heap," decided Nick

Ella and Gerald now became aware that the tarpaulins had hidden a couple of hulls. But they still couldn't fathom what was going on. These objects had nothing that Gerr would have described as 'bits, and ropes and things.' How could you sail a hull without 'bits'? However, it dawned upon the two Stanleighs that they were seeing two trailers that were carrying the basics of Nick's GP14, the *Frolic*, and of the Enterprise that they had been lent

"I say!" Gerald had examined the Enterprise. "She's called *Percy*. So she's a 'he'!"
"No boat's a 'he'" argued Carol.
"Well, this one is. Wonder why they called her – er – I mean, him – '*Percy*'?"
"Funny sort of name! Come on. We'll roll her and *Frolic* down to the beach."
"Him!"
"Er... Him and *Frolic*... No! Dash it – a boat *has* to be a she! We'll roll *them* down to the beach."

That was easy, and with so many people to lend a hand it was not difficult to lift the fibreglass Enterprise off its trailer and onto the sand, especially as the gateman wandered over to see what was going on and was pressed into service. It was a different matter when they had to do the same to Nick's weighty GP that was made from very dense local juniper wood.

"We'll never do it without help," sighed the owner who knew his boat of old.

"Aw! Come off it! We managed fine with old *Percy* here."

Gerr felt confident but the girls were silent. In their opinion *Percy* had been tricky to manoeuvre out of his cradle without bashing his hull against the bumpers of his trailer; and it had been an effort to carry him to the edge of the water. *Frolic* was much heavier and, to make matters worse, the GP's trailer had unusually tall and sharp-cornered mudguards. They'd have to lift Nick's boat very high to avoid those. What a pity *Frolic's* trailer wasn't the sort that could be rolled into the water. Then they could have floated the GP off her trolley without any difficulty.

"Oh well... We'll just have to try," sighed Nick.

Everyone exerted the greatest force possible – or as Gerald crudely expressed it:

"I've strained a gut trying to lift your blimmin boat, Nick!"

But they only just managed to raise the heavy dinghy a few inches. It was plain that to get *Frolic* out of her trailer without seriously scratching or bumping her on those viciously pointed and high mudguards was more than they could achieve. They mopped red, sweating faces.

"We'll have to get help somehow," groaned Nell rubbing her back, which felt as if it had twisted into two pieces. They stood about wondering. But in Africa there is usually no lack of manpower so the guard was not dismayed. He went to the gate and looked along the track. Very soon he was calling out to a friend and a little later Dizzy was being begged not to chew up a stranger who said his name was 'Wiston'. When the dog had been persuaded not to gnaw a chunk out of the newcomer's leg, he permitted Wiston to remove his boots and roll up his trousers. Then their new helper added his muscles to the task of moving *Frolic*.

"They were first class muscles too," recalled Ella later. "They positively rippled through his tee shirt and we got the GP onto the beach in two ticks."

They rolled the trailers back under the trees. Surprisingly Nick didn't help. He was standing aside deep in thought.

"The masts and booms are in that shed; and I see that its door is locked with a massive great padlock."

Everyone turned to look at the padlock and faces fell.

"Who's got the key?"

"Fisheries people, I suppose; and they're all on holiday, and today is Friday so we won't see them till Monday! If the Sampsons were here, Mr. Sampson would have a key, of course."

"Oh... DA... I mean BOTHER!"

"Yes. Nothing's going to plan."

"Possums! We've just *got* to find the key." Nick turned to the watchman.

"Who has the key?" he pointed to the shed.

"The key?" The watchman would have like to be helpful. He just hadn't been warned that strangers would be arriving so he was worried about assisting them. Nick took the man across to the shed and rattled the padlock.

"The opener for this. We need to get inside here." He banged on the door. "Who has the key for this small house?"

Silence.

"Who is in charge of this place?"

"Bwana Sampson."

"Yes. We know that. But he is away. Who is after Mr. Sampson?"

"Eh?" As well as being scared of blame for helping strangers, the man had very little knowledge of English.

"Oh I do wish I could talk Kangi and make myself understood! People are only awkward because they don't understand. Which people are working in the office here?"

"Ah! Maybe Mr. Merwamma."

"Good. Where is the house of Mr. Merwamma?"

The location was dragged out of the guard.

"Lucky it's near the Depot. I'll go and see if he's got the key and will lend it to us," said Nick not very hopefully. Then bitterly he added:

"We've had so many problems so far... We'll probably find he's gone away for the long weekend! El can you make yourself seem old and respectable and come with me?"

"I'll come too," offered Gerald who did not fancy sitting around.

"It's a bit hot for walking," objected Ella. She was not a great one for exercise.

"It's only just down the road. Come on. No thanks, Gerr. You look too debonair – or whatever it is – and too devilish – as if you enjoy getting up to mischief!"

"Hmph!" snorted Gerald. "What about you?"

"Oh, me? Butter wouldn't melt in my angelic mouth!"

"I thought you said we looked identical."

"Only when you're wearing a heavenly expression!"

To laughter from the Australians, Nick and Nell plodded off. The guard settled into his pillbox near the gate and Wiston took Gerald to inspect the boats. Kirstin challenged Carol to a game of ducks and drakes but they soon abandoned that in favour of bird watching. There were almost tame Egrets and Hammerkops standing on a barge just off shore. Black and white Cormorants swam about close at hand, their bodies under water but visible because the lake water was so clear. Only their long, sinuous necks and small heads popped up between dives. They eyed the humans with hard suspicious glares.

"Their necks're like rubber snakes," said Carol. "Look how blue their eyes are!"

On rocks that were white with bird droppings deposited over centuries, Darters, very like Cormorants but entirely black, stood with wings spread open to dry. Waders, Ducks, Eagles and Wagtails were not at all shy. Pied

Kingfishers, resembling flecks of ebony and ivory, shrieked and hovered like tiny helicopters, then plummeted without a splash after fish.

The bay was so beautiful, the birds and butterflies so fascinating that no one minded waiting till Ella and Nicky returned, dusty, rather weary, and simmering with suppressed irritation. They had an unwilling Mr. Merwamma in tow, and it was clear that he was justifiably not at all keen to open the shed. He was voicing difficulties: He had not been told… Permission had not been given… He had not heard that there would be visitors… Why were private boats in the Fisheries compound anyway? His superiors would be angry with him for issuing equipment…

"They're not Fisheries equipment. They're *our* masts," Nick explained patiently for the umpteenth time. He could sympathise with the conscientious Mr. Merwamma and he knew that all the official's arguments were perfectly in order. He also appreciated the man's kindness in leaving his home on a bank holiday. Thank goodness that Ella and Mrs. Merwamma had hit it off so well that the lady had encouraged her husband to help the sailors.

Reluctantly the Fisheries' secretary unlocked the padlock and allowed Wiston to open the shed door. The boys were inside like two shots. But at first no masts or booms could be seen. Bewildered, Gerald turned to the girls who were just behind him, looking equally worried. As their eyes adjusted to the gloom they saw Nick clambering onto a barrel and loosening a rope.

"Look out!" he said. "I'll let this one down first. We hang them up to keep them away from the White Ants… Get ready to ease it, Gerr, will you?" Wiston was already up on a crate releasing another rope to lower the far end of the GP mast, which had been hanging horizontally in the air below the roof.

"Catting kangas!" exclaimed Carol. "It's awfully long."

Mr. Merwamma and Wiston stared at her.

"We *must* remind the Aussies not to use that expression in this country" said Nick softly to Gerald. "People here don't understand it refers to kangaroos. They think it means them – Kangalians!"

Gerald laughed, but Nick knew the matter was serious.

As Ella and Wiston carried the GP mast out of the shed it seemed to go on forever. The boom, another nice, but weighty, piece of timber, was lowered next. Gerald laid it on the beach beside the mast.

Kirstin had unaccountably disappeared. Suddenly she materialised beside the Fisheries official who, mesmerised, was watching the cousins' antics.

"Oh, Mr. Merwamma," she said in dulcet tones. "Please will you show me where the freezer is? We must put this small container into it." She showed him the plastic box that held the now melted, but still cold, Bolognese sauce.

"Eh? What?" asked the puzzled secretary.

"It won't take much space and we'll need it the day we return."

Assaulted by so many surprises this morning, poor Mr. Merwamma seemed dazed. Without fuss, he turned to lead Kirstin to a freezer inside the office building.

"Wait," called Ella taking the sauce from Kirstin. "I'll bring the box in a minute. You go and see where the freezer is."

Quickly she threw the last few things out of Pythagoras and parked him beside the boat trailers. She locked up carefully, then, when no one was looking, she slipped the keys inside the sauce and clipped down the lid.

"There!" she announced to herself. "We don't want to take that enormous bunch with us and lose them overboard! So that's a good, safe place to hide them. Too bad if they sink down through the sauce. I wonder if they'll alter the flavour?"

"Better not come with me," advised Kirstin when she emerged from the office building. "I've just seen inside that freezer. It's full of all sorts of gory specimens: cut up fish with fantastic whiskers, innards of all kinds, incredible fishy jaws, fins, tails, eyes... and goodness knows what else; I even saw a couple of things that looked like tiny pickled mermaids. No! Really! *Dinkum!* You won't like it at all, El."

Paling visibly, Ella handed the box — which was *not* small! — to her cousin without a word. Indeed she wouldn't like the contents of that freezer — not one little bit! She felt decidedly queasy at the mere thought of its sights and formalin-laden smells. Kirstin, unaffected by goggling eyes, and alarming body parts, found a niche at the back of the bottom shelf where she hoped the sauce would not be opened and used for fishy experiments. Thanking Mr. Merwamma very sweetly she allowed him to relock the building. As usual Kirstin's loveliness and deceptively innocent charm had worked.

"Well done, Kirstin," said Nell. "I'd forgotten all about that wretched sauce. Good thing you remembered it."

"How did you know they had a freezer?" marvelled Carol.

"Oh — I didn't!" Kirsty assured them airily. "But I guessed it would be best to just assume that they had one and also that we'd be allowed to use it. Things always work if you assume a great air of confidence."

She smiled, even more innocently than usual.

"Hmph! You're a designing female!"

"I know!" laughed Kirstin grinning as she flicked her long blonde hair back with a saucy movement of head and hand. Then she ran across to help Wiston and the boys.

Percy's hollow mast and boom, both made of aluminium and therefore unacceptable to hungry termites, were lying against the rear wall of the shed. They had to be excavated from below a heap of fishing nets, big floats, and some plastic drums that were sometimes used as buoys. This mast was shorter than *Frolic*'s because an Enterprise's mast is stepped on deck and does not stand with its foot in the bottom of the boat. The mast was soon balanced in its mount on the foredeck. Gerald supported it until the Australians, who were familiar with Enterprises, had fastened the forestay and shrouds (cables that keep the mast in position).

Meanwhile Ella, Wiston and Nick struggled to insert the GP mast into its slot. This was always a tricky job because cleats and other fittings attached to its lower end prevent the mast from being slipped straight down into its hole. It has to slide slightly sideways as well as moving down while being held vertical.

"Let's turn *Frolic* onto her side. It's easier that way," puffed Nick whose face was bright red from the effort of trying to balance in an unstable boat and holding a heavy mast upright while simultaneously attempting to wriggle the square lower end into its slot. So Ella and Gerald held *Frolic* on her side while, with some difficulty, Wiston and Nick negotiated the cumbersome mast into place. After that it was routine work to turn the boats into the wind, raise the sails and then to lift or push the rigged boats into the water, before finally attaching rudders and tillers. Stowing the gear was more exciting.

"Is that your camera, Gerr? – In the Tupperware box? Good. Strap it under the thwart with these bungees. Then you can get at it easily and it won't be in the way or get kicked or anything."

Gerald took the elastic straps, each with a hook at either end, that Nick was offering him, and fastened the waterproof box below the seat that the other boy was pointing at. It went across the boat.

"Shall I put the other camera in the same place in *Percy?*"
"Yes. And the two pairs of binoculars in plastic bags go on the other side of the thwarts – underneath, like the cameras."
"O.K."

"Bedrolls? – Right up at the front behind the buoyancy bag under the foredeck of *Frolic* or up against *Percy's* front buoyancy tank. They won't weigh down the bows too much. That could be dangerous if we run into heavy weather."
Kirstin looked up.
"Bad weather? A mere zephyr, I'd say."
Ella had noted the gentle breeze with relief and didn't echo Kirstin's scorn at all. If the wind remained like this for the entire cruise Nell wouldn't mind a bit!
"Oh yes. But it can blow up very suddenly. It's sometimes called the 'Lake of Sparkles' but don't forget that one of the

early explorers named it 'The Storm Sea'. It can be really murderous."

Ella's heart did its usual sinking trick.

"Do you... ?" But she gave up in the flurry of stowing the heavy food boxes below the rear decks.

"Oh possums!" exclaimed Kirstin waving two small triangular flags. "We've forgotten to fix on the burgees."

"Oh yes! Bother it!" *(Burgee pic/diagrams pages x, 22 & 36.)*

"Come on then. Turn the boats onto their sides. This one first. It'll be a good test anyway, to see if we've tied the gear in properly."

They tilted *Frolic* till the top of her mast was low enough for Kirstin to reach up and slip the burgee stick into its clips on the masthead. Then they did the same for *Percy*.

"There," said Kirstin. "That wasn't so bad after all. I'm glad we bothered."

"You had the easy bit. You weren't pushing the boats over."

Suddenly there was a commotion in the shed. Dizzy, who had been following an interesting scent connected with Giant Cane Rats, had been locked inside and was now pursuing his prey with verve and frantic, deep barks. Luckily Mr. Merwamma was still around, watching the strange antics of these extraordinary young foreigners, and chatting to the gate guard. He handed the keys to Gerald so that he could release Dizzy and sort out the shambles that the dog's hunt had caused.

When the door opened an enormous Cane Rat, as big as a respectably-sized cat, shot out into the bright sunlight, crossed the rough grass and vanished towards a patch of reeds. Yelping feverishly, Dizzy was not far behind his grey quarry. Poor Dizzy! Not being familiar with this bit of marsh, and having much more momentum than the rat, he came to grief, landing heavily, and with a great splatter, in swamp. Still barking frenziedly, but undeterred, though up to the neck in squelchy mud, which he had expected to be dry land, he struggled on, battling between clumps of papyrus, pushing through weeds and forcing his way among assorted submerged vegetation. He snorted and splashed and gave tongue in huge delight.

"I say! Don't tell Dizzy," said Kirstin pointing to a tree stump on the nearer side of bulrushes. There, grooming his whiskers, and watching the dog's departure with arrogant calm, sat the Cane Rat!

"Cheeky thing!" exclaimed Ella. "Isn't he *huge* though?"

A little later, Carol bending over to re-adjust her personal bundle under a seat that ran up *Percy's* side, suddenly felt a soggy prod in the back of her shorts. Ugh!

"Caterwauling Kangas!" she shrieked. Then she laughed. Dizzy, draped incredibly in the *slimiest* weeds, daubed all over in filthy mud, was offering her a stinking object and inviting her to share his pleasure in this latest trophy. The rat forgotten, he had caught this disgusting, rotting piece of something-or-other.

"Go away, Dizzy! *Flick off!*"

"Gosh!" sweated Gerald when at last all was set and the boats, with carefully balanced cargoes were floating level. "Let's have a swim. Race you to that launch, Nick."

Without bothering to change or undress the boys ran into the water and splashed towards a moored speedboat. *Frolic* and *Percy* bobbed about, head to wind, a yard or two off the beach.

"Come on," urged Kirsty. "Let's get the boats beached a little way up so they don't sail off by themselves. Typical boys! – Abandoning them just like that!"

"They knew we'd see to it. Or at least, Nick did," said Carol. "I bet Gerald doesn't even know yet that boats don't look after themselves".

With Wiston's help they dragged and pushed the stern of each dinghy up onto the beach.

"That'll do," said Kirstin knowledgably.

"But the bows are still in water," Ella pointed out.

"Yes, I know. But there're scarcely any waves and I don't think the boats will be lifted off. Anyway, it's not for long and we're not going far, so we'll keep an eye on them."

The girls withdrew behind the famous shed and changed into bathers. Then they slowly swam after the boys, diving as they went for white snail-like shells that lay here and there on the sandy bottom. Some were inhabited by tiny fish. Others still protected their original "snail" occupants, and many were just empty.

"Are you looking forward to sailing, Ella?" asked Caro.
"Er – I don't really know."
"Well, you'll find out as soon as we've finished swimming," Kirstin told her. "And once we're under way it will be too late to decide that you want to stay ashore!"

23. Frolic trying to get under way with no burgee and a strange combination of mainsail, genoa and small spinnaker

CHAPTER 16

"We're off!"

"D'you know what?" asked Ella ruefully looking at her arms as they dressed after the swim.
"No. I never met him."
"What?"
"Yes. Watt. Never met him so I don't know him!"
"Kirs-*tin*! Ha! HA!" exclaimed Nell sarcastically drawing out her cousin's name to great lengths in exasperation. "You know very well I wasn't talking about anyone called Watt!"
"What then?" replied Kirstin perfectly solemnly except that there was a twinkle in her eyes. Ella sighed.
"I was going to say… We never daubed ourselves with anti-sunburn cream. And we never put on our long-sleeved shirts either. After all Maddy's warnings too! I'm already going bright pink!"
"Gosh! It must be dreadful to burn so easily," sympathised Kirsty, "and to have such a delicate skin."
"I don't understand it. Your hair is just as fair as mine, and Carol's is pure gold," grumbled Nell. "Why don't you two burn like me?"
"We do brown – a bit. I don't know why we don't go all puce like you, and peel like a snake changing its skin – as you do."
"Something to do with cretins," suggested Carol doing up her cuffs. She and her sister had automatically left out long-sleeved shirts, hats and dark glasses in readiness for sailing. They knew that the combination of sun and wind would attack even their tough hides if they sailed unprotected for several hours; and it was better to put up with the boys' teasing about tie-on hats and Panda Bear dark glasses rather than suffer the effects of light reflected from the water.

"Cretins? No, not cretins, Carol, you cretin yourself!" guffawed Kirstin. "You mean keratin… No. That's in your hair and nails… and rhino horn… What's the word she's trying to use, El? The stuff that's in our skins… "

"Pigment perhaps," suggested Ella half heartedly and a bit dubiously as she examined her shoulder. "Obviously I haven't got enough of it – whatever it is. I'll have to unpack to get out my anti-sunburn stuff."

The boys were not best pleased with this but they waited silently as Ella untied her bag, unwrapped its plastic covering, took out what she needed, re-packed, rewrapped the plastic layers and tied the bundle back in its place. They were itching to be off.

"Anyone want some anti-burn cream?" offered Ella generously. Everyone patted on some of the stuff and the Australian girls also had thick white triangles of zinc oxide on their noses.

"Special Ozzie trick to stop peeling conks," they explained.

"Makes you look like clowns," laughed Nick.

"Oh well. Better amuse you than get a raw snout."

"Ten thirty one" said Gerald consulting his new watch. "For goodness sake BUCK UP! Do let's *get going*!"

Carol lifted an armful of lifejackets with a view to handing them out; and there, below the jackets, were two anchors which the pile had hidden.

"Oh Possums!" she exclaimed. "We haven't packed the anchors."

"Caterwauling Kangas!"

Nick looked over his shoulder to see if Kirstin had offended any Kangalians. Luckily no one who might have taken umbrage had heard.

"Oh! Blow!"

"Where-ever are we to put them now? Nasty spiky beasts!"

They tried hard to find somewhere to lash an anchor into each boat, and became more and more impatient as the heavy, awkward things refused to fit anywhere convenient.

"Oh dash it!" said Nick eventually. "We should have buried them in *takunda*; but I am not going to re-pack! Now they'll stub our toes and stab our legs a million times a day."

"Where else can we put them? We've tried everywhere."

"I don't know."

"Let's leave them behind."

"Wailing Wallabies, Gerr. You must be mad! How'll we manage without them?"

"Easily," said Nick deciding that Gerald was right. "We were planning to pull the boats up onto beaches every night, anyway. Now we'll just have to pull them higher."

"Well – leave the wailing things. That's what I say."

In the end they lashed the anchors to the boat trailers and hoped for the best.

"Bet we regret this," muttered Kirstin darkly.

"Oh! Pooh!" said her sister cheekily. "I hate anchors. Horrid prickly things!"

She started handing out five lifejackets for the second time.

"Put it on," she ordered standing small and square in front of her tall cousin, Gerr, who had started to stow his lifejacket inside *Percy*.

"Admiral Maddy's orders," said Carol firmly and bravely.

"And my dad's orders too," said Kirstin. "He says 'Only idiots sail without wearing a life jacket'."

"But I can swim. I've won all sorts of swimming cups at school… " No one would ever suggest that Gerald was modest! "We can all swim – like fishes," he went on. "If we fall overboard we won't come to any harm. We'll just swim."

"You might get knocked out – in two senses – by the boom say – Then you might find it a bit difficult to swim when you're unconscious. Or if you get a broken arm or ribs, and the weather is very rough, it might be jolly hard to stay afloat till we can go about and get back to pick you up."

Grudgingly Gerald donned his lifejacket.

"What charming ideas you do have," he grumbled sarcastically.

"How are we going to sort ourselves out?" asked Nick. "Kirsty and Caro you'd better start in *Percy*, I suppose. You're used to sailing Enterprises so you'll soon get the feel of this one."

They nodded.

"What about you two?" Nick looked at the Stanleighs doubtfully. He would helm his GP to start with.

"You take Gerr and teach him how to crew," suggested Kirstin, who didn't fancy having to coach her admirer. "It's nice easy weather so he'll pick it up quickly."

Gerald looked affronted. "And you're more patient than I am, Nick," added Kirstin honestly. Her cousin looked even more offended.

"OK, then" agreed the Cruise Commodore. "And you teach Ella."

He expected Gerr to get the hang of sailing much more quickly and more easily than Nell and was glad to have been allocated his male cousin to teach. Besides, with Carol crewing for Kirstin, Ella would have little to do and could take life in the Enterprise easily. Taking life easily was very much to her taste. And, having a placid nature, she wouldn't mind obeying orders. Kirsty was relieved not to have been allocated Gerald as her pupil. That might have been embarrassing.

Dizzy whined. He was not partial to boats and he had a feeling that his new friends were about to disappear in the unpleasant way humans did in these strange floating objects.

"Sorry, Dizzy, old boy," said Nick patting the dog. "We'll be back next Thursday." With a sudden premonition that things might not turn out as planned, he added:

"That is – if all goes well. See you then. O.K?"

He turned to Gerr. "Hop in Crew-boy, and I'll push off."

Nick's command was rapidly obeyed and in a minute or two the GP was heading towards the middle of the bay.

"Centreboard down," ordered Skipper Nick.

"Hey? What?" asked Gerald. He would have been furious if he'd known that his reply made Nick think of the Sampsons' *bezan*! But assuming that his cousin had just not heard the order, Nick repeated it. Then he twigged that his Crew hadn't the foggiest idea what he was going on about.

"Centre board... Oh... Look – that knob. Pull it hard back and the centreboard – that's a sort of movable keel... Sometimes it's called 'the plate'. At the moment it's up out of the water, see? Looks like a slab of metal... Pull the knob – That's right. Pull it as far back as it'll go. There. Now the centreboard's down. It's no longer out of the water but is down below the boat, acting like a keel. Wedge it in position with that sliver of wood."

"Bit of wood?"

"The wedge that's hanging from the centreboard casing by a bit of red twine. Yes. That's it. Now ram the wedge in between the centreboard and its casing. Done? You'll find that the way of fixing the plate in the Enterprise is a little different, but the main idea's the same: having got the plate down you want to fix it there. Is it jammed?"

"Yes."

"Good. Now we won't make leeway."

"Leeway?"

"Making leeway means crabbing: going sideways. The centreboard stops us going sideways – well – up to a point it does."

"Why doesn't *Frolic* have a proper keel?

"Dinghies don't have keels. They have centreboards or dagger boards. You have to moor in deep water if you've got a keel. In a dinghy you can just pull up a centreboard or dagger board and float the boat right in to the beach."

"Oh."

"And it's handy to be able to adjust the plate when you're racing too."

"Oh?"

"Look – Sit over on the other side, please Gerr. OOPs! Gently – man! Don't rush about like an angry rhino."

Very unsure about what to do as well as unused to being lectured Gerald was, at the moment, feeling exactly like an angry rhino, but he gallantly bit back a nasty reply and sat where Nick was pointing.

Caro and Kirsty had pushed Percy off with Ella already installed near the mast. Then they splashed inboard. Carol lowered the plate and took the jibsheet.

"This little sail is called the jib," she said pointing to the sail that was over the bow. "Today we're using the big jib that's called… "

"I thought you said the jib was a small sail?"

"Yes. See the big sail at the back of the boat? That's the mainsail. The one in front of the mast is called the jib. There are two sizes of jib. Both are usually (but not always) smaller than the mainsail. Today we're using the big jib because there's not much wind."

"Oh."

"The big jib is called the 'genoa' – 'genny' for short."

"So what's the small jib called?"

"Ey? Oh – er – I think it's just called the jib."

"When do you use that smaller sail?"

"When the wind's stronger. The little jib allows us to point better."

Kirstin saw Nell's look of confusion.

"To point means to sail closer to the wind."

That didn't seem to make sense to Ella either.

"Look at the little flag at the top of the mast," said Kirstin. "That's the burgee. It tells you which way the wind is blowing."

"Yes. So…?"

"Well – are we moving towards the wind?

"No. We're going at an angle to the wind."

"With the small jib I could, if I wanted to, make that angle smaller. Then the boat'd be moving closer into the wind. That's called pointing. I can't go close to the wind with the genny."

"I'll never remember all these things."

"Never mind. You'll get it soon. Until then we'll just tell you what to do. OK?"

"Fine by me."

Today both boats were using genoas to catch as much of the light wind as possible. Carol let her genny billow out as far as it would go without collapsing, then she cleated the jibsheet. Nell watched everything with round eyes and was soon listening to Carol's instructions as to how to operate the small sail when it moved onto Ella's side.

"OK," she said. "I'll try," and she started to pull on the rope that Carol had indicated.

"No. No," laughed Kirstin. "Not *now* El. You pull on that sheet – rope – when we go about. That means when we change direction slightly and the sails cross to the other side of the boat. When we do that it will be your turn to handle the jibsheet.

"Oh," said Ella vaguely. 'Well!' she thought. 'I suppose I'll understand what they mean in time.' But dubiously she added: 'Perhaps.'

Wiston, already some distance away, was waving goodbye from beside the reeds. They had given him a handsome tip and he had promised to help them de-rig the boats on their return. Now they called repeated thanks and waved again.

"Oh no! Dizzy's following," Kirstin shouted across to *Frolic*.

"It's OK," answered Nick looking back. "He'll swim about a bit. Then he'll turn back and go home. Don't worry."

Sure enough Dizzy, who was a wader and wallower but not a swimmer, splashed round in a big circle and then paddled back to shore. They saw his big black shape slowly making its way along the sands and over rocks back to his home beach. On the way he enjoyed few exciting chases after vervets.

"Cheerio, Dizzy!" called Ella. "See you next week."

"Hurray!" shouted Carol. "We're off!"

"Never thought we'd make it! One flipping problem after another flaming difficulty" growled Nick.

"We're off to re-discover the ancient explorers' lake," sang Kirstin, as happy as her sister. She let her boat glide away from the boys in the GP. The Enterprise was the faster boat in light breezes and Gerald was having a spot of trouble with his genoa.

"Don't pull it in as hard as a board, you goof!" Nick was saying. "In light winds you want to let the sails out as far as they'll go without losing tension. Loosen the jibsheet – that's the rope you're hanging onto like grim death. Yes. That's right. Let the wind take the genny out. Yes. OK. Now back in a smidgin... Fine. Now you can cleat it."

Gerald looked puzzled so Nick left the tiller and leant forward to show his cousin how to squeeze the rope between the jaws of the jamming cleat.

"To loosen the jibsheet – that's this rope – you pull it upwards, out of the cleat's jaws, like this. See – now the sheet's in the air. It's loose. When it's free like this you can let it out or pull it in. Got it? But if you clamp the rope – by pulling it down between the jaws of the cleat, like this... then it's fixed and you can relax – so long as the cleat works – and you can admire the view. Only you've got to watch the genny, or the little jib – whichever is being used – and adjust the sheet when necessary.

"Hm," said Gerr. "Hey! The sails're flapping all over the place!"

"That's because I've left the tiller and the boat's going head-to-wind – automatically. She's very good at that. It's awfully handy. When she's facing into the wind she stops."

Nick went back to the tiller and waggled it. Slowly *Frolic* turned, then gathered enough speed to respond to the helm, and the boys set off after the girls.

As Nick had predicted it didn't take Gerald long to get the hang of operating the genny. They went about a few times to give him practice and then they looked round for the Enterprise. It had crossed to the far side of the bay, taken a squint at the small ships in the tiny harbour, inspected the floating dry dock, and now on a new tack, was returning towards the hills on the Fisheries' side from which the girls had set sail. *Percy* was well ahead of the GP and he looked tiny. Suddenly the huge size of the bay came home to Gerald.

"The girls are chatting," said Nick. "Look at the way their boat's moving. Kirsty's not concentrating on her sailing. Come on, Gerr. You've got it now. We're going to overtake those girls!"

CHAPTER 17

Lunch at sea. Gambolling in the deeps.

Catching up with the girls wasn't as easy as Nick had anticipated, but *Frolic* eventually came abreast with *Percy* as they were approaching the big island that almost shuts the mouth of Baboon Bay. Both boats had tacked several times, crossing and re-crossing the width of the rectangular inlet. Now the vessels in the shipyard looked insignificant; yet the cousins were still not beyond the sheltering bluffs on each side of the long cove.

As the dinghies sailed side by side Kirstin called out:
"*Percy* really *is* a 'he' boat. We don't know why, but he's definitely not a 'she'!"
"How odd!" muttered Nick but he didn't explain whether he thought it was odd that *Percy* should be male, or whether he considered it strange that the boat could convey this to the people who were sailing him.
"I thought that all boats *had* to be 'shes'," said Gerald.
"Well, apparently that one's not. He's a 'he'. I suppose that's why he's called *Percy*."

This illuminating, if not very elevating, conversation was interrupted by an imposing sentinel baboon on the island. From high on a rock that towered from the beach he barked warnings at the sailors as they drew near. Sitting on the sand or inland under trees, members of his troupe were staring into space or grooming each other. Coming down to the edge of the water some stuck tails in the air and bent to drink.
"Just look at that!" exclaimed Gerald. "See how they scoop a little basin in the gravel and slurp the water from that. Isn't it amazing?"
"Stops them getting their feet wet, which would happen if they came to the edge of the lake where waves lap up and down," commented Carol, full of admiration. "Clever, aren't they?"

Youngsters were gambolling everywhere, swinging on convenient creepers, playing a form of 'catch', and whisking about their elders till they tweaked the tail of a sober adult just once too often. Then they were reprimanded with a shrill shriek of baboon abuse. Suddenly a screaming squabble was in full swing.

"My goodness!" exclaimed Ella who was training to become a nursery nurse. "They're even worse than my little horrors at college! Crikey! What a din!"

The baboon grandfather gave another bark. This was an abrupt, sharp, authoritative warning. The fighting stopped. For a second the monkeys stood like statues. Some of them glared at the passing cousins. Babies leapt for the safety of parents; and mothers, grabbing more independent youngsters swept them under their tummies. At another short grunt, the whole company lolloped off into the trees. Granddad had decided that the boats had crept up too close for baboon comfort. When the last fleeing tail had disappeared the old fellow went ponderously up the beach in the rear.

"Ready about," said Nick. "Pity they couldn't wait another minute. I wish humans could explain to animals that we aren't going to hurt them."

"Ready," replied Gerald, deftly uncleating the jibsheet as he had been taught and preparing to move smoothly to the other side of the dinghy.

"Lee O!" said Nick putting the tiller across, and *Frolic*, responding beautifully, veered gracefully away from the island.

"Gee! Gerald! You're a real expert," called Kirstin, half mocking and half serious.

"Oh! Aren't we going to land?" wailed Carol disappointed.

"Can't we have lunch on that beach?" suggested Ella.

"Well – we could – if you insist," Nick called back dubiously. "But with the wind this light it'll take us ages to get even to Colander Cove let alone into the further bay. Probably be better to eat as we go along. We were hoping to reach

Elephant Island this evening but with a delayed start and the wind as it is, we've no hope of getting that far."

"Oh Lor'!" moaned Nell. "I was looking forward to stretching my legs."

"Whatever for?" asked Caro. "There's heaps of room in an Enterprise – not like in a Mirror that ... "

"Ready about," interrupted Kirstin.

"Ready," replied the obedient Carol sadly casting a look at 'The island on which we didn't land' as she named it to herself.

"Lee O!" ordered Kirstin.

Her sister manipulated the genoa.

"Pull your rope, El," she said as she slackened off on her side.

"What? — Oh! Er – oh yes!" Ella took her eyes off the vanishing baboons and turned them to the jib.

"Oh heavens! What's gone wrong? What do I do now?"

Carol nipped across the boat and sorted out Nell's tangled jibsheet.

"There you are," she said, cleating it and going back to her own side of *Percy*.

"See how much room there is for both of us? Especially as we're both small. Try sailing a Mirror or a Miracle. Not much space there. Always getting bumped by the boom unless you're really awake."

"Oh, caramba!" was all the learner could say. Gingerly she stretched one leg and then the other trying to decide which was more cramped and which was going redder with sunburn.

"Pass me the anti-burn cream, Caro, please. It's wedged under that rope over there. Thanks."

Later Kirsty shouted:

"When are we going to eat? I'm starving!"

"So're we," answered Nick. "But we'll wait till we're properly out into the lake, shall we?"

"It's still early. It's only twelve twenty two." Gerr's new watch had been well splashed so he was glad it was waterproof.

"Then we'll be in a howling gale in mid-lake, when we're out of the shelter of Baboon Bay," said Carol exaggerating picturesquely as usual, "and we'll be so busy holding the boat that we won't have a spare hand to eat with."

Ella turned green and gave a suppressed groan.

"Oh no, you shonky idiot," Kirstin contradicted her sister amiably. "Just look at the horizon. Flat as a pancake! Nick is absolutely right. We've got to use what wind there is while it lasts."

"Um. Yes. I suppose so."

"I wouldn't be surprised if the wind drops completely and we have to paddle most of the way" added Kirstin after studying the sky and tree tops; so Ella, plunging from the idea of one form of misery to a picture of perhaps a worse sort of agony groaned out loud this time.

"I do hope not," she said; and her unsympathetic cousins merely laughed.

"Might give you an appetite, Nell," they said. "I say – do watch that jib! Pull in a bit. We're heading more into the wind now. It's a pity but we've got to get round that headland somehow."

"Let's have another drink."

Bailing mugs were dipped into the lake and thirsty mariners were glad to down large quantities of clear, cool water.

"And we're supposed to be doing this for pleasure," said Ella in disgust. "Here, Carol, I'm sure you're dying to operate the jibsheet. I'm going to read one of my books." The Aussies swapped glances and shrugged.

When Ella's bundle was unpacked – yet again – there was no sign of her books. On careful consideration she remembered having temporarily stuffed them under one of *Frolic's* buoyancy bags. Bookless and disconsolate she moved about on the edge of *Percy's* little side deck which seemed to have become extraordinarily hard and uncomfortable. She tried to keep as much as possible of her aching body in the shade of the sail.

"For pleasure!" she murmured again, bitterly. Her cousins grinned. They knew exactly how Ella was feeling. All would be well once the wind started to blow. They were sure of that.

But all they could offer as amusement were frequent and necessary cups of fresh lake water.

Gerald was surprised how fast (or so it seemed to him) the boats were swishing over the water, even in this light wind. It was great gliding along with little waves splashing away from *Frolic* and soft chuckling sounds coming from under the bow.

"Pooh! This is putsi!" he thought with his usual confidence. "I might even get bored later on."

He didn't know how fickle the weather on inland seas can be, and he had no idea of how quickly conditions can change. He was also unaware that down at the coast of Bafandoland the Indian Ocean was stirring up trouble – bad trouble. A hurricane was brewing and when Bafandoland suffered a cyclone, its tail usually lashed Lake Kangi. Gerald was innocent of the fact that tomorrow he and the others would be battling to stay afloat – struggling, in fact, to stay alive!

By one o'clock Baboon Bay was far behind. It was actually still in sight and low on the horizon, but not always directly astern because they changed direction each time they started a new beat. Their objective, Colander Cove, was much further away so, with the wind scarcely existing any more, it was going to be difficult to reach it by nightfall. They had each nibbled so much of their individual lunch packs that it hardly seemed worth going head-to-wind and having a nautical picnic.

"We're not even moving," moaned Carol "We've been opposite that huge cliff for *hours!*"

"I think we *are* just moving," Nell consoled her, trying hard to persuade herself as well.

"It's just that we're so far out at 'sea' that we don't seem to be making any progress or passing things on shore," hoped Kirstin doubtfully. She saw a leaf in the bottom of the boat and dropped it overboard. Slowly – ever so slowly – it floated sternwards and then moved beyond the rudder.

"See – We *are* moving – a *bit!*" she confirmed.

There was a splash! Gerald bored beyond endurance with the slow pace, and sizzling in the heat, had let himself topple over backwards off the edge of *Frolic* into the water.
"Super!" he spluttered coming up and shaking drops out of his hair.
"Can I go in too?" asked Carol eagerly.
"Go ahead," allowed her sister. "Ella too, if you like."
Nell looked round and saw with a shiver of fright how terrifyingly remote and small the coast looked.
"Are you sure it's OK to be so far from land in such a cockleshell?" she asked. In panic she looked the other way. Had they gone so far that they were now near to the dangerous eastern coast? But the lake is 50 miles wide and at present she had absolutely no need to be anxious. Then she gazed over the side and shuddered. She could see down, down, down – and still further down – through clear turquoise depths that turned progressively greener and more mysterious. The water looked exquisitely cool, but so agonisingly deep! Caro stood up, said:
"Watch it!" and jumped overboard. She had been careful so *Percy* rocked only a little.

"Go on, El," encouraged Kirstin. "It'll be lovely in. Just take care not to tilt *Percy* too much as you go."
The plump girl stood up cautiously. The unending depths were terribly daunting. She'd never even *imagined* such bottomless water. Her heart thumped horribly. But she felt unbearably HOT! Would she be able to balance on the unstable edge of the boat? Clutching the mast, she stepped momentarily onto the side, then more firmly onto the foredeck. Could she muster the courage to jump? Suddenly, holding her nose and giving a squawk, she stepped off.

With a huge splash Nell went under... Deep... Deeper yet. Was she going right to the bottom? Was she going to drown? No! Threshing arms and legs hard, she was now coming up again. Thank goodness for that!

"Lovely! Gorgeous!" she spluttered as she popped out of the surface looking surprised and relieved. Catching her breath she realised that she really meant it. How easy it was to swim here. Of course! She was still wearing her life jacket. They all were. Sailing orders...

Ella was delighted to find that she could open her eyes underwater without being attacked by salt sea or chlorinated pool. But she had a shock when she tested this new pleasure by dipping her head and trying to see the lake floor. Although the water was absolutely crystal clear, the depths were so tremendous that the lower levels looked deep ultramarine and didn't reveal their secrets. The bottom was nowhere in sight. Nell suddenly felt as if she was unbearably high and nearly suffered vertigo! Then she understood that even if she did become giddy, she wouldn't fall. The water was supporting her. She gazed up at the wonderfully clear sky with relief. Open blue heavens above, limpid turquoise water below...

"Kirstin," she shouted. "You remember that chunk of amber that Granny's got? The one with an insect caught inside it?"

"Yes."

"Well – When I'm under water here, I feel like an insect in sapphire!"

Kirstin laughed. What strange ideas Ella had!

The three swimmers enjoyed themselves immensely, cavorting round the dinghies like otters and, with life jackets removed, even diving under one side and coming up on the other of the solitary skippers.

"Get together, you two," called Gerald. "I'm going to swim below *both* boats." So Nick and Kirstin steered closely parallel courses. Gerr took a deep breath and disappeared with a neat kick. In a few moments he was on the far side laughing at his sister's worried expression.

"'Seasy," he assured her.

"Hop in," said Nick, longing for his chance to dive below the two hulls. "I'm dying of heat. My turn to swim now."

"Gosh! Er – yes. O.K." Gulping, Gerr suddenly grasped that Nicky expected him to cope with *Frolic* alone. He'd taken the tiller once during the morning but that had been briefly and under his skipper's eye. Would he remember what to do?

Nick steadied the boat as his cousin tried to clamber in over the side.

"No! No!" he said, patting the back of the boat. "Always come in over the transom if you can. It doesn't jiggle things so much."

So Gerald swam round to *Frolic's* stern. Tall, and with powerful muscles, he had no trouble hauling himself in; but over in the other dinghy, now some distance away, Carol was having a tough time trying to get aboard. There wasn't a chance of her making it over *Percy's* stern. Not only did the rear deck make it difficult to get a grip, but the Enterprise seemed awfully high up out of the water, and Caro was short for her twelve years. The jibsheet was clamped so, grabbing its loose end, Kirstin threw the middle portion of the free rope over the side. With this loop as a step, and with a heave from Ella, Carol slithered head first and amidships into *Percy*.

"Not so good for the jamming cleat," said Kirsty. "However… Hang about El. Then, when I'm in I'll give you a shove up."

"Not yet. I'm enjoying this," said Nell wallowing about idly, letting her life jacket support her.

Carol settled down with the tiller in one hand and the mainsheet in the other. There was really very little for her to do because the wind had almost dropped. The jib was correctly set and cleated so she concentrated on keeping the sails as full as possible. Over in *Frolic* Nick was giving his cousin a crash course in helming. For once Gerald did not exude preposterous confidence.

"OK," he said somewhat doubtfully. "I'll try."

The water was so flat. It seemed impossible that any novice could do anything wrong. Nor was there the slightest indication of the storm that would soon hit them with frightening suddenness.

CHAPTER 18

Flocks round fishing boat. Hard paddling.

24. Carol in her mermaid flippers visiting the depths.

Nick slipped overboard, careful not to rock his boat; and Gerald gripped the tiller as if he feared it would take off with both dinghies and leave them all floundering helplessly. Coming up with a mouthful of lake, Nicholas blew the water like a fountain into the air.

"Phew!" he said happily. Then, with grim humour he swam up beside *Frolic* and challenged:

"Beat you to the camp site, Gerr."

Kirstin, worried, was at *Percy's* transom kicking and pushing and trying to make the hull move a trifle less slowly. If the wind didn't rise soon they'd be forced to paddle or they'd never arrive before sunset; and even in daylight locating a small, unlit and concealed cove on a stretch of totally uninhabited, wild stretch of African coastline is extremely difficult. Would they find anywhere to land in the dark?

"Catting Kangas! It's hard work," she puffed giving up at last. Then she exploded a huge hoot of laughter.

"Wailing Wallabies! Gerr, you *can't* gybe in this non-wind!"

"Can't he though?" laughed Nicky as Gerald's sail again snapped slowly across *Frolic* and the bewildered new skipper ducked only just in time to avoid the boom cracking his skull. In a flurry he jabbed the tiller. Over went the boom for the third time. Down bobbed the distracted Gerald.

"Puking Possums!" the others heard him exclaim bitterly as his vessel rocked, and the sail flapped, and the boom whacked across yet again. Flustered, Gerr stood up.

"Can't gybe?" exclaimed Nicky, laughing. "I'd say he was going for a record! Four gybes in under three seconds! Push the tiller over, man!"

"Eh? What?" Thoroughly bemused Gerald turned to look at him and was hit in the back by the boom on its fifth traverse.

"Oh Heck! Come and sort out your stupid boat, Nick!"

Kirstin who by now was closer to *Frolic* took pity on her panicking cousin.

"Give us a paw, Gerr," she said coming up to the transom. "I'm coming aboard."

Looking sheepish and self-conscious, Gerald tried to

remember what it was that Kirsty had done to help her sister aboard. Something to do with a jamming cleat and a rope...? He leant over towards the jibsheet.

"No, just leave the tiller and give me a hand." said Kirstin. Splashing all over the small rear deck she slid inboard.

"Thanks. Look... Sit there and... OOPS!" Back came the boom again! Kirstin gave her confused and scared cousin another lesson in helming while Ella bobbed about half listening, and Nick swam round the slowly moving pair of boats. But gradually Nell noticed that she was actually having to swim hard to keep up. The breeze was strengthening. Good oh!

"I think I'll get back on board, Nicky." Ella spoke in slight panic. "Will you give me a leg up?"

"No. But I'll give you a shove. Hey, Caro, throw down a loop please."

With one foot in the loop and an almighty heave from Nick, Nell clawed her plump way inboard. Nick disappeared under water! Carol was leaning well out on the far side to keep *Percy* level. Much merriment resounded from everyone except for poor Nell.

"Oops! OUCH!" she slipped and stabbed a toe painfully, then hit her knee on the centreboard casing. "Gosh! Caterwauling Kangas! Ow!"

Grinning but sympathetic, Carol moved nimbly to counteract her ample cousin's plunges about the boat till she gradually regained her balance and stopped staggering about.

"Caramba!" said the sufferer in a final sort of voice.

Nick was now struggling to keep up with the 'fleet', which was starting to pick up speed. He glanced across at *Frolic*. Kirstin and Gerald were managing nicely.

"Hey, Caro! I'm coming aboard," he called and put on a fine turn of speed to reach *Percy* whose bows, now that they were biting into the water, were chuckling really happily and giving him a cheeky white moustache. "Get over a bit more, Ella. OK? You'll balance the boat as I heave myself in."

Carol went pink because she was a trifle shy to skipper with her idol (her big sailor cousin) as Crew, but scattering drops he sat opposite to Ella and took charge of the jib.

"Come on, Old Salt," he urged. "Let's make the most of this. I don't think it's going to last."

Pessimistic Nicholas, was right. For a blissful, but all too brief, forty minutes the wind picked up till the boats were skimming rapidly over small choppy waves. At first Ella and Gerald were worried by the way the dinghies heeled, but they soon got the feel of proper sailing and even learnt how to lean out to counteract the effects of sudden squalls. As these unpredictable puffs came dancing over the water each gust ruffled the surface into a patch of tiny pointed wavelets that bounced together over the bigger waves like a million frogs hopping independently over an elephant's crinkled back.

Kirstin, helming the GP, was getting every ounce from the blow so the two boats flew along together. Then, gradually, the wind dropped.

"Well. It was nice while it lasted," smiled Carol some time later. "But now I'm bored stiff by that penguin-shaped rocky outcrop. We've been parallel with it for *hours!*"

Exaggeration was her forte.

"Let's have tea," suggested Ella.

Bananas and biscuits were handed round and bailing cups used yet again to dip water from the lake. And still they seemed to remain opposite that wretched penguin shape. Or had they actually drifted backwards?

A small, motorised fishing boat, which had been just a blob on the horizon, came puffing southwards to unload its catch at the commercial fishing company south of Baboon Bay. An extraordinary number of African Fish Eagles swooped about the miniscule tanker as sea-gulls do in other climes. Here the few gulls in the swirling flock were ultra careful to keep out of the way of ponderous eagles which did not swerve as zippily as smaller birds. They were all after fish or pieces of fish, that dropped from the boat or which the fishermen threw up to them. With a powerful SWOOSSSH an eagle swooped to the lake surface and rose with a tilapia in its claws. Two other predators, which had been after the same booty achieved incredible aerobatics to avoid smashing into the victor and into each other. The fascinated cousins couldn't help applauding. The gulls screamed. There was another spectacular display of hefty aerial manoeuvres as several imposing Fish Eagles zoomed onto a chunk that had been thrown high into the air. The birds seemed to miss each other by less than a fish scale, as, with great swishing wings the group exploded into separate birds again. When the winner fumbled, and dropped his prize, a different eagle, swerving with forceful grace, swung his legs backwards then forwards in a vigorous arc, and caught the falling trophy in his big claws.

"Fantastic!" breathed Gerald, fascinated. He reached under the thwart for the binoculars' waterproof bundle and watched till the fishing boat had chugged into the distance. In *Percy* Nicky had also seized the binoculars and was sharing them with Ella and Carol. The excitement was quickly over and the 'fleet' was again floating on a vast, terribly flat sea.

"I'm going to paddle," announced *Percy's* crewman extracting two implements of torture. "Here you are, Ella. You can use this one to work on your side."

"Hm," replied his cousin unimpressed.

Kirstin and Gerald soon followed suit. But whereas Nick and Ella advanced, if not rapidly, at least noticeably and in a straight line, *Frolic* floundered in circles.

"What on earth?" spluttered Gerr. "Don't paddle so flipping hard, Kirsty."

"I'm not. It's you... Oops!" The GP started a reverse chassé. "It's because we've got nobody steering. It's hopeless with the tiller swinging free and swaying all over the place. We must control it. Do you want to paddle for a bit and I'll steer? Or vice versa?"

"Then we'll swap?" asked Gerald cannily.

"Of course."

"I'll paddle first then."

Things went better after that though, naturally, with only one worker, heavy *Frolic* lagged behind the lighter *Percy* with his two paddlers and independent steerswoman.

"Wailing Wallabies!" fulminated Kirstin, who didn't number patience among her virtues. "I'll steer with my bottom and paddle at the same time!" This succeeded up to a point but it was difficult to maintain a straight course.

"Let's try to lash the tiller," suggested Gerald, but they couldn't locate any spare cord.

"Where d'you keep your spare rope?" yelled Kirstin ahead to Nick.

"What's that?"

"Rope. Where d'you keep spare string?"

"Tied to the bars of the seats." But there was none to be seen.

"Here! I'll use this bungee," said Gerald impatiently unstrapping the camera from under the thwart."

"Bit dangerous to have the camera loose," observed Kirstin.

"Oh dash it! In this dead calm, nothing can happen."

If he had known this huge inland sea and its varying moods Gerr would never have made such a rash statement. But he was, as yet, happily unconscious of how vicious this lake could become. Ramming the camera box between two bundles, he twisted the bungee round the tiller and linked the end hooks to struts of the seats on each side of the helm. This held the arm fairly straight and, by paddling assiduously they made good progress. But how long would they be able to keep this up? The tremendous cliffs lining the coast made it impossible to land anywhere before Colander Cove. Would they make that before nightfall?

25. An African Fish Eagle – 'paddling' in order to drink.

CHAPTER 19

Galley slaves.

Over in *Percy* Ella was flagging.
"Let's change sides," she puffed as matter-of-factly as she could. She had a stitch in her right side and her arms were hurting dreadfully. Her back ached. Nick was happy to swap positions with her. He too had painful stitches and cramps.
"I'll take a turn," offered Carol from her post at the tiller.
"In a minute," said Nell gritting her teeth and plying her paddle bravely. Heavens! How slowly they were going! That beastly penguin outcrop was still just about opposite.
In fact they had moved a considerable distance but as they were now heading partially in towards the shore their apparent motion past points along the coast seemed negligible.
After a while Nell and Carol changed places. Just as Nick thought the agony in his arms and back would be impossible to bear for another moment he got his second wind and when Ella offered to swap seats, he said:
"No... Thanks... I'll go on... a bit longer."
The water was like a mirror: smooth and untroubled by any movement at all. Hot afternoon sun scorched down cruelly and sizzled round the boat. As if their miseries weren't enough two huge flying insects buzzed aboard.
"Pretty," said El admiring their yellow and brown bodies and fine big, cellophane-like wings.
"Oh! No!" groaned Nick. "Hippo flies! Where on earth – or on lake – do the flipping things come from? We're absolutely *miles* from shore. It was partly to escape hippo flies that we came so far out – as well as to avoid being carried onto that awful cliffy shoreline."
"Isn't it amazing how, whenever there's little or no wind, they *always* find us?" said Carol who, glad of an excuse, dropped her paddle and swatted – and missed – and swiped – and missed. "Cunning things!" she exploded. "They're always the

same. Got eyes all round. I'm certain of it. Watch out Ella! If one of those brutes gets you — my word! — You'll know all about it!"

"They sting like red hot crochet hooks drilling oil wells into your flesh," warned Nick. He rested, and then aimed a plastic sandal at a hippo fly. The crafty creature evaded his blow. He looked back at *Frolic*.

"Better wait for the others," he suggested taking another futile bash at their assailants. "I'm not happy about this weather. At this time of the year we should be enjoying nice steady breezes from the southeast; but first it came from the wrong direction this morning and now this dead calm is ominous. I don't like it!"

"Where's the place we're heading for this evening?" panted Kirstin rubbing her back as *Frolic* glided alongside the other three in *Percy*. She and Gerald had changed sides several times and now they didn't know which arms or which sides of their bodies hurt the most.

"Can we see it yet?"

"Colander Cove. It's round that headland."

"Possums! That's *galaxies* away!"

"Yes. Sorry. If only the wind had behaved properly."

"How're you two coping?" asked Ella. "Would you like someone to relieve you while one of you steers?"

"No thanks." Gerr quite literally gritted his teeth. "We'll manage." He was not going to be beaten by stupid paddling or by collapsing muscles, and definitely not in front of Kirstin.

An hour later they were still labouring, not as fast as before, but with desperate purpose. They had to reach a place where they could land before nightfall.

"Can't we sleep somewhere before Colander Cove?" suggested Caro even later. She was almost sobbing with fatigue as she came off a paddling shift. "Why don't we just go ashore at the nearest spot?"

Grimly Nick unhooked binoculars from under the thwart.

"Look through these," he said in an apologetic tone. Carol gazed and gave another sob. An unbroken line of tall, sheer

KANGALIA

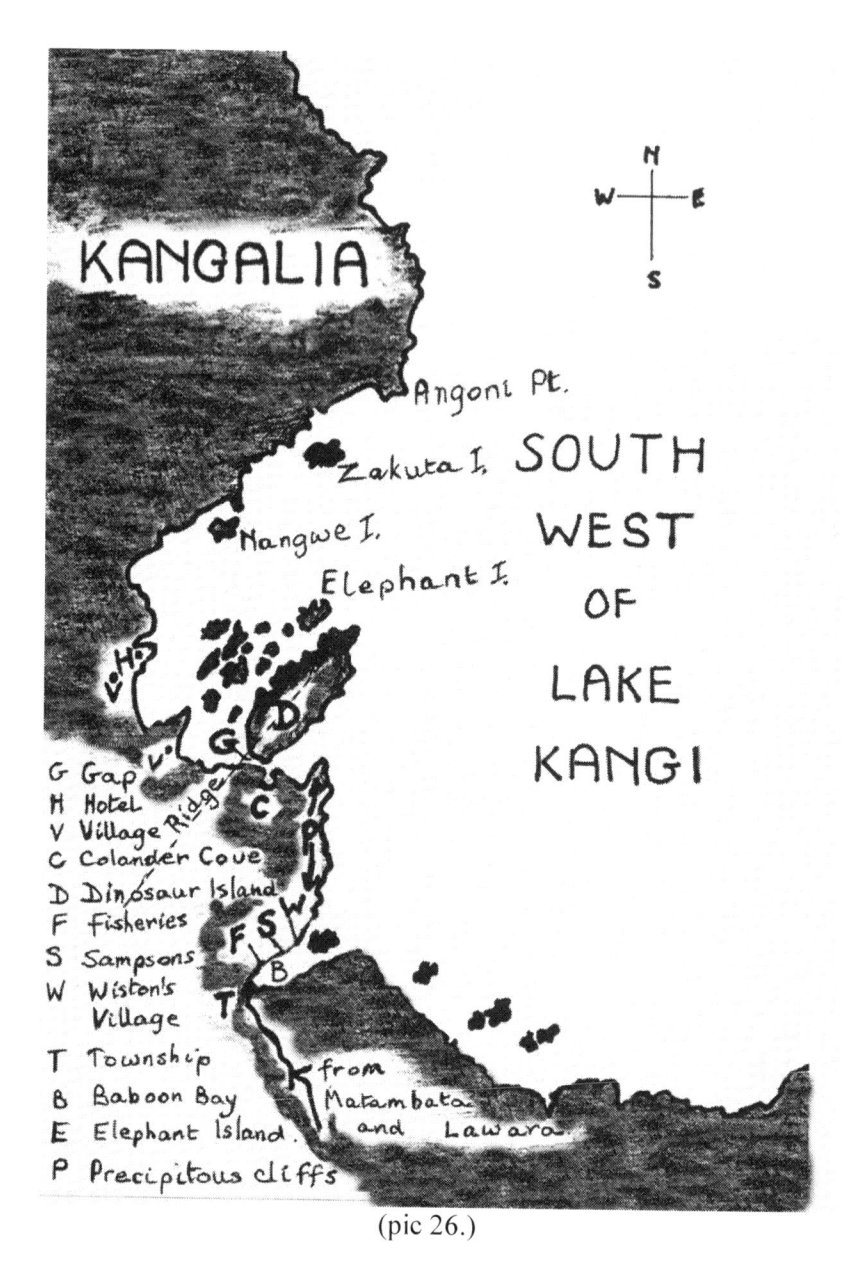

Angoni Pt.
Zakuta I.
Nangwe I.
Elephant I.

SOUTH WEST OF LAKE KANGI

G Gap
H Hotel
V Village
C Colander Cove
D Dinosaur Island
F Fisheries
S Sampsons
W Wiston's Village
T Township
B Baboon Bay
E Elephant Island
P Precipitous cliffs

from Matambata and Lawara

(pic 26.)

cliffs stretched from as far behind as she could see to the distant promontory, which blocked the view ahead.
"There isn't even a native hamlet – not even a fishing shack *anywhere*," she gulped.
"No, of course not. There isn't any path down from the top of

even one of the precipices. They're just vertical all the way."

Immense tumbled boulders lay scattered at the feet of the terrifying walls, which offered neither the tiniest cove where a dinghy might shelter nor any inch where they could spread sleeping bags. Despite the lack of wind small wavelets were breaking unpleasantly on countless small and big rocks all along the murderous coastline. It would have to be Colander Cove – or Bust! In her case Carol thought it would probably be the latter.

"The only thing to be grateful for," said Nick soberly, waving towards the crags, "is that we're not being blown up against those killers by a storm."

Frolic was still nearby. Gerald and Kirstin had changed places for the umpteenth time and Gerr had just readjusted the bungee holding the helm, yet again. The tiller kept on creeping out of the straight and letting the rudder push them crooked. They had tried taking the rudder off but the result had not been satisfactory and, as Kirstin pointed out, if the wind did suddenly blow up they would need to use it and might not have time to fiddle about upside down trying to re-ship it.

"Is Colander Cove it's real name?" asked Gerald.

"No. I've forgotten what the local fishermen call it. It's not big enough to have a name on the chart."

"So why do you call it Colander Cove, then?" asked Ella, hoping that the conversation would give them a respite from paddling even though, like the others, she was desperate to get to the spot before sunset.

"Because it's as full of rocks as a colander is of holes."

"Oh! Delightful! But how does that make it into a colander?"

"I suppose that, since there *are* a few holes between the rocks it must be like a kind of sieve."

"Huh!"

"We'll have to take the boats from hole to hole."

"It's sort of round, you know, with a little crescent beach on the west, and the cliff on this side curling round to complete the circle.

When we get past the big promontory there you'll see the embracing cliff sticking out from the mountainside."

"Oh!" There didn't seem to be much else to say.

They paddled on, pausing when rests became essential, forcing themselves to carry on beyond reasonable limits. Nicky and Kirstin swapped boats. The boys now had the heavier boat and the girls put their backs into making *Percy* move.

"Why don't you have rowlocks and oars, for goodness sakes?" asked Gerald crossly.

"Don't know, really. We keep on meaning to fit them," Nick panted. "But we've never got round to doing it."

"Wish you had."

"So do I."

Slowly – dreadfully slowly – the rocks came almost imperceptibly closer. Then it was possible to notice individual trees and bushes. They paused for apples and biscuits – and laboured on like galley slaves.

A small naval boat came bustling over the northern horizon. At what seemed like enormous speed it bore straight towards them. The officer in charge was wondering how two tiny dinghies could possibly have reached this incredibly remote spot.

'Even local fishermen don't bring their dugouts to this dangerous part of the coast,' he thought.

Fine-cut bows started to look bigger and bigger. Gerald panicked.

"Help!" he exclaimed. "It's going to run us down!"

"No. Just the Kangi Navy doing a snoop," explained Nick. "Pretty routine I suppose. Especially these days when there's so much trouble on the other side of the lake."

"I expect they keep checking to try to make sure that no bandits come across over to this side," said Ella. "Kangalia's got enough problems dealing with all the refugees who come streaming across from Bafandoland to escape the horrors over there. Wallabies! They're heading awfully directly towards us, aren't they?"

She eyed the rapid advance of the elegant little ship with admiration tinged with alarm.

"D'you think they've seen us?" asked Carol desperately.

"Shall we paddle like fiends to get out of the way?"

"No. Just keep a straight course then they'll know what we're doing. Anyway, we'd never get clear."

"But perhaps they don't know that steam gives way to sail."

"We're not sailing. We're paddling."

"And maybe they haven't seen us."

"They *must* have spotted us. They have to keep their eyes open so as not to run down fishermen."

"Come to that... Why haven't we seen any dugouts today?"

"It's this awful coast. It's so steep and rugged – nowhere to pull up a canoe or to land their catch. No villages... besides, all along here is Game Reserve."

"Caramba! Are we going to camp among wild animals?"

"Well – sort of. But they won't hurt us."

"Are you sure it will be safe?"

Closer came the speeding sloop. Its bow wave curled up gracefully. At any other time they would have admired its lines and action; but right now it seemed determined to mow them down and send them all to Davy Jones' locker.

"Only it can't be Davy Jones' locker," Carol pointed out. "He's in the sea. It must be somebody else's locker here, down at the bottom of the lake. Mlungu's (a local deity) perhaps"

Suddenly the bow wave diminished and vanished. The thump of powerful engines went into subdued neutral and the sloop was no longer surging ahead. It slowed down, and almost stopped. A dark-skinned officer, smart in crisp white uniform, held a loud hailer to his mouth and shouted.

"Where have you come from?"

"Baboon Bay." It seemed a silly thing to say since at present they appeared to be coming from the other side of the lake. Oh dear! Would the officer think they were spies from Bafandaland? Would they be forced aboard and carried all the way back to Baboon Bay? The man studied them through binoculars.

"Where are you going?"
"Colan..." shouted Nick. Then he muttered: "No. That's not its real name. How can I explain?"
"Er... We're going through The Gap."

The officer looked round the huge uninterrupted expanse of lake and wondered at the audacity of people who hoped to go so large a distance in such tiny vessels. They wouldn't get far in this calm – that was certain. Should he order them on board and take them back to Baboon Bay? No. Their boats would be a nuisance... In this weather it was unlikely that they'd be driven against the terrible cliffs and, anyway, it wasn't his job to do Lifeboat duties... He decided that they were just a bunch of idiots who posed no danger to Kangalia. He hoped that they would not come to grief but...
"Don't go near to the Other Side." He waved eastwards where, 50 miles away, they could see a faint blue line of distant mountains.
"You hear?"
"Yes. OK. We most definitely plan to stay on this side."
"Too many rebels over there. These days too much trouble. They are pinching many boats. Stay away from them."
"Sure thing. Thank you. We absolutely will."
"Very bad men in Bafandoland. Too dangerous. Be careful."
"Charming!" muttered Ella.
"Yes. OK. Thank you."

The sailor seemed satisfied. Engines roared. The sloop gathered speed and flashed past with lots of room to spare. Carol breathed again. Big waves surged across towards them. The GP and the Enterprise bobbed like useless corks.
"Oh well, come on then," urged Nick. "Pointless sitting about here. I don't want to be paddling through the night even if you lot fancy doing that." He studied his hands for blisters, then wiped the palms down the front of his life jacket and seized his paddle viciously. His cousins groaned but agreed with him. The painful, boring, exhausting effort was resumed.

"I know exactly how galley slaves felt," grumbled Ella. She and Kirstin were now wearing sailing gloves, not to protect their hands from ropes cutting into their flesh but to reduce paddle blisters as much as possible. Gerald and Nick noticed this and pulled on gloves as well. Why had none of them thought about gloves at first?

The sails flapped and shook uselessly. Their idle noise was aggravating.

But at last the merest suspicion of wrinkled water hesitated in the distance on the mirror-like surface. The faint ripples went left... and then right... and then crawled towards them.

The sails filled briefly, but clacked empty again.

"Oh come *on*, wind," pleaded Carol. "*Please* blow!"

They worked on. The heat of the day was past now but still they scooped up water and poured it over themselves and over each other, over their heads, and onto their clothes and down their throats. They paddled on, and on, and on.

Another cat's paw disturbed the lake's immobility. Then a third danced past. Six or seven tiny gusts were disporting themselves about their part of the lake. Till suddenly:

"Watch it!" said Commodore Nicholas. "Here it comes. I'll take the helm, Gerald." He dropped his paddle into the bottom of *Frolic*.

"If you like – I can't see why though."

"Look out, Kirstin," Nick called to the other boat and pointed to troubled wavelets in the distance. But that experienced sailor, looking simultaneously hopeful and wary, was already taking the helm from Ella.

"Centreboard down," ordered both skippers together; then, as if telepathically, they simultaneously decided to change their genoas for small jibs.

"Tricky to manage a genny if it's going to blow. Better safe than sorry," explained Kirstin to Ella.

When the squall came it was strong but they were ready for it. Both boats took off in style, heeling a good bit more than either Ella or Gerald liked, but cutting through sizeable waves at great speed.

CHAPTER 20

Reach the beach – or die!

Splendid! Super! Marvellous! Ella and Gerr might not have enjoyed the tilting boats, but they 'held on tight' and rejoiced in the speed. Perhaps they'd reach Colander Cove before nightfall after all. The dinghies rounded that frustrating headland which their crews had been glaring at for such ages that they felt they knew every cranny in its cliffs. Now it was behind them, and abruptly, the precipices on shore changed into steep but ordinary mountainsides that became less and less vertical the further forward the cousins cast their anxious eyes.

Behind that horrible promontory, which they were sure had been staring insolently back at them, the slopes slipped away inland to form what looked like a large triangular bay. Its far side was a ridge that jutted out into the lake. This shoulder now shut off most of the horizon ahead.

"Hey! Are we planning to bump into that long bit of land that's sticking out into the lake?"

"No. And it's not a peninsular, actually, but an island – Dinosaur Island I call it, because of its shape. I know it looks simply like a continuation of the mainland, but that's because the channel between it and the Mainland is so terribly narrow that we can't see The Gap just now."

Nick planned to slip through that slim cutting the next morning. He was a little worried because it was a finicky route between boulders. The others, however, weren't thinking any further ahead than hoping to land *soon*.

"Where's Colander Cove?" asked Gerald.

"It's just this side of The Gap. When we go round that buttress that's sticking out fairly close to us, you'll see that on its other side the cliffs curve like an arm almost all the way round Colander Cove."

And then the wind dropped as suddenly as it had arrived! Spirits plummeted as the sailors felt that the lake was deliberately conjuring up trouble. The cousins were shocked! Very close... and now no more wind! The sun was low in the sky so they set to paddling in grim earnest. There was no chat, no banter. Encompassing *Percy* and *Frolic* there was just an almost tangible miasma of determination to 'get there or die.'

To give the boys a break from tricky steering El moved into *Frolic*. Later Kirstin remarked to no one in particular:

"Why do distances *look* so small across water but are really gi-*normous* to cross – even when you're travelling at a good lick?"

When they finally rounded the curving bluff they had no energy left to feel happy or to cheer. They were just full of unbounded relief. Some of them had begun to doubt whether that inhospitable coastline would ever allow a tiny haven of beach to exist. Perhaps the bay was a figment of Nicky's imagination... a mere mistake on the charts... a squiggle that was not true. But there it was at last. To be sure they couldn't see it very well because the sun was so low that the cove was in deep shadow cast by humpy Dinosaur Island rearing on their right. Nevertheless... There it was – ahead, to their left: a beach of rough sand in a tiny indentation on the mountainside, with a hill sloping up in a perfectly normal way behind it. Oh joy!

Ella took Gerald's paddle and he was sent into *Frolic's* bows to watch out for danger. He didn't feel that the precaution had been in vain. The region was littered with hazards: massive blocks, small rocks, huge boulders, piled stones. They lay about as if some petulant monster had dropped handfuls of giant-sized gravel all over the beach and into the water – and of course it was big submerged threats that were the killers.

"Left a bit, Nicky – I mean, 'Go to port'," said Gerr. "Starboard now. Careful. We're about to go between two underwater whoppers, and there's another one ahead."

The Aussies followed carefully in *Frolic's* wake.

"Wouldn't like to do this in rough weather," said Gerald.

Next morning he didn't have time to recall those prophetic words; but now, dodging rocks above and below water, they paddled the boats shorewards and gratefully pulled them up the pebbly slope.

"Thank Goodness!" said Kirsty with immense feeling. She studied her blisters and watched the others collapsing onto the beach, stretching arms and legs, and flexing painful fingers. How she sympathised with them! All she wanted to do was to lie down and sleep till morning. But she pushed away the temptation.

"I say! We can't relax yet. The sun will very soon have completely gone and we'd better get organised as quickly as possible – don't you think?"

"Slave driver!" grumbled the others, but started to unpack the dinghies.

"We must rope the boats to rocks or trees in case a storm blows up during the night," said Nick. "The anchors would have made it easier if we'd brought them."

Gerr stared at him as if their recent labours had affected his cousin's brain.

"Tie the boats?" he gasped in amazement. "Why! – There isn't even a breath of a zephyr! There'll never be a storm strong enough to wash waves to where we've lugged the flipping boats. I've never had to work so hard in all my life."

Gerald had hated the tussle entailed in hauling *Frolic* and *Percy* up the beach; but the Commodore was adamant.

"If this was a wider beach we could haul the boats right up out of danger. But I don't care what you say. This lake is renowned for being thoroughly unpredictable. Never trust it. Whatever the weather it's absolutely breathtakingly beautiful. Often – no – usually – it gives superb fun sailing. But it can be devilish. Sorry. We *must* attach the boats securely so they can't swing about and hit rocks."

"Swing about and hit rocks! My foot!" snorted Gerald. "Swing about on dry land! A heavy thing like *Frolic*! I *ask* you!"

He was *blowed* if he was going to waste energy on such a useless project. Instead he left Kirstin and Nick to lash the hulls and slowly followed Carol up the hill in search of firewood.

Ella was unrolling sleeping bags.
"Sorry about my brother," she said, feeling bad. "Don't take any notice."
"It's all right. We're all exhausted and acting crotchety. It's this weird calm," Nick explained. "Why aren't we getting the nice steady blows that should arrive at this time of the year? I'm not happy about all the changes in the wind; and now what does this unusual lack of even a breeze mean?"

"Caterwauling Kangas!" complained Carol as she picked up a nice dry branch. "Do your arms and back ache, Gerald? Mine are absolute agony!"
"Well – er – yes, actually. They *are* a bit sore," admitted her cousin grossly underplaying his pains. "Why don't dinghies have outboards?"
"We've got one for our boat in Oz. You have to strengthen the transom otherwise the vibrations shake the craft to pieces. Dad did that for us so we can use our Enterprise without sails. But the engine's awfully heavy lying in the boat when you're sailing, and it gets terribly in the way. Usually we decide at the start whether to take sails and mast and boom or to fit the engine. It's better that way."
"Yes. I suppose so. But it would be fun to have an engine just the same. Just think! We could water-ski then!"
Caro laughed.
"Oh no we couldn't! Not even with a strong transom. It's only safe to use a small engine, you know. We'd never go fast enough to ski. It wouldn't be anything like your Dad's super speedboat."

"Didn't we have fun last year?" grinned Gerald his eyes sparkling at the memories of their last adventure-packed waterskiing and windsurfing holiday."
"Yes," said his young cousin thoughtfully. "It was exciting while it happened. But, on the whole I don't like adventures much. Well, anyway – not until they're over. Gerr, are you

ever going to pick up some wood, or are you just sleepwalking?"

Gerald was not listening.

"I say! Look!" he exclaimed in delight. They had reached the top of a low ridge and were now able to see over it onto the far side. "See? Below us, there's the famous Gap, between the mainland and Dinosaur Island... Gosh! It's a really narrow channel, isn't it? – And disgustingly murky in shadows at this time of day. I'm glad we're not trying to go through there just now."

"Look further," comforted Carol, pointing to the vast sunset-blazing bay beyond. It was neither a deep rectangle cut between long promontories like Baboon Bay, nor a tiny circle like Colander Cove, but an unbelievably enormous spread of calm blueness. It reflected the setting sun in a long dazzling streak of red and gold. Fringed with acacias as well as with baobabs, palms and banana trees, an arc of golden sand stretched for several miles out to a distant sand spit. Tumbled boulders, which were white by day, now shone rosy-tinted.

"It's straight out of a South Sea adventure story," breathed Gerald. "What are those blobs on the beach near the sand spit? They're hard to figure out, so far away?"

Carol could tell him:

"They're dugouts and small boats with outboard motors. They belong to the village that's hidden under Flamboyant trees." Carol collected another dry branch. "Beyond this huge bay is another, just like this one, except that at its very far end is a tiny hotel. We towed *Frolic* overland there last time we visited Kangalia and sailed about in the two bays. It was great going from island to island. I expect we'll visit a couple of them tomorrow."

Gerr shielded his eyes. Against the overall fiery splendour a string of large and small islands 'floated' on the flat water. They made an intriguing pattern of overlapping black shapes.

"Some of the islands have crew cuts," said Gerald noticing the fuzz of trees on hilltops. "Golly, but it's beautiful!"

"Yes," agreed Carol. "Even my Dad, who's been to all sorts of places, says it's one of the loveliest spots in the world." Then she added matter-of-factly:
"Do buck up Gerr. It'll be dark in two ticks and I'm famished."
"Me too." He applied himself to the job of collecting fuel.

After a rest and then supper they all felt much more human. They even wondered why they had been so cross, depressed and exhausted before. The moon turned everything silver when it shone into their cove. Crickets made a scratchy sort of music; bats flickered about in the indigo sky, clinking metallically; and soft rustles in long grass whispered about small creatures waking to forage in the dark.

Tonight no one lay awake stargazing and looking for satellites. Strangely their muscles ached more as they relaxed so there were grunts and sighs and complaints. But in spite of pains and stiffness they were all asleep almost before they had slipped into sleeping bags. Carol did not even have time to wriggle a comfortable shape in the very coarse gravelly surface. Her eyes closed as she lay down. Ella stayed awake long enough to wonder whether or not to light mosquito coils and dropped off in mid-ponder.

The moon, sailing serenely overhead, watched a procession of small creatures emerge cautiously from grass and bushes onto the tiny beach. Sniffing warily they skirted round the cousins' five cocooned shapes and sank muzzles into the lake. Mongooses, duikers, bushbuck, monitor lizards, two genet cats and a civet drank and then melted away back into the shadows. Later, in absolute silence, without even so much as the clink of hoof on pebble, a majestic male kudu stood suddenly clear in the moonlight. His magnificent horns spiralled high and strong. He held himself proudly, but paused warily for a moment or two before stepping gracefully down to the water's edge. Like the other animals he drank quietly and economically, constantly on the *qui vive*. And then, like them, he vanished, ghostlike.
There was nothing but a few prints here and there to show that the little inlet had ever been visited.

27. Kudu

CHAPTER 21

High jinks in Colander Cove.

Resentful little puffs, which had scarcely disturbed the supper fire, developed into a steady breeze only just strong enough to keep off mosquitoes. For hours it seemed undecided whether to die or whether to grow into a full-sized storm; but after barely ruffling the kudu's mane, the zephyr finally made up its mind. It grew steadily stronger till it was plucking at corners of sleeping bags, tossing branches, and whipping up the lake. Miniature whirlwinds pranced over the beach obliterating signs of four-footed visitors. Waves stopped chortling quietly and started to roar. They frothed higher and higher, snatching at last round the sterns of both dinghies. But the cousins, undisturbed by the surrounding noise and movement, were deep in the sleep of the extremely tired.

Persistent twists of wind yanked and teased jibs, both neatly coiled round its forestay. Little by little the foot of each rolled-up sail worked loose and then *Frolic's* canvas came completely untied leaving the foresail free to fly and flap, which it did with tremendous verve. Nick and Kirstin opened sleepy eyes almost simultaneously, took in what was happening, and wriggled out of sleeping bags. They weighted their bedding, then tried to rewind *Frolic's* exuberant triangle round the forestay but each gust and blast kept on snatching it from their hands and whipping it in every direction till they admitted:

"It's no good. *Frolic's* jib just *won't* be controlled."
"We'll have to lower it."

Unclipping the sail from the forestay they bundled it below the foredeck. Having tied an extra length of cord round the energetic lower end of *Percy's* jib, they considered the boats.

The sterns were lifting as each wave arrived with a great slap, and the hulls were chopping up and down on the coarse gravel. The paint was suffering.

"We'll have to wake Gerald."

The three of them, pushing and straining, shoved *Frolic* and *Percy* still higher up the beach into a mass of rotting vegetation.

"They're slack now," said Gerald flipping one of the ropes that were meant to hold the craft stationary.

"Yes. But I'm not going to re-tie them," said Nicholas. If the waves reach the boats here they'll wet us first so we're bound to wake. Let's just make sure that none of the food or clothes are going to be blown away. Then I'm going back to sleep."

Later the daily screams, cackles, warbles and shrills of the dawn chorus were lost in the clatter of buffeting wind and crashing waves; but the cousins slept on till just after sunrise.

"Crikey!" said Gerald not knowing whether to be delighted or scared. "It'll be really something – sailing today!"

"Yes. *Frolic* will leave *Percy* standing in this blow," said Nick complacently. He glanced sideways at Kirstin. "She always shoots along in strong winds."

"Rubbish!" replied his cousin staunchly. *Frolic* may go well but *Percy* will go faster. You wait and see!"

"We'll see," agreed Nicky, smiling like a Cheshire cat. "Hey, Gerr?"

"Sure thing!"

Certain she'd be seasick, Ella looked at the waves and sighed. She hoped she didn't look as green as she felt. Like everyone she had found yesterday's hot, slow, exhausting progress exceedingly tedious; but if she had to choose she'd settle for boring old doldrums rather than terrifying winds, any day!

"Ouch!" she squeaked as Carol backed into her by mistake. "Do be careful of my sunburn!"

"Sorry!" said Carol. "Who's for a boiled egg? Do you people want two each? They're smaller than eggs in Oz or in the U.K."

"Yes please," they answered in unison – except for Ella, who opted for just one.

The wind was from the west, whistling out through The Gap towards the main lake. Some of the blow was then reflected

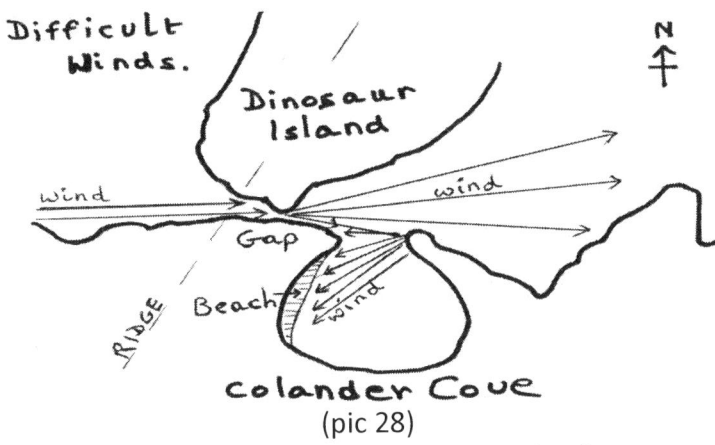

Difficult Winds. Dinosaur Island. wind. wind. Gap. Ridge. Beach. wind. N

Colander Cove
(pic 28)

off the curved cliff that partially enclosed Colander Cove on its east side, and this bounced onslaught came back, straight at them. Nick watched a fishing dugout being laboriously paddled from the east of Dinosaur Island back through the strait towards the big double bay. His conclusions were not particularly happy.

"Going to be tricky getting out of here," he remarked through a mouthful of bread and marge. (Margarine keeps better than butter in un-refrigerated conditions.) "We're on a lee shore here... which is *horrid!*"

"That means the wind is blowing straight onshore – towards us," Kirstin explained to the Stanleighs. "So it will be difficult to sail away."

"But the second we get out of the cove the wind will come from a completely different direction – and it'll be stronger!" said Nick solemnly. "And dead against the way we want to go."

As they ate, another two canoes, going the same away as the previous dugout, laboured towards The Gap. The straining paddlers managed a wave as they vanished behind boulders.

"Fishermen going back to their village with the night's catch, I suppose," remarked Nick as they all waved back.

"I thought you said fishermen didn't come along this coast," said Gerald.

"They don't go much where we were yesterday - *south* of Dinosaur Island, but they do venture northwards on the east side of the island."

"Looks like dreadfully hard work," said Carol thinking about the paddlers. "*Much* tougher than yesterday."

"Of course," said her sister. "Yesterday all we had to do was get the hulls through the water. Today they've got to fight against wind and waves as well as pushing their canoe along."

"And those hollowed-out trees are really heavy brutes."

"I suppose they live in the village we saw yesterday evening, far, far away on the shore of the big bay. It's a long way for them to go. Why don't they fish in the bay – on the west side of Dinosaur Island?"

"Some of them do. But the Bay is shallower than the main part of the lake, on this eastern side. I expect the fish are better or something in deeper waters."

"Well, I wouldn't like to head back into the teeth of the storm like that."

"Nor would I!"

"Where're *we* aiming for today?" asked Carol with an awful premonition.

"We could plan on going to Elephant Island. That's the one furthest out into the bay on the other side of Dinosaur Island."

"Oh good!" said Kirstin. "That's a lovely spot. I really liked it last year."

"Yes. It's a gem of a campsite."

"Much nicer than this one which is in shadow morning and evening."

"We'll have to go though The Gap, then?" Ella's voice was fearful.

"Yes. But we've got to go that way in any case. If we sail on along the east side of the Dinosaur there's nothing but water for hundreds of miles – nowhere to camp.

"It'll only take us about three hours to reach Elephant Island in this wind. Don't you think we could try to press on further

north – to see if we can get far enough to collect some samples of Lake Flies?"
"Yes."
"Mm."
Nick was in a quandary. He felt they should get into the big bays where the weather would be less blustery, but this storm made going after the Flies a great temptation.
"I was hoping to sleep at Elephant Island yesterday, but with that awful calm… "
"Well – we didn't."
"No," said someone grimly. "We didn't. And we jolly nearly didn't make it to here either."
"Well, let's see how it goes. We could have early lunch on Elephant Island and then press on into the lake proper to Nangwe Island perhaps, or to Zakuta Island, or Angoni Point."
They settled for that plan and decided to swim before packing up. (*Map on page 106.*)

Another dugout fighting the wind came into view. No craft of any sort were heading the other way – into the main body of the lake. Instead of struggling on towards the passage this canoe seemed to waver and then the two canoeists made up their minds to paddle into the cove where the cousins were changing into bathers. The larger of the paddlers appeared to be very exhausted and, as the canoe touched shore they all moved forward to help pull it up the beach. Hollowed out tree trunks are not only very unstable but they are also extremely heavy and cumbersome.

The older man gasped a 'thank you' and went to lie on the shingle. The youth, evidently his son, smiled shyly and accepted their help. Then he went to sit beside his father. In the canoe was a fine catch of tilapia but it must have made the dugout extra heavy. The lad started to collect a few twigs and asked permission to take a glowing ember from the cousins' fire. They invited him to use their small blaze instead of lighting his own.
"Shall we give them something to eat?" suggested Carol.
"Good idea."

Brewing another billy of tea, they laced it with lashings of sugar and offered that, together with two empty mugs and thick slices of bread and peanut butter, to the newcomers. The old man and the boy accepted gladly. As father and son ate, they told in broken English (helped by Nick's limited knowledge of Kangi) that it had been a rough night out on the lake. Under the circumstances they had been lucky to catch any fish at all so the pleasing haul that they had netted would be a marvellous bonus for their family. They poked the small flames into a bigger blaze and sat happily drying, getting warm and recouping strength after the exhausting effort they'd made to reach Colander Cove.

Surprisingly quickly the old man recovered and declared himself fit to continue. His son explained that, once through The Gap, there would be many beaches where they could rest if necessary.
"Not like sunrise side," he said. "Here – this side – is too many big stones. (He meant boulders.) No canoe safety. Not at all!"
The cousins remembered those grim cliffs and understood clearly what the lad meant.
"In my family plenty females," said the youth proudly. "Good for fetching water. Good for digging gardens. (i.e. ploughing fields.) Good for marriage money." He sighed. That was the happy aspect of life. But sadly, to be successful from a canoe two people are needed and, as he was the only surviving son, his father still had to struggle out in the dugout to fish for the family's living. If only he had a brother the old man could have stayed at home like the other elders and spent his time talking and smoking under the Baobabs.

The cousins helped to launch the canoe with its glittering load, and watched till it was out of sight.
"Bit of a fight for them. Hope they get back safely."
"Sure to. They had a good rest and they must know how to thread The Gap."
"These choppy waves are quite exciting, aren't they? But I'm glad I don't have to paddle through them."

"Come on," said Gerald. "Let's go and jump off that whopping, great boulder."

He pointed to a massive chunk of granite, which had evidently fallen from the cliff-side at some time in the not-so-very-distant past. The place from which it had broken free was bare and rocky, as yet without any regenerated vegetation; and the scar where the monster had skidded down to the water was still obvious.

"What a din it must have made breaking off and tumbling down!" said Kirstin.

"And what a huge splash!" added Carol. "I bet it happened in a thunder storm with lightning sizzling everywhere and thunderbolts crashing about like nobody's business!"

"And hailstones the size of our heads smashing all round," added Ella not to be outdone. Then another thought struck her: "Good thing there wasn't a village below when it came down!"

Carol looked over her shoulder and up at the hills as if expecting another landslide.

It was exhilarating fighting chest high through turbulent waves to reach the vast scar, which was surprisingly far off. Boisterous swirls did their best to bash them against dozens of underwater boulders as well as onto others poking above the thrashing spray. Then it was a challenge to scramble out of the water and climb the steep sides of the granite lump when they reached it.

"Oh no!" said Nell firmly when they climbed to the top. "I'm definitely not going to jump from here! It's absolutely terrifying."

Her brother had been standing on the edge gazing intently into deep water on the far side of the boulder. Now, without a word of warning, he dived way down into swooshing waves. – "Rather like a plummeting kingfisher going in after a fish" was how Kirstin described it later. Ella screamed and Carol gasped, wrapping her arms round herself in fright.

They all watched anxiously for him to reappear.

"Damn stupid thing to do," groused Nick. "The water's so churned up there's no way to see where it's safe to dive." Looking half conceited and half relieved Gerald surfaced with a wide grin, and the others breathed again.

"Come on!" he called treading water below them. "'Slovely. Last one in's a two-toed platypus." He shook his head to sweep the hair out of his eyes.

"Ho!" shouted Nick screwing up his courage. Then he added, "That's cheating!" as Kirstin ran down a sloping part of the rock and jumped from a lower level. They each found a jumping off point, which suited their individual courage and abilities, and were enjoying themselves immensely when Carol pointed to the beach.

"Oh help!" she shouted, her face a mixture of horror, fear and fury. "Look!

29. Baboons pinching the bread.

CHAPTER 22

Greedy baboons. Getting *Frolic* through The Gap.

A troupe of baboons was disposed about the hillside and round the boats. Some were already beside the lake digging holes and drinking. Others were sitting – baboon fashion – on the beach and still more, in trees and bushes, were preparing to venture down into the cove. Carol's anguished cry was caused by a couple of braver creatures busy investigating the humans' food. One was sampling their last (rather mushy) banana, eating it skin and all. Two others were squabbling over a big plastic sack that held the expedition's bread supply.
"Oh NO! Shoo! Rock off!" yelled Kirstin jumping up and down on the boulder, waving her arms frantically. Nick shouted the same message in the idiom of Southern Africa by screaming rudely:
"Voetsak!" (It's said that every second dog there thinks its name is 'Voetsak'!)
The baboons all looked towards them. A few of the more nervous monkeys began to edge away.
"Cor! Geroff, you blighters!"

Nick, Kirsty and Gerr plunged into the waves and, closely followed by the other two, all bellowing and splashing as hard as they could, got themselves to the beach as rapidly as possible. They were so furious that they forgot that a baboon, close up, is a large animal with long vicious fangs and dangerous claws. When angry it can easily kill a man or rip even a big dog to pieces. There would have been no escape if the monkeys had decided to turn nasty. Luckily, although two males stood up temporarily with eyes glowing red, the troupe fled. But one dragged the bread sack after her. Loaves fell all over the gravelly beach; but they didn't stay there. Lolloping monkeys picked them up, tasted them, fought over them, and ran off on three legs clutching their spoils in the remaining hand.

"Oh, goodness!" cried Ella in mingled dismay and rage.
"Puking Possums!" That was Kirstin, shaking her fists impotently.

"Now what'll we do? We'll never last out without bread." All eyes turned to Nick.

"Possums! Kangas! Wallabies! And everything else as well!" he exploded, half wrathfully and half trying to ease the situation by making his cousins laugh. "We may be able to buy bread in the village, or at the hotel – per*haps* – if we're incredibly lucky," he suggested. "But it will delay us dreadfully. We'll never make Nangwe or Zakuta if we have to cross the bay to reach the hotel first."

"Oh blow!"

"Who *wants* to go and get mixed up with civilisation, anyway?" asked Kirstin elevating to dizzy heights the primitive village and its very isolated neighbour, the extremely basic hotel that was five miles further on.

"Who wants to see an ancient old broken-down hotel?" said her sister scornfully.

"Well – I'd quite like to," said Nell who really preferred modern comforts to the bush, and whose mother used to run a large, ultra-smart residential sports club.

"You won't know what's hit you when you see *that* hotel" laughed Nick.

"I think it'd be fun to sail across that wizard bay," added Gerr. "Bother the daft old Lake Flies. Let's go and see if we can get bread and enjoy the bay too."

"Well – I *do* want to try to catch Lake Flies," said Nick. "It's a challenge."

"I know it was my dad who suggested it, but I'm certain he never actually meant it," said Kirsty. "It sounds like a horribly dangerous thing to try and do," she admitted.

"Yes – but – I'd at least like to try."

"But we can't manage without bread!"

"No. Oh *bother* the baboons!"

"Yes. *Bothersome baboons!* in fact," laughed Kirstin.

"Precisely!"

"OK. I give in. We'll sail across the bay hunting for bread."
Then Nicky added: "Anyway, I suppose that Ella and Gerald ought to see where Granddad landed during World War II."
"What do you mean?"
Between them Nick, Kirstin and Carol unfolded the story:
"You know that Granddad was in South Africa for a spell during the Second World War?"
"Was he?"
"Yes. He flew back north to Egypt on a flying boat."
"Flying boat? A boat with wings? Are you having us on?"
"No. You know – one of those seaplane things. What were they called? Sunderlands, I think... Anyway, they flew through the air but didn't land on runways. They used to come down on water."
"Sounds terribly dangerous to me," said Ella.
"I've seen pictures of them," murmured Gerald dubiously. "They landed on their 'tummies' but had floats on their wings – to balance them. They took off from water as well."
"Of course they did, you shonky idiot! D'you think they clambered out of the water onto the beach and changed out of their swimming floats into dry wheels for take off?"
"Oh, do shut up being stupid and get on with the story," said Gerr the impatient.
"OK. OK. Keep your hair on."
"The flying boats used to stop every night. They stayed at Laurenço Marques (in Mozambique), Cape Maclear (in Nyasaland), and ... and... oh... and at Entebbe... and... Oh – lots of places... and this big double bay was one of them."
"Gracious!"
"Yes. That's why there's a little hotel here in this extremely wild back-of-beyond spot. The passengers and crew slept each night in a hotel beside the water they'd landed on."
"Caterwauling Kangas! The trip must have taken *years!*"
"Not quite. Six or seven days from Durban harbour to the Nile at Cairo, I think."
"Good grief!"

"So: Granddad landed – I mean splashed down – here, and slept in that hotel?"
"Yes. In 1943 – or thereabouts, I think."
"Did they *have* 'planes then?"
"Car-*ol!* Of course they did."

"Don't you to want to see the bay and the village and the hotel?" asked Ella of the Australians.
"Seen it – last time we visited Nick," said Kirstin briefly. "The great bay's lovely, but the hotel's grim. Might have been nice once when the airline used it."
Carol filled out this laconic statement by adding:
"Hotels aren't our sorts of places and this one's terribly run down these days. Lots of grisly caravans messing up the shore as well... "
"You go and get bread (if you can) and see the hotel. I'll do a painting of that huge fig tree growing out of the rock over there," said Kirsty. "Carol and I will join you later – on Elephant Island – at tonight's campsite. You'll have your work cut out beating across the bay and then reaching Elephant Island by afternoon."
"Yes," said Nick glumly. "Bang goes our chance of collecting Lake Flies I suppose."
"And a good thing, too, probably," said Nell.
"Oh well! You never know. We may be lucky with fabulous winds or something."
Ella who had been feeling quite happy and healthy suddenly went green again.

"What d'you want to paint that tree for?" asked Gerr of Kirstin.
"I like the shape and colours of the boulder and the way the tree seems to grow out of an invisible crack and the tremendous white roots sort of pouring themselves down the rock. It'll make a nice picture – if it works. And that wonderful Fish Eagle amongst all that splendid fig foliage, is great against the deep blue sky... It'll look good enlarged later in oils."
"Well – *chaqu'un a son gout,*" clowned Nick deliberately miss-pronouncing the last word to sound like 'gout' in English.

"Come on, then. Let's get packing. Will you two be all right coming along alone later?"
"Sure."
"You do know how to get to Elephant Island, don't you?"
"Of course. You took us there last year. Remember?"
"Yes... but... There're several islands. Make sure you don't get the wrong one."
"Stop worrying. Look!" Kirstin drew on the sand with a stick left over from the fire. "We're here on the mainland in this little circular cove." She sketched in the coastline continuing on each side of Colander Cove. "OK? Here is Dinosaur Island, with its tail almost opposite us now. And this is the channel between the mainland and the Dinosaur's tail."
"Yes."
"Well... You lot go through The Gap, and across the bay. Then you bounce off the hotel beach back towards Elephant Island." Kirstin drew two lines representing the *Frolic*'s route.
"Yes. Yes. We know what *we're* planning to do. But where will you be aiming for?"
"We shoot through the channel behind you – but we'll be some hours later."
"Neither you nor we will *shoot* through The Gap. The wind will be buffeting straight against us, remember. Both boats'll have to work hard in lots of nasty short beats, tacking and tacking and tacking all the way. Watch out for a hideous big submerged rock right in the middle of everything! There's a metal pole sticking up from the rock out of the water, and it's got a big bucket welded to its top. The Sailing Club organised that to warn people of the dangerous spot. It's – well – about here – I should say." Nick jabbed another stick into Kirstin's sand map. "It won't be easy to see the rock with all the spray smashing about."
"Right. We'll give that a miss."
"I hope so."
"OK. *Percy's* through the Channel. Then we turn to starboard and sail up the western side of Dinosaur Island, and go on and

on… We ignore all the islands and aim for the one which is furthest out in the bay – almost beyond the Dinosaur's nose."
"Correct. And the camp site is?"
"On the farther side from the mainland. A nice bay with super soft sand – not gravelly stuff like here in this cove."
"See you there then. If we're late don't forget to light a fire to guide us in."
"Oke. Have a good trip."

They all helped to push the two dinghies down to the edge of the water and then they turned them into the wind and raised *Frolic's* sails. These flapped about furiously but uselessly. Nick frowned at the churning water. He had a difficult decision to make. If Ella took the helm he and Gerald would find it easier to paddle effectively, but there'd be no one watching out over the bows for underwater dangers. On the other hand, if Nell was a look out, although *Frolic* might miss more of the killers, he and Gerald would find it difficult to head the dinghy in useful directions. Suddenly he appreciated that clinging onto the slippery deck in *Frolic's* bows, a look out would be in great danger of being shaken off the plunging boat.

"El will you take the tiller, please?" he said reaching his conclusion. "Gerr and I will paddle – and shove off against the rocks on each side."

For another long moment everyone waited in mystified silence as Nicholas worried about another problem. The Australians would have only one paddle wielder, or two paddlers but no-one at the tiller. Then he remembered that Kirstin was a very competent sailor. He thought: 'Perhaps the wind will have dropped by the time they try to leave.'
"Will you remind me about helming?" asked Nell, and Nick forgot about his anxieties.
"What? Oh! All right."
Kirstin and Carol pushed them off.
"Cheerio," shouted Ella. "See you this evening."
"Hope you find bread."
"So do we!"

30. Strange rocks are OK *in water as calm as it is in this picture.*

    To get *Frolic* out of the cove the boys had to paddle strongly against the wind which was reflected forcefully off the curved cliff that reared opposite the beach. Scary explosions of spray showed where rocks lay everywhere, waiting to wreck them. They had to miss those somehow. As soon as there was enough depth of water they shoved down *Frolic's* centreboard to stop the boat crabbing and to give greater control.
"I hope those two manage all right," Ella shouted dubiously. "It's nasty – even for the three of us, and you two are much stronger than they are." Her voice was scattered by the wind.
"They'll be OK," grunted Nick, still working hard. *"Percy's* fibreglass – much lighter than us. Easier to manoeuvre."
Frolic was being badly bashed despite the boys' efforts. Nick winced as he thought of the damage to paint every time another rock struck the hull and he dreaded *Frolic* being holed.
    It seemed like light years before they were just about clear of the gusts reflected off the opposite concave cliff. Blasts of air bursting out from the Channel started to snatch at the sails and they would soon no longer be head-to-wind.

Instead, for the second or two before they turned to face The Gap, they would have the blow coming from dead astern.

"I'll take the helm now, El," said Nick pulling on the mainsheet and taking Nell's place. "Ready to stop paddling soon, Gerr. Haul in the jibsheet, Ella. No! Not that rope. The other one, on the other side. Yes – that's it."

Apart from the thunder of waves smashing on rocks and the bashing of spray off boulders there was a tense, expectant silence in the boat. Gerald paddled steadily though his arms ached badly. After a moment or two Nick said briskly: "Right. Stop paddling. You take the jibsheet now, Gerr. Ella, stay where you are. Pull in the jib a bit. I say! Good thing we're using the small sail and not the genny, eh?"

"We'd have been daft to have flown the genoa," said Gerald who had learnt fast. "Wind's far and away too strong."

Suddenly *Frolic* caught the blast and sprang into action They went roaring across a frothing sea. On a broad reach they rushed northwards almost parallel to the eastern side of Dinosaur Island. Then, as suddenly as the wind had hit *Frolic*, it died to a breeze.

"We're in Dinosaur's wind shadow," yelled Nick into the sudden relative calm. "Ready about?"

"Ready."

"Lee O!"

Soon they were heading back southwards towards the Channel.

"We're going to creep up to The Gap in this shadow of the island," Nick briefed his inexperienced crew. "Then the wind will hit us again. After that we'll be tacking against the blow. Try to keep the boat trimmed – that means keep it balanced. It's important."

The other two nodded. They needed no warning about the dangerous situation.

"Gerald, you go on managing the jib. Nell, every time that Gerr crosses the boat you move the other way. OK? Move smoothly, mind! We don't want to capsize in that maelstrom."

Ella nodded again and gulped a bit.
It seemed a long way back to The Gap as they crawled down in the lee of the island. Then Nick warned them:
"Here it comes!"

Still on the beach the Australian girls watched *Frolic* heel and start skipping along. She had a splendid bone in her teeth.
"Say! Look how those two are leaning back like professionals," admired Kirstin. "They're doing a fine job balancing *Frolic*." With sails pulled right in, the dinghy came dashing back as if about to re-enter the cove. But before he could be caught in the nasty swirls of gusts that were being reflected off the concave cliff Nick went about. Ella and Gerald swapped sides fairly efficiently as the jib snapped over. The girls were now presented with *Frolic's* stern. Close-hauled as before, but now on a different tack, she was again shooting off, but towards a different section of the Dinosaur – a part closer to The Gap this time. *Frolic's* wake frothed white and straight but was quickly caught up and dispersed by the waves. Kirstin wondered what Ella and Gerald were thinking. Were they terrified out of their wits by the tricky sailing?

Suddenly, in spite of all the crashing of waves and wind, the cove seemed empty and desolate. Kirstin gave herself a mental shake. 'Don't be *galah* (daft). We'll see them this evening,' she told herself.
"They'll be into the Channel on the next beat," said Carol. "I'm going up onto the ridge to watch them through."

Kirstin was on her heels. Unknowingly they stepped where the Kudu had stood, and pushed aside grasses that he had slipped between. They followed one of the trails that the disappearing baboons had used and Carol found a porcupine quill that had not been there when she and Gerald had come down the same path, laden with firewood, the evening before.

Puffing, they reached the ridge and looked across into the big bay and down into the narrow space between the

Mainland and the Dinosaur. *Frolic* had already tacked several times and was now at the further end, in the wider part of the Channel. The girls watched as the tacks gradually grew longer and longer and finally, the two triangular sails co-operating elegantly, swept *Frolic* over choppy waters, till the boat was free of the Channel, and out in the bay.

"She's whizzing along as fast as that navy sloop!" exclaimed Carol excitedly, exaggerating as usual.

"She's on a broad reach," said Kirstin as if that explained everything – which, indeed, it did!

They watched *Frolic* a little longer and admired the view before turning to clamber down into the cove.

"Phew! I hope that we manage as well as they did," remarked Kirstin thoughtfully. She held back her long hair which the wind was trying to snatch away. "We don't have nearly as much weight as they did to balance with, and a fibreglass Enterprise isn't as stable as that heavy GP."

Nick was thinking the same as he pulled on the tiller. He hoped the Aussies would be alright and wondered whether he should have insisted on them all keeping together. His mother always told them not to separate. They were tough, those girls, but they were not big and neither carried an ounce of extra weight. Both would have to paddle so their exit from Colander Cove would be very difficult with no one at the helm... He shook his head to dispel nasty worries.

Gerald looked back towards the ridge wondering if the girls were up there, watching *Frolic*'s progress. He hoped Kirstin had appreciated his excellent crewing! It was far away but he thought he could see a spot of red. Perhaps that was Carol's shorts. Kirstin might be with her. He waved – just in case. The girls waved back, but Nick had just said "Ready about?" so Gerr didn't see their movement.

The Australians wandered a little way along the mountainside as they watched their cousins sailing away; then they clambered down via a different track. It, too, had been used during the night by some of the smaller four-legged visitors that had come to drink. The larger creatures had learnt to avoid this path because it was cursed with lot of smilax creepers which grabbed at everything that passed. The sharp curved thorns slashed at the girls' arms and legs and became incredibly enmeshed in shorts and shirts and hair.

When they reached the cove *Percy* was bobbing up and down with his bows afloat.

"He doesn't like being left behind," said Carol. "He's trying to follow *Frolic*."

"Have to yank him up a smidgen," decided Kirstin.

They heaved and pushed and shoved and groaned. But they were trying to push him uphill so they made scant headway. *Percy* resisted every effort to move him into a safer position. It was almost as if Caro had been right and he didn't want to stay on the beach.

"Tell you what," said Kirsty. "We'll dig a hole at his stern – at the higher end – and push gravel under his bows, then his back'll tip down into the hole and his bows will be out of the water."

"Good on you!" admired her sister.

They excavated a huge pit under the transom and then, sweating and panting, had to have a short rest before they went round to the front of *Percy* and sat on the sand on each side of the bows. With legs working like pistons they pushed more and more gravel under the hull. Without realising what tribulations they were laying up for themselves they pressed it in. They kicked it down. They prodded it under. It was good fun in a way – but exhausting.

Then Carol sat on the rear deck and *Percy*'s stern finally tilted into the hole as Kirsty heeled more gravel under the raised bows.

"Kangas!" she exclaimed at last. "I guess that'll do now."

Both the Aussies collapsed onto their backs and, breathing hard, spread themselves on the sand.

"Gosh! I'm exhausted already!" groaned Kirstin.

Carol laughed. "Me too!"

Later she would remember that laugh very ruefully.

31. The Dinosaur at dawn – seen from Elephant Island.

CHAPTER 23

Painting. Scary Visitors. Rising wind. Catastrophe!

The girls admired the angle at which they had tilted *Percy* then Carol turned away saying:
"Better get your picture. I'm going up the hill to watch the hyrax on that rocky outcrop. Did you hear them squealing last night?"
"Yeah. OK. But put some zinc oxide on your nose before you go. Where is it? I'll have some on my snout too."

A long time later, the painting almost complete, above sounds of the storm Kirstin became aware of strange noises. *Percy* was shifting as before! DRAT! All that mountain of hard work had been neatly eroded by encroaching waves and the boat was again jerking about, bashing his paint.

She tried to haul him up. In vain! With his stern still in the hole he was extra difficult to move. She looked round for Caro. Where on earth had her sister gone? Surely by now she must have seen enough hyrax to last her for several centuries. Gosh! It was two hours since the younger girl had set off up the mountainside. Time just melts away when you're painting. Kirstin made another muscle-cracking, but useless, effort to budge *Percy*.

"Car-*ro!*" she yelled. "Car-*ro!*"
What on earth had happened to the pesky girl? The wind snatched Kirsty's voice and shredded it into unrecognisable snippets. As she turned back to the dinghy she noticed a dugout outside the cove with two rougher-than-usual-looking men in it. These were stragglers, going home like the others with the night's catch. There had been no passers for a long time. Working energetically against the wind they were evidently aiming to get through The Gap; but unlike the old man who had come in for a rest, these two were big, strapping young louts. Obviously not tired, they were putting powerful backs into their paddling and making good headway.

Noticing a girl on the beach they shouted to each other and then turned their canoe to head into the cove. Suddenly Kirstin, usually so calm and confident, was terrified.

'Oh help! Why have they changed course?' she wondered. 'Those chaps don't need a rest. They've got evil intentions.'

'Oh kangas! Possums and wailing wallabies! Help!'

Should she run up the hill? Or should she stay to protect the dinghy – and all its cargo? The food, camera, binoculars, sleeping bags, sailing gear... All that stuff would mean a fortune to these simple fishermen. Kirstin's mind began to seize up.

She stood her ground. She would not desert her boat and the Expedition goods. Thank goodness Carol was *not* here. Kirstin was glad of that now. She'd fight if necessary. Oh yes - she *would*! If only Nick and Gerald were here. But of course, these coarse-looking individuals only dared to approach because she was alone. However, she had teeth and nails and she could kick like a kangaroo... Yes. She'd fight all right!

The dugout was almost on the beach. The prow grounded. The men jumped into the waves. Easily they pulled their canoe a little way up the gravel. Kirstin stood watching, adrenalin pounding through her. She didn't know it but her fists were clenched. All this gear would be a great temptation... Also – there was no false modesty about Kirstin – she knew that she was an attractive miss, with a well-shaped body. She was very fair. She had heard that black men fancied blonde girls... This was an utterly deserted spot...

She gave herself a mental shake. Then she started shivering again. Could they be bandits from the other side? She tried to believe that the fellows were just thieves, ready to take everything and to leave her on the beach. Well, if she and Carol were stranded here they wouldn't be able to turn up at Elephant Island this evening. Then Nick and C⁰ would come back to see what had happened.

The men were approaching. Kirstin swallowed hard.

Remembering the Kangi greeting, she said: "Matins!" trying to sound cheerful and totally unconcerned; but the word came out in a sort of croak. That wouldn't do at all. She cleared her throat. The ruffians smiled. What kind of smiles were they? Friendly? Wicked? Lustful? Triumphant? She found it impossible to interpret the grimaces. Possums! What ugly, hulking brutes the revolting creatures were! She decided to run but discovered that she was completely frozen.

They came up to *Percy*.
"Matins," they said. Although their voices were harsh they almost sounded peaceful. No doubt they were trying to trick her into feeling safe! They put their hands on the boat. Kirstin gulped and managed a jerky step forwards.
"No!" she ordered and was proud of the firmness in her tone.
"O.K.?" asked one of the young men. "O.K.?" He made motions of pushing *Percy* up the beach. Kirstin's legs nearly gave way beneath her.
"Oh! Thank you!" she gasped tottering forward to lend a hand. "Thank you very much!"

In no time at all the two husky fellows had *Percy* out of the hole and higher than the wild waters. Still smiling, they turned back towards their dugout, waved and were about to leave.
"No! Wait! Wait!" cried Kirstin. Hastily she rummaged till she found something suitable. – A packet of biscuits would do fine. She thought hard and remembered the Kangi word for thanks. The men smiled even more broadly and, with a small bow, one of them took the biscuits in two hands. This showed that it was a large gift. To receive it in one hand would be rude. It would indicate that the gift was paltry. They bowed again, said "Thank you" in Kangi and pushed off their canoe. As they turned out of the cove into the head wind they shook paddles in a farewell motion before they started battling against the weather once more.

Kirstin swung her arms in reply and then sat down very suddenly on the gravel. She was interested to discover that she was shaking and gasping.

"Hello," said Carol from behind her. "That was nice of those blokes. I thought they looked like out and out baddies at first."

"Where the possums have you been? I've been worried out of my mind!" snapped Kirstin getting rid of some pent-up tension.

"Er… " stuttered Carol, taken aback. "I… er… well… I watched the hyrax for a bit. They're not nearly so furry as the ones we saw up the mountain, when we did the peaks with Nick, remember?"

"It's warmer here at this low altitude," said Kirstin automatically. "These hyrax don't need the covering that those high altitude animals do. Why were you so long?"

"I could see that you were still hard at painting so I climbed a long way and crossed the ridge, high up there – where there's a magnificent fig tree. It's all sticky with sap. I wanted to see if I could spot *Frolic*; and I did. I watched them for a long time. They stopped at the village but they obviously didn't find bread because after calling there they didn't turn off towards Elephant Island. They went on beating against the wind towards the hotel, well – not really towards the hotel because, of course they can't sail in that direction… They'd be going directly into the wind if they did; and even Nick can't magic any boat to do that. They're making huge zigzags, if you see what I mean. They must be having great sailing."

"Oh." Kirsty was beginning to feel better. "You shouldn't wander about like that without telling someone where you're off to."

It was rare for Kirstin to lecture in such a 'big sisterly' voice, but she was still a bit shaken. "Suppose you'd slipped and sprained your ankle or hurt your leg or something!"

"Yes," agreed Carol surprisingly meekly. She saw the older girl's point and had also correctly interpreted her jitteriness. 'Better go on with my story. It'll give her a little longer to calm down,' thought Carol, and then she nearly said:

"It was getting rather rough… " but, noting that Kirstin was still unusually pale, she changed this to:

"Then, I thought I'd better see if you were ready so I nipped back over the ridge – and I saw you trying to heave the boat – I started to run... and... and... well... I *did* slip! The slope was a bit steep. I shouldn't have hurried. One of those wretched smilax creepers right across the path caught my foot. I tripped and went flying.

It had hurt like billy-o, remembered Carol. The thorns were small but they were like razor blades. She had looked at the wound in amazement. The creeper clung all round her leg and those little daggers dug in viciously. No wonder it hurt so much. For some moments she had to sit and get herself under control. However, no point mentioning that now...

"I wounded my ankle – twisted it a bit." She underplayed the event. "I had to hobble. I'm better now."
Kirstin looked down. One of Carol's ankles was red and swollen, criss-crossed with cuts.
"Go and sit on that rock and put your leg in the water," she ordered. "That will cool it and reduce the swelling. I'm going to brew us a quick cuppa and make a snack. Then we'd better be off. If the others go bread-hunting right across to the hotel before doubling back, they might be quite late reaching Elephant Island. You never know; and we might not find it as easy as we expect to get there. We'd better try to arrive early and get camp set up, with lots of fuel for a bonfire in case they need guiding in after dark."

"Yes," agreed Carol. There was nothing else to say. Being an astute young thing she didn't let on that she was thinking:
'We want to rush away because we don't want to be found here alone by any other rough-looking tykes who may not turn out to be as nice as the last two.'
Instead, holding out what looked like a polished green egg, she said:
"Look what I found for Tony's birthday, next Saturday."
"Oh! How lovely!" gasped her sister. "It's absolutely magic! Where was it?"

"In a sort of hole in a rock, with a lot of other big pebbles. The colour's even better when it's wet. Look!" She spat on the stone and its markings were revealed in still greater splendour. "We'll varnish it. Then it will look like this always."
"Oh yes. What a beaut! D'you think it might be malachite?"
"D'you think it could be?" asked Carol hopefully.
"Well, not honestly. But it's really super. I think you should give it to Mum or to Maddy. They'd appreciate it more than Tony would. I'm sure we can find something else for him."
"Yes. Maybe. That's a good idea. I could give him the porcupine quill. He'd like that."
"Yes, but we'll try to find something else because that's a bit dangerous, really."
"Mm."

The girls were both on edge and eager to leave. They had suddenly become aware of how vulnerable they were. Other unwanted visitors might have unpleasant intentions. As Kirstin bustled about Carol ruminated over the weather. From her vantage point high on the mountainside she had noticed, as Kirstin in the sheltered cove had not, that the wind was strengthening. That was why she had started to hurry down to the beach – long before the dugout men had appeared. Kirsty was still engrossed in her painting but Carol knew that it was high time to abandon art. It had become imperative to leave as soon as possible – 'If it isn't already too late," she thought desperately.

The others often accused Carol of looking on the black side but for once all her present forebodings later turned out to have been justified, though not, perhaps, in the ways that she had anticipated. For the present, not knowing what was in store, she soaked her ankle and munched some cheese and an apple. When they had eaten, the girls carefully doused the fire with plenty of water.
"The next problem, *cobber* (friend)," Kirstin addressed her sister, "is to launch this here boat – jolly old *Percy*. Those blokes were just what we needed at the time but if it's as hard

pushing the dinghy to water as it was hauling him away from it, I think we'll be stranded until we can get help."

Carol said nothing. She feared Kirstin was right. However, the slope helped considerably and they managed to wiggle and push the boat into the water without too much trouble. Once he was floating, they turned him head-to-wind and, timing their shoves to coincide with large waves that helped to lift *Percy,* they pushed the stern just far enough up the sand to keep him more or less stationary, in a suitable position, until they were packed up and ready to repeat Nick's manoeuvres as he left the cove.

They lashed the tiller since, with only two people aboard, they couldn't spare one of them to be a helmswoman. They'd both be needed to paddle and to fend off from dangerous rocks. Carol splashed into the water to hold *Percy's* forestay so that he wouldn't suddenly veer about while her sister hauled away to raise both sails. Suddenly overcome by shocking feelings of dread she never made it to the bow but stood frozen as waves bashed her and sent spray flying over her head. Ghastly visions filled her mind.

"Hurry up!" shouted Kirsten, her hands on the halyards; but the younger girl couldn't respond. Her faced was pale and set, with a glazed expression.

"What's up? Caro, you O.K?"

Hearing her name and her sister's anxious tone Carol recovered enough to ask:

"D'you think we'll make it – out of the cove?"

Kirsty knew they were taking a huge risk. She looked round at the awful conditions with almost as much terror as that of her Crew.

"Either we give it a shake," she said harshly, "or we stay till we're rescued."

Carol took a step forward and grabbed the forestay. Kirsten raised the canvas. As in *Frolic's* case, mainsail and jib now clattered and flapped unpleasantly but they'd be ready as soon as they were needed. The girls pushed *Percy* into the waves, slithered inboard and grabbed a paddle each.

There was no turning back now. It was 'be wrecked – or survive'. They laboured very hard into the wind that, having come howling through The Gap, was then reflected straight towards them off the curved cliff. *(Wind diagram on page 121).*

Their headway was painfully slow and each time water crashed into the Enterprise the sideways slither was terrible. No matter how hard they fought, *Percy* was battered unmercifully.

"Get the centreboard down as soon as poss.," panted Kirstin, paddling desperately. "We're making a lot of leeway. We don't want to be bashed against foul rocks on both sides."

The sails flapped uselessly because *Percy* was still head-to-wind. This was intended, but the clatter was irritating. Caro had already twice tried to lower the centreboard to give them better control of their movements, but she'd had no luck.

'Funny,' she thought. 'I'm certain the water's deep enough for the plate to go down… " She tried again – then she made another huge effort. And then yet again she fought the immovable beast!

"The centreboard's stuck," she told Kirstin with a note of panic in her voice.

"Oh strewth! – Blast it! Jiggle it about. I expect it's got a piece of gravel stuck in it. Gosh no! PADDLE!"

By working desperately they just avoided a nasty crunch on a submerged monster. But they kept on smashing into hazards above and below water with such force that the terrified skipper was just waiting for a hole to appear. She managed to control her voice enough to say:

"Try jiggling now. The stone might fall out if you wiggle the plate really viciously and pull down hard at the same time."

Carol alternately paddled frantically and waggled like mad. She fought to move the board either up or down. She even struggled to try and make it move sideways. Every effort failed. Whatever was causing the jam, it was well and truly wedged solid.

"Leave it," gasped Kirstin who, had been paddling flat out the whole time. "You'll have to help me. I can't manage alone."

They scraped past a rock just averting tragedy by a well-placed shove from Carol; but it seemed for many tense moments that crashing waves would win and smash them to smithereens against some huge boulder.

"Keep paddling – HARD!" screamed Kirstin having a violent go at the centreboard herself.

"Shove off! – Starboard!" yelled Carol unable to ward off another looming lump of granite by her own unaided efforts. Kirstin abandoned the plate and bent her back desperately. Another close shave! The sails continued to clatter and snap.

Whatever would become of them if the plate didn't go down soon? They'd never manage to paddle *Percy* through The Gap and up the Channel against such a howling wind. And even if they did manage that... well... *even* if they *did* – which was impossible – there'd be an awful long way to go on paddling – and against the wind – till they made it to the first beach... and if they became too exhausted to get there... the gale would blow them back against the rocks on the far side of the Channel. When she reached that conclusion Carol was sweating with fear as much as she was from the physical labour.

Kirstin was struggling against the elements so desperately that she couldn't think. That centreboard just *had* to go down. Or should they give up and return to the cove, risking the arrival of evil-doers? In fact going back was probably beyond their powers now... Both scenarios flashed through her mind in a series of rapid and very disturbing pictures. All she could visualise was a smashed *Percy* and two bodies swirling about in waves.

They reached the vortex of winds where gusts from The Gap were equalled by reflections off the cliff, and also by buffets from surrounding boulders. Sails were cracking madly, half filling one way, then puffing out on the other side. The horrified girls had to take great care not to be knocked overboard by the too-mobile boom. *Percy* was bouncing about, up and down, leaning over to port, to starboard and all over the place. It was terrible! They had enormous difficulty keeping the dinghy balanced and it was almost more than they could do to avoid being thrown overboard.

What should they do? What *could* they do? Nothing, but try to maintain such momentum as they had. If they stopped paddling for even an instant they would be at the mercy of the conflicting winds and there could be only one end to any boat in that situation – a conclusion that Kirstin preferred not to consider. Their arms ached unbearably. Their entire bodies hurt terribly. Their backs were agony. There wasn't even time to change sides and thus alter the pain.

"*Paddle*!" shrieked Kirstin. "*Paddle*! It's our only chance!"

Carol was beyond thought. She had become an automation, acting only instinctively. Her whole body cried out:
"I *can't*. The pain's too much! *I can't go on!*"
Yet her arms went on moving, struggling, battling. If either of them gave up they were doomed. Her mind blanked out but her body fought on.

The wind was making their eyes water fearfully and now Kirstin realised that she was really crying as well. She knew they'd never make it. Salty tears rolled down her cheeks as she imagined her little sister's body swirling lifeless in these shocking whirlpools.

Suddenly – like a cannon shot – the sails gave an almighty CRACK! – Then *Percy* hit something! Carol screamed. Kirstin's hands released her paddle. She found herself flying forwards terrifyingly fast, straight towards the mast. The boat was at a frightful angle. Water was pouring inboard.

"This is *it*!" thought Kirsty as her head smashed against the boom. (pic 32.)

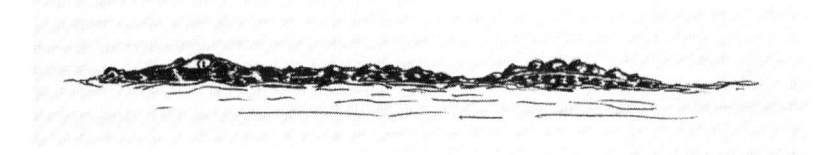

CHAPTER 24

Hunting for bread.

The Stanleighs and Nick were battling directly into the blast. They had to zigzag first one way then the other, gaining a little on each diagonal move. While they were still in the dangerous strait their tacks were short and they went about often. But once they were through the narrows and then out of the Channel there was plenty of space between the long gold beach of the Mainland (to their left) and the fluffy green tops of islands out in the vast bay (to their right). Once there they could take long beats and enjoy vigorous sailing.

Although this kept them busy, they still had time to be impressed by the tremendous beauty of the scenery: peaking waves flashed blue; tall palms danced frenetically and bowed almost to the ground. *Frolic's* crew stared at amazingly long, dazzling beaches. In the dry background ochre-coloured hills dotted with Baobabs and magical mounds of huge, grey, balancing boulders, turned mauve as they rolled away into the distance. It was all utterly wild and exciting.

The big bays across which *Frolic* was speeding were so enormous that they could not be considered as a harbour, but they were shielded from the worst of the storm by mountains to the west. There was no doubt that the gusts here were not as powerful as they were out on the lake proper to the east of Dinosaur Island. There, if they couldn't get through The Gap, the Chorton girls would be bashed to pieces, or exposed to the full buffeting of a heavy gale.

"Can anyone see *Percy*?" asked Ella looking back towards Dinosaur Island and the narrow channel.
"Not yet," said Nick. "If I know Kirstin, she'll take at least a couple of hours over her painting.
"Yes. I s'pose you're right," agreed Nell; but she squinted hopefully over her shoulder nonetheless.

About an hour later they landed on a wide beach below a cluster of mud huts. Women were bent over, washing clothes in the lake. Although naked above their waists, they wore ankle-length skirts which were wet to the knee.

"Any buledi?" asked Nicky.

The ladies pointed with their chins and wet elbows to a small house made of mud that had been slapped on over bluegum poles. The roof of corrugated iron instead of the usual scruffy thatch marked out the owner as a person of means. The hut was also special because it had a large opening in one wall. This had a shutter made from a sheet of wood which was hinged to the window's upper edge. It would fall and close the hole when the slanting pole, that was at the moment keeping it more or less horizontal, was removed. Two guy ropes stopped the wind from tossing the shutter about.

A man on the covered veranda was pedalling hard on an ancient sewing machine, stitching a brightly striped shirt. More of his products, gaily coloured frocks and blouses, hung for sale from the rafters of the porch and in today's gale they were flapping about wildly as if being worn by frenetic dancers. This establishment turned out to be a shop, which the sailors trooped into. They just about filled all the space between sacks of mealie flour, 5-gallon tins of paraffin, bags of rice, bicycle tyres, paraffin lamps, fishing nets, batteries, ropes and lots of other items needed by the villagers.

When Ella asked for 'buledi' the chap behind the counter indicated a worn, wooden shelf bearing three very solid-looking loaves.

"Golly! We can't use these cobblestones!" exclaimed Nell feeling how hard and weighty they were.

"Better than nothing," said Gerr paying the shopkeeper.

As they got under way again they studied The Gap hoping to see *Percy's* bright blue mainsail and white jib. But there were no watercraft in sight anywhere. Even the local fishermen thought it too rough to go out in their dugouts.

"Still a bit early, perhaps," said Nick in consoling tones.

When they reached the second bay the waves were slightly less frantic. *Frolic* met a speedboat, which had come from the hotel with a water-skier in tow. It was definitely not suitable weather for skiers but this one managed a cheery wave before splashing into the water.

Like a hippo fly crawling across a huge canvas the GP zigzagged on, tacking through a fairly narrow strait between two small islands just for the fun of it. A different launch came roaring towards this passage from the other side. When they were spotted, the motorboat slowed courteously so as not to distress them with big waves in the narrows.

"Why's your wake so crooked?" shouted the people in the speedboat, laughing loudly. "Don't you know how to sail straight?"

"Had too many beers," answered Nick who knew that hoary chestnut of old. With more friendly laughter the speedboat people passed and revved off, leaving the GP to continue her short beats up the miniature Gap. Gerald was helming under strict supervision and, despite Nick's rude comments and nervousness for his boat, the novice was coping reasonably well.

Closer to the hotel, a windsurfer was having a tough time even in the shelter of the hilly western arm of the bay. His bright little triangle of sail was continually lifting – only to splat down again almost immediately. Carol's 'grisly caravans' came into view, each parked in its own small garden. A few were well maintained. Some were dreadfully dilapidated. The whole area looked horribly run-down.

When the hotel finally appeared the Stanleighs were flabbergasted. It was a small, rambling, bungalow that nestled under a hill. Enveloped in Bougainvillea and shrouded under Flamboyant trees it was so old-fashioned that it looked as if the building had escaped from the previous century. It seemed incredibly decayed.

"I told you it was nothing like your mum's swish place," said Nick grinning at his cousins' appalled expressions. "Of course most people who brave the shocking road to get here just camp – It's more comfortable than staying in the hotel. The proprietress once found a leopard on her bed."

"Good grief! What did she do?"

"She shot it."
"Poor thing!"
"Who – the leopard or the lady? I bet she got a shock, too!"
"Where's the golf course?"
"There isn't one. There's nothing all round except wild bush – and animals. And to get here you have to bash through a marsh, then go up and down hills on appalling tracks."
"Where are the tennis courts?"

Remembering the establishments that their mother had run, the Stanleighs just could not imagine a hotel without what they considered to be essentials.
"There aren't any. And there aren't any squash courts either." Nick was thoroughly enjoying his cousins' horror.
"Well – what's that tall building then?"
"Oh, that was the control tower for the old airport – or old air-harbour. What did they call the places where seaplanes landed?
"I don't know."
"What's the place used for these days?"
"Pigs."
"Pigs!?"
"That's what I said. – A local farmer keeps his hogs on the ground floor. The upper levels are no longer safe."
"Well! I'll be…"
"Catting Kangas!"

Nick laughed again at his cousins' scandalised expressions.
"There isn't a swimming pool either. You don't really need one – with the lake so handy. And there's no sauna, no Jacuzzi, no disco, no television, no telephone… no… Oh I've run out of no's! You suggest 'whatever'… You won't find it at this 'hotel'. Your mum would love to be in charge here – wouldn't she?"
"There must be bedrooms, and a bar – and a dining room… "
"There's a bar of sorts. To cool the drinks the fridge runs off paraffin – when they've got any, and if the fridge isn't broken, of course. The bedrooms are those round mud huts with palm

thatching. They're just tacky. You wouldn't get me sleeping in them – not with all the mozzies and creepy crawlies. Much better to sleep out in the breeze."
Nell shuddered.
"I had thought we might get lunch here," she said in a quenched voice.
"You can ask a huge Kangalian who works a sweaty, old wood stove. He cooks your food if you want him to. You pay him of course."
"You mean you have to provide your own food?"
"Well, yes. It's quite usual in Eastern Africa, you know, when you're far from shops. The stores in Baboon Bay – the ones Kirstin classified as so grotty – they're the closest provisioning sources."
"Wailing wallabies! I wish Mum could take a look at this hole that calls itself a hotel!"
"It's just that we're really at the back of beyond, and the further up north we go the wilder it gets."
After a moment of horrified silence, Gerald said:
"Well, anyway, the site is utterly superb, with the magnificent bay; the fabulous beaches, more or less empty; incredible masses of bright flowers..."

"Look at those cormorants over there on the rock," said Ella pointing to a row of black birds. "Why are they holding out their wings like that?"

"Most of those are darters, actually," said her brother who was a bit of a twitcher on British birds and had been reading up about African species. "They're drying their wings after diving for fish. There're some cormorants, over in those bare trees. They're bigger and they've got some white on them."

A sunbather watched idly as they crunched *Frolic* onto the coarse sand. Gerald jumped smartly into the waves to hold the forestay as Nick had instructed him and he looked very professional as he held the boat head-to-wind.
"Jolly good, Gerr. No one would ever think it was the very first time you'd done it." Both boys' sunburnt faces broke into wide grins.

They pulled *Frolic* a short way up the beach.

"One of us had better stay within view of the boat," said Nick. "I'm going to try and rout out the cook to see if he's got any bread, or rolls, or anything. If he hasn't we may have to push further inland, where there's another hamlet."

"I'll watch the boat," said Ella firmly. "You two can do the shopping. It's too hot for walking and I'd rather not see the black pit where cooking is done."

"El," urged Nick seriously, "if *Frolic* starts to wiggle about please get someone to help you haul her up a bit higher. OK? We've lowered the mainsail, and stowed it, so you won't have any trouble with that. If the jib starts to unroll – which it might in this wind – just lower it and take it off."

"Aye, aye, Commodore," said Nell, a trifle caustically. "I'll do my best. No – really – I'll watch her like a darter hunting for fish."

"Hm. There're some fine chaps over there playing volleyball. Flutter your eyelashes at them if you need any help. I'm sure they'll be delighted to oblige."

"What! Looking like a lobster!" The sun-scorched girl held out blotchy limbs to exhibit her sunburn. "I bet I look a sight!"

"Nothing more than usual," murmured her irrepressible brother provocatively; but he gazed sympathetically at her blisters and she knew that he didn't really mean his teasing, so she just shot him a mock murderous look, wrinkled her nose at him, and said comfortably:

"I'll hide myself where no one can see me."

"Got your book, have you?" asked Gerald knowledgably. "Well, keep one eye on the boat as well as two on the book and three on the handsome young fellows."

Nell was immune to her brother's baiting so she just hunched a shoulder and pretended to punch him.

"Come on, Gerr," called Nick.

"Sure." Gerald hopped out of Ella's way and scampered after his cousin. "Cheerio. See you later, El."

Clutching purse and plastic bags the boys set off hopefully. Nell was annoyed to find that she'd left her books in *Percy*. *Why* did she *always* seem to leave them in the wrong boat? But she was happy enough watching the volley ball players and dipping herself in the water now and again. She wondered which of the players she could fancy. There was a Kangalian with a superb physique. But then again, on the other side of the net that fair fellow, probably a Scandinavian decided Nell, had the most devastating smile. When he laughed Ella's heart turned over. She thought it might be fun to have a little doze and try to dream about those chaps.

After a while she located Gerald's pack, unwrapped its waterproof layers and started delving into its depths. When the boys came back they were astounded to find her togged out in Gerr's pyjamas. Being so much shorter than her brother she'd had to roll up a lot of the sleeves and trousers.

"Heavens! What a sight! Why have you pinched my night clothes?"

"I got so sunburnt yesterday, and this morning I got windburn as well as *more* sunburn. It's *agony*! I hope you don't mind, Gerr. These cotton sleeves and trousers will protect my arms and legs. Ouch! – Even so, they hurt where they touch."

"Mind! What am I to sleep in?"

"A tee shirt and running shorts – like Nick."

"Oh – so you've got it all settled? Why don't you wear your own jeans and a long-sleeved shirt?"

"They'd scratch even more than these soft jimjams do."

"What if *I* get sunburnt?"

Ella laughed bitterly. "Gerald *dear!* You never burn. You just go a marvellous mahogany colour. You boys are so lucky to be so dark – and tall."

"Oh well! I s'pose I'll have to be a martyr! But I do wish you could see what you look like!"

"I don't wish to do so!" said Nell with huge conviction and so much dignity, that the boys laughed heartily.

"Mum would have fit if she was here! As for your William-the-Conqueror boyfriend – what was his name again? – the fellow in Hastings... "

"Norman."

"Ah! That's right. He'd roar his head off if he could see you."
Poor Ella! Taking after her mother, she was usually so particular about her clothes and make-up, and her hair.
"Why didn't you wear a long-sleeved blouse like the Aussies?"
"I thought the anti-burn lotion would be enough. But it's not! What have you got in your bags?"
"The hotel cook sold us some strange things that he calls 'rolls'. Anyway, perhaps they're better than the 'logs' we got in the hamlet behind the hotel." He clunked some of the 'logs' together and laughed. "I bet these won't go mildew in a hurry. They're harder than dog biscuits."
"We can soak them in milk and they'll fill us up, I s'pose," said Nell eyeing them dubiously. "Rather like curling stones, aren't they? *You* can sharpen your teeth on those. *I'll* specialise in the cobbles we bought in the first village."
With a resounding 'thump' the boys dropped their trophy into *Frolic*.
"What about lunch?"
"I've set it out – over there under the palm tree."
"Good-oh! But I'm going to cool down first. It was horribly hot walking up that path behind the pig tower."
They swam in the incredibly clear water and snorkelled briefly round rocks where thousands of colourful little fish glinted like roving rainbows.
"Stupendous!" said Gerald surfacing and puffing a spurt of water from the tip of his breathing pipe
"Absolutely whizz!"
"Exactly like swimming in an aquarium," said Ella happily.
"Why didn't we see fish round the rocks at Colander Cove?"
"Because we weren't looking."
"Yes, and also because it was much choppier there so a) the fish were skulking in protected crannies; and b) it was much more difficult to spot them through the churned-up water."
"And, besides, we didn't do any goggling."
"A pity," said Gerr, hungrily biting into a 'cobble stone'.
"I wonder what the others are eating."
(Maps on p106 and 171 may be useful in the next chapters.)

CHAPTER 25

Fast trip to Elephant Island.

After lunch Gerald proudly took the helm as they left the hotel. Now they had the wind coming from their port side so they were on a broad reach and making for Elephant Island as fast as they could. There was a long way to go.
"Did you spot Percy while we were away?" asked Gerr.
"Not a sausage." Ella's tone was worried.
"Weird!" said Nick. "They should've been through The Gap ages ago, and well on their way to Elephant Island by now."

The wind blew Nell's hair till it looked like spun silk. She could see that her brother was excited to be skippering the boat as it heeled, with water swishing past the lower gunwale. The mainsheet tugged very satisfactorily. No one objected to wearing a life jacket today; and although he was enjoying himself, Gerr was glad that Nick was handy and keeping an eye on the situation.

They sped past a long island where most of the trees were black with Cormorants and Darters. Fish Eagles oversaw everything from the highest boughs, and little black and white Pied Kingfishers wings fluttering fast, twittered shrilly, as they searched the depths with sharp eyes. From time to time they plummeted stone-like, and vanished under water. More often than not, they came up with silvery shimmers in their beaks. They took ages to eat their catch for the fish had to be swallowed head first; and if it wasn't in the correct position it was a tricky business manoeuvring the slippery, wriggling captive until at last it lay with its head towards the bird's gullet and its tail waving wildly from the tip of the beak. Sometimes as the kingfisher juggled its still-living meal the fish fell back into the lake and escaped.

"Would you like a turn at helming, Nell?" asked Nicky keeping his fingers crossed. He was relieved when she soon yielded her place to him saying:
"It's pulling a bit too strongly for my liking. I'll look out for

Percy and sometimes have a turn with the jib. O.K.?"
"You'll be useful helping to keep the boat trimmed. We'll be leaning out a lot to balance the force of the wind."
"It's super when you're leaning right out," Gerald told his sister. "Shove your toes under the toe straps to brace yourself, El, so you can look right down into the water under the boat and you'll see the centreboard! Imagine! The water seems to be sheer green glass, and through it, there's the plate clearly visible when – according to me – it should be well below us and out of sight."
"It's because the boat's heeling so much," explained Nick. "See how the gunwale on the other side from you is frothing almost through the very surface of the lake."
Emma thought it was extremely dangerous and looked away.
"I don't care about the reasons," said Gerald gazing down. "It's just such a beautiful fascinating sight."

Later, in a sheltered region to windward of an island, they heard snorts and grunts and then spotted the flick of ears just above the surface of the water.

"Hippo!" said Nick.
"Oh gosh, yes!" exclaimed Gerr as huge heads came into focus. He was thrilled. "Just look at the enormous yawns! Thousands of teeth," he exaggerated. "I didn't expect hippos to have tusks, Nick."
"Well they do. And it's as well not to annoy them or they'll chomp you up with their teeth and tusks. Like that mother for example – she'll lunge out at us if we sail too close to her baby that she's keeping just beside her shoulder."
"Oh look!" Ella pointed to a 'teenage' hippo that was lumbering up onto a submerged rock. "Its skin is fantastically shiny – exactly like pink and brownish wet plastic."
"Hippo skins exude a special grease," said Nick. "That's why they gleam."

"Let's go closer and take photos," urged Gerald. "The way they constantly swing their short flat tails over their fat bottoms is so funny. It spatters their pooh all over the place!"
"No," said Nicky. "We don't want to antagonise them." The

young hippo sploshed off the rock and, as they sailed away, only a shoulder here or a rump there surfaced momentarily, but mostly only beady, watchful eyes and enormous nostrils showed above the water, together with the flicking ears that were being pestered by hippo flies.

Frolic was giving a second group of hippos a wide berth when they narrowly passed a monstrous beast that must have been plodding about underwater far from the rest of the herd. Suddenly it rose just astern and lifted itself amazingly out of the waves. He fell back with a mighty, spectacular splash. The creature was obviously extremely cross! *(Drawing on page 176.)*

"Thank goodness he missed us!" said Ella emphatically. Nick quickly took evasive action and didn't dally about to ask the beast what it felt like to be almost run over by a GP14.

They were far from the Mainland when, to make a change from dramatic reaching, they turned to starboard and ran before the wind straight towards the Dinosaur.

"We didn't see the Aussies in the big bay so presumably they're making their way towards Elephant Island up between the Dinosaur and the bunch of minor islands that we're heading for," said Nick. "We might see *Percy* when we get to the far side of the string of islets."

"Probably they're dotting around the islands and we keep on having a rock or something between the two boats so we keep on missing seeing each other," suggested Gerald.

Not one of the sailors in *Frolic* imagined how far from them the Enterprise was, or dreamt of the terrible plight that their cousins were in.

"Goose wing, Gerr."

"Eh?"

"Oh. Sorry! You're getting so expert that I forgot you'd never been on a proper run before."

"I've been on *millions* of runs. Every time the snow is too deep for rugger we have to puff flipping miles round Beg's Bush!"

"I didn't mean that sort of run, you twit. I suffer from that sort as well, and I bet we get a lot more snow in Scotland than...

To prevent a boring argument about which school inflicted the worse torture Ella butted in:

"You told Gerr to 'goose wing', remember?"

"Oh yes. When you're *'on a run'* you're sailing with the wind pushing from dead astern, as we are now."

"I like it," said Nell. "It's nice and quiet."

"That's when we can 'goose wing'. We keep the mainsail out on one side of the boat and we use the jib on the other side. Up to now we've always had them both out on the same side."

"And each time we go about they both cross over to the other side together," said Gerald showing how clever he had become.

"Nuff chat! Goose wing! Pull the jib over to the other side." Gerald did as he was told.

"OK. Will you come and take the tiller now, Gerr? I'll show you how to use the whisker pole."

Nick found the pole in its clamp under the foredeck, and slipped the pointed end of the pole through an eyelet in the free corner of the jib. Then, adjusting its sheet to keep the small sail taut, he slipped a hook at the other end of the pole into a loop on the front of the mast.

"There," he said, setting the foresail better. "The whisker pole's like a sort of boom for the jib. Good eh? One sail on each side – like a goose spreading her wings. Now – UP with the centreboard, El"

Nell was horrified! "Oh - no, Nick! We'll lean over! We don't want to capsize!"

"You said it! We most definitely do not want to capsize. Awfully messy business it would be with all this cargo aboard. We won't go over, though. Don't worry. When we were 'leaning over' as you put it, we were heading north and the wind was coming from our port – our left – and making us heel. The centreboard doesn't stop us heeling. It's not weighted like a keel, you know."

Ella, who could really have skipped the lecture, just said: "Oh!" But her brother was all ears and taking everything in.

"What's it for then?" he asked.
"The centreboard? I explained that before."
"Well, I've forgotten. Sorry."
"It stops us making leeway – going sideways. If the centreboard is *up* there's no opposition to sideways motion. With the plate *down* the boat does crab a bit, but not much."
"Why don't we want the centreboard down now?"
"Because the wind's behind us," said Nick patiently. He thought it was so obvious! "The wind's pushing us forwards at the moment – not sideways."
"Yes, I see... so the less drag in the water the faster we go."
"Exactly."

"I like running," said Ella again later. "It's so calm – not noisy as it was when we were beating. And the boat's on an even keel too."
"Yes," agreed Nick. "But it's jolly tricky just the same."
"Why?"
"Well – er – it's a bit difficult to explain." Nick was about to wade into a discussion about sailing by the lee and gybing when you didn't want to. But he didn't feel like going into all that so he just said:
"One thing is that a running boat tends to dip her nose. In a bad case she could sail herself under."
"Oh no!" That was Ella, of course.
"Well move back towards the stern," urged her cousin moving back himself. "That brings the bow up out of the waves. Oops! Gently does it! A running boat can roll most terribly."
Frolic, responding to Nell's sudden move, had done just that.

As they carefully shuffled back he leant out and slightly tweaked the mainsheet that Gerald was holding. It was a trifling adjustment.
"Phew! Jiminy! What's happening?" screeched the fledgling helmsman.
"We're planing!" shouted Nick excitedly. "Isn't it super? We're *skidding* over the surface of the water – no longer *cutting* our way *through* it. The GP's good at that. She's got a flattish bottom."

"Lovely," agreed Ella as the boat settled again and the planing stopped. "That was really great!"

"Show me how it's done," commanded Gerr. So, taking the tiller, Nick did his best to explain how to catch the wind and wave together. "Try it. But mind you don't start sailing by the lee and gybe! Gybing's the easiest way to capsize a boat, I reckon."

Nell clutched the spinnaker cleat.

"You have control," Nick said as he handed Gerald the tiller.

"Eh? What? Crikey! Yes. I have control!"

"Don't puff yourself up! It's just a formality. When you give someone else the tiller you're supposed to say: 'You have control' so that everyone knows that the skipper's changed."

"Do you think it's safe to let Gerr… " began Ella.

"I hope so."

"Of course it is!" claimed her brother stoutly, and he was nearly as good as his ambitions. It took a few attempts before he was shouting with joy and excitement. Planing was indeed *wonderful!*

Gerald was less confident when they were just south of Elephant Island. Nick mentioned:

"There's an interesting nest somewhere round here. Shall we sail round this little islet and see if we can find it?"

"Yes. Let's."

"OK. We'll have to change direction then. Pull the tiller towards you and we'll do a controlled gybe."

"Er… " said Gerald remembering the unpleasant gybes he had performed unintentionally the day before in virtually no wind. "Perhaps you'd better take over… I'll learn to gybe properly one day when the wind isn't so strong."

"Good idea," put in Ella with emphasis. So Nick and Gerr changed places and, with Nick at the helm, *Frolic* began to circle the tiny island.

"Look for a tremendous Baobab," said Nick. "In one of the multiple forks of its branches there's an enormous collection of twigs." They all studied the trees but it was Nick, who knew what he was looking for, who first spotted the untidy heap.

"There:" he said pointing with the hand that held the mainsheet. "Just above that loofah creeper with the pods hanging down like big cucumbers, and all the yellow flowers."
"Oh yes. My goodness! What a whopping nest!"
"Looks shockingly uncomfortable, doesn't it?"
"Not half! Did you say it was a Fish Eagle's nest, Nick?"
"Yes – and no. The Fish Eagles actually *construct* this bundle of brushwood and live in the top flat – so to speak. Their nest is on the crown of the pile."
"You'd think that a magnificent bird like a Fish Eagle would make itself a superior high-class home. I wouldn't be satisfied with that dreadful muddle of branches… "
"But then you're not a Fish Eagle, El! Snuggling in the middle of the conglomeration of sticks there's a hollow – nicely lined with mud and feathers – which is the real nest."
"Look. There're a couple of Fish Eagles perched way up high in the very summit of the tree. Perhaps they're the owners of the nest," exclaimed Gerald.
"Sure to be. The builders wouldn't let any other eagles come so close."
"They look shockingly smug, and proud!"
"I think they have a right to look haughty. They're such splendid birds."
"But what's so special about this nest – apart from its size?"
"Oh – the size isn't particularly special. Fish Eagles add twigs year after year so this monster must be pretty old, I suppose."
"Jolly nearly a Historical Monument, I should say," said Gerr.
"Built by the 'First Fish Eagle Earl' in the 9th century' – sort of thing," agreed Nicky. "What's special about it is that it isn't only a stately home. It's a block of flats!"
"I *beg* your pardon!"
"Well not exactly a block – more like a maisonette, with the eagles upstairs and a pair of Hammerkops nesting in the middle. Right in the centre of the bundle."
"Jiminy! I hope this 25th Earl doesn't drop his boots on the ceiling late at night."
"Yes. I say – look – You can see the entrance now."

33. The mansion of the Twenty-fifth Fish Eagle Earl.

"Oops!" Nicky had forgotten about sailing.
"Sorry!" he said as he corrected his mistake.
"Anyway – see that hole? That's the Hammerkops' front door. They live in the basement – rent free!"
"Oh yes. There it is!"
"Well, I'll be bothered! Don't the eagles get fed up with the

Hammerkops or vice versa?"

"Apparently not. Last year when we camped on Elephant Island – my Mum, and Uncle Ken, and Kirstin and Carol and Tony and I – we spent a lot of time studying this nest. All the birds seem to get along famously."

"Look! Down on the rocks below. There are two sort-of-coppery birds: the Hammerkops."

"That's them all right!"

"It's an absolute hoot watching the Hammerkops going home," said Nick with a huge grin. "The entrance to their flat is only just big enough for them to get through and there are no rocks or branches nearby, so they can't kind of waddle in as other birds might. Oh no! They dive in – using a horizontal racing dive of course. They fly up to the nest, shut their wings and *shoot* inside. It's really quite spectacular"

"Good heavens!" said Ella grinning at the picture that Nick had conjured.

"Wouldn't do for a Hammerkop to come home drunk!" chortled Gerr.

"Jolly handy," said Nell."If you need a loofah you just grab one from outside your front door."

"First you'd have to peel and then dry it," said Nicky. "*And* get all the big seeds out – or they'd fall everywhere in your bath!"

The great ball of twigs was behind them now and Nick could no longer turn round easily to watch it or the birds.

"We may as well push on right round this islet," he said, "and approach Elephant Island from the south-*east*. That'll give Kirstin and Carol a surprise. They'll be expecting us to arrive from the south-*west*. Shall I take her in? Or do you want another go at skippering, either of you?"

Gerald had enjoyed a long 'innings' at helming and was wary about rocks that might lurk at the entrance to the Elephant Island approach. Ella was happy doing 'nothing in particular'; so Nick stayed where he was and they went to port just before reaching a cove in the Dinosaur's bulging tummy.

"We're right through the islands now," said Nell, "and we still

haven't seen *Percy's* blue sail. Where *can* they have got to?"
"Wish I knew!" Like Ella, Nick sounded worried.
But Gerald suggested: "A snack will stop us fretting."
"Good idea." agreed Nick. "I'm hollow as a tree that's been struck by lightning!"
"But you both had enormous lunches," objected Ella who did not fancy untying a food parcel and digging around in it to find something that would satisfy the boys. The boat was heeling more than she liked. Her companions paid no attention to her arguments and nagged her to get something edible out of the cargo.
"*You* rummage for it then," she told her brother.
"Oh no I'm busy! I'm crewing! I've got to look after the jib," said Gerr with his tongue in his cheek, and the jibsheet firmly clamped in a jamming cleat. He was, in fact, taking a leaf out of his sister's book and doing nothing in particular. Ella sighed.
"You've both got worms!" she grumbled. "That's why you're always so hungry! I think I'll ask Maddy to dose you both – with *double* doses too – when we get back."
She bent over the bundles in *Frolic*. Where had they stowed the biscuits? Which parcel held the fruit?
"Mm!" said Nick when she finally handed round apples. "These are imported. Lovely aren't they? Apples don't grow well in Kangalia."

The other two, who normally took apples completely for granted, now looked at their fruit with respect, and tasted the refreshing tartness with unusual appreciation.
'How odd,' thought Gerald, 'to treat *apples* as particularly special! But then, I reckon that Nick wouldn't give a 'thank you' for a pawpaw or a mango or even a pineapple. I s'pose it all depends on what you're used to. We take for granted what's ordinarily around and we forget that what to us is a boring, everyday thing is, to other folk, a high treat.' He shook his head and stopped thinking. Philosophising was not his strong point.
"Will you pass another biscuit, please Ella?" he said, and when she looked amazed he explained: "Got to feed the worms, you

know! And we'll need energy to pitch camp."
"Baloney! We don't use tents!" replied his sister sharply.

34. <u>Elephants</u> enjoy playing in water and will happily swim or wade across rivers or from island to island. In this picture the line between pale (dry) backs and dark(wet) bodies shows the depth of the river which these elephants have just crossed. If you can spot the baby at the back (third from left) you'll see he is totally wet showing that, as they crossed, he was completely submerged and had to use his trunk as a snorkel.

CHAPTER 26

Waiting for the Aussies.

It was late afternoon when they beached *Frolic* safely in the small bay on the northern side of Elephant Island.
"Why is it called 'Elephant Island'? I see that's even its proper name on the map."
"Sometimes the creatures are found here"
"What! Right out here in the middle of the lake?"
"We're not anywhere near the middle of the lake, you know. You keep on forgetting that there are hundreds of miles of water stretching further north from here."
"Well it jolly well feels as if we're hundreds of miles from *everywhere*! Anyway – why do the elephants come here?"
"They like the hard round fruits that grow on those vegetable ivory palms over there, and the long grass and other stuff as well I expect. I'm not an expert on the big beasts."
"But how do they *get* here?"
"They swim, of course!"
"You're joking!"
"No. Really. Elephants swim well – when they want to."
"All the way from the Mainland?"
"I imagine they swim or wade from island to island. I haven't ever stopped one to ask him, actually!"
"Idiot!"
"Have you ever seen elephants on the islands?"
"Well, no, I haven't. I don't think they bother to come out here very often these days. What with civilisation and Game Parks and things… " said Nick vaguely. Ella looked round, half hopefully and half fearfully.

"'Sfunny that the other two aren't here," said Nick. I thought they'd arrive before us."
"You know what Kirstin's like when she's painting. I expect Carol's busy bird watching or collecting all sorts of things. They will have completely forgotten the time."

"Yes. Their whole family's a bit scatty about art and time," said Nick, conveniently forgetting his own mother's artistic tendencies.

"But they can't *still* be in Colander Cove," said Gerald. "I wonder why we didn't see them on our way here."

"Probably the various islands got in the way," suggested his sister. Nicky had nagging fears so he avoided commenting.

"Let's get everything shipshape before they turn up. They must be almost here by now," he said hoping against hope.

When all had been done to make camp comfortable and ready to prepare supper, thoughts turned again to their two missing relatives.

"Let's go to the top of the hill and see if we can spot them."

It was more of a tiny, low plateau than a hill. From a border of beach the island rose fairly steeply to a flattish area where trees and bushes were almost horizontal because of their constant battle against the wind. Sundown was again casting a red glow over the evening world. When they reached the small plain they turned their backs on the sunset's brilliance and gazed east and south expecting to see a blue mainsail and a white jib now tinged by the setting sun.

There were no sails anywhere. Not even the dark silhouette of a dugout disturbed the scene's deserted splendour. This evening the dirty weather was still keeping fishermen ashore, and any men who had not managed to return from the previous night's work would either never be seen again or were still battling on the far side of the Dinosaur. Nick, Ella and Gerald seemed to be utterly alone in a wild and beautiful, but now rather hostile, world.

"Where *are* they?" Nell sounded worried, as well she might.

"Perhaps they went for a spin round the islands and it's taken longer than they thought it would."

The three lookouts rotated slowly, scanning the waters in all directions. The entire region appeared to be devoid of any sign of humanity. The village far across the bay, and the hotel in the distant corner were both obscured by intervening islands.

Not one of the watchers admitted to gnawing anxiety. They were definitely starting to feel jittery. Where on *earth* were the girls? Nick thought about the difficulties of escaping from Colander Cove. The wind had been rising all day. Had the Chortons waited too long? Had they found it impossible to get out? Sweating with horrible premonitions, he wondered: 'Had they come to grief?'

"Maybe they've gone to the wrong island," suggested Gerr.

"It's not at all likely. I mean – they were here last year. They know it pretty well."

"Could something have happened so they're stuck on one of the other islands?"

"I doubt it. Listen! I think we'd better make a big bonfire to guide them in... In case they try to reach us after dark. It'd be a loony thing to do but you never know what they might try."

They collected as much wood as they could find. There didn't seem to be much. Perhaps local fishermen had taken branches back to their villages. Or maybe elephants had destroyed all the potential fuel before it had had time to grow, fall and dry.

Nick was so anxious he was almost at the point of biting his finger nails. His thoughts were going round in circles:

'I should never have allowed the fleet to separate. Those two are excellent sailors but I should have remembered that they are physically small. Perhaps they just didn't have the strength to fight this morning's conditions.'

He understood much better than the other two how very dangerous their exit from Colander Cove had been. He just prayed that *Percy* hadn't been wrecked. Could the girls have survived such a tragedy? No! Survival would be totally impossible. If *Percy* was broken up by those hideous rocks in Colander Cove there'd be no hope whatsoever for anyone on board.

None of them felt like going back down to the bay to start cooking. They were so concerned that they didn't even feel like a cup of tea, though that would have done them a lot of good. The misery and fear of what might have happened became worse and worse as the evening shut in.

"Where on earth can they be?" worried Ella for the umpteenth time.

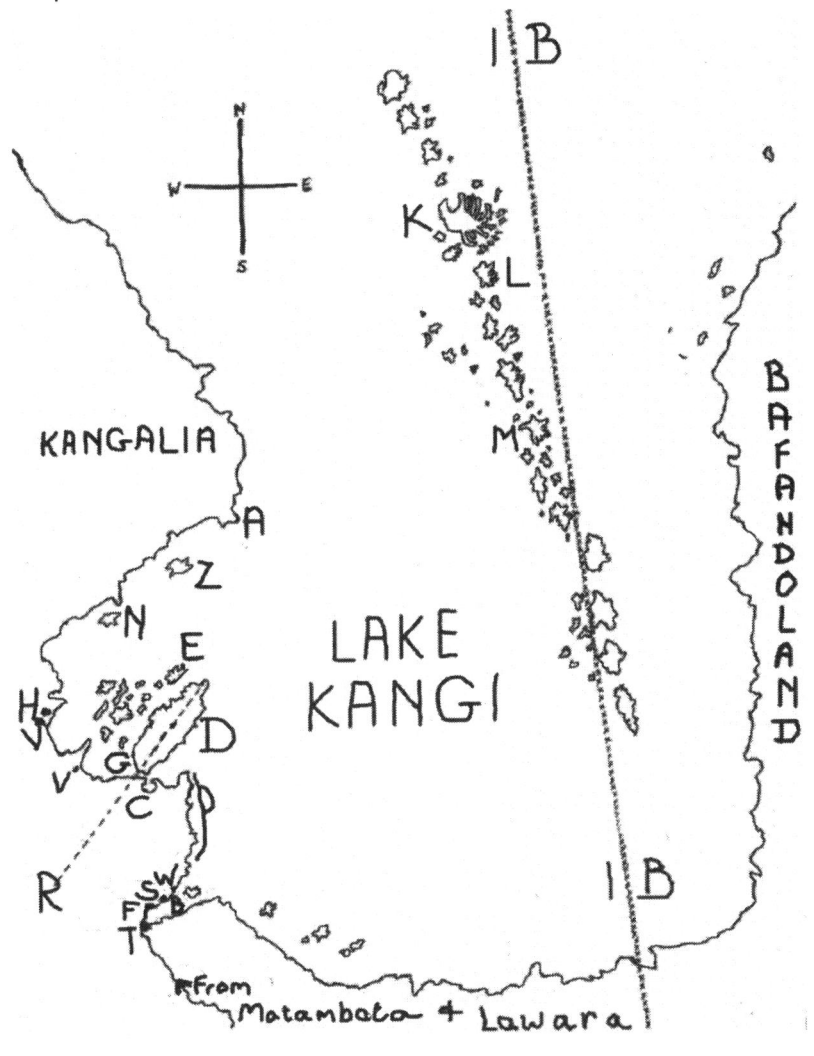

35. Southern part of Lake Kangi
IB = International Border. K: Kadenzi Island. L: Lumbo Island.
M: Midimi Island. Otherwise: Same key as map on page 106.

CHAPTER 27

Worried on Elephant Island.

Headlong towards the cannibals.

By the time the three on Elephant Island had collected a good pile of firewood a violent sun was about to vanish behind the far-off western hills with a final dazzling burst of crimson; but *Percy* and the girls were still nowhere in sight. Apart from mutters of "Where *can* they be" from Ella, which she couldn't suppress, the three on Elephant Island were stoically trying to say nothing that would show the others how anxious each was feeling.

"Where *can* they be," muttered Nell yet again, like a tenacious dog with a bone. It was the last straw for Gerald.
"For goodness sake, El, SHUT UP! If you say that again I'll... I'll... go *berserk*!"

At last, however, they could no longer pretend that all was going to plan – not even to a very delayed schedule.
"Er – six-eighteen," said Gerr. "Isn't there something we can *do*? Shall we go and look for them?"
"Don't be daft," answered his sister snappishly because she was so anxious. "We'd be bound to miss them in the dark. And what about our promise not to sail at night?
What do you think has happened, Nick?"
"I don't know any more than you do."
"Well, what do you think *might* have happened?"
"Gosh! How should I know?" Nick refused to voice his fears. They were too depressing – too ghastly.
"Perhaps they couldn't get out of Colander Cove," suggested Gerald.
"Yes," agreed Ella, putting into words all the thoughts that had been driving Nick mad. "That's a possibility, you know. The wind's not so strong now but it did rise a lot after we left this morning. Maybe they just couldn't paddle out against it."

"It was *very tricky* in that sort of whirlwind when we were getting gusts from The Gap... " agreed Gerr, "and more wind reflected off boulders and from the curved cliff bashed us terribly – all at the same time... " His mumbles died away.

"They could easily have capsized there," said Nick voicing all their greatest fears.

"They'd swim back to the beach," suggested Nell trying to believe that. She hesitated to go on but somehow she could not stop herself. "In that case, of course, *Percy* would undoubtedly have had it – on those fiendish rocks."

"Yes. Most likely." Nick couldn't bear to think about that so he dealt with the possibility brusquely.

"But I think they themselves would be able to swim ashore alright. Don't you, Gerr?" persisted Ella with optimism born of ignorance. She simply hadn't appreciated the terrible dangers of their emergence from Colander Cove earlier in the day. Nick, however, was certain that if Kirstin and Carol had lost control of *Percy* and had been tipped into that swirling cauldron of frothing water... they would not still be alive.

"Yes. Yes. Perhaps they'd have managed that." said Gerald, as ignorant as his sister. "Even Carol," he went on; yet his brow was deeply furrowed with worry. They're both very good little swimmers. Of course if they got a bonk on the head as *Percy* went over... "

"Ger- *ald!* For heaven's sake!" exploded Ella.

"Well, we're trying to fit facts together to decide what may have happened. Perha... "

Gerr's voice died. He suddenly dashed into bushes and was terribly sick. A vision of Kirstin lying on a wave-bashed rock; her face under water; limbs twisted and broken; fair hair being tossed this way and that, turned his face yellow-green.

****

A few moments after crashing into the mast Kirstin regained consciousness. She felt decidedly groggy but, gingerly touching her head, she decided that she was still alive. Her eyes weren't working quite correctly but she figured that by some miracle *Percy* had been swept right over a submerged boulder and into the temporary lee of another, even bigger, monster. Thank goodness his centreboard had *not* been down. Scraping over the submerged rock would have ripped the plate right out and left a huge hole in the dinghy's hull. In less than a minute the boat and crew would have been down at the bottom, rolling this way and that, helpless at the mercy of cruel currents – fulfilling Gerr's vision!

O.K. – Incredibly *Percy* seemed to be all right, apart from a dreadfully scarred bottom. But where was Caro? Kirstin's heart seized up. Her sister? ... She gulped with relief, but then almost started howling, when she spotted a body rolling about beside the centreboard casing, washed in water. Even as the older girl started desperately to bend to towards her sister, *Percy* lurched. The sail cracked again. She knew she had to deal urgently with the boat.

Wisely the paddles were tied to thwarts so they were nearby, noisily banging against the dinghy. Kirstin tugged on one cord and grabbed the paddle that had been floating beside *Percy* bashing him irritatingly. Instinctively she started paddling. Not far to go now till they were past that last barrier. But would her unaided efforts be enough? And even supposing she could get them past that stretch of rock, they would then be hit unmercifully by the appalling gusts coming straight from The Gap. The terrified girl moaned. She'd never manage to deal with that situation alone. And she *had* to get Carol's head out of the sloshing water.

"Caro!" she called between panting with her struggles. "Caro! Wake up! *Please* wake up!" Was her sister dead? Kirstin nudged the collapsed shape gently with a foot. It took several frightening seconds but at last the younger girl moved. Her eyelids flickered and then opened. Looking dazed she struggled and sat up. Kirstin watched while an expression of amazement slowly crossed that re-awakening face. It blinked as realisation dawned: '*Percy* has escaped being wrecked!' "Carol!" screamed Kirstin. "Wake up! I need your help!"

Both hardly conscious, the girls managed to claw their way out of the cove. Then the situation was almost worse. They were in a whirlwind of conflicting winds and big crashing waves. The centreboard was desperately needed to provide control. Without the plate they had absolutely no hope of choosing where to go, let alone of veering into the wind and tacking through the channel. The gusts blasting out from the strait were driving them further and further from The Gap.

"We'll run with the wind for a while," shouted Kirstin above the roar of swirling crests and the smashing of dark water on hideous boulders. Their minds were still foggy but they felt less dizzy now. Although her sister's face was pale and tense there was no fear in it – just determination to survive. They would weather this somehow. They'd been in tight corners before and lived to tell the tales.

"Maybe we'll be able to shake the blockage out when we're moving fast," explained Kirstin. "Anyway, there's nothing else we can even try now," she added as strong flurries from The Gap caught them and filled the sails. Besides, they were both completely shattered. It would be foolish to attempt anything that required brute force until they had recuperated.

Automatically Kirstin took the helm, releasing the bungee that had held it in as fixed a position as possible, and adjusted the mainsail. Mechanically Carol set the jib. The shocking wind made all this very difficult. They were doing the only thing possible – running before the wind. Like a race horse with the bit firmly clamped between his teeth *Percy* swooshed off in tremendous style.

'Gosh! If we were racing now... ' thought Kirstin. But, of course, any regatta would have been cancelled in such weather. She studied the foaming white caps with respect.
"Gee! What speed!" gulped Carol. She cleated the jibsheet and attacked the centreboard again. More and more vigorously she shoved, and heaved, yanked, and pulled. She even kicked. At last she had to pause; and then, puffing, she renewed her efforts. After each tussle the exhausted girl

waited hopefully but nothing happened. Time and again she renewed her increasingly frantic onslaughts.

"It's absolutely no good," she admitted quietly at last. "You try. D'you think I can manage *Percy* while you have a bash?"

"Just mind you don't run by the lee and you'll be all right."

Carol took the tiller and Kirstin moved forward. But at the end of ten minutes they had to admit that the centreboard was jammed so completely that nothing short of beaching the boat and investigating from below would loosen whatever it was that was causing the trouble.

They had been tearing through the water so fast that by this time Dinosaur Island was far astern. Colander Cove was just a mere crack behind a cliff.

"I say – " said Carol in a small voice, "do you realise, Kirstin, we're heading straight for the other side – the dangerous country which is full of rebels and bandits? The tribes who eat their captives... and we've got no means whatsoever of turning round!"

"The fact had not escaped me," replied Kirstin grimly, "but we're not *heading* that way. We're blimmin well, blinking, *rushing headlong* onto their coast. And I can't see how we can avoid it."

36. Angry Hippo. It doesn't do to sail too close! – Story: page 159. (Good in colour. See it on www.Daphne.es Click on Fateful Flies.)

CHAPTER 28

Flares.   Caught in Bafandoland?

Nick decided that they had to try and look on the brighter side. A good Commodore wouldn't let his fleet become depressed.

"Maybe they didn't manage to beat through the channel. Perhaps they gave up, ran before the wind for a bit and then did a reach round the other way. Perhaps the only thing they could do was to sail right round the Dinosaur."

"Wouldn't that be terribly dangerous – with all that wind on the east of the big island?"

"Yes. But if they couldn't get through The Gap that's all that was left for them to attempt."

Immediately all eyes switched from southeast or southwest to northeast. There the Dinosaur's snout was just showing above the waves. The creature appeared to be crouching on the water and at that moment the last ray of sunset was painting the cliff which rose out of the lake to form the nose. A crimson nostril was reflected in waves so it looked as if the Dinosaur was breathing red flames like a real dragon.

The heat had suddenly gone. They were wet from swimming and from the spray splashing into the boat and also, hunting for fuel had been a sweaty business so now, lashed as much by their worries as by the unmerciful wind, they shivered. There was no tiny sail in view.

"It would take them *ages* to go right round the Dinosaur."

"Well – not really. If all had gone well they'd be round the snout and here by now... if they set out in good time."

"If! If! If!" squawked Ella, working herself up into a real panic. "What can we *do*?" she repeated – yet again!

There was silence as they all wracked brains to try to solve the mystery or think of something helpful; but with no facts to go on, and with only suppositions to juggle, they got nowhere. After a ghastly pause, Gerald moaned:

"Gosh! I wish I knew what to do! The sun's completely gone."
"Yes. We should have started the fire! What's the time?"
"Six thirty one."
"Right. We've got till 7. Remember, in case of emergency we send up a flare on the hour – every hour if need be."
"Yes."
"We must light the fire *right away*. I suggest Gerald stays up here to keep it stoked and to see that it doesn't spread. Ella and I can go down to camp and fetch something to eat and bring up the flares. Then at seven o'clock we'll put up a flare and hope to see an answer from them."
"Yes. OK. Anyone got a match to light this beacon?"
"They were in bathers or, in Nell's case, pyjamas, so no one had matches.
"I'll nip down with you and come straight back up to light the fire," said Gerr.
"O.K."

They hurried down to the small bay. Gerald found a box of dry matches and went sprinting up the hill. Nick rustled among the life jackets and grabbed two packets of flares. Then he and Ella carried saucepans, water and food up to the highest point of the flattish summit where Gerald was tending huge flames.

When they eventually had it, the food and tea did them good. So did the warmth and light of the fire. But before they started supper they realised that 7pm – flare time – was approaching fast.

"Let's go over the emergency rules to make sure we know what to do."
"Point One," said Gerr: "The lost boat, or boat in danger, fires a flare – a red flare if it is in need of urgent assistance, or a white flare if help is not needed. Either flare will indicate the lost boat's position to Base Camp."
That seemed straight forward enough. But where was Base Camp?
"I suppose that *we* are Base Camp," said Nick. "I mean – F*rolic* is where she's meant to be – where we're *all* supposed to be."

He paused and then went on: "So *Percy* is the lost boat. Yes?"
"Yes," agreed the other two in subdued tones.
"Right. So *they* must fire the first flare."
"Yes."
"If it's white it means they're not in an emergency situation. If it's red… " Nick's voice trailed away. Whatever would they do, in the dark, if they saw a red flare?

Point Two was considered next.
"On seeing the flare from the lost boat, or boat in danger, Base Camp will send up a reply. A white flare will merely acknowledge that the first boat's signal has been seen. A red reply flare informs the boat in danger that rescue will set out as soon as possible."
"That's very clear," said Ella. "But will we really set out in the dark to rescue them?"
"I don't know," said Nick miserably. "We'll discuss that if necessary."

"I say! Do buck up. It's almost 7pm," said Gerr urgently. "Let the fire die down and stand with your backs to it. We'll be able to see their message better without firelight blinding us."

Nell went on reciting the emergency rules that Aunt Maddy, that conscientious Admiral in Lawara, had insisted on them all studying till they had them almost by heart.
"Point Three: On seeing the reply flare from Base Camp the boat in danger will endeavour to remain as static as she can so that the rescue party can find her as rapidly as possible."
"Hm," muttered Nick. "Easier said than done. Especially in this stormy weather."
"Both staying still (for them) *and* us finding them will be darn difficult," put in Gerald, brutally expanding Nick's thoughts.
"That tells us what to do if they are in danger," said Nicky grimly. "Perhaps they won't send up a flare at all. That would be… " He couldn't finish the sentence. "Go on, El, what if they're not in danger but just lost?"
"Point Three continued: On seeing a white flare from Base Camp the lost boat will fire a second signal: white if she is

capable of returning to Base Camp unaided; but a red flare will mean that she needs help, when convenient."

"Hm," said Nick again. "Let's hope we get two white explosions from the Aussies. Here, Gerr, you hold the red packet. El here's the white lot."

"Seven o'clock!" announced Gerald in a strange tense voice. Ella seemed be panting.

"Oh gosh!" gasped Nick. "Gerald, you'd better watch that way. Nell, will you look out over there? If I focus this way we'll have the whole horizon covered. We must keep our eyes peeled."

"And our fingers crossed," said Nell seriously.

Then, in a totally different voice, before she'd managed to get all four pairs of fingers crossed, she cried:

"There! There! There it is!" She pointed way off to the northeast.

"Can't be!" grunted Nick, swivelling round and moving to Ella's side of the fire. As he and Gerr gazed in the direction of her finger Nick muttered again:

"Can't be! They *can't* have got so far – surely? And *why*?"

They could definitely see a very distant white star. Nell had spotted it shooting up like a firework, and then it burst, as if celebrating midnight on New Year's Eve. Now it was falling very slowly back to earth, oscillating from side to side and spitting out fountains of white sparks that, from this distance, looked like incredibly thin silvery lines.

"Oh! Thank Goodness," breathed Ella. "They're all right!"

"Phew!" agreed Nick.

"Jiminy," exploded Gerald happily. Then he added jealously: "Gee whizz! What a sail they must've had!"

"Let's hope they fire off another white flare," said Nick hopefully. "Oh my gosh! We've got to let off a white one to tell them that we've seen their signal." He turned to Ella to ask for a white flare; then he suddenly remembered something else, and croaked:

"Oh Crikey!" Harassed, he looked at the distant signal, which had now all but fizzled out, and scratched a line on the ground. The scratch was vital. It showed the direction of that far-away spark.

"Quick. Does that seem to be pointing the right way?"

His cousins looked at the line, which was clear in the light of the dying fire.

"Yes," they said confidently.

"Come on," urged Ella. "Let's send them a white so that they know we've seen their signal. It'll put their hearts at rest."

Nick took the tiny canister that Nell was offering. He removed the cap and placed the cylinder in the bailer bucket of water where it bobbed about in the vertical position.

"Stand back," he ordered.

It felt like a month of Sundays before anything began to happen, but in fact it was only a few seconds that the plastic floater sizzled and hissed; and then suddenly it zoomed off into the sky. Although they had been tensed up, waiting for the explosion they all three gasped and jumped even further back. Above their heads a long silver line glistened higher and higher, until, with a slight 'POP!' the streamer turned into a shower. Like the first signal, this one floated down ultra slowly throwing out more and more bursts of sparks as it sank towards the lake on the leeward side of Elephant Island. All the time that it was dropping the flare was emitting the most mournful moaning that set their teeth on edge.

"What a horrible, eerie groan!" exclaimed Ella.

"That's to attract attention. If potential rescuers don't spot the flare they might be induced to notice it if they hear the wails."

"Oah!" shivered Nell. "I don't like it!"

"It's really creepy! Why don't they make the thing say something cheerful?" asked Gerald crossly as he felt the hackles rising on the back of his neck.

"I don't know. Maybe it's to announce that below there are people in dire distress who need help. What a grisly thought!"

"Anyway, it doesn't matter, now that we've found them," said

Ella in a satisfied tone. "I'll survive the doleful whistle because the flare has done its job."

"Well, sort-of," said Nick refusing to be comforted too easily. "We'll take a compass bearing along that line, of course, but that doesn't mean it will be easy to find them if we have to rescue them. It may not be too bad if they are on land... but if they're still afloat... Well – Let's hope they give us another white flare."

"That'll mean that we have to stay put on Elephant Island till they get here," said Gerald, disappointed.

"Yes. We can't help that. They ought to manage to get here in less than a day. We can sail around close by here, and fish, and go goggling."

"Mm. That will be fun, but it will delay our sail northwards to catch Lake Flies."

"Oh well! Hang the Flies! I'd rather meet up with Kirsty and Caro than collect a whole TON of flies."

"Me too," agreed both his cousins.

"Why aren't they putting up a second signal?"

"Give them a chance. Maybe they're finding it a bit tricky."

"But nothing could be easier," said Gerr who had only watched Nick setting off their flare.

"That's what you think. It's putsi easy when you're standing on dry land; when you're warm and dry and have enough light to read the instructions; when you're protected from the wind... Nothing could be easier then. But sometimes it's not so simple, you know."

Gerald was silenced. He grimly imagined his cousins trying to organise the flare as *Percy* bounced about in huge waves. Were the girls actually hanging on to a capsized boat? The three cousins stood expectantly, glad that the wind was keeping off mosquitoes, but desperately hoping to see another firework-like shower of sparks. At last Nick asked dubiously:

"It *was* a signal we saw, wasn't it? You don't think we could have mistaken something else for a flare and missed the real sign while we watched that wrong light." He stopped and gulped. "– that came from somewhere else? – Could we?"

"It *was* terribly – I mean – surprisingly – far north… " agreed Gerald adding fuel to Nicky's misgivings.

"No," said Ella confidently. "It was definitely a flare. I saw it go up and I watched it float down. It was just like the one we sent up. Only it was far away. It was their signal all right."

"Yes. And it would really be too much of a coincidence if someone else had the same type of rocket and fired it off at precisely the second that we were expecting them to send a message."

"Well, why aren't they completing the message? Why aren't they shooting off a second signal – a white one – or a red one? Then we'd know what was going on."

"That would tell us what to do."

"I don't know."

"Perhaps they only just managed to send off that one signal. Perhaps they can't get another off for some reason… "

"Anyway, they're not in an emergency. That's one good thing."

"What will we do then? Will we wait here, or shall we go and rescue them?"

"Gosh! I don't know. Mum didn't think of a situation like this. The way that Nick scratched his head showed how desperate he was for ideas. "The rules don't tell us what to do in a case like this."

"I think we'll have to go to them," said Ella thoughtfully. "After all – if they were completely alright they'd be able to send up another flare, wouldn't they?"

"Ye-es. I imagine so."

"So it stands to reason: If they can't shoot up signal number two they're not entirely OK. But I expect they don't want to frighten us by showing a red if they are more or less safe. Probably everything's fine except for something to do with *Percy* that we can get fixed if we all help but which they can't manage on their own."

"Sounds sensible," agreed Nick.

"We'll have to go and rescue them," decided Gerald, eagerly.

"Yes. I suppose so. I don't think the Admiral and other officers in Lawara would approve of us going towards the border, but I don't see what else we can do."

"Towards the border?" gulped Nell.

"Obviously. They're near the border, or on it, or actually *over* it. Sure to be from the direction of that signal. Maybe that's why they don't want to put up another light which could advertise their position."

"Oh! Migosh! Maybe they were captured in the act of sending up flare number one and that's why they haven't been able to fire off flare number two."

"If they've been caught firing off signals they'll be had for spies – sure as eggs!"

"You *do* have the most *ghastly* ideas!"

"Yes. Well – but... It might be true! Very likely, you know."

"Hell! Yes! I wonder where on earth they are! We'll have to look at the charts. Anyway – Let's be glad they first sent up a white and not a red. But of course that's meaningless if the bandits caught them just after they'd sent off the white flare."

"Crikey! Yes!"

"So we'll set off at first light to find them?"

"Yes. But we'll have to be jolly careful not to fall into rebel hands ourselves."

"Oh heavens! If the bandits spot us there'll be nothing we can do to stop them capturing us. We won't be able to save ourselves or rescue the others."

"Maybe the guerrillas don't have any boats so if we stay out deep they won't be able to catch us."

"How far can rifles shoot?"

"Don't even think about that sort of thing. We can't leave the girls stranded."

"There's nothing for it. We'll have to go."

They paused, still hoping desperately for a second message. At last, Nick, the Commodore on this trip, said:

"We'll have to send off a red rocket. D'you want to fire it, Gerr?"

Quickly Gerald selected one of the red flares from his

packet. He peeled off the cap, and dropped the canister into the water at their feet. They all stepped well back. Nick had shown most efficiently how very easy it was to send off a flare. Or had he? The plastic tube bobbed about in the bucket and neither hissed nor sizzled. They were tempted to lean over and prod it, or to try and find out why it wasn't soaring up towards the stars.

"No! Keep back," Ella reminded the boys. "It might suddenly decide to whizz off and we don't want anyone's eye to be in its way."

"Gosh, no!"

At last their patience ran out.

"Must be a dud. Try another," suggested Nick. Gerald selected another red plastic tube.

"Your turn," he said, handing it to his sister. She peeled off the lid and dropped the device into the bucket of water. It floated beside the one which had failed to ignite. Suddenly there were two sizzles, two dragon-like hisses, and both flares shot simultaneously into the sky.

"Jiminy!" shouted Gerald excitedly.

"Caramba!" yelled Ella. "Aren't they absolutely *beautiful?*"

"Wallabies!" choked Nick. "But what a *ghastly*, blood-curdling racket! Well – nobody could possibly miss that display! At least they must know that we're coming to save them."

If he had had second sight he might *not* have concluded with: "Roll on tomorrow."

They were subdued as they watched the last red spark flicker and finally die, and then while they munched supper. After finishing up with cocoa they doused the fire with the water from the bailer bucket, which was now devoid of small plastic cylinders. A melancholy trio, they stumbled down, through bushes, back to the bay where *Frolic*, a silvery, magic-looking ship in the strong moonlight, sat peacefully on the sand. She was extremely well protected from the wind by the two high arms of the bay but nonetheless they now roped her firmly to convenient trees. There had not been time to do this before.

"Maybe we should leave Ella here when we set off tomorrow," suggested Gerald as they met again after tying the ropes.

"*What*?!" His sister was appalled by the prospect of being marooned alone on Elephant Island.

"And if you don't come back? How will I survive? How'll I get off the island?"

"You can fire off flares until somebody spots them from the shore and arrives to rescue you..."

"Then, if none of us come back you can dispatch an armed rescue party."

"I am *not* going to stay alone on the island!"

"Oh all right! All right! Keep your hair on. Calm down. Perhaps we'll talk about it tomorrow."

Ella fumed in silence, determined not to be left behind.

Having learnt from experience, the sailors wrapped all food and hid it in the boat where vervets, baboons, monitor lizards and other predators were less likely to venture. Tooth brushing was quickly over and they rolled into sleeping bags beside *Frolic* to lie for some time silently wondering what would happen the next day. But eventually, one by one, they nodded – fearing the worst – hoping for the best – not knowing what to expect – just drowsing – till at last they fell asleep and the moon sent dappled shadows over the scene.

What had happened to Kirsty and Caro? Why had they sent up only one flare? What complication – or tragedy – had overtaken their Aussie cousins?

37.
<u>A sociable group:</u>
1 Pelican,
2 Sacred Ibises,
((hard-to-spot)
&
15 Cormorants.

CHAPTER 29

Terrifying flight across the waves. Mystery Cloud.

"You know, Caro," said Kirstin conversationally after an electric pause. "I can't help thinking that Nick was exaggerating when he told us that those people on the Bafando side eat anyone who arrives on their shores."

She was again poised over the maddening centreboard, which remained obstinately stuck. Her sister, at the helm, was thinking: 'Nick doesn't usually exaggerate; and there are other things that could happen to us that would be worse than being eaten.' However she kept quiet and quoted to herself: 'The Crew person has to support and cheer the Skipper. Crew should uphold Skipper's morale. Crew should not make uncalled-for remarks.' She'd had it all drummed into her at various regattas. Now she told her memory: 'O.K. O.K. I haven't said it. I've been a good Crew.' She wiggled her painful foot surreptitiously. The ankle was hurting rather a lot!

Her arms and Kirstin's were still aching from today's paddling to escape from Colander Cove and from yesterday's efforts as well. They continued to be sore for many days to come, but the future had become so fraught that mere pains in arms, legs and back seemed negligible compared with their greater worries. At the moment, having let *Percy* run before the wind for some time, the girls felt a little rested and were facing their problems.

"Shall we lower the jib?" Carol shouted to be heard above the buffeting gusts. "We'd go slower. Like that we wouldn't reach the dangerous regions so soon."

"We could lower both sails," Kirstin pondered aloud as she gave up struggling with the plate and sat on the side of the boat. "But would that be sensible? If we needed to raise them again I reckon that, in this blow, we'd find it excruciatingly difficult... and completely impossible if we had to do it in a hurry. No. Leave it for now - especially as those little clips come off the forestay if the jib is allowed to go slack."

"Catting Kangas!" shrieked Carol in fright as a sea broke over *Percy's* bows and smashed inside the boat. "Do sit back a bit. We don't want to run her under. This wind's a real brute!"

"Oh *blue*! Sorry! I was thinking," apologised Kirstin as they both moved as far aft as possible. "Does this chap have self-bailers? Oh good!" She bent into the bottom of the dinghy and opened them both. At the pace at which they were flying through the waves the hull was soon sucked dry and she was able to lower the levers again. (Blue! = Fright! in Aussie slang.) "Better than our leaky self-bailers at home," she smiled at her sister. "These don't need to be kicked to make them work!."

"D'you want to take the helm back?" suggested Carol whose arms were feeling the strain of the mainsheet.

"Not specially. You're doing fine and I'm trying to think. Besides, we'd better take turns so we don't get fagged. Who knows how long we'll be sailing... "

"At this speed we'll hit the other side by evening," said Carol pessimistically.

"Perhaps not. The lake's very wide. Over fifty miles... Maybe we might manage to land after dark. But of course – what's the difference? Day or night – we'll either be found, and captured – or end up starving in the bush or eaten by wild animals. There's absolutely nothing over there, you know."

"Except wilderness devastated by revolutionaries, and possibly a handful of brutalised Government troops who'd think we were rebels anyway. And the rebels will assume that we are Government spies... "

"And they're all starving. So there's not much in it really... "

"No."

"Maybe we'll be able to land, and loosen the centreboard, and sail away again without being seen."

"And maybe pigs will fly."

"You're very depressing."

"Yes!"

It was an effort shouting to be heard so they sailed on automatically, each trying to think of a way out of their dilemma.

From time to time, although they were both well back in the stern, a heavy wave broke in over *Percy's* port quarter so they left the self-bailers open to work continuously and were glad of their efficiency. At one stage Carol instinctively pulled on the mainsheet and for a few glorious moments they planed over the waves at incredible speed. Then Kirstin 'came to'!

"For heavens' sakes, Caro!" she yelled. "We don't want to get there any quicker than we *have* to!"

"Sorry!" gulped her sister. "Jiminy! I just did it without thinking."

From then on she tried valiantly to spill wind – which, of course, is almost impossible when a sailing boat is running under such conditions. But it gave Kirstin an idea.

"Listen," she said. "We don't *have* to run. We'll jolly well reach, or at any rate go as close to the wind as we catting well can."

"But we'll make hideous leeway."

"Who cares? We'll crab all the way up the 300 miles of lake that are left to us, if necessary, so long as we never make enough leeway to cross the border – or anyway – so long as we don't get marooned on the wrong shore."

"Mm..." murmured Caro appreciatively. "Good on you, Sis." Suddenly, uncharacteristically hopeful, she added: "And surely the wind can't stay this hard and in this same direction for long."

"I wouldn't be too sure about that. Shall I take over and we'll see what we can do about changing direction?"

"Yes," said Carol gladly, relieved to be handing over the tiller. "You have control," she said formally.

"Oh no I don't" replied Kirsty grimly. "But I'll do what I can. I'll try to go to port. There are more miles on that side than to starboard. And also the lake is wider up north. And port is further from the dangerous Bafando Side than starboard is."

Gently she put the tiller over and obediently *Percy* turned his nose northwards. Carol leaned out to port, balancing the boat as it heeled. They were still speeding; and with no centreboard to stop their sideways motion they were also slithering to starboard (towards Bafandoland) as well as shooting forwards. *But,* they were still in control!

They would, of course, inevitably hit the eastern shore eventually – so long as they didn't go under – but at least it would now happen later rather than sooner. They were no longer heading directly towards the perilous coast. Their line of motion was definitely oblique and Kirstin was successfully spilling wind, which slightly reduced their mad speed. Whether or not spilling wind reduced their slide to leeward they couldn't decide but their spirits rose a little.

After some time Kirstin asked:
"Have we got the charts, Carol, or are they in *Frolic* ?"
"We've both go copies, *drongo* (silly)!"
"Oh yes. Thank goodness."
"Admiral Maddy's orders, remember? We all thought she was being over dram-... over dra... what's the word Ella used?"
"Over dramatising the situation."
"Yes. That was it."
"Get our charts out, mate."
"You'll have to go with the wind a bit more while I'm doing it. Without me hanging out here beside you the boat will heel too far over."
"Yes. I'll have to change course while you're not helping to balance things. Anyway it'll be a relief not to be leaning backwards so drastically. My tummy muscles are really sore. I suppose yours are too."
"Yes," answered Carol. She could have added: 'So are my arms, and legs, and ankle.'
As Kirsty let the boat go round her Crew started to move gently forward and chose a package from among the cargo, untied it from its place, unwrapped the plastic cover, and withdrew a large envelope in which she proceeded to rummage.
"Watch it!" screamed Kirstin. "Don't let bits blow away!"

Carefully Carol poked through the envelope till, looking mystified, she found the sheet that the older girl wanted. Kirstin sat on it while her sister re-wrapped the rest of the charts and secured the bundle in its place.

"Unfold the chart on the floor of the boat, will you?" said the skipper and when that had been done she put her foot on it to stop the paper flying away. The chart was decidedly damp but that couldn't be helped.

"Look there," Kirstin pointed with her toe. "A string of islands. Thought so... OOPS! Possums! Sorry! Caro, open the bailers. Oh heck! They're already open. I forgot. Is the map soaked?"

When order had been restored as much as possible in a tiny craft bouncing about on big waves, Kirsty said: "Here, take over will you? I'm going to swot the chart."
They changed places.
"You have control."

Kirstin crouched on the boards studying the paper, which had its own ideas about taking wings.
"Warn me if I'm needed to sit out, mate," she said.
"Sure." Carol was concentrating hard on helming. A little later her sister looked up.
"You've got a horrid cut on your head," said Caro. Kirstin put up a hand and touched the place that was sore. Her fingers came away slightly bloody; but she didn't have time to bother with that now.

"There's a string of islands right down the middle of the lake." she said. "Do you remember the map?"
"Vaguely."
"To be precise they're not exactly down the centre. They're a bit squiff. The southern quarter are more to the east than the northern three-quarters of the line. So the southern islands are in enemy territory, but the northern, more westerly lot belong to Kangalia." *(Map on page 171.)*
"Um," said Carol, starting to catch on.
"So we've got to get up as far north as we can."
"Yes. I get you."
"If we can manage to get past the first... er, one, two... the first five, no – the first six – main islands – there seem to be

millions of tiny circles – I expect those are just sort of heaps of rocks… But it makes it difficult to figure out how we'll be able to count the proper islands… if we get that close… Well – If we get past the first six decent-sized chunks of land and then aim for any of the rest we should be all right."

"You mean less un-O.K. than elsewhere," argued Job's comforter. "You know everyone says it's not safe to get near the border *anywhere*."

"There's nothing else we can do – unless you can cook up a better idea. If we get as far north as the islands and we are still to the west of them, then we'll be darn lucky. That's what I say."

"If we get past the first six before slipping leewards over the border we'll be luckier still. For goodness sakes, hurry up and sit out with me so I can head more north and less east."

Kirstin hastened to comply with this request and Carol, in sarcastic mood, went on:

"And if we *do* manage to go 'bump' into some friendly island – with no rebels on it, and a splendid sandy beach with no rocks, where we can land, – and with a village of people – friendly people of course – to help us tip *Percy* onto his side so we can find out what's wrong with the plate, it will be a hem miracle!"

"Well – Yes – the first bit. But you know perfectly well that the islands aren't inhabited. They're too near the border… too dangerous."

Carol sighed.

"We'll just have to pray for a miracle but not expect a miracle squared," she said. "Sandy beach and no humans of any kind at all."

"Yes," agreed Kirstin. "Now – to lower the jib or not to lower it…"

They argued the pros and cons for some time but in the end left it up.

"Time for tucker," suggested Caro. "I'm famished!"

She could have added: 'and my ankle's throbbing terribly,' but as nothing could be done about that she didn't mention it. Some sustenance would distract her, perhaps.

"Yes, my tummy's rumbling too. Shove over. I'll take a turn at the helm, if you like."

"*Bludger*! (Lazy)" accused Carol; but gladly she handed her sister the tiller and found the lunch pack. Extracting the food little by little they ate deliberately slowly, spinning out every morsel for as long as possible and keeping some for later – just in case. Under present conditions the prospect of having to open one of the big food parcels was not enticing.

"Look!" shouted Caro with her mouth full of pineapple. She waved backwards towards the southwest.

"It's all right for you," grumbled Kirstin. "You can look round and admire the view. It's different if you're helming." But she took a quick glance back just the same.

"Very, very odd!" she exclaimed. "What is it?"

A tiny black cloud was billowing along towards them at not much above mast height. It constantly changed shape and travelled at a speed that no cloud had ever attained, as far as Kirsty was concerned. Astounded, Carol stared with her mouth open. She couldn't figure out what it was that was bearing down on them out of a sky where there were few clouds and those were dashing about high in the heavens. This particular dark blob was incredibly low over the water! Was it going to hit them?

Kirstin glanced up at the burgee. It was straining very slightly to one side with every thread. She looked backwards. What could that worrying cloud be? A specially ghastly gust? Now that it was closer it seemed to be made of rotating blobs. What was the cloud bringing? Danger – no doubt!

"It's birds!" blurted the younger girl in amazement.

"Birds?"

"Yes. I'm sure it's birds." After a while she added: "They're tumbling about all over the place. Seems as if some are having trouble flying. They look like poor swimmers floundering about in big breakers back home in Oz."

Her sister was alarmed. Again she glanced over her shoulder. Carol was right! A flock of assorted land and water birds, all fluttering desperately, was being buffeted along at a great pace. Below the birds the water was churned into peculiar peaks.

"Gust ho!" she yelled. "Watch out, Crew! Ready to let fly the jib if necessary."

Quickly letting out the mainsail, she pulled up the tiller and *Percy* turned to run before the wind. Now the boat was temporarily on an even keel and speeding almost silently, compared with the previous battering. The change from battling motion was intensely welcome. But before they had time to savour the relative peace, *Percy* was tossing and bucking in a fierce gust that slammed past like a tornado. The birds, which had been caught up in an offshore blast many miles away, were struggling desperately to stay in the air. They flapped and fluttered in the heavy wind and looked, as Carol later said, 'like umbrellas turned inside out.'

"My! Am I glad they missed us!" gasped Kirstin as the agitated cloud of ruffled feathers tossed and twisted away across the lake. "Hope we don't get any more gusts like that!"

"Too right!" agreed Caro who was still clinging to the gunwale. "Even being caught in only the edge of that squall was ghastly! Imagine how *Percy* would have bucked about if we'd been in the middle."

Bravely she volunteered:

"Shall I take my turn at helming? You've had a long session. And it's a good chance to swap while the boat's stable before we turn north again."

Taking turn and turn about at the tiller they were far from bored.

There was plenty to do just keeping the dinghy trimmed and the hull as free of water as possible.

"I'm exhausted emptying *Percy* with the bucket when the self-bailers need help," groaned Carol.

"And constantly struggling to keep as northerly a course as we can," said Kirstin. "I hate the noise and thumping about."

Despite all their efforts the mountains on the western – friendly – side of the lake dwindled and those on the east grew steadily, though luckily slowly, larger. All the time each girl was worrying about how this mad caper over hideous waves would end.

38A. & 38B. They *had* to find an island with a beach. In rough waves it would be fatal to try to go ashore on islands like these.

CHAPTER 30

The bobbing 'mine'.

As they roared terrifyingly across deep, rough waters the girls saw no other boats of any kind. It was Saturday so the commercial fishing trawlers were not operating, and presumably the navy did not patrol at weekends.
"Other people all round obviously consider it's too risky to put out," suggested Kirstin. "Probably no one likes the look of the breakers."

She had hated the huge waves at first, but now that *Percy's* course was settled and they were managing to hold the dinghy fairly stable she was enjoying the sail. Of course it would have been marvellous to have had someone with strong muscles to relieve her frequently from the strain of the tiller and mainsheet. Her body was a huge, silent, scream of pain. Carol did her best but she couldn't cope for long.

Kirstin looked down at their feet stuck under the toe straps. Sitting on the very edge of the gunwale, holding on with the seats of their shorts, and by the 'skin of their toenails' they were able to hang so far out over the water that, like Gerald, they could have seen the centreboard if it had been behaving properly. But it wasn't apparent today. It was not doing its job of stopping their sideways gallop. However, the further she and Carol leaned out the closer the *Enterprise* could sail to the wind so the more north-easterly instead of easterly the boat rushed.

Stretching back for so long and always on the same side was hard on tummy muscles and thighs. Sometimes when they couldn't bear the pain any longer Kirstin bore away from the wind and let *Percy* run for a while, or held a course which allowed them to sit more comfortably on his port gunwale. 'Using toe straps must be awful for Carol's ankle' thought Kirstin. 'It should be rested, not strained to cracking point.' Yet to escape falling overboard while bending back 'impossibly' far, the toe straps were essential.

"How's the ankle?" she asked.
"Sore," said Carol. "But I'll survive." – 'So long as we don't drown,' she added to herself.

If any canoes *were* bobbing miserably in the waves the girls never spotted them. Perhaps fishermen had given in and were letting the wind blow their dugouts wherever it willed. The girls thought about the men who had struggled back through the storm past Colander Cove, and they wondered how many others had not made it home.

'Well, in our case, at least the wind's not taking us *quite* where it wills,' thought Kirsty with relief. 'We may be making tremendous leeway but we're not just running headlong towards the east.'

Sometime during the afternoon she noticed an odd object bouncing over the white horses. It was low in the water but did not move like a canoe. An untended dugout would have wallowed heavily but this object skittered across the waves. There was no shape of anyone sitting up to paddle. In fact it was peculiarly shapeless altogether and, as far as the girls could make out, it was turning this way and that as it bounded along.

"It's a bomb!" declared Carol. "Keep away from it!"

"You're bonkers, Caro."

"I know. But it's fun being mad!"

"As if we haven't got enough to deal with, without having to avoid floating bombs!"

"Well. It made a good story! You looked really shocked for a moment."

"We don't need any of your *drongo* (silly) stories right now. Anyway – bombs don't float! And if they did they wouldn't leap about like beach balls as they went along."

"Don't bombs float? Well – It's a mine, then. They float *and* they explode. Steer clear of it!"

"For Heaven's sakes!" Kirstin studied the distant red and brown blob. "It does look as though it could be one of those nasty things we saw in the Maritime Museum. Now you've got me all of a jitter, you *shonky ghalah*! (silly idiot)

And all for nothing, I bet!" Kirsty gave herself a mental shake and brought herself back to reality. "Don't be daft, Caro. How should a mine come to be floating in the middle of an African inland sea?"

"After the war. You know, even these days, sometimes old mines are found on the beaches of Britain. Remember how Ella and Gerald saw one all cordoned off before the experts blew it up near Hastings?"

"But there wasn't any war *here*."

"Oh yes there was. It's in that book — abut this lake. You read it last year and I've just finished it recently."

"That was the *first* world war — a huge time ago. The mines would now be long gone. And anyway, Carol, there were only two boats on the entire lake at that time — well only two that could be involved in battles, and they were both tiny things — One was German... what was she called... ?

"The *Wissman*-something perhaps?" Carol, who had just read the saga, suggested vaguely.

" ...and the other was a British naval boat of sorts. The two captains were *friends* so I'm certain they didn't litter the lake with mines to sink each other, and damage dugouts."

"Oh well," said Carol philosophically. "I liked the story of how the English captain heard the news that their two countries were at war and the Bavarian chappie didn't know about that. The British sailors went and shelled the *Wissman* when she was in port undergoing repairs."

"Didn't you laugh at the victim's captain who was woken from his siesta? Still half asleep, wearing only his underpants and bare feet he leapt into his rowing boat and rushed out to the attacker yelling: 'Vor Vy you are bombs throwing?' He thought his pal was just playing jokes."

"And when he climbed aboard he was taken prisoner."

"They say that the two friends had a great time for the rest of the war playing bridge and drinking whisky!"

"I bet they did... and admiring the beauties of this glorious lake — well — glorious when it's not chucking storms at us."

The girls laughed at their own version of history.

There was a short silence until Caro noticed that the 'mine' was appreciably closer.

"Kirsty, watch out for the 'bomb' – or whatever it is."

"I'm just going to hold my course. If it comes too close I'll have to head off – if essential. But we don't want to do that unless we're forced to."

Kirstin meant what she said but she was also curious to know what the weird 'thing' could be; so although Carol, half believing her own fiction, was vaguely unhappy to notice that *Percy* and the unidentified object were drawing steadily closer, Kirsty was secretly quite pleased about the reducing separation. She held herself ready to let *Percy* slide away from this mystery that was bobbing so rapidly along, making much worse leeway than their own. Suddenly she laughed.

"It's an inflatable dinghy!" she said. Carol looked again.

"Yoiks - yes! The sort of toy that Tony's friend, Alan, has at home. It's a jolly big one – but not a proper 'rubber duck' like your pal Tim's huge Zodiac. You know what? It's a plastic duckling!"

"I hope there's no one in it!"

"Can't be. It's turning over and over."

"Well, I hope there's no one hanging on to it. It's obviously been blown off from some lakeshore weekend cottage."

"Probably it was left on the beach and the gale blew it away during the night." Now Carol felt completely differently.

"We must catch it," she said. "If anybody's hanging onto that dinghy we must rescue him."

Kirstin agreed, so instead of trying to avoid the mystery float they tried to meet up with it. Would they succeed? Was that an arm waving desperately from the far side of the little plastic bubble?

"We're going to miss."

"No we're not."

"Go more to port."

"Can't!"

Carried away by the excitement of the chase Kirstin put the tiller over too fast and rather more than she should have.

Percy heeled frantically. The plastic dinghy bumped against his stern. Kirstin, trying to manoeuvre to prevent what might become a terrible accident, had both hands fully occupied: one with the tiller and the other with the mainsheet. She could do nothing to catch the toy. The younger girl made a grab, but she was too far forward so her hand never even touched the bouncing toy. She couldn't bear to see it bob out of reach. With a yell she stopped leaning backwards. Immediately *Percy* became desperately unbalanced. The starboard gunwale skidded under the waves. The situation worsened drastically when, trying to grab the tiny boat, Carol skipped nimbly to the lower side of the Enterprise. *Percy* immediately heeled even further and shipped a horrifying quantity of lake. As he shuddered, preliminary to capsizing, the twelve-year-old slipped and cried out. The waves came crashing up to meet her and she plunged headlong into the churning waves.

Kirstin screamed in horror. Even if *Percy* stayed afloat, in this weather she didn't need time to realise that it would be impossible to go about safely, and even more difficult to pick up a floundering swimmer.

39. Man overboard!
(Don't miss seeing this in colour on www.daphne.es.)

CHAPTER 31

Unexpected events on Elephant Island.

The next morning Ella, Gerald and Nick woke early, roused not so much by the dawn chorus but by some internal alarm that warned them that they had important things to achieve. Supper saucepans were scrubbed rather faster than efficiently, and a hearty breakfast (*with* cobblestone bread!) was devoured for, said Ella, they didn't know what was ahead of them or what they might have to do.

By 07.15 all was packed and they were almost ready to be off. Gerald was on the foredeck about to raise the sails. The end of the mainsail halyard, which was dangling from the top of the mast had swung out of his hand. He reached up to catch it.

"Here," he said to his sister who was on the beach. "Use that shackle to fasten the top of the mainsail to this rope."

"Peak. Halyard," said Nick automatically. He was rummaging in the 'Essentials' bag.

"What?" asked Ella.

"You should say: the 'mainsail peak' – not the 'top of the mainsail', and that 'rope' is called a 'halyard.' It hauls up the mainsail," explained Nick absently. He had found the compass and was thinking about other matters. "I'm just going to the top up there to take a bearing along the line where we sighted their flare last night. We should have done that straight away. Lucky it didn't rain during the night."

"It's OK. I got the bearing yesterday – with the compass on my watch," said Gerald.

"Oh." Nick hesitated. Then he came to a decision. He'd made one mistake by allowing the fleet to split up. He'd better do everything correctly now.

"Well, I'll just take another reading to confirm yours. After all, your compass may not be as accurate as the prismatic one."

Gerald was offended by this bit of tactlessness, but he had to agree that the bigger, nautical compass might well give a more exact bearing than the compass incorporated with so many other gadgets on his watch. So, nobly, he replied:

"All right. You check the bearing. After all it was tricky trying to reading it by firelight last night. Nell and I will get the sails up. Small jib? – like yesterday?"

"Yes," said Nick, trying to gauge the size of the waves outside their bay. "We wound the jib round the forestay last night. All you have to do with that is unwrap it." He went off towards the place where they had lit the beacon.

On the way he stubbed his toe on a very large iron tent peg. It was old and rusty but still strong.

'Odd!' thought Nick. 'Someone must have camped here sometime and left this behind. I wonder if that was us, last year.'

Deciding that the peg might come in useful he put the compass on a rock and spent some minutes tussling to wrench the chunk of metal out of its niche. Suddenly it came loose and he staggered backwards holding his prize aloft. Collecting the compass he went on up the hill to the 'plateau'. There he shoved the peg temporarily through his belt and having set the instrument, he noted the direction of the line they had drawn.

"39 degrees," he muttered blissfully unaware of the effect that the iron peg was exerting on the magnet in the compass.

In the cove below Ella stretched up and pulled on the mainsail halyard that Gerald had handed down to her. She tugged it still lower to a convenient waist level (thus, of course, pulling the other end higher). With a shackle she attached it to the peak of the mainsail. Meanwhile Gerr unfurled the jib from the forestay and decided to haul it up a little more tightly. He climbed back into the boat and bent to the bottom of the mast.

On a GP14 the halyards i.e. the ropes that pull up the sails, run down *inside* the mast. Each halyard comes from the top (the peak) of its sail and enters the mast high up over its

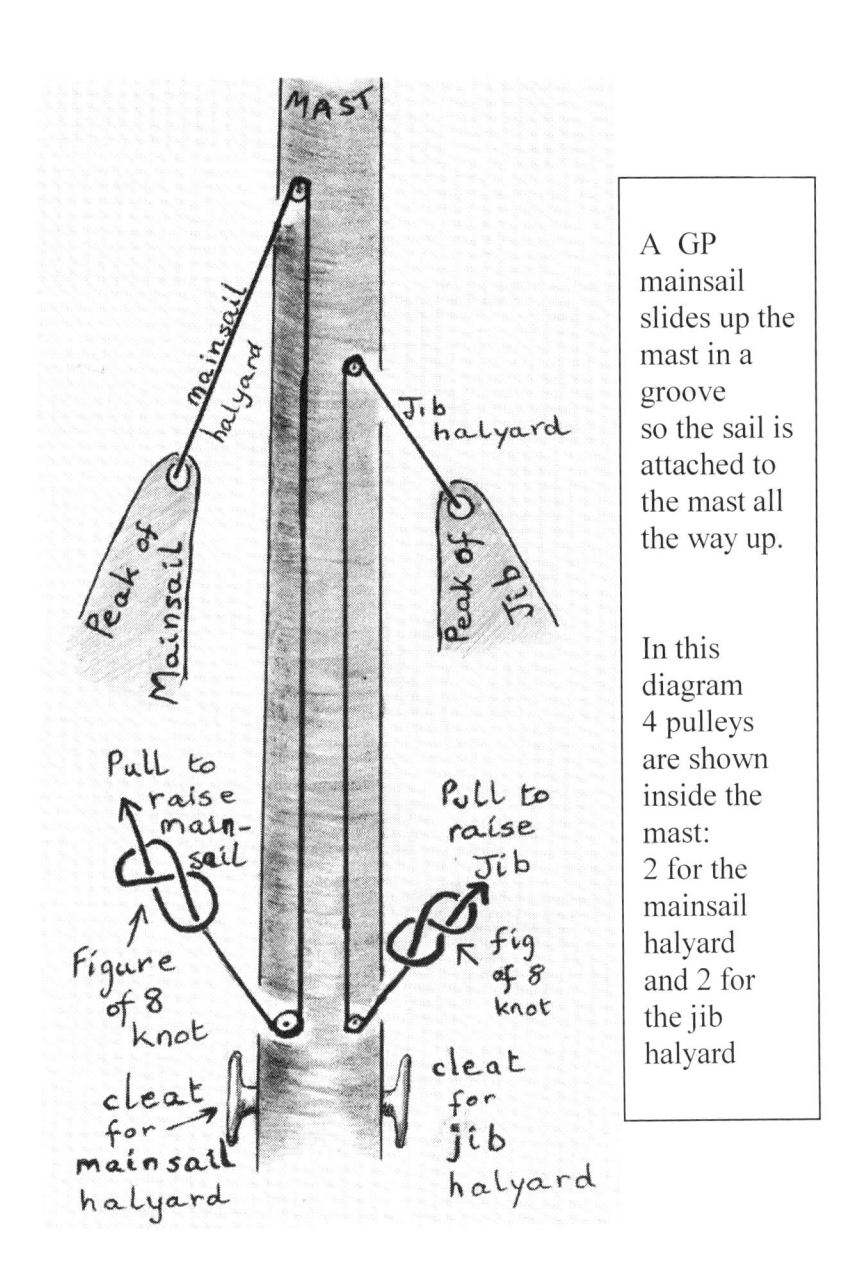

A GP mainsail slides up the mast in a groove so the sail is attached to the mast all the way up.

In this diagram 4 pulleys are shown inside the mast: 2 for the mainsail halyard and 2 for the jib halyard

40. To show how halyards pass down inside the mast

own pulley. The halyard then passes down the hollow centre of the mast, right down to a hole near the base of the mast where it exits, again over its own pulley. Each of the two

203

halyards does this and each has its own entrance to and exit from the mast. When Gerald grabbed the halyard that was cleated beside the lower, starboard (right hand) pulley, and yanked it, the jib rose a little further up the forestay.

"Ella," he said, "bend the forestay."

"What do you mean?"

"While I haul up the jib you pull the forestay with one hand and push it in a different place with the other hand so it's got a small S bend in it," explained her brother.

"That way, Nick says, we get the jib up really tight."

"OK." said Ella obligingly climbing onto the foredeck and doing what she was told. "You *are* getting expert, Gerr!"

With the foresail nicely up Gerald re-cleated the jib halyard.

"Ready to feed the mainsail into its groove?" he asked.

"Yes," said Ella. "You can haul away now."

Her brother bent once more to the other hole low down in the mast. This time he would get hold of the port (left hand) halyard and pull on that rope as Nell carefully fed the sail into the groove on the outside of the mast. Up would go the mainsail – right up to the masthead, sliding all the way up in its slot that kept the sail attached to the mast.

But as he bent there came the sound of a speedboat. It flashed past the opening of their bay. Gerald in *Frolic,* Ella on the beach, and Nick on the plateau saw it make a spectacular spray-spreading turn. Then, throttling down, it chortled less noisily into the bay and crunched its nose onto the beach beside the dinghy.

"Say!" said a man in a peaked cap, which, for some inscrutable reason, he was wearing backwards,

"Say! Have you gotten yourselves a swell campsite! Mighty fine harbour too! Sure is!" His accent was strongly from 'across the pond'.

"Gee, Pop!" exclaimed the only other person in the speedboat – a small boy whose bright red hair was cut like a toothbrush. "Gee! Look! They made a fire!"

Ella and Gerald glanced at the doused embers of their fire and wondered what was so special about them. For once they were both speechless. They felt as if Eden had been invaded. How *dare* these people import their nasty, noisy, smelly, over-rapid machine into this peaceful bay? *Their* cove – which they had been thinking of as remote and wild and far from civilisation.

"Were you guys shooting off firecrackers in the night?" asked the man.

"Firecrackers? No," replied Gerald, puzzled.

"Perhaps he means the flares," said Ella coldly. She turned to the invaders.

"Yes," she said. "We were signalling to our friends."

"Gee!" said the boy again. "See, Pop! Toldya!"

"Junior here wuz convinced you wuz sending up distress messages. Acted real crazy. Wouldn'a go ta bed till I promised ta come right over in the morning and take a snoop. Well – we're sure glad you ain't in any kinda trouble."

"And we're glad we didn't have to wait for your help," said Gerr sarcastically; but the irony was lost on the American.

"Why-ya shooting off signals?" asked the boy.

"Our cousins got lost. They sent up flares so we answered them," explained Ella kindly.

"We're going to rescue them today," Gerald told the man proudly.

"Huh! Nice fun'n games, hey?" The fellow sounded condescending.

"You can think so, if you like," answered Gerald annoyed. "But we hope the girls're all right. It's not too good these days being stuck in Bafandoland territory."

"With bandits and rebels and all," added Ella.

"Sure. Sure," said the man, taking off his cap and scratching his head. "Well, Junior, can we quit looking all about the islands for ya sailors in trouble? Are ya satisfied?"

"Sure," said the boy. "Let's go water-ski."

"Suits me," said his father. Then, with a flash of inspiration, he turned to Gerald.

"Do ya ski, Bud? Wanna hava turn?"

Gerr's eyes lit up; but the spark died.

"No thanks," he said. "We're in a hurry to get away."

Nick, arriving down at the beach would also have loved a spin on skis. Suddenly he thought: 'Why not? Gerald can have a whizz round while Ella and I finish rigging the boat and start sailing. Then, when we're clear of the islands, the Stanleighs can sail *Frolic* while I have a quick turn. The speedboat can easily circle round *Frolic* while I'm skiing.'
So he said:
"Go on Gerr. Have a quick bash. El and I'll sail on and you can catch us up. Will that be all right?" he asked the American.
"Sure. Hop in!"

Gerald didn't need to be asked twice. Grabbing a life jacket he climbed over the high side of the speedboat. Nick and Ella pushed it off, called "See you soon!" and returned to the dinghy. She was head-to-wind with the jib flapping.
"Will you feed the mainsail into the groove while I haul up?" asked Nick. "It climbs more easily if it's guided in at first. Then, if you lift the boom later on, I'll get the peak well up."
"Haul away," said Ella.

Nicky stepped into the dinghy, stowed the compass and tent peg, pushed away piles of mainsail and bent to take hold of the lower end of the port halyard, which he expected to find hanging out of the hole in the bottom of the mast. Then a very rude exclamation escaped his lips.
"There's no mainsail halyard," he said in a deadly voice. Desperately he shoved away heaps of sail as if he hoped to discover that he had made a mistake. Ella looked puzzled.

"The bottom of the halyard isn't appearing out of the lower hole in the mast." Nick confirmed this as, with the mainsail out of the way, he stared at the empty pulley. "What have you and Gerald done? Have you hauled the halyard right up through the mast?"
"I don't know," said poor Nell, completely bewildered, but miserably aware that some calamity seemed to have taken place. Nick snorted, found the mainsail peak and saw that it was correctly attached to the upper end of its halyard. He followed the rope with his eyes till it reached the masthead.

Far too much length of halyard was outside the mast. There was no doubt about it. Either the vital knot at the bottom had come undone or in a fit of excess zeal Gerald had untied it! Without the tied figure-of-eight, when Ella had pulled the rope down to her level, the halyard had been drawn up inside the mast and its lower end was lost, out of sight within the mast and well beyond reach!

"That's completely torn it," announced Nick bitterly. "We'll have to dismast, unscrew and remove four pulleys, try to pass a weighted nylon thread down the bore that runs through the mast from top to bottom, and then use that fine cord to carefully pull the halyard through again to where it should be. After that we'll have to fix the pulleys back in place, before replacing the mast."

His cousin gazed at him horrified by this catalogue of mysteries.

"Lucky you know how to cope," she said tentatively.

"It happened once before – soon after we got *Frolic,* and didn't know about the knot. I should have warned you both."

"Well, let's get on with it then," suggested Ella.

Nick stared at her aghast.

"Don't you understand? We'll have to take the mast out!" he said as if speaking to an idiot. "We'd never manage that – just you and me. Don't you remember the struggle we had at Baboon Bay to ship the beastly thing? Even with Wiston's strength we had a tough tussle. It's even more possums difficult to get the wretched pole out; then it will be still more impossible to reship it. We'll have to wait till Gerald gets back, and even then we may not manage it."

"Maybe the American chap will lend a hand," suggested Ella.

"Yes, we'll ask him. Might take ages to thread. It's a finicky business. That's why we keep a length of fishing nylon in the tool kit. I say – " suddenly a nightmare thought struck him. "Have *we* got the tool kit or is it in *Percy*?"

They moved the sail completely out of the boat and found the tools in their appointed place.

"Phew!" Nick let out a deep breath! "Thank goodness for that. We'd never do it without thin nylon and the fishing weight."

There was nothing else to say and nothing to do so they sat on the beach in glum silence. Half an hour passed. They had expected to see El's brother long ago, skimming over the waves as the speedboat passed the opening of the bay, and sinking slowly as he released the towrope. But no! Neither Gerald, with his rather bow-legged style of water skiing, nor the speedboat appeared. The sun rose higher. Ella moved as the patch of shade in which she was sitting changed position. She was boiling over, not only with heat but with worry about the Aussies. How desperately did they need help? She was also simmering cross with her brother for staying away for such a long time.

Nicky was tense too. He went up the hill to see if he could spot Gerald and signal that he was needed. To his horror the water in all directions was completely empty. There wasn't a sign of any speedboat, water skier, canoe, fisherman, dugout, or craft of any kind. After a despondent amble round the top of the island he made his way back down the slope to Ella. She was just emerging from the water where she had submerged, Gerald's pyjamas and all, to cool herself.
"Can't see a single human or any kind of boat, not *anywhere*," Nick told her in shocked tones. He still could not believe that Gerald and the speedboat could have gone so far as to disappear.

"Can't see them?" Ella was equally astonished. "Where have they gone?"
"Haven't a clue," answered Nick crossly.
After a while, in desperation, he suggested:
"If you can hold the boat, I'll try to get the mast out. It'll save time if we can manage that."

So that the mast was no longer tied to *Frolic* they unfastened the bottle screws that hold shrouds and forestay to the deck. Then they tipped the dinghy, fully laden as she was, onto her side. With Nick's height and strength this was not difficult. Nell balanced *Frolic* while Nick struggled to remove the mast. It had been tricky sliding it into its slot, past cleats when they first rigged the GP in Baboon Bay, but now that extra shackles, jubilee clips and other fittings had been added, it was impossible for one person to extract the heavy piece of timber. With Nick heaving madly and jolting the boat wildly, Ella found it very difficult to keep her balance; and without someone to support the weight of the mast, Nick was unable to manoeuvre its bottom section correctly. Puffing and exhausted, they gave up. Nick helped Nell to lower *Frolic's* hull back onto the beach.

They tried repeatedly, but to no avail. All this took time. By now they were desperately worried. Had the speedboat struck a rock? Had there been a nasty accident? They climbed together to have another look – again with no result. Short of paddling *Frolic* out and hunting for the speedboat there was nothing they could do. The chances of never finding their quarry among all those little islands and of missing each other was too great a risk to take. Besides, paddling the dinghy through wind and waves would be utterly exhausting as well as probably useless. Had Gerr been hurt? Had he *drowned*? Then another frightful thought struck Nell: "I hope they haven't gone whizzing way out there trying to catch us up," she said. "After all, we did say we'd start sailing."

In the horrified and depressed silence she handed out a ration of biscuits and an apple each to keep up their spirits. There was plenty of lake to drink as they munched, miserably speechless because there was no more to discuss about what might or might not have happened. They became steadily more angry, frustrated and anxious. Nick kept on getting up and clambering about boulders, hoping to see something to end their worries. From time to time they dipped themselves into the lake to cool down. Hours were passing and they should long since have been on their way to rescue their cruise mates. They became frantic. What had happened to Gerald? Had the Aussies survived the night? It was *terrible* to think of how this delay might be increasing their troubles.

CHAPTER 32

Arrival of the plastic duckling.   Is it Midimi Island?

"*Caro!*" shrieked Kirstin in terror as she felt the boat going over and saw her sister plunge headlong into the waves. The plastic toy bumped past *Percy's* stern. Shipping what felt like a ton of water the Enterprise juddered again. Was he going over or just straight under? Luckily Kirsty didn't instinctively jump forward to grab at her sister. The sailor in her reacted automatically and she turned the boat off the wind. Had she thought, she might have tried to head the other way so as not to sail over Carol. Luckily she didn't have time to think, and fortunately, in spite of his load of sloshing water, *Percy* responded fast to her rapid nautical reaction and stopped fighting his way as much northwards as possible. The boat settled heavily and uneasily onto an even keel. There was deep water in the well, crashing from side to side in the rolling boat that was still moving forward as well as juddering about under the impulse of the gale and its surging cargo.

Slowly and sullenly the water began to stop hurling itself from side to side and just sloshed ponderously in the bottom. Kirstin fought desperately to keep *Percy* upright. Incredibly Carol was still with the boat. She had unconsciously tightened her clutch on the jibsheet that she had been holding when she took her dive and this was now towing her along beside the Enterprise. With a white face, looking deeply shocked, she surfaced spluttering, and spitting out great quantities of water. Her nose was full of the stuff and as she sped through the waves she sneezed repeatedly. Luckily she didn't release the jibsheet and also luckily she had the sense to wait as motionless as possible until her sister had *Percy* under control. Then, with the gunwale being so low in the water because of the huge volume of lake that they had shipped, apart from the force pushing her backwards, Carol had no difficulty climbing inboard again.
"Sorry, Kirsty," she said in a small voice. "*Very* sorry!"

"I could never have gone about to pick you up," replied Kirstin very shakily. "You'd have been a goner. I'd have tried of course, so then I'd have been a goner as well." There was a silence as the awful implications attacked their minds. Both girls were trembling, stunned with the horror of what could have happened.

"You might have had us right over. And all for the sake of a stupid little rubber toy! I'm glad it's gone!"

"It hasn't! I've got it!" Carol herself was surprised. She opened her hands and let the jibsheet, which had saved her life, fall into the waves in *Percy's* well. But she kept hold of a fine green nylon cord. She didn't remember grabbing this slender rope, and she looked at it wonderingly. The other end of the cord must have been attached to the plastic 'duckling' for now it bobbed merrily along behind *Percy.*

"Well, I'll be… " exploded Kirstin. "Hurry and open the bailers, you idiot.

"They're open. We left them open."

"Oh yes. Well, you'd better buck up and start bailing – FAST!"

Kirstin maintained a disapproving silence as Carol attached her prize to the spinnaker cleat and started exhausting work with the bailer bucket. Thoroughly ashamed of herself, the youngster stayed very quiet. But she couldn't avoid glancing back towards the bubble that they had in tow. There was that little pink thing waving again. What *was* it?

"You'd better pull it up and see what it is," said Kirstin rather grudgingly. "I can't believe it can possibly be a hand but I can't figure out what it is."

Carol pulled on the green nylon cord and the little air-filled boat bounced up towards *Percy's* transom.

"A doll!" exclaimed Kirsty. "Well! Really! Caught up in the rowlocks and that green string somehow. How extraordinary! NO – Leave it!" she added hastily. "Let it be."

"I wasn't going to touch it," said Caro defensively. "I've learnt my lesson." She paid out the green painter and let the prize fall back in their wake.

"You know," she said a few minutes later. "That bubble is being pushed by the wind and it's pulling round *Percy's* stern so it's helping to keep us heading away from the wrong side of the lake – or maybe it's pulling us east. I can't tell"
"Hm. Perhaps it's slowing us down as well."
"No. I'm sure it's not doing that. It's so light it's not drawing any water at all. Anyway, it'll be a Good Thing if we are slowed. We don't want to get too far away from the others."
"NO. We need to get up north as far as the Kangalian islands, don't forget. The islands further south – nearer to us – are Bafando territory."
"Um. It must have come right across the lake, bobbing for miles and miles, crossing way in front of the Dinosaur's nose."

When *Percy* was empty and riding properly Kirstin asked:
"Are you cold? D'you need to change?"
In wet clothing, which was evaporating fast in the wind, Carol was absolutely frozen; but she was so desperate to get out of their perilous situation that she answered:
"No. I'm alright. Let's get back on course."
"Yes. Too right! Wailing wallabies! – After all that shermozzle we're *bound* to miss the islands and slide to starboard between them onto the enemy's coast! If we don't I'll eat my Sunday hat!"
"You haven't got one!"
"Well, I'll... Oh – I don't know... I'll do *something*!"

It was a good while later that Carol yelled:
"Island! No – island**S**. Maybe you'll have to eat your plastic rain cap after all!"

It was difficult to be certain that those small blobs were not merely bits of peninsulas sticking out from the Bafandoland shore. Kirstin suggested:
"Use the binoculars. Are they terribly wet?"
"Not too bad," said Carol thankfully while she steadied herself as best she could in the careering boat. After a long scrutiny she concluded:
"Yes. Islands. I *think*. Here. You have a squint."

Their approach towards rocky blobs was a mixed blessing. The idea of drawing closer to what was probably rebel-held terrain did not appeal to either girl; but they knew they were reaching the end of their strength. They couldn't keep up this fight against the elements for much longer. *Percy* was inexorably slipping sideways towards the archipelago and there was nothing they could do to avoid a collision. They just hoped that contact would be later and not sooner.

Some time after 3 o'clock they were close enough to distinguish different aspects of the chips of land. Many were mere chunks of rock, sometimes surmounted by tufts of vegetation.

"But which of the bigger lumps count as proper islands?" wondered Kirstin. "And which are the first six that we must avoid at all costs because they belong to Bafandoland?"

"The islands overlap each other so I can't tell how many I can see," moaned Carol. "I'm completely confused. And since there are no buildings, no pylons, no fields, towers, roads... no signs at all of human habitation... one patch of coastline looks exactly like another."

"We can be glad there aren't any huts," said Kirstin grimly.

By 4.40 they were very close to the intermittent land and details were easily seen, but it would not be long before the sun started to sink.

"We'll have to decide on an island soon," worried Kirstin. "We can't risk slipping between two of them because then we'd eventually and inevitably land on the enemy coast. Better to be stuck on a perilous islet, and hopefully not be found, rather than to drift ashore onto the rebels' mainland. If we're not seen we'll be able to fix the centreboard and sail off again... " As an afterthought she added: "Or if we can't loosen the plate... well, we'll just wait till the wind changes then we'll run back with the new wind direction."

"Yes." Carol's answer sounded unconvinced.

"There's a longer one," pointed Kirstin. "Can we recognise a particularly lengthy island on the map? Take the helm, will you? I'll see if anything makes sense on the chart."

After muttering to herself as she tried to sort out shapes and relative positions of specs of land, she said dubiously:

"That bigger one might do... Midimi – I *think* we could try for that. Perhaps... D'you agree?"

But Carol was intent on managing *Percy* and had no eyes to spare for studying the chart, so Kirstin tapped the paper and explained:

"Just here, below my finger, after the fairly long island that we're passing, there're two un-named minor islets, quite close together. After them, going north, there's a smallish gap. Then comes a bigger island, called Midimi."

She looked fiercely at the specs of land that lay ahead, as if she was daring them not to agree with her. "That seems to fit what we can see; but I wish the next bit was visible from here. That might confirm where we are... "

"I think I can make out a pretty long gap after that bigger island which is ahead," said Carol a little later. "There're rocks and bits as well, of course; but they can't count as islands."

After a minute or two she added:

"No. Beyond the big island there's definitely a long stretch of just water and a few rocky bumps."

"That settles it then. We can't afford to risk crabbing through that wide gap and hitting one of the rocks or end up sliding on towards the enemy coast. I think we should try to land on the biggish island that might be Midimi. What do you think, Carol?"

"Has it got a beach?"

"What?"

"Has the big island on the map got a beach where we can land?"

"If it *is* Midimi it has. The chart shows what might be a beach of sorts somewhere about the middle. At least, it doesn't look like cliffs. Most of the islands are marked as steep on their eastern sides and not so abrupt on their western edges. We're approaching from the southwest... You have a look."

Kirstin took the helm, her eyes trying to find something that might be a beach

"I'm turning," she told Carol presently. "We're going to run in. I'd rather not approach so fast but apart from lowering the sails, which could leave us on a lee shore, we can't do anything but run in and be ready to reach off very quickly. OK? If I've timed it wrongly we'll have to paddle, so get them ready."
"Oh no!" wailed Carol. "I'm absolutely whacked. I can't paddle – not another stroke!"
"My arms are aching too; and I'm fagged out tugging on the mainsheet. But if it comes to a choice between shipwreck and paddling, I'll paddle!"

Carol made a sound that could have been a sob or a groan or just a choke; but she set the paddles ready to be grabbed and turned to study the approaching shore. Was this land deserted or was it peopled by dangerous rebels? Could *Percy* creep up to it unobserved, or were bandits even now watching their progress and planning to seize their boat and take them prisoners? There was no means of telling.

"I reckon I can see what could be a beach so I'm going to head for that," said Kirstin in a scared tone.
Although she was glad that her ankle would have a rest when she no longer had to lean out to balance the boat, Carol wondered if they were wise to turn in so soon. What if they hadn't yet passed rebel islands? Perhaps they should have tried to reach the next spec of land... She crossed her fingers. They were stiff with cold. Her clothes drying in the wind had left her shivering.
"Anyway I'm turning."
This was it! There could be no second chance.
"Oke," said Carol in a gritty voice. They really had no option.

CHAPTER 33

Landfall.

When the Aussies decided to steer *Percy* to starboard and run towards the island that might – or might not – be Midimi, the wind seemed lighter than it had been in the morning. So, although the dinghy was still swishing along at a fine pace they were not speeding as madly as they had earlier in the day.

"Let the foresail fly," counselled Kirstin. "We'll be slower like that, but we can still pull in the jib and use it if need be. Just pray the clips don't come off the forestay."

Loose, the small sail flew about freely – irritatingly. But it was a good plan.

"There," said Carol, pointing. "There! – See? A stretch of sand. Thank goodness for that!"

"Hm! Not just where I was expecting it to be. Perhaps it's not Midimi Island after all. Oh possums! I hope we're not about to land slap on some rebel territory in spite of our efforts."

"Well, we can't do anything about it now," said Caro coolly and sensibly. "If we turn and start reaching again we'll never make the next island. We'd only come a *guster* (cropper) on one of those rocky islets – I bet – or slip straight through and hit the eastern shore."

"You're a fine, comforting Crew, you are!"

"But it's true! Anyway, I don't think I can go on much longer. I'm completely *cactus*, (shattered) aren't you?"

"Yes – worse than kaput – totally pooped! Stand by to lower the mainsail."

"But if we go in fast we can get *Percy* higher and not have to haul him up the beach – which we aren't strong enough to do anyway."

"And we may smash onto a rock as well. No. Stand by to lower sail. At least the wind is pushing us exactly where we want to go. We'll still have the jib to use if necessary and, going fairly

slowly, we can use paddles to avoid rocks. I'm so glad you spotted the beach."
"Ready," said the Crew girl up near the mast.
"O.K. Lower away."
For a few tense minutes as the mainsail dropped, the unstable little craft rocked alarmingly.
'Help!' thought Kirstin.
"Wallabies!" said Carol in a matter-of-fact voice.

Despite their fears they got the mainsail down and the boom inboard without anything dipping into the water. Their friends back home would have been proud of them. With yards of 'canvas' tumbled about their feet, there was scarcely any room to move and, despite all the previous discussion, the paddles weren't handy. Crew had to dive under piles of sail to excavate them.

Kirstin played the jib and then let it fly again.
"Right! Paddles into action! No! Wait. I'll lash the tiller."

Carol didn't wait. She changed sides and started paddling to push *Percy's* nose more towards the beach.
When Kirstin had fixed the rudder she said:
"OK, mate. Be ready to back paddle if necessary."

With the Enterprise bobbing forwards at a comfortable pace it turned out to be very easy to guide him to the beach.

"No need to remind you to raise the centreboard!" said Kirsty with dry humour.
"Hmph!" snorted her sister.

When they were close to shore Carol limped onto the foredeck and stared hard into the water.
"No rocks at all ahead," she called back happily. "You can sail in on the jib and try to get as high up the beach as possible. Shall I try to raise the mainsail?"
"No – that would be just asking for trouble, I reckon. But get the jib operational."

They swished up onto very fine gravel in great style. Carol jumped overboard and held the bottom of the forestay but there was little need. Even with only the jib, the wind was strong enough to have punched the bow well into the soft surface. They heaved *Percy* as far as they could manage and collapsed beside him, both suddenly feeling remarkably weak.

"Possums!" gasped Kirstin looking left and right. "We only just managed to avoid the heaped-up boulders that are on each end of this bit of sand by a *coo-ee*. (a little) Phew! Can't lie like this for long, though. Wind'll soon wiggle *Percy* about and push him along the beach to the rocks. We must hide him – and ourselves – if possible."

For the time being they had no strength to cope with *anything*. They lay on the sand like stranded fish, surprised and thankful to have reached shore safely, and tried to recoup energy for the next burst of effort that would undoubtedly be needed.

"Phew!" exclaimed Kirstin again. "Am I glad we've rocked up here! My whole body is just one mass of pain!"
"Me too," agreed Carol. "Every muscle is aching like mad! I didn't know I had so many different bits to my body. I'm completely *dead*!"
"I wonder where the others are now. What'll they think when we don't turn up at Elephant Island tonight?"

Despite their good intentions, and although the girls knew that they should get on with urgent tasks, they continued to lie on the long, narrow beach, physically and emotionally drained. Boulders in a scattered line separated the gently sloping sand from steeper terrain that rose to a long, low hill with one minor peak. This spine, covered with shaggy shoulder-high grass that shook and crackled in the wind, stretched along the entire island. Tangled thorns crept over shrubby trees, anthills, cacti and incredibly tumbled, rocky outcrops. Here and there a monster boulder balanced, apparently impossibly on its fellows. Dry bracken filled any remaining gaps with impenetrable efficiency. Over it all the wind continued to blow strongly though not as fiercely as before. Trees swung about as if in agony. Waves crashed onto rocks, now and again sending up great fan-shaped explosions of spray. The sun had started its descent and the heat of the day was well past.

At last Kirstin sat up and shook sand out of her hair. *Percy,* evidently unwilling to stop his headlong career across the churning lake, fidgeted as the wind buffeted against his mast and transom. While the girls had been resting gusts had found their ways under the mainsail and puffed it up. The peak was tormenting its halyard, as Dizzy would have shaken the Cane Rat had he managed to catch it.

The plastic dinghy on its long painter had drifted downwind and blown up onto the sand. As it bounced in each gust it tugged at *Percy's* stern, tending to pull him round parallel to the edge of the water. Kirstin watched the boats with a worried expression, and Carol, still flat on her back, had an identical look on her face as she gazed up at her sister and wondered what Kirstin was thinking.

"Shall we empty *Percy?* – Hide all the stuff?" she asked at last propping herself up on one arm.

"Yes. No. Let's look round. But first we ought to eat to keep up our strength."

"I s'pose so, but I can't be bothered."

"Yes. I feel like that too. But we'd better make the effort."

"There's some of that Pro Nutro stuff in the bundle, I think – if we divided the stores up properly. That's very easy to eat and it's very nourishing."

"I'll try and find it. Will you untie the *Queen Mary* from *Percy* and stow her somewhere where she doesn't show – and where she won't blow away again?"

"The *Queen Mary*?"

"Yes. The *Queen Mary* – *y*our wretched little bubble boat. Good name for it – don't you think? It's tending to pull *Percy* round and we can do without that."

"All right," said Carol hauling herself up with an effort and brushing sand off her shorts. She hobbled off to secure their new, tiny craft in a sheltered spot between rocks and bracken.

Kirstin found the powdery cereal that looked like baby food. Dousing two bowls of it liberally with powdered milk and sugar she mixed it all with lake water into a porridge. At the same time as swallowing the vitamin-enriched mush they drank water and ate segments of orange. It was surprising how well this unorthodox snack revived them. Then, by timing their efforts to coincide with the biggest of the waves which were slapping in they were able to haul *Percy* a little above the waterline.

On land there was no lack of rocks or trees so they contrived a sort of spider's web of ropes to hold the boat as stationary as possible. Feeling that the time they had used, though precious, had been well spent they issued themselves a round of toffees and peanuts, pulled on their plastic sandals and set off hoping to find a safe and concealed harbour where *Percy* could lie hidden.

Kirstin began leaping, and Carol limped, from boulder to boulder round the edge of the island. They tried to bash through the vegetation that started sparsely but became increasingly thick the further they tried to push inland. Two facts quickly became obvious. The first was that the scramble was doing Carol's ankle no good at all. The second was that they would never have time before sunset to explore even partially round the island.

"We're going back," decided Kirstin. "You stay beside the boat and I'll try to go straight over and see if there's any shelter on the lee side of the island. It'll also be a chance to check if there are any other human inhabitants. We've got to make sure that there isn't a dangerous camp of vicious crooks on this lump of land."

Carol gave a sudden shocked gasp of realisation. "You'll take huge care not to be caught?" she begged.
She wouldn't like being left alone, but her ankle was giving her quite a lot of pain. She knew she wasn't up to going with her sister, so she made no objection.

"Tell you what," she suggested. "I'll unload the cargo and hide it. Even if we're hoping to punt *Percy* round to a safer harbour it'll be easier if he's empty. OH!" she squealed as a pair of francolins suddenly whirred up from the undergrowth just below their feet.

"But," Kirstin pointed out, "it won't do your ankle much good if you trudge backwards and forwards to hide things in bushes; and we don't want *Percy* in one place and our goods elsewhere."

"I wouldn't be too sure. Things may turn out that we're glad not to have all our eggs in one basket."

Kirstin stared at her, startled by this idea. Then she nodded.

"Yes, *cobber* (friend), ye're right. Go ahead. But don't overwork the ankle. Try and rest it as much as you can."

"Aye, Aye, Cap'n." said Carol cheerfully, hiding the nagging thought that she'd be alone. "I hope you find an ace harbour."

It was a very long time before Kirstin got back, exhausted, thirsty, bedraggled and torn by thorns. Carol had unpacked completely. Stores and sailing gear were nowhere to be seen. There was not even an inch of spare rope in sight, and the *Queen Mary* had also vanished.

"Kangas!" exclaimed Kirstin. "You *have* done well! Where's all the *takunda*?"

Carol pointed to various clumps of bushes and rocks.

"Hidden," she said. "A mixture of food and gear and so on at each spot. But I couldn't hide *Percy*."

"My! My! My! Efficiency double plus! Good on you, mate! I just hope *ants* and *animals* don't find the food and that we *do* locate whatever we hunt for."

"Did you discover a harbour?"

"The other side isn't a lot higher than here but it's steep and vertical near the water. The whole island, as we noticed while we approached it, is fairly low-lying. There're only a couple of cracks in the tiny cliffs as far as I could see, and both inlets are far too narrow to take a boat. Of course I only had time for a short snoop around... There's a lot of it I haven't inspected. Maybe if we hunted for longer we'd find a good place."

"There's not much time. Shall we turn *Percy* onto his side and investigate the centreboard?"

Kirstin looked at the sun and at her watch. She was desperately tired. They had been up early, swum and leapt about on the huge rock. They'd packed off Frolic, worked hard to raise *Percy* out of the water, painted a picture or climbed to the ridge behind Colander Cove, and sustained a considerable shock when the two 'ruffians' had landed. The strain of struggling out of the wind-torn cove had been greater than either of them realised. After a spell of unconsciousness, they'd unceasingly fought the storm and waves for about six hours, worrying for most of that time about where they were going to end up and in what condition they would then be in. They'd explored and battled to pull *Percy* up the beach. Anyone would be dead beat after all that.

"It'll soon be dark," said Kirstin, listening to deafening vespers of birds singing, tweeting, croaking, warbling...
"But the moon will be up and on this beach we won't have any shadows, except for little ones."
"Oh – all right. Let's have a bash. But it means untying all this bird's nest of ropes which are keeping *Percy* safely in place."
"We only have to undo two of them. The others will just go slack of we roll him over that way."
"Right. Obstinate beast, aren't you?" Untying a few knots was easy but they then approached the next task hesitatingly. It was going to be a bit of an effort to get the dinghy onto its side. Suddenly Kirstin looked at her watch.
"We'll do it tomorrow," she said with more confidence than she felt. "But now we'd better get on with telling the others where we are."
"Oo! Flares?" asked Carol breathlessly.
"Yes. Of course."

Like their cousins on Elephant Island they rehearsed Aunt Maddy's emergency rules.
"Get two white flares out of my life jacket," ordered Kirstin.
"I'll take one from your jacket and one from mine," said Carol trying to remember where she'd stashed the life jackets.
"Then we'll each have the same number left."
"O.K. *Good oil*." (Smart thinking)

By torchlight they read the instructions on each flare to make certain that they really did know how to operate the device. They studied the chart to see if they could decide the direction in which Elephant Island lay.

"Well – if we *are* on Midimi Island… " said Kirstin slowly and thoughtfully, "*if* we are – then – I reckon, Elephant Island is somewhere over there."

As she pointed they both noticed a miniscule pinprick of light. It was not *exactly* where Kirstin was indicating but it was pretty close to where they estimated Elephant Island might be. And it was definitely not a star.

"I bet it's them," said Carol excitedly. "I bet they've lit a beacon fire for us. Good on them!"

"Um." Kirstin wished they were all five sitting companionably round that fire, far from the horrible eastern coast and remote from vicious rebels. Now that the sun had set this spot had become altogether too isolated and much too lonely – even spooky .

"Looks a heck of a long way off, doesn't it?"

"We sailed a mighty long way today."

"Um. Help! Only ten minutes to go! We'll never make it to the top of the hill, such as it is."

"Will it make much difference if we fire the flares from here or from higher up?"

"Shouldn't think so. It's only about fifty feet or so. But then, supposing that's not *their* fire? Perhaps we're not as far north as we think we may be. That tiny twinkle may be on a little islet somewhere: a solitary fisherman's fire to dry himself out. Or perhaps it's a remote village on the far eastern side of the lake. "

"Perhaps Dinosaur Island is still between Elephant Island and us. Some bits of the Dinosaur have a very high ridge. What if our flares don't go high enough for them to be seen from the other side of the Dinosaur?"

"We'd better get as high as we can."

"Yes. You carry the flares and start up that way." Kirstin indicated the opening between trees from which she had appeared after her solo tour of part of the island. "I'll get the bailer bucket and fill it with water. Then I'll catch you up."

Carol vanished, limping, into dark jungle and Kirstin was suddenly consumed with worries. She shouldn't have sent Carol off on her own. Her sister hadn't crossed the island earlier on and didn't know the way. She hoped that Caro wouldn't get lost or fall into an ant bear's hole. Were there any dangerous animals – or snakes – that might be lurking about after dark? She hoped that they'd manage the flares correctly. She prayed that the others would see their signal... Desperately she dipped a bucketful of water from the lake and rushed as fast as the weight allowed into the tangly bush after the younger girl.

42. Midimi beach on a calm day.

CHAPTER 34

Signalling from Midimi.

It was easy to hear Carol breaking through bushes so her sister soon joined her. They found an exposed boulder fairly high up.
"This will have to do," decided Kirstin. "It's quite a good place for a signalling station and there's no time to climb further. There're only 90 seconds to go till 7pm – signalling time."
She took off her watch and handed it to her sister. Then she stood ready with the flare in her hands and the bucket of water, now rather less full than before, at her feet. Carol gave the countdown:
"Twenty, nineteen, eighteen… three, two, one, NOW"
Kirstin dropped the uncapped canister into the water. It made a plop and sent up a spurt of splash when it landed on its side. Then it proceeded to bob madly as the weight in the base acted to pull the cylinder into the vertical position. The girls retreated hastily behind one of the nearby rocks that were balancing on the monolith. Hiss! Sizzle! And ZOOM! Away went their brilliant white flare.
"How odd! Why didn't it go straight up?" asked Carol.
"Don't know. Very strange the way it went off at an angle! Maybe I did something wrong."
"No. I'm sure we did everything that the instructions told us to. Probably it went off when it was still bobbing about – not vertical."
"Anyway, it's burst all right! Not exactly overhead though, is it? Possums!"
"But it's absolutely *beaut*"
"Smashing!"
"I hope the others have spotted it."
"So do I. And I hope our next one goes straight up, to give them a proper bearing. Mind you, that's not important because we'll be sailing back to meet them… I hope!"

"We'll know soon whether or not they've seen our signal. Either we'll see their white flare or we'll see nothing."
"Yes."
"Doesn't it make a revolting noise?"
"Utterly blood-curdling!"

They waited in silence trying not to concentrate on that flickering mote which they hoped like billy-o was a fire lit by their cousins.
"We must watch *all* round," said Kirstin. "We *think* we know where we are but we may be anywhere. We can't be sure which part of the sky their flare will zoom up into."
"There it is!" shouted Carol with enormous satisfaction. "I just *knew* that beacon was theirs."
"So we *are* on Midimi Island," said Kirstin. Suddenly it didn't seem *quite* so isolated and remote. "Right. Your turn with the next flare."

Carol took off the cap and very gently – too gently – placed the little cylinder in the water. The exposed top didn't get wet so the signal didn't ignite. Behind their protective rock they waited and waited.
"No. Don't go near it! It's like a firework. It could be dangerous." Kirstin pulled Carol back as the younger girl started forward to investigate. "I'll get a stick."

She had difficulty finding one long enough for her liking but returned at last with a splendid branch that she had, with difficulty, ripped off a young tree. She was sucking her palm where thorns had jabbed her. Kirsty poked the flare - not quite knowing exactly what she thought this would achieve but she hoped the result might be the exploding of the signal. Her wishes were answered. The small canister, now so rudely submerged and released, not once but several times, suddenly sizzled. It shot off. But the silver flash travelled only a couple of metres. The flare had been almost horizontal when the rocket had started and now it just missed the top of the bucket and streaked slap into a rock! It crashed off that, whipped past the girls, missing them by centimetres, and, at great speed, vanished into a cranny between three other boulders. The girls leapt into safety behind their original protector.

"Well! Blow me down!" yelled Kirstin furiously. "If we'd tried to aim through that narrow crack we could never have succeeded. No – not in a thousand years."

In the confined space between the boulders the flare burst and burst and continued to explode. Dazzling sparks filled the hole. The cylinder was hitting one rock face after another and being reflected off, each time with a sharp explosive impact. The girls covered their ears and shut their eyes against the blinding close-up brilliance – much more dazzling than the previous flare which had obediently burst right up high in the sky. The moaning, whistling noise was excruciating. It made the hairs on the napes of their necks feel as if they were standing up like hackles on an angry dog. The girls clutched each other as they watched the antics of the sparks with slitted and shielded eyes. Finally the cylinder must have smashed for there was a thunderous bang and a huge smother of sparks, and then nothing more. Carol uncovered her ears and, pale in the moonlight, stared at her sister with a dark disturbed expression.

"Puking, absolutely *puking* Possums!" said Kirsty bitterly. "They'll never have seen that!"

"Oh Wallabies! Oh *dear*!"

"I'll have to run my hardest to fetch another flare. Don't move. I'll be back as quickly as I can." Kirstin was gone almost before she had finished speaking.

She fought her way down through thick undergrowth. It was pitchy under trees and bright moonlight elsewhere. The dark and bright contrasts made it difficult to see where to put her feet. They didn't want *two* maimed sailors so she took such a lot of care not to fall and hurt herself, that she never saw creepers and thorns higher up. They tried to strangle her and clawed at her face, arms, legs, hair and clothes. Despite their clinging brakes she reached the beach and stumbled as quickly as she could through the sand to where she knew that one of the life jackets was hidden. She turned it this way and that, trying to find the pocket. The flap was open. She had the packet out. Damn! It was a red packet! "Quick! Where's the other pocket?" She found that and extracted the second packet. Yes. It was a white set. Good.

Kirstin turned and started to run across the sand. She felt like a chameleon because she couldn't seem to move fast; and also because one eye was watching where to put her feet while the second kept glancing over her shoulder to see if the others were sending any further signals. She was into the undergrowth. 'Stop looking back,' she told herself. 'Concentrate on getting up to that rock.' Breathless, she burst out of the trees and, puffing terribly, handed the flare to Carol, before sinking to the ground exhausted.

"Here," she panted. "Send it off quickly."

"They've just shot off a red," said Carol. "Why didn't you fire from the beach?"

Open mouthed and still gasping Kirsty stared at her.

"Never thought of it," she said at last.

"Nor did I till after you'd gone. I did shout, but I suppose you didn't hear."

"No. I didn't. I made as much noise as a herd of frightened buffaloes bashing through the bush. I wouldn't even have heard a gun!"

Slowly Kirstin got to her feet. Carol watched sympathetically.

"Now what?" she asked. "Shall we send up this flare?"

"They won't have a clue what that would mean. It'd just confuse things."

"Yes."

"We'll have to stay put – if we're not caught in the meantime. As soon as we see them we'll set sail and turn them back, and go back with them."

"So long as nobody sees us – or them."

"Yes. And so long as no one saw, or heard, our flares."

"Oh wallabies!"

"The whole point of flares is to attract attention."

"Oh! *Wailing!*" exclaimed Carol full of despair.

"Yes. Oh well! Nothing more that we can do about it now. Let's have some supper, re-tie old *Percy,* and turn in. I'm fair scuppered."

"So'm I!"

43. Rambling hippo

CHAPTER 35

Island Spirits.   Enormous visitors.

Unbeknownst to the cousins, as well as to certain officials who thought they knew everything about the lake, the line of islands down the "middle" of the inland sea, though very rarely visited, were not entirely unfrequented. In particular, during storms, fishermen blown out of their normal haunts, sheltered on parts of the archipelago and afterwards made their ways from island to island before finally crossing back to the eastern or western shores where their villages lay.

As it happened, on the evening when flares were conveying messages between Elephant and Midimi Islands, a pair of Kangi men, crouching in a cleft between some chunks of granite, were scared almost out of their wits when an appalling moaning filled the air. With grey faces, and eyes starting from their sockets, the terrified fishermen stared at each other. Too afraid to move, unable to utter, they cowered, with mouths agape. When the nerve–searing sound stopped they continued to sit like frozen statues depicting horror. After a very long time one whispered hoarsely:
"The Spirits! The Spirits of Midimi! We are as dead!"
His companion gulped and shambled a bit further into their dark crack where the embers of a fire scarcely glowed. There they squatted, petrified and uncertain how to react, eyes red with fear, until at last the man who had found some sort of voice whispered:
"We must move! We must go!"
The other waved a weak hand towards the waters. Collecting their few scanty, sodden possessions, and still shivering with dread, they cast frightened looks over shoulders and tottered a couple of metres down to their dugout that was drawn up on a minute patch of gravel under trees. They threw two small bundles into the canoe and dragged the heavy log down to the water.

"Where… " began the man in front as they launched the dugout. At that instant his croaking whisper was silenced. The Spirits were groaning again. A weird, melancholy ululation, as of souls in direst distress, reverberated through the night.

The men did not turn round. Terror coated them with burning perspiration but kept them shivering as if they were dreadfully cold. It also gave them the strength to drive their canoe at immense speed through churning waves, from which they had only recently come ashore to rest. Resembling the demented maniacs from which they thought they were fleeing, their eyes goggled as they worked their paddles. Not until they had put three islands between themselves and the vengeful spirits of Midimi did they pause, and hesitatingly turn their unstable craft towards another spec of land, seeking some tiny crevice where, they hoped, dangerous men and evil spirits would not be able to find them.

****

After supper Kirstin and Carol relaxed with their backs against a boulder.
"Their fire's gone out. They've gone to bed," said Carol.
"And very soon we'll be in our sacks too. I'll not be sorry for it. Pass the coffee, please, Carol. I wish *we'd* taken the cocoa and not *them*."
"Same here. But d'you know what, Kirstin?"
"No?"
"*We've* got the fishing things and Ella's books!"
"Oh my! I bet Gerald and Ella were mad when they found out!"
"Yes. And d'you know what?"
"No. For goodness sake, stop asking me if I know what!"
"Sorry. But d'you know wh… Oops! … Sorry! – Nell had just shoved in her books any old how, not decently wrapped, you know… So they're absolutely sopping. Pages all stuck together… "
"Oh wallabies! Well, we'll try to unstick them in the morning.

We'll have plenty of time before they are near enough for us to set out to meet them."

"*If* we can get the gravel out of the centreboard casing, that is. Kirsty – What's that noise?"

"I'm not sure. It's been getting nearer and nearer for some time."

"No need to tell me that!" retorted Carol who had been only too aware of the approaching sounds.

"Funny sorts of walloping grunts, aren't they?"

"I think it's hippos."

"I would agree, but what is there for hippos here? We haven't seen any swamps, or reeds, or lush grass... "

"Heaps of grass on shore. Dry, of course."

"Yes." They lay listening to the snorts. Undoubtedly they were coming nearer.

"That's them splashing as well," said Carol sitting up.

"Yes." Kirstin also sat up and then she pointed. "There they are! Look."

In the moonlight a couple of huge beasts were clearly visible wallowing along through shallows and no longer snorting now that they didn't have to surface to breathe.

"How super!" whispered Kirstin.

"I hope they don't decide to come ashore," answered Carol equally quietly. "They'll hate it and go bonkers if they get mixed up in *Percy's* spider web of retaining ropes."

"Bit pongy – aren't they?"

Thrilled but anxious, the girls watched as their visitors sploshed past. The two massive, homely creatures turned up towards the beach and paused.

"I'm going up behind the rocks," breathed Carol.

"Stop!" ordered Kirstin. "Don't panic them. Wait till they are looking the other way."

Carol froze until the hippos turned their heads and considered a small patch of reeds. It was so insignificant that it scarcely seemed worth the big beasts' attention. Then the girls scrambled up and ran to hide behind convenient bushes.

Despite their vast bulk the animals turned amazingly quickly.

Suspiciously and doubtfully they looked round out of small piggy eyes. After a dithering pause, during which the hidden pair hardly dared to breathe, the reeds were forgotten and abandoned. Lumbering gently, no longer completely at ease, the giants slowly returned to the water and continued ponderously along the edge of the island.

Presently the snorting started again and, as the girls wriggled into sleeping bags, the grunts faded into the distance.

"Well that just proves that we haven't seen all the island," said Kirstin. There must be a swamp or lots of greenery not too far away, otherwise they wouldn't survive."

"Maybe they're just en route somewhere – on a sort of journey," suggested the younger girl.

"Yes. Hippos and crocs do travel immense distances – even across dry land if they have to... "

"Well, I'm glad we're sleeping right up beside *Percy*. If they come back they're bound to hit the ropes before they get near us and that will wake us in time for us to escape."

"Yes. I'm asleep."

"So'm I... G'night."

"'Night."

Both girls thought, but neither mentioned: 'Crocs are much lower than hippos. They wouldn't get mixed up in *Percy's* ropes as they waddled up the beach towards us.'

44. Waddling croc. They move surprisingly fast.

CHAPTER 36

Lonely Vigil.

The next morning, as we know, on Elephant Island there were strange events followed by desperately frustrating inactivity and great anxiety. On Midimi, however, the Aussies didn't open eyes early nor, once they were awake, did they hurry themselves for, as Kirstin said:
"The others can't possibly be here before lunch time." Nevertheless, when they had finally stirred out of their sacks and finished a leisurely breakfast, they attacked the problem of *Percy's* centreboard in a very business-like manner.

Ropes holding the boat in place were loosened. They had done their job and restrained *Percy* from shifting along the beach or even from floating right off, but his bow, which they'd faced into the wind and therefore also into the waves, had been very close to the water. It had come in for quite a battering, being lifted from time to time as bigger surges roared ashore. However, this morning the wind was a great deal less boisterous than yesterday and still dropping; so the dinghy had been left higher and drier than he would have been if the storm had not lost a lot of its force.

The girls swung the Enterprise round parallel to the water's edge and heaved mightily. They were rested now so with the help of the shelving beach *Percy* rolled obligingly and without too much difficulty. Kirstin held him on his side while Carol peered into the centreboard cavity. As the sun was still fairly low, its rays lit the dark interior clearly.
"Absolutely bung full of small stones," she said. "I'll go and find a stick to poke them out."
"No. I'll go. You did too much walking yesterday. Try to rest the ankle today. Can you manage to hold *Percy?*"
"Of course. It's easy now that he's over."

Kirstin came back with an assortment of sticks and reeds. After prodding around for a while she said:

"Trouble is – the twigs are all either green and bendy or dry and brittle-snappy."

The branch that she was using broke as she spoke. An intensive search produced nothing better. Stronger sticks were too thick to go between the board and its casing. Others thin enough to slide in and touch the chips of gravel were too supple or not strong enough to dislodge the pebbles.

"It must have happened when we kicked the stuff under *Percy* to raise him out of the waves at Colander Cove," said Kirstin as Carol, prodded away in her turn. They winkled out a handful of small stones but some obstinate troublemakers still kept the plate completely immovable.

"We'll have to remove the bolt that the centreboard swivels on and hope to be able to hammer the plate right out using brute force," said Kirstin despondently. "The gravel will just *have* to let itself be scraped out if we do that."

Her sister agreed glumly. The strenuous job had no appeal.

Percy was lowered back onto his stem, and turned head to wind once more. The girls searched the rock crannies and bushes where Carol had hidden their *takunda* the previous evening. Disaster! The tool kit was not in their cargo.

"Wailing wallabies!" groaned Kirstin. "We're really properly stumped now! Why oh why didn't we have a tool kit in each boat? We've got just about everything else in duplicate."

"Tools are so bulky and heavy. We didn't expect to split up… "

"Possums! Now we're forced to wait till the others arrive. Can't possibly undo those nuts without a couple of spanners."

There was a dull silence until she spoke again with determined cheerfulness.

"Oh well… I'm going to fish. What about you, Caro? We might as well use the fishing gear since we've got it."

"I don't feel like fishing – unless we could catch some bread. I really didn't enjoy breakfast without bread. Besides – we've got no bait."

"I'll find an anthill. Fish love termites. Or there must be some worms, or something… "

"Should we try to hide *Percy?*"

"Well – " Kirstin pondered, and felt lazy. "No. It's not worth it. As soon as we see the others we'll sail out to meet them."

"But we *can't*! We'd have to sail into the wind and the centreboard's still stuck."

"Oh! Puking possums! Yes! I was so certain that we'd get the gravel out... I had it all planned: how we'd go out and meet *Frolic*. BOTHER IT!"

"You go and take it out on the fish. I think I'll climb to the top of the island – not to the outcrop where we sent off the flares last evening, but up to the peak of the hill."

"Hill?"

"Well – that bump thing. I'll get a better view of *Frolic* coming round the Dinosaur's nose from there."

"I doubt you'll be able to see her so far off. She'll look absolutely minute."

"I'll try anyway."

"Don't tire your ankle. Let's put a bandage on it. Why didn't we think of that yesterday?"

Even though the 'hill' wasn't a big one, the top of the island was far along the ridge and it was slow, hot work battling up. Thorns caught in the huge crêpe bandage that was round Carol's ankle. It was much too long but they hadn't liked to cut it. She almost wished she hadn't decided to be Look Out; but when the explorer finally perched on a stone near the top of the knoll that constituted the highest point of Midimi Island she was glad she had persevered. The view was marvellous. Small white horses danced over ultramarine water that sparkled as it stretched to 'infinity'.

Close at hand the vegetation waved lush greens and rich ochres. More than anything else Carol wanted the fleet to be reunited and away from this dangerous area so the sooner she caught sight of her cousins' boat the happier she would be. Thank goodness for the flares. At least she knew that her mates were on their way – or that was what she *thought*!

To both north and south a ragged string of islands stretched into the distance. She couldn't tell how far along the chain she was but since there appeared to be a satisfactory number to her south Carol felt fairly confident that *Percy* had reached a shore on the correct side of the border. To east and west the views were similar: far-off mountains dwarfed by distance and painted in delicate blues and mauves. They were dotted with a few darker tones where occasional clouds speeding overhead cast fast-moving shadows. Evidently the wind was still strong in the higher atmosphere though here at lake level it was dropping steadily.

Why hadn't she brought a bottle of water? She wished they had managed to hide *Percy*. Of course the rebels were really interested in bigger vessels with engines... Still, a boat was a boat... She and Kirsty should not have let the languorous climate of the low-altitude lake make them lazy. It had been so much easier just to leave the dinghy in full view!

Shaking herself free of dismal thoughts, Carol studied the freshwater sea. If there were any small islands to the east, close in along the Bafando shore, they blended with the coast and could not be distinguished. Looking south-westward, and back where the wind had propelled *Percy* so frighteningly, she could make out the very distant Dinosaur squatting as if in deep thought. The once-terrifying cliffs behind the beast were now a mere insignificant line on the horizon. To the right (west) of the snout, with binoculars, Carol could just make out a few tiny smears of green. Although she couldn't distinguish one from the other she knew that they were some of the islands in the Double Bay and, presumably, one spec was Elephant Island where Nick and C$^{\underline{o}}$ had slept last night.

It was ages before a boat of any kind appeared. This was partly because Carol had not expected any vessel to look so miniscule, and partly because she had been looking too far south. When a tiny dot finally materialised there was no means of telling whether it was *Frolic's* sail or the sail of some other craft, or perhaps not a sail at all but light reflected from a fishing trawler or a small steamship. Even through binoculars the inconspicuous spec refused to reveal any details. Nonetheless, feeling like Robinson Crusoe, the Look Out stood up on her rock to shout and wave madly. Up and down she jumped till her ankle gave a particularly nasty twinge. Then she giggled to realise how stupidly she was behaving. No one could see or hear her and she certainly hoped that her antics hadn't attracted the attention of any dangerous Bafandoland bandits. She sat down feeling silly.

(pic 45.)

Gradually the rock rabbits, which she had startled with her yells, began to creep out from their burrows again to bask in the sunshine. By now Carol was thoroughly blasée about hyrax, but they were something to watch. They were so unused to humans that the little creatures ventured close beside her. She was able to take very close-up snaps that she hoped would come out particularly well.

(pic 46.)

A couple of highly-coloured agama lizards also posed obligingly, showing off the serrated spines down the centres of their backs. They glittered in the sunlight.

'I wonder why their skins are slightly knobbly,' thought Carol idly. 'But, gosh! Those startling puce heads and brilliant yellow rumps... together with the metallic blue bodies – WOW!'

Rather bored and definitely sleepy she slumped in the shade of a big cactus. A ghastly BOOMING suddenly brought her very much awake. 'What on earth was that? Where did it come from?' She jumped with fright as another tremendous roar answered the first. A stealthy rustle terrified her. It didn't sound like a four-legged creature and there was none of the pulling and scrunching noises that grazing animals might have made.

Carol became more and more keyed up. Had her stupid antics, shouting and jumping been seen? Was a band of frightful murderers about to encircle her? She remembered lurid pictures she'd seen in old books of South Sea Islanders with bones through their noses and spears in their hands making weird noises with big conch shells.

The soft, stealthy sounds came gradually closer. Careful not to make any stick crack, Carol crept behind a bush. A small stone rattled from under her sandal and she shook with fright. What *was* it that was approaching so furtively? She felt like screaming with tension. It was all she could do not to make a dash for the beach but she knew she'd never make it. She'd be caught. And then Kirstin would inevitably be implicated as well. Panting with fear Caro stuck it out behind her shrub. Her eyes were glued to the spot from which the surreptitious scratches were advancing.

The petrified girl was nearly at shrieking point. Gradually, nearby underbrush started to shake. She stared with increased horror! An evil human would have been awful enough... but the thing that was approaching was definitely *not* a person.

CHAPTER 37

Where is Frolic?

Suddenly, from below a leafy branch appeared a monstrous scaly foot. Was the creature carnivorous? Was it dangerous? Did dinosaurs still live in Kangalia? Carol had no idea. The way the vegetation was being pushed about it seemed as if there were several of them – whatever they were. And they were *big*! Would they pounce?

47. The monster's foot

Again she felt like running away; but she knew that in this thick vegetation she'd never get away from any predator.

Besides – running from a killer invariably made it chase you. No she *had* to grit her teeth and stay put. But it wasn't easy to stand her ground. That fearful booming sound came again. This time it was right up close – obviously from the hungry throat of the approaching horror.

Then a huge, horny beak poked into view. Carol breathed with a little less panic, but she thought: 'I bet that could inflict a shocking wound.' The dangerous-looking weapon was topped by an impressive casque. Then came a sharp eye surrounded by bright red flesh. The same gory colour flamed from hideous wattles: a bulbous kind of bag that wobbled about below the bird's 'chin'.

"Ground Hornbill" breathed the watcher, almost fainting with relief. 'Gosh!' she thought. 'I've never been so close to one of those before. And I thought they only boomed in the evening... '

A male waddled into full view and soon afterwards two females, with shiny blue faces and without the red wattles, followed. How enormous they were – 'Well over a metre long and at least a metre high', estimated the hidden girl. 'Crickey! *Bonza* to see them so clearly!'

Feeling a twinge of cramp she risked a slight movement. Immediately the birds froze, staring in her direction. But either they didn't spot her, or the island was so unvisited by humans that they were not frightened. After a suspicious moment they continued waddling forward, pecking at whatever it was they seemed to fancy. Only when Carol tried to use the camera did they move off, uneasy though not particularly frightened.

'Pompous looking things – full of self importance! Just like old Colonel McKorphet!' She couldn't suppress a giggle. That did it! The Hornbills looked reproachfully at her and without hurry lifted huge wings. Heavily they glided off towards another part of the ridge.

It was a huge relief to be able to stand up and stretch! And it was great to see movement on the lake. As well as the original northbound spec that she had seen, now, in the far distance, a small steamer was churning southwards from some Kangi port up north. She must be heading for Baboon Bay. How remote in time and distance Baboon Bay seemed to be! Aeons away...

Mr. and Mrs. Ground Hornbill

The steamer's course went about half way between Lake Kangi's central chain of islands and the Dinosaur. Studied through binocs the small square vessel was seen to be tossing more than might have been expected. This was because she had been constructed with a particularly shallow draft that allowed her to pull in very close to the coastal villages that she served.

The Chorton family had once been on a week's voyage on this little ship so Caro knew that the boat was the only contact that simple villagers living in isolated lakeshore hamlets had with the outside world. Her cargo ranged from goats to sitting room suites, from bicycles to sets of drums, wheelbarrows, food, crops, tools and hundreds of squashed-in people. Everything, passengers and cargo, was taken ashore or came out to her by dugout because Baboon Bay was the only place on Lake Kangi with a proper harbour and quay.

Carol deliberately stopped herself from gazing at the point that she hoped was *Frolic*. On the principle that a watched pot never boils she decided that an anticipated boat never moves. Certainly this particle never seemed to advance. She allowed herself only occasional glimpses towards what she was now thinking of as their 'rescuers'.

In fact that dot was actually clipping along at commendable speed in the steady, though no longer over-strong, west-by-north wind. After what seemed like centuries, the watcher persuaded herself that she could recognise the boat. Much later, when she was thoroughly bored with her self-imposed job, she figured that, although the wind would have allowed *Frolic* to head directly towards 'her' island – Midimi – the GP, if it was the GP, was most definitely heading towards some place a good deal further north.

Again Carol stood up; but after prancing about, shouting and waving, she concluded that her efforts couldn't possibly be seen and decided to hobble down to the beach. Besides, it was long past lunchtime, and in spite of the late and ample, though breadless, breakfast, she was hungry. In dancing round on the rock she must have done something nasty to her ankle for it was certainly hurting more now.

She was quite close to the beach and had reached the part of the island where 'jungle' and exposed boulders mingled in roughly equal proportions when a sly rustle in the undergrowth startled her. It was not the sound of scampering or hurried hyrax. Nor was it the bounding noise of disappearing duiker or klipspringer. It definitely wasn't the crackle of Ground Hornbills... Swivelling alertly to investigate, she stood transfixed one foot still in the air and her eyes bulging from their sockets. Then turning rapidly, as fast as her ankle would let her, she sped down to the beach.

"Gosh! You've been ages!" said Kirstin lifting a red face from the fire. "If I hadn't been afraid of missing you I'd have come to fetch you. I've cooked fish for lunch."
"Gee! Good on you! Am I glad I wasn't here to help clean them! I'm famished."

"Hmph! Well, here you are. Eat up! Did you spot anything? I haven't been able to see a sausage from down here... apart from monitor lizards and masses of birds, and a splendid pair of otters gambolling about like nobody's business. That was real *spiffy*!"

"From up top I saw lots of hyrax and birds too, plus a steamer and the ship that we went on last year, both going south. And *Frolic's* on her way!"

"Oh hurray! Are you sure it's her? I'd have thought she'd have been nearly here by now."

"She's sailing towards the wrong island, I think."

"Oh strewth! We'd better get a smoky fire going. – Or is she close enough to make a smoke bomb work? I hope it doesn't attract other people as well as *Frolic*!"

"Wallabies! Yes!"

As they finished lunch Carol remarked nonchalantly:
"I saw a python up there... miles and miles of python."

"WHAT?"

"I saw a python – a snake – you know – one of those big things with beautifully patterned skins."

Transfixed, Kirstin *stared* at her.

"I know what a python is, *dill*! (idiot)" she said. "You lucky beast! Where was it?"

"Up there. Not very far away. Up among that jumble of boulders. I didn't see all of him, but I saw lots of bits moving very, very slowly along on the other side of various bushes and rocks and things. Don't snakes move in a funny way? Sort of squeezing up one section of body from behind and then unsqueezing it in the forward direction... "

"Catting Kangas! You lucky so-and-so!" repeated her sister enviously. "Perhaps he'll still be around later. We'll go up and look; but in the meantime we'd better be careful not to bump into him or any of his mates when we're collecting firewood."

Enlarging the fire was easy but making a smoke signal was a different matter. To produce a column that rose vertically to indicate their position turned out to be impossible. First it was hard work gathering greenery to put on the flames. Living branches were loath to be parted from their parent trees or shrubs. When placed on the fire they either doused it almost to extinction or produced what the girls considered to be very inadequate quantities of smoke. No one would think it was a sign, or even notice it in particular. And although the wind was now not at all strong it still had the power to disperse any puffs that they could produce. The fumes were blown in every direction except upwards. Mostly they scudded along the beach. It was very disappointing. A lot of time passed and there was little to show for their efforts except for sooty bodies and filthy clothes.

"Amazing isn't it how a fire kippers you when you want it to just burn brightly," said Kirstin bitterly, wiping a sweating brow with a disgustingly charcoal-ly hand. "But when you actually *want* smoke, it jolly well won't let itself be made!"

Frolic still had not come into view. Carol was not surprised because she had seen how far off the boat had been, but Kirsty felt frustrated. Yet she managed to sound fairly positive when she said:
"After lunch the signal seemed most urgent, but we've failed to make decent smoke. Now we'll try something else. I had an idea while I was fishing but I couldn't start without your help."
"What is it?"
"I thought that maybe a batten might be thin enough, yet strong enough, to dislodge our flipping gravel."
"*Bottler*! (Brainwave) Let's try."
Carol limped happily towards the boat.

So yet again *Percy* was untied and pushed over onto his side. The younger girl held him while Kirstin poked with a batten taken from the mainsail. It slipped easily inside the centreboard casing.
"Good oh," breathed the patient support crossing her fingers – with difficulty because she was holding the boat.
"I... think... " The poker was concentrating hard. "Yes that's one piece out! *Ripper* (Three cheers)!"

Another piece of agate, whose beauty was completely missed by the girls, plopped onto the beach as the plastic rod dislodged it.

"Hurray!" shouted Carol.

"Hang on! Don't get too optimistic!" warned her sister. "There are lots more bits still to go."

Little by little, one by one, the obstinate chips of stone yielded to the poking batten.

"It's not doing the whatsit's varnish any good," remarked the older girl looking at the batten ruefully.

"We'll re-varnish it when we get back," consoled Caro happily.

"If the rebels don't get us first," said Kirstin whose turn it seemed to be getting jittery.

With *Percy* operational again they felt much happier. Mainsail, jib, paddles and bailer bucket were retrieved from hiding places. The girls donned life jackets and were about to push off into the light wind with a view to meeting their cousins. But why had *Frolic* not yet appeared?

"Perhaps we'd better just pop up to the rock where we fired off the flares to see if we can spot her," suggested Kirsty. Neither of them wanted to waste time but it would be no good sailing in the wrong direction and missing the others.

"I'll get the compass to take a bearing," said Kirstin.

With grass flattened and bushes pushed aside from their previous trips, the going was much easier than it had been on the previous evening and they were soon standing on the boulder gazing out to 'sea'.

"There," said Carol, who knew roughly where to look. She lifted the binoculars.

"But she's miles off course!" Kirstin started to exclaim. She paused doubtfully. Even without the glasses, and although the sail was far away, she could tell that it definitely was *not Frolic's.* It was one large rectangle not two small triangles.

"It's a dhow!" said Caro in disgust. "The sort they used in the last century to carry slaves across the lake. Look." She handed the binoculars to her sister. Kirstin saw a cumbersome hull, which somehow managed to look graceful. It was difficult to tell from so far off but the deck appeared to be crowded with humanity and cargo. The bulky sail was hanging from a boom that was roped high on the single mast and set across the boat. The boom was actually made from several long poles lashed together. It hung in a downward curve with drooping ends, like a depressed mouth. The patched canvas billowed blowsily and untidily but the vessel was skipping over the waves and moving quite fast.

"It looks like a plump old lady teetering on very high stilettos rushing along to catch a bus," said Carol screwing up her eyes. They laughed. It was an excellent description.

"That solves the problem of why that sail was heading so far north," said Kirstin. "She's obviously taking advantage of the wind to run across to the big inhabited island. That's a long way north from here but a good bit west as well. Those dhows can more or less only run with the wind, you know."

"But where's *Frolic*?" said Kirstin voicing both their worries as she turned slowly, scanning the surface of the water with binoculars poised ready for use. All sorts of possibilities were whizzing through her head. Had Carol missed *Frolic's* sail because she had been concentrating on the very much bigger blob that was the dhow? But, if so: why had their cousins not arrived long ago? Had Nick, Ella and Gerald sailed to the wrong island and been caught by rebels? Surely they wouldn't have had trouble sailing across the lake on a day like this? The weather couldn't have been more ideal for their course. She and Carol hadn't mistaken last night's signals, had they?'

For the moment Kirstin was stumped. Vaguely she felt that she ought to be doing something about the situation. But her mind was an unaccustomed vacuum. She couldn't think of a single action to take. Turning to Carol she met an expression of blank bewilderment that matched her own, and found that they were both saying to each other:

"But where on earth has *Frolic* got to? What's *happened*?"

49. A small and unusually empty dhow.
(Good in colour – Look it up on www.daphne.es
Then, on the menu, click on Fateful Flies.)

CHAPTER 38

Frustrating delays. Stranded speedboat. Turtle.

Rescue Mission at last.

"Hello! Terribly sorry I was so long!"
A jaunty voice startled Nick and Ella out of their stupor.
"Gerald! Where have you *been*?" squealed Nell.
"Where have *you* sprung from?" snapped Nick.
"Out of the waves – like Aphrodite," grinned the returned prodigal.
"*What?*" Two irate voices rebuked his levity.
"Oh – you know – the goddess of love who was born in a seashell off Paphos in Cyprus, and who rose out of the waves."
"Botticelli painted her," said Ella weakly.
"What in *Hades* has all that got to do with us *now*?" exclaimed Nick irritated beyond bounds. "We've been waiting *years* for you. We need your help."
"Thank goodness you waited. I was afraid you might be half way across the lake by now," said Gerald soberly.
"Why have you appeared round those boulders? Where's the speedboat? What *happened*?" His sister was full of questions.
"It's a long story."
"Oh POSSUMS!" groaned Nick. "That's the final straw!"
"We set off in fine style," started Gerald as they picked their way over rocks back to the beach.
"Yes. We saw you."
"We did a few ins and outs round the islands... It was wonderful. Apart from the exciting skiing conditions the scenery is blimmin super."
"I bet. Then what?"
"Stupid engine ran out of petrol. Well, it wasn't really the motor's fault. Would you believe it? That fool of a man just jumped into a borrowed boat this morning and whizzed off without checking the fuel in the tank!"

"Not possible!"

"Well, he did! So there we were – out on the blue – behind that pointed shaped island – you know the one… "

His listeners nodded.

"The engine choked and stopped. Yank thought it'd gone wrong and started fiddling around with it. I swam up to the boat – wasn't so easy dragging those skis in this rough sea, I can tell you, even though the waves are tiddly compared to those of yesterday…

"Anyway – I got to the boat, and there he was, his cigarette hanging from his lips, taking the engine to bits. Petrol fumes *everywhere!* Imagine! – How we didn't get blown to smithereens I don't know! I dropped the skis and dived under… Came out some distance away.

'Whassamatta?' he yelled, so I told him as politely as I could manage that I thought he should put out his fag. He dropped it overboard… just dropped it right into the middle of where he'd been rinsing out parts of the engine. I could see the shine of oil and petrol on the surface. Gosh!"

Nick and Ella gasped and went pale.

"After that hadn't caused an explosion I decided it might be safe to go aboard. We fiddled about till I thought of looking in the fuel tank. Empty! We were *miles* from shore… "

"Yes," agreed Nicky, "that pointed island is a very long way out."

"There wasn't another boat of any kind in sight," Gerr continued. "We started to paddle… "

"He actually had paddles!" snorted Nick sarcastically.

"He'd borrowed the boat, remember? I expect the owner keeps them in the boat," guessed Gerald. "Anyway – there were paddles clipped in place. But have you ever tried paddling a speedboat, and in a wind? Well don't! It's impossible! Monstrous heavy – and incredibly high out of the water! It catches every blast… "

"So how did you get here?"

"Swam."

"You're joking!"

"Never been more serious. Had my life jacket on, of course, so I knew I wouldn't sink. But it doesn't exactly help the speed aspect. It took an age. I swam to the pointed island, walked as much as I could along that – my goodness I was glad I had my plastic sandals! The thorny underbrush on these islands doesn't bear thinking about. And the rocks are like razor blades! Then I swam to the next island... and so on... till I got here.

"Well I'll be… " said Nick, looking at Gerald with respect.

"You must be exhausted." That was Ella.

"Not really. Bit cold though in the wind. Is there any fodder? Oh yes!" added Gerr, "I saw a turtle."

"You lucky beast!"

"Lucky? Well – yes – I s'pose I was... But I didn't think so at the time – coming eyeball to eyeball with a nasty snake-y face!"

"Ugh!" His sister shivered.

"But they're actually nice, harmless creatures," said Nick mildly.

"What did it look like?" Nell wanted to know. "I mean – apart from its reptile-y face?"

"Oh – I don't know... sort of turtlish really," suggested Gerald unhelpfully, "About the size and shape of a toilet seat cover."

"Gerald!" exploded his sister.

"You asked what it was like, didn't you? Yes," he meditated. "It was something like an old leather loo cover." He grinned naughtily. "It was fast asleep, basking on the surface."

"What did you do?"

"I did an ultra rapid reverse turn – just like the Olympic swimmers on TV. – So did the turtle, actually."

"Can you blame him?" asked Nick chuckling. "He probably disliked your phys as much as you hated his!"

"Well! Of all the cheek!"

"Where's the speedboat? Have we got to go and rescue them?

"Maybe. They were just drifting about when I left them. Junior was moaning like mad about being bored and wanting his momma... I expect Momma might miss them in due

course, if she's not rejoicing too much at their absence. Though why anyone should want that little brat back puzzles me. A real terror, that's what he is!"
"They may end up on some rocks."
"Yes," agreed Gerr callously.

"Wailing Wallabies!" groaned Nick. "And we were trying to get away quickly. "I only hope the girls aren't in desperate straits," he added through clamped teeth. "Come on! Let's get cracking." He explained what had happened.
"Oh," admitted Gerald. "Yes. I untied that knot in the bottom of the halyard. I thought it looked untidy and had got there by accident."
"Untidy!" spluttered Nick raising his arms in anguish. A perfectly good, *essential* figure-of-eight knot! Untidy!"

The sinner was told that he'd have to wait for sustenance, ("The exercise will warm you" said Nick heartlessly.) and they tackled the problem of making *Frolic* seaworthy. With Gerald helping, the mast was winkled out with only slight problems and it was soon being held vertical beside a tree. Nick and Ella had already removed the pulleys so gaping holes showed at the top and bottom, and also about one third of the way down from the top, where the jib halyard entered the mast. Now Nick climbed the tree to a branch more or less at the height of the uppermost hole.
"Crickey Moses!" he exclaimed. "This bark's prickly!" Balancing on the branch he added: "OUCH! Twenty million thorns are scratching my posterior."

He dropped a long slender fishing weight tied to a nylon thread into the highest hole. Carefully the Commodore lowered the torpedo-shaped lump of lead down through the centre of the wooden mast. As expected, in spite of its shape and smooth surface it snagged on the upper opening of the jib halyard, but as the pulley had been removed, a few jerks on the cord and simultaneous wiggles of the mast persuaded the heavy lozenge to slip past the tricky section.

"Got it!" shouted Gerald happily as the weight appeared at the lowest hole.

"Well, pull – *Gently!*"

Nick had taped the lower end of the halyard to the nylon and now, as Gerald drew yards of thread out of the bottom gap, from his high perch Nick fed the halyard into the top of the mast.

"O.K.," called Gerald. "I've got the lower end of the halyard in my hand."

"TIE A KNOT IN IT," ordered Nick urgently. "I'm coming down. Ouch!"

While Nick and Ella screwed in four pulleys and made sure that their ropes were passing correctly, Gerr rummaged for vegemite, which the Australians had brought from Perth, and made some sandwiches. Then Nell pushed against the boat during their tussle to re-ship the mast.

It was an enormous effort; but finally patience and brawn prevailed. Gerald munched as the other two reconnected bottle screws.

"Ten twenty," said Nick looking at his watch despairingly. "The girls will think we're lost or something."

Ella gave a sad gulp.

After some discussion it was decided they had better go in search of the speedboat.

"After all," said Ella, "We won't like to read later in a newspaper that a man and a boy drowned when their boat smashed on rocks in this big bay."

They found the American father and son, very hot and disconsolate in their still-drifting boat. The boy's chirpiness had evaporated. They greeted *Frolic* with relief and took the towrope gladly, but had to be helped to tie it to a part of their machine, which would not rip off, and with a knot that would not come undone. Then dreadfully slowly, for the speedboat had great wind resistance, they sailed shorewards.

It was not until they were out of the band of islands that their plight was noticed and then it was only by an inquisitive boy in a small dugout. They sent him hurrying off for help and some time later they saw another speedboat tending their way.

50. The lad in his small dugout.

"Help's on the way," called Nick to the American. "We're in a hurry so will you untie our rope, please? We have to go the other way now." Gerald received the towrope and coiled it. Then *Frolic* went about.

"Thanks," shouted the man and his son as the boats passed. They waved. Then *Frolic* headed north-north-east and both crews became engrossed in their own affairs. Minutes later Ella, looking back, noticed a jerry can and a huge funnel being passed between the speedboats. Soon afterwards they both zoomed off towards the shore.

"Altogether we've been delayed more than 4 hours," fumed Nick. "And the wind's dropping."

As they sailed closely past Elephant Island they set the compass. Far ahead something was bowling merrily over the lake. Ella got out the binoculars and handed them up to Gerr who balanced precariously on the foredeck to gain height so as to see better.

"It's a big sailing vessel," he reported. "A very odd-looking thing... Got a sort of rectangular sail. The boom's set across the mast and it droops at each end."

"Probably a dhow," suggested Nick. Gerald thought of pictures he'd seen in travel books.

"Yes," he agreed. "I suppose it could be called a dhow."

Frolic's course diverged from that of the dhow, which was bound much further north, so after they had all studied the laden craft through binoculars, they turned eyes to the horizon ahead. Being right down at water level they could see the archipelago's string of islands only as tiny smudges of green above blue waves.

When Nick had set the course Gerald had nearly contradicted him, but with unusual modesty, the owner of the posh watch, with compass and goodness-knew-how-many-other-gadgets, wondered whether the morning's adventures had made him forgetful. He couldn't be precisely certain of the bearing he had taken the evening before so, wearing a puzzled frown, he remained uncharacteristically silent and acquiescent. Had his bearing been a couple of degrees further north than the course on which *Frolic* was now sailing? By heading so far south was Frolic tossing straight into danger?

CHAPTER 39

Fires and a ghostly ship.

"But where *is* Frolic?" said Kirstin again. No answer was forthcoming. From the lookout boulder the dismayed girls searched the completely empty lake for signs of two small triangles, flushed pink perhaps by the setting sun. There was silence except for rustling wind and various bird noises. They turned slowly, scanning the surface with straining eyes. Kirstin held binoculars at chest level, ready for instant use.

Should they sail off taking large beats, making themselves as obvious as possible? No. That would be silly. The less visible they were the safer they might all be, and also: "If we can't see them from up here," said Kirsty correctly, "it stands to reason that they won't see us from water level if we're down in a boat as well."

"But what if they've landed somewhere and are hoping that we'll show ourselves?" asked Carol. They pondered that for a while until Caro answered herself. "They never saw our second flare so they don't know if we are mobile or not."

"That's true. So they won't bank on us showing ourselves. I think we'd better try that smoky fire again, then if we sight them we'll use a smoke bomb."

They returned to the beach, and once again hid all *Percy's* gear. It was tedious work in the heat but if they were attacked by bandits they might be glad to have their possessions out of sight and disposed in different places. With matches, smoke bomb and a small mirror, to act as heliograph if possible, they climbed slowly and thoughtfully to Carol's earlier lookout on the highest point of the island.

Midimi was obviously uninhabited and unvisited because there was plenty of firewood lying about. They soon collected a fine heap of dry branches; but, as before, tearing off greenery for making smoke was difficult. When a middling-sized pile was ready Kirsty pointed.

"I think… Look that way… between those two islands… Is it?"

"Yes," said Carol. "Oh – thank goodness! It's *Frolic* all right but why the wallabies are they so far south?"
"Our flare blew off southwards."
"But not that far."

Full of plans to set sail, meet their cousins and bring them to Midimi, the girls started to dash down to *Percy*. Excited, but panicking because *Frolic* was far away and evening was setting in, the girls forgot about using the fire, the smoke bomb, and the mirror. They didn't like the idea of Ella, Gerald and Nick sailing so far south where the islands were horribly close to the border. Neither did Kirsty and Caro fancy another night alone with the pythons and perhaps other terrifying creatures. Besides, they *did* want to have the fleet re-united so that they could all sail away from this perilous region as soon as possible.

But after the first rush Kirstin pulled up.
"We're bonkers," she said.
"So what's new?" asked Carol. "Why are we *dill galahs* (silly idiots) this time?"
"What the wallabies good is it for us to go sailing off and perhaps miss them as they go round an island, or else meet them and not be able to find our way back here, where we know there is a hospitable beach? Because it will be dark by the time they get here – if they get here."
"Hm," agreed her sister.

They climbed sadly back to their unlit fire. With dry leaves and a match they quickly had it crackling and when it was burning fiercely they dumped greenery onto the flames. The wind was now very light so acceptable volumes of smoke rose fairly well into the sky. Kirstin walked a little way to leeward along the ridge and set off a smoke bomb while Carol did her best to flash signals with the mirror.

It had become plain that *Frolic* was circling each island as she came up the chain. The Australians were overcome by the bravery of their cousins in doing this, but petrified. They were exposing themselves to all sorts of possible dangers.

"I suppose they had no option," said Kirstin. "If we weren't on the first island they sailed to, and we didn't show ourselves elsewhere, what else could they do?"
"I wonder why we didn't see them approaching?"
"Compared to the vastness of the lake their sails are really tiny. We'd have had to be watching every single minute, I reckon, in order to spot them. And we weren't watching during the several hours that passed when we were tackling the centreboard and trying to make the smoke fire down on the beach."
"Yes."
"Gosh! I hope that no one else has seen them."
"Yes."
"I say! That smoke bomb's quite effective, isn't it?"
"Yes."
"I hope they see it soon. At any rate let's pray they see it before the wind disperses it."
"Yes."
"Good conversationalist, aren't you?"
"Yes."
"Are you able to say anything else apart from 'yes'?"
"Yes."

They both laughed and went on watching the distant dinghy whose crew couldn't be made out with the naked eye, and the light was too dim for binoculars to help, so they observed in desperate silence till the far-away sail changed its tactics and, instead of circling the next isle, turned and was definitely heading northwards up the western side of the archipelago.
"They've seen us," said Kirstin with immense relief.
"*Spiffy ripper*!" exclaimed Carol. "And only just in time, too!"

Slowly – painfully slowly – *Frolic* crept northwards. The girls watched fearfully, hoping like mad that they wouldn't see some powerful boat zooming out from a hidden cove to capture their cousins. At last it became too dark to follow the pale spot. Would *Frolic* be safer now that she couldn't be seen?

"We'd better keep the flames bright," said Kirstin throwing another dead branch onto the fire. "What a blessing there's so much dry stuff around!"

It was decidedly spooky tending the beacon up there on the hill with only primitive bush all round. Everything had become very black and they could see nothing outside their circle of firelight. Extraordinarily large bats flittered past at high speed, clinking metallically. Night birds called. Moths: huge, small, plain and fantastic, committed suicide by flying into the flames. The girls were kept busy rescuing them as well as millipedes, beetles, crickets and other insects, which persisted in creeping, crawling and jumping into the embers. Their brethren screeched all round. A scorpion scuttled out of a burning branch and hurried away from the flames.

51. A deadly escaper..

"I'm glad the nasty beast went that way," said Kirstin. "Don't think I'd have had the nerve to rescue him if he'd gone towards the fire."

"Pity we aren't insect eaters," remarked Carol thoughtfully. "We'd have had a good roast dinner this evening."

A light wind rustled mysteriously through long dry grasses as the Aussies fed the pyre conscientiously and hoped to see the approaching boat later, by moonlight. Eighty minutes after sunset, two days after the full, a slightly lopsided moon began to paint its welcome silver everywhere.

"Looks as if it's got a touch of mumps," giggled Carol. It was a relief to have something to laugh at. Kirstin was studying the waters.

"I think they're over there," she said pointing dubiously. "But it's hard to tell. I wish these stupid clouds would go away. We'll have to go down soon and make a lighthouse on the beach – to guide them in."

The prospect of stumbling through dense undergrowth in the dark sent shivers of fear through them both but neither mentioned the dangers that might be lurking in gaunt bare branches or behind stark silhouettes of giant cactuses; and not a word was breathed about pythons, mambas or any other kind of snake. Did scorpions wander round at night?

They had not brought a torch. When the time seemed right they cleared an ample bare patch round the fire to make sure it wouldn't spread, and stoked on fuel to ensure that flames would last as long as possible. Then, feeling like ancient cave women, carrying a lighted branch apiece, they started down to regain the beach.

The walk seemed endless. Each bush sprouted thorns that were determined to stop their progress. The wounded ankle was aching; but finally, covered in burrs, and punctured – as Carol said – in ten million places, they staggered out onto the sand. The remains of their afternoon attempts at signalling were still spread over rocks so it was easy to start a new blaze, and to keep it burning with the fuel they had collected earlier in the day. Then, in tense silence, they had to wait – and w-a-i-t. At last the faint sound of a distant whistle wavered over quietly-swishing waves, and through the mist.

"It's them!" said Caro thankfully.

Apart from being physically exhausted she was sick of feeding fires and would be glad to feed herself instead. Briefly the hope that the others might be bringing bread flashed through her mind. Then she ran – hobbled – to find a torch.

Kirstin took it away from the flames to a place on the beach where *Frolic* could land safely and there she waved the little light up and down, up and down. A thin, acknowledging pipe shrilled from the darkness. Perhaps it was fairly close but still nothing could be seen. Sounds carry well over water and a diaphanous gauze-like haze was rising from the lake. Muffled noises that seemed unreal came across the whisper of small waves. Sails were softly flapping loose. Murmured orders, fuzzy and incomprehensible were impossible to pinpoint. Almost shining through the clouds, a vague disc surrounded by a hazy circle was all that showed of the moon, but muffled sploshes, nearer now, indicated that paddles were being used. Like the girls before him, Nick was advancing cautiously.

Suddenly out of the gloom a misty patch, lighter than the surrounding blackness was just discernable. Gradually it turned silvery, and ethereal. Still its shape was uncertain. It could have been a faint cloud of shimmering faeries. When weak moonlight started to penetrate the mist, the dancing pixies turned into a weird ghost that slowly became triangular. Tinged here and there with flickering red from the fire, a sail loomed disproportionately huge, and ghoul-like, as if it had escaped from hell. It was awesome, and the girls on the beach were trembling, dumbstruck.

Somehow shouting didn't seem appropriate. The vision seemed too insubstantial and despite muted splashes, it appeared to be advancing magically, incredibly slowly, with no visible means of propulsion.

'This was what the mystical boat that carried King Arthur's body must have looked like,' thought Kirstin overcome with emotion. When she realised that she was shaking, she took several gulps of air before saying, in a quiet but carrying tone: "Hold your course. You'll be fine. Sand all the way."

"Aye, Aye," came Nick's voice, equally hushed and subdued.

Carol abandoned the fire. It was no longer needed as a beacon. Brushing sudden tears from her eyes, she ran to stand beside her sister. The silent, mysterious-looking vessel, that appeared to be made of faintly-sparkling spiders' webs, slid softly closer. Almost stealthily it became less ghostly. And then it was grounding. With a splash Gerald jumped overboard to hold the forestay. A small strange figure in voluminous clothes fell off the dinghy into shallow waves and spoke as Gerr stretched out a hand to help:

"Ouch!" came Ella's voice. "Do watch out for my sunburn."

Everyone laughed and the bewitched silence, which had encompassed them all like a magic eggshell, suddenly shattered. Nick unshipped the rudder and soon he was helping the others to push his boat out of the waves. As they heaved *Frolic* up the beach they knew by her weight that she was definitely no fairy vessel.

The relief they all felt was overwhelming. Gerald was hugging Kirstin.

"Thank goodness you're both safe!" he almost groaned.

Carol was hugging Nick and crying:

"Great to have you lot with us on Midimi. It's been so lonely!"

"Best of all we're all together and we're unharmed!" repeated Nell over and over again as she went round hugging *everyone!*

Splashing noisily they jumped about with excitement, never realising what a racket they were making and forgetting how far noises carry over water. Everybody was talking at once. If there were any Bafando baddies on Midimi Island or its neighbours they'd know without doubt that strangers had invaded their territory. Were there any evil men on nearby islands?

Questions and answers and stories and explanations tumbled about till no one could understand what was being said by anyone else. Suddenly there was an unexpected lull and into the silence Gerald's voice, pitched loud to dominate over the previous hubbub, announced clearly and imperatively:

"I'm *hungry!*"

"So'm I!" came a chorus from four happy voices as the general laugh subsided.

"Did you manage to buy bread?" added Carol in a small, not very hopeful tone.

CHAPTER 40

Midnight armada.

Supper was late. There was so much to say, and everyone was so famished that it was also an extremely long meal that started with chicken-cube soup and finished with fresh pineapple and dried dates. In between came a strange variety of courses, which in other circumstances, might not have mixed very well. On this occasion everything tasted delicious. It was washed down with countless mugs of cocoa.

When at last conversation became less urgent it was found that Ella and Carol, who had been sitting back to back, had subsided into a little mixed-up heap and were sound asleep. Sorting them out and helping them into their sleeping bags the others did their best to avoid touching Nell's sunburn but in a half-awake tone she muttered:"Ouch!"

They smiled sympathetically. Then they gathered up all the supper things, together with other items that were lying about and stuffed everything into the boats.

"What a higgle piggle!" said Kirstin. "We ought to hide it all."

"We should put the boats out of sight too," said Nick. "We'd be completely scuppered if they got pinched."

"Nowhere to hide 'em," said Kirstin rather sweepingly considering that she and Carol had not, as yet, been able to search far afield.

"Oh well," yawned Gerald. "You've been here and unmolested for over 24 hours. No reason why we should receive a visitation now."

"Oh yes there is," argued Nick, who was worried. "The girls sailed straight here, and in a storm, when probably any rebels were sheltering in a cave or tents and not keeping a look out. But not only did we arrive in good weather, but we really showed ourselves, sailing right round several islands and islets as we hunted for the Aussies. And *they* advertised this place good and proper by sending up flares."

"And a smoke bomb, and making murky fires." added Kirsty.

"Oh lummy!" Gerr did not care to have all the details spelled out.

"Nicky's right," said Kirstin anxiously, "and until the sun went down you were still very conspicuous as you sailed on past three or four more islands to reach us here."

"But we didn't see anybody," said Gerald obstinately. "Nobody was aware of our arrival."

"Just because *we* didn't see *them* doesn't mean that the rebels weren't skulking on one or more islands watching *us*. It's easy to spy on the lake, you know, when you're hidden in the branches of a tree or in the shadow of a rock," said Nick.

"Like leopards," said Kirstin enigmatically, "or koala bears."

"*What*?" Gerald looked at her as if she'd gone mad. What on earth was she on about? His cousin looked back in surprise. She thought she'd made it all perfectly clear.

"You know – in a game park – heaps of creatures see you, including a koala, or a leopard up a tree perhaps; but you may not see any of them. In any case, whether you see game or not, you can be sure that such specimens as you *do* see are only a tiny percentage of the animals that are all round."

"Oh... Um... Well... " said Gerald stretching and yawning enormously again.

Although the moon was now high and the clouds had dispersed, there was no question of going off to hunt for hiding places. They were all much too exhausted and sleepy to relish a major expedition round a big island, and Kirstin was sure there wasn't a nearby creek or cove where one, let alone two, dinghies could be concealed. They stood around in uncertain silence till at last Gerr announced:

"I'm turning in."

"Doesn't seem to be much we can do," Nick admitted. It had been a very long day. "We must just hope we don't get visitors during the night."

Nick's wish was not to be fulfilled. He and Kirstin lit a few mosquito coils because the wind was threatening to die completely, and soon they were asleep beside the others.

Ella woke to the sound of yells and the clatter of boats coming ashore. Her heart started pounding. Clouds were again covering the moon and everything was opaquely dark. She turned over and looked at the blackness of the lake. As far as she could make out a lot of shapes were close inshore, advancing fast towards the beach where the cousins were lying. Two small craft were already aground and it was the shouts of their crews as the keels crunched up the gravel that had woken her.

Nell lay frozen with terror. What appeared to be a regular flotilla of dugouts followed four larger boats (such as the one shown on page 4) onto the beach. Between 20 and 30 men gathered in the far corner of the rocks. They were talking, shouting and arguing about something in their midst. Ella was very surprised that none of the rest of her party had been disturbed by the commotion. Carefully she edged across until she was close enough to her brother to shake him gently. When he showed signs of waking she whispered in his ear:
"Gerald – don't move. Wake up, but lie still." He started to lever himself onto one elbow but El put her hand on his chest and pushed him down. Again she breathed into his ear:
"Don't move. Lie still. We have visitors."

Looking at her blearily, he opened his mouth to ask whatever was going on and found Ella's hand over it. Coming properly awake he raised his head and turned to see what his sister was indicating. The clouds had shifted; so now a pale light was casting deep shadows. With grim features he studied the huge group of men and boys at the far end of the beach. Had bandits come to capture them? Then, still in his sleeping bag, as Ella had, he wriggled across the sand till he reached Nick.
"Nick," he said softly. "Nick!"
As his cousin stirred Gerald, pushed him down and repeated his sister's words.
"Wake up, but don't move. We've got visitors."
Ella wormed her way across the sand after her brother and three worried people tried to fathom what was going on.

A huge armada of canoes, drawn up out of the waves, clustered round four fishing-type boats whose bows were ashore. The rough-looking crews were now congregated in several gangs with small fires starting to twinkle in the centre of each group. Now and again, as the flames brightened, silhouettes of men squatting or standing round the fires were clear. Shadows flickered grotesquely on big rocks.

"Do you think they're guerrillas?" breathed Nell.

"Can't tell," answered Nick.

"What d'you think they're up to?" queried Gerr.

The other two shook their heads.

"We'd be no good against that mob. Even counting all of us we're outnumbered five or six to one. And they're a really burly bunch."

For some time the three lay quietly watching. The invaders paid them no attention. Each party seemed to be intent on its own fire and there came the smell of fish.

"I believe they're cooking and eating," murmured Gerald at last.

"And that far group is fiddling with a faulty Tilley lamp – or something. Or maybe they're using the lamp to see as they tinker with that outboard motor."

"You go back to sleep," Nell told the boys eventually. "I'll wake you if you're needed."

They were having such difficulty repressing cavernous yawns that, after a few murmurs of disagreement, they found it easier to give in.

"Be sure to call us if necessary," they said.

"And wake us to take a turn at keeping guard if they stay too long," added Nick.

Ella could never have slept with those barbarous characters around. Fearful and anxious she eased herself a little way up the slope and slumped against a rock with the strangers in view. Why had they landed here? She was glad they had so far taken no interest in the sleeping five or in their boats, but she worried about how long it would be before the pack of scoundrels wandered across to the cousins' camp.

After some time the separate parties split up. Men and youths ambled here and there, but when an inquisitive couple wandered towards *Frolic* and *Percy,* a muted but authoritative voice called them back. Many of the wild-looking fellows just lay down and slept.

Ella began to feel less frightened. Whoever these characters were, a large vocal 'committee' now appeared concerned only with something that they were working on by the light of the Tilley lamp. They kept the lantern shielded by large rocks and seemed to be hiding from notice.

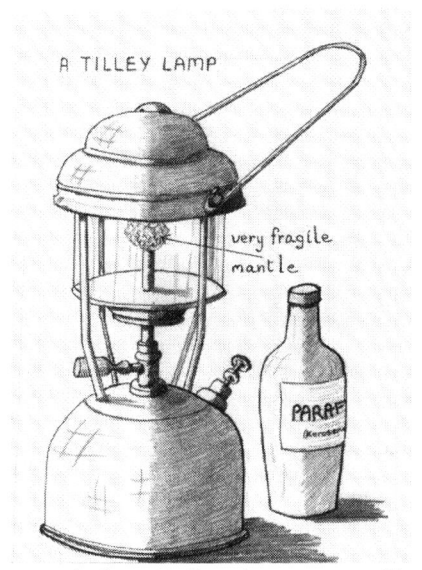

A TILLEY LAMP

very fragile mantle

PARRF

pic 52.

Time dragged for Nell who was still stressed, and starting to get painful cramp. After what seemed like centuries, she was relieved when there was a general movement back to the fishing craft. Paddles struck each other with sharp 'clacks' and made hollow drum-like 'clunks' as they hit the sides of dugouts. Splashes, raucous shouts and the loud crunch of keels sliding over shingle were very much out of place in the velvet night that had recently been filled only with stealthy murmurs. All should have been soft and peaceful with only gentle sounds of the African bush and waves lapping quietly upon this wild, uninhabited shore that was so isolated in a vast inland sea.

The tense watcher wondered how her companions could sleep through the disturbance. But sleep they did, so only she saw the large fleet paddle off without lights, into the now relatively calm lake. Once afloat the departing men fell completely silent. It was weird to watch their dark, silver-grey shapes melt into the night. Gradually they became less and less substantial. The movement of paddlers could no longer be discerned as they forced their craft west-north-west, and then – suddenly, Ella shook her head and did a double take. She was staring at nothing. The visitors had vanished.

Who were they? Why had they paused on this beach? Where were they going? Were they revolutionaries bound for some destructive mission on the Kangi side of the border – and therefore too busy to bother with small fry such as *Frolic* and *Percy*? Were they fugitives who had escaped from the bandits? Questions went round and round in Nell's brain until the moon was low on the horizon. Then finally, she gave up her voluntary watch and allowed her lids to close.

The next morning Kirstin and Carol were furious.
"Why didn't you wake us?" they demanded.
The visitation was discussed from all angles and it was finally decided, with reservations, that since the invaders had taken absolutely no interest in boats already on the beach, they could have had no evil intentions, and must have been Kangi fishermen, blown across by the storm and now taking advantage of the calmer weather, and of darkness, to slip up the islands till they were closer to the western (Kangalian) shore and felt able to tackle the long crossing homewards.
"Rubbish!" said Kirstin stoutly. "Kangi fishermen don't work in packs. They operate with not more than two, or perhaps three, dugouts working together. Besides, how would so many stranded fishermen find each other and get organised to paddle back all together in a fleet like that?"
"I know they work in pairs," said Carol, "but sometimes you see lots of pairs working close together."

53. Dugout Armada.

"And it *is* feasible," suggested Nick, "I mean – normally the winds on this lake come from the south or the north. They sort of whistle up and down the Rift Valley – in line with the lake."

"So?"

"Hang on. Give a chap a chance. The type of winds coming *across* the lake from the west – or east – only happen rarely, when there's a cyclone down on the east coast of Africa. Then we get the tail end of the hurricane up here inland in the mountains, and then the winds tear westwards or eastwards across the lake – as we had recently."

"Oh. So…"

"So – m*aybe* – the Kangi locals are moderately used to being blown across to the central string of islands. Perhaps they have a secret gathering place where they can meet if they've been forced to go with the weather and get stranded on the islands."

"Under the biggest Baobab on the third island… " murmured Ella half sarcastically.

"No!" said more fanciful Carol. "By a sacred stone on a symbol shaped island… "

"Well. It's an idea, anyway."

Gerald caught onto Nick's theory and took up the argument for him.

"They *could* do that, you know. I mean, have a special meeting place. And then, when the weather has calmed down, which it started to do last night, and there has since been time for all the stranded fishermen to gather at that place. Well, then they set off home in a big band. An armada large enough to fight off any rebels who may decide to attack them."

"Hm," murmured Kirsty again, but less dubiously.

"I wish we'd joined them," sighed Ella. "For safety. I don't at all like being so close to the wrong side of the lake."

Well," concluded Kirstin, "the fact that they landed here proves that there aren't too many sandy beaches around.

We were jolly lucky to have found this spot."

54. "The biggest Baobab on the third island" ?
Maybe it was a sacred tree with offerings made to it: coffee libations poured over its roots, and rags fastened with thorns to its trunk.

CHAPTER 41

Python.

Although at breakfast time Ella had bemoaned not having left Midimi Island with the midnight armada, when the others started to pack and to discuss the day's sailing plans she was not at all inclined to move. She was tired of sitting in a small boat on bobbing waves. Her sunburn was painful and she would have liked to spend the day lathered in cooling lotion lying idly in shade. She was also sick of Gerald's pyjamas. But as she daren't take them off she wanted to give them a thorough scrubbing before setting sail once again.
"Besides!" she exclaimed. "Look at you! All of you. You're just like me: *filthy*. Your shirts need a good wash. Kirstin and Carol are black with soot... "
"Oh – Ella!" said the others. "Stop fussing!"
Kirstin had a brainwave.
"If Nell wants to do washing," she suggested, "Caro can take us up to the python's rock and we'll try to spot him."
Gerald stared open-mouthed.
"Python?" queried Nick, interested. "How big is he?"
"Oh – Big," replied Caro un-informatively. She had to repeat her story. Nell listened aghast.
"You mean to say you let us sleep on the beach with that monstrous creature prancing about close by, all ready to gobble us up?"
"*Do* snakes *prance*?" asked her brother sotto voce.
"Well – er – sorry we didn't warn you," apologised Kirstin not at all contritely. "We'd forgotten all about the python till just now. But I *would* like to see him."
"You bet!" enthused Gerr.
"Of course," said Nick. "Are you coming with us Ella?"
"No!" said his eldest cousin emphatically. "No. I'm most definitely *not* coming. Let's get away as soon as possible."
"Oh, El," laughed Carol. "You are funny! First you wished we'd

left the islands with the armada in the middle of the night. Then you wanted to stay and get clean. Now you're all for the off again!"

Nell looked a trifle put out.

"Besides," said Nick, "There are lots of pythons all round the islands and the lakeshore. By leaving here you'd only be heading for another python home. Ella stared at him with a comical expression of sheer horror.

"Come on," said Nick taking her arm. "Come and view Ye Olde Python living in Ye Olde Bush and all. You may not have another chance you know!"

"I *hate* snakes!" said Nell.

"But pythons are so pretty," said Carol persuasively, giving Ella a little push from behind.

"Where to?" asked Gerald, seizing his sister's other arm.

"Watch out for my sunburn!"

"Over here," said Kirsty. "Go ahead, Caro. You know the way."

They retraced Carol's route as quietly as possible. Ella, terrified of stepping on a sleeping brute, would happily have made as much din as voices, dead sticks and rattling stones could have created; but Nick urged:

"Try to tread lightly, and don't talk. We don't want to frighten him."

"Snakes don't have ears."

"Don't they? Well, anyway – they jolly well feel vibrations that tell them which animals are around."

"And they smell with their tongues."

"You shouldn't tell such porkies, Carol!"

"No. Really. *Dinkum deadset* (it's true)... When a forked tongue flips in and out a snake isn't licking his chops. He's smelling the news from all around. Honest!"

"In that case," said Nick wickedly, "Gerr had better stay on the beach. After all, we don't want to asphyxiate the poor old reptile!"

The girls giggled but Gerald, who could not think of a sufficiently rude retort, pointedly ignored Nick's remark. He pretended great interest in an anthill that they were passing.

"I don't care how frightened the python is," said Ella. "The further he skedaddles away from me the happier I'll be."

"How d'you know he's a 'he'?" asked Gerald.

"Well – er – we don't," admitted Kirstin.

"I believe it's very difficult to tell," said Nick

He and his mother had once been in the front row of the audience at a Fauna Society lecture, and Maddy had drawn both her legs right up onto her chair when a puff adder had started to creep out of its glass-fronted box.

"No doubt snakes can tell, and that's all that matters," decided Kirsty. "Now which way, Caro?"

"Round that boulder. We're quite close now."

"Keep your eyes peeled and your mouths shut."

"Aye! Aye! Commodore!"

There was no sign of their quarry or of his relatives lurking in the underbrush. Cautiously they spread out over the rocks and advanced with some misgivings, even on the part of the bravest amongst them.

"Do pythons eat humans?" whispered Gerald.

"Well … er… It depends on how big the creature is and how small the human is. If he's as big as Carol says, I expect he'd gladly coil himself around you and squash your bones to pulp. Then he'd dislocate his mouth so that he could swallow you – especially if he was ravenous. If you trod on him, then of course, it would be reflex action. As quick as a flash he'd have you wrapped up whether he was hungry or not!"

"Oh – er… well… er… yes," said Gerr lifting his feet high into the air and paying exaggerated attention to where he placed his next step.

"There was a python who took up residence near the football field at Lawara High School once," said Nick who had now given up all hope of seeing any wildlife. He was sure that all creatures for miles around had become aware of them ages ago and quickly slithered or scampered out of sight.

"They eventually caught him and later let him loose in the bush. Actually I think that one laid eggs while she was temporarily kept in the zoo, so he must have been a female.

Anyway – when she was first spotted the headmaster announced in morning prayers that the lower football field would be out of bounds to first, second and third formers until the creature was removed. It seemed that the older pupils could go there to be squeezed and eaten! We all thought it was a huge joke – till we saw the monster when she was brought round on display to the various schools.
I was still at primary school in Lawara at the time, before I went to boarding school in Scotland."
"Wallabies!" said Carol.
"No – Pythons!" laughed Gerald.
"Oh well," Kirstin chuckled, "give me emus, any day!"

"Er………. " gurgled Ella as if she was being strangled. Coming to a dead stop, she stood as still as an African carving, her face chalk white under its puce sunburn, and her mouth wide open. One shaking arm was held out with the hand pointing. The others looked at the spot her finger indicated.
Carol rapidly took a huge step backwards.
"Crikey!" gasped Gerald copying her.
Kirsty leaned forward.
"Catting Kangas!" she breathed. "What a *beaut*, eh?"
Resting on the edge of the giant rock outcrop on which they were standing was a large triangular head. The stony eyes were watching them sleepily, but without much interest.
"Gosh!"
"*Ripper!*"
"My golly!"
"Puking possums!"
They edged backwards, awed by the splendour and size of the head, and by the magnificent length of a section of body which showed over the rim of the boulder.
"If we go round there," suggested Nick, pointing, "and climb among those rocks, we may be able to see the rest of him-er-her." The others followed as he retraced his steps and took a detour at some distance from the snake.

55. Python-watching from the nearby kopje.

"There," he soon murmured with satisfaction. By peering between two huge lumps of granite they could see the snake draped along a ledge on the side of the first boulder. His neck extended upwards so that he could rest his head higher on a flat part of the monolith, where the visitors had spotted it.
"What a size!" whispered Kirstin.
"*Spiffy*!" said Carol, feeling braver now that they were not quite on top of 'her' snake.
"I'm going to climb higher," declared Gerald pointing to the top of their kopje. "From up there we'll get a super view of his entire length. Did anyone bring a camera?"
Kirstin waved hers by its straps.
"Oh, good."
    From the top of the knoll they looked across at the enormous reptile.
"I say! He's peeling. He's sloughing his skin."

"Like Ella!"

"No. He's got glorious new skin everywhere except that tiny bit that seems to have stuck. I'd say he finished peeling sometime ago."

"I thought that snakes cast the whole skin all in one piece – like the entire skin we found in Nick's garden – with the shape of the head and all."

"That's only smaller snakes. Really big ones – like this chap – do it in bits."

"Oh."

"What a massive bulge he's got! Must've had a whacking great meal. I bet he's feeling bilious now."

"A hyrax or two, I guess."

"That proves that he's finished sloughing. They don't usually eat when they're peeling."

"Gosh, Nick, how do you know so much about pythons?"

"I don't really. But when you live in a country you can't help learning about the fauna and stuff... Kirsty and Caro must know oodles about echidnas and duck billed platypi, and ..."

"PlatypusES!" interrupted Gerr.

"Dominus – domini... Fungus – fungi... Platypus – platypi !"

"What about walrus? – Walri, then?"

"Poor hyrax!" said Carol who hadn't studied Latin and didn't know or care what Gerald and Nick were going on about.

"But lucky us!" said Kirstin. "If he wasn't so busy digesting he'd have slithered off by now. See how he's turned his head to watch. He doesn't like having us around. But he's too full to be bothered to move."

Having taken a couple of snaps, she began to scramble down the rock.

"I'm going up close to get an ace shot," she announced.

"No!" Ella was horrified! "No! Don't! You're mad! You're not to. It's not safe!"

"Rubbish!" said Kirstin. "He's absolutely stuffed full of hyrax. He won't move for a month of Sundays."

"Be careful," pleaded Carol clasping her hands together.

Kirsty clambered down and squeezed through a crack between the boulders. Slowly, cautiously, she advanced towards the bulging python. It watched her intently with eyes glistening like polished pebbles. They seemed to reveal deadly knowledge. The four on top of the kopje held their breaths.
"Watch out!" squealed Carol suddenly. "He's moving!"

Nell was gripping Gerald's arm painfully but it was not until later that he noticed the bruises. Kirstin quickly raised her camera and clicked the shutter. She was about to sprint away when she noticed that the reptile was moving only sluggishly and not towards her. Deliberately he lowered his head and lazily, as if it was an incredible effort, he began to slide away from her, retracing his length along the ledge so that his body was looped back upon itself.
"Aw, man! Leave the poor chap alone," said Nick. "Let him be."
Kirstin took another quick snap then squeezed back to rejoin her friends as they climbed off the rock.

"Give us a hand, Gerr," begged Ella finding the descent tricky. Her brother turned to help, then he stepped back.
"Ta-ta, El!" he laughed. "We'll come back in a week – perhaps – and see how you're getting on. Have a good time with your pal the python!"
"Ger-*ald!*" squeaked Ella. "Come on! Don't be such a beast! I can't get down."
Her heartless brother and cousins laughed harder till Carol, still chuckling, went back to help. Nick and Gerr weren't far behind so Nell was assisted down like royalty.

They returned to the beach via a route which would disturb the snake no more.
"Crumbs! That was *great!*" exclaimed Gerald enthusiastically. "Super!"
"Aren't you glad you came with us, Ella?" asked Nick.
"Er – well – Let's get moving, anyway, now" she replied ambiguously. "Who'm I sailing with today?"
They all laughed.

"But Nell, what about the washing?" teased Nick.

"I'll do that tomorrow."

"Don't remind your sister," said Nick quietly to Gerr as they pushed off *Frolic*, "but there are pythons on just about all the islands. Millions of them," he exaggerated. The boys chortled but would not share the joke with the girls.

"Oh! All right! We'll have our own back on you one day," threatened Kirstin who was fastening the Queen Mary's painter onto an eyehook in *Percy's* stern. The bailer bucket (inside the dinghy) was also attached to this loop.

"Just you wait," glowered Carol darkly, taking *Percy's* helm.

"We'll wait," agreed Nick affably. "Have you noticed, by the way, how the wind has changed? It's coming nicely from the south-south-east now. Obviously the cyclone down at the coast is over, and the weather here is almost back to what it should be."

"*Bonza!*" rejoiced Carol. Then she added soberly: "But with the wind this way we'll have to beat all the way back to Baboon Bay. It'll be really *cranky* (nasty)."

"Will we make it back to Elephant Island tonight?" asked Nell.

"Seems a pity to start back already," murmured Carol.

"No fear!" said Kirstin robustly. "We're nearly up to the Lake Flies region. *Give it a burl.*" (Give it a try.)

"D'you think we really ought to?"

"Aw – come on, man!"

"We've been out three nights. Let's go on for one more day. Then – if we start back tomorrow, we'll have three full days to get back. That should be enough."

"Well... "

"Right. That's settled then. Get the chart out Kirstin and we'll see which island to aim at for tonight."

"Island!" exclaimed Ella alarmed. "Surely we're not going to stay in the middle of the lake? What about bandits?"

"Of course. It'd take too long to cross back to the Kangalian shore and then go north from there."

"Oh, gosh!"

"Listen. It'll be OK. As we sail more and more north we'll be safely on our side of the border, going further and further from the baddies."

"Why do the wretched Lake Flies only appear so far north?"

"Because they hatch on the surface of very deep water. They seldom swarm in the shallower section of the lake further south."

Kirstin compounded Nell's horror by adding:

"This is one of the deepest lakes in the world. Did you know?"

Poor Ella! Sailing had been horrendous enough so far. Now she looked down through beautifully clear water and did not notice the sparkling clarity and colourful fish. Instead she imagined deep, dark, ominous layers. Awful depths stared up and *Percy* seemed like an unstable plastic bottle top.

"Looks as if there are precious few islands with beaches. Most have steep sides and they'll be rocky, I suppose," said Kirstin who was studying the chart. There's one where we could perhaps land. It's a funny shaped *thingo* that's roughly the right distance away."

"Look out for your boom, Nick!" shrieked Carol as Nick steered closer to *Percy* and tried to look across from *Frolic* at the chart that Kirstin was holding up for him.

"Oops! Sorry!" He corrected his steering and sheered off.

"Phew!" said Gerald addressing a cormorant, which was swimming alongside the boat. "Some people haven't the first idea of how to sail, have they?"

The bird eyed him impassively. Then, as if deciding that the youth was not nice to know, it raised its beak insolently, blinked a pale blue fishy eye, and dived out of sight.

"We'll aim for your island, Kirstin," called Nick. "Why do you say it's funny shaped?"

"It's like a spread-out hand – sort of – a right hand seen from above with … er – one thumb and one, two… eight – no nine, fingers. All the fingers point northeast. Sure to be corker coves and rocks to hide the boats in between the 'fingers'. Room for a regular army of boats, I reckon."

"Fleet, not army," corrected Carol.

"Sounds good," said Nick. "What's it called?"
"It's called... I can't see the name. Oh yes! Here it is. It's called Kadenzi Island." It was a name that they would regret ever having heard. However, for the time being it sounded promising.
"O.K. Kadenzi Island – here we come!" chanted Gerald happily.

Ella spread another layer of sun cream over her suffering body. "Ouch! I hate sunburn!"
"And snakes!" laughed Carol.
"Yes!" agreed Nell with intense feeling. "And deep water, and tiny little sailing dinghies, and... "
"Soon you'll be peeling just like a reptile," laughed her unfeeling brother. "Ha! Ha! El's peeling like a python!"
His sister found a piece of bark in the bottom of *Percy* and threw it at him. It fell between the two boats with scarcely a splash.
"Better luck next time," teased Gerald. "No wonder you never made the cricket team."
"Good thing for you, though, that I took up hockey instead," laughed Nell.

56. Small fish being dried to stop them from going bad.
Carol called them fish lollipops.

CHAPTER 42

<u>Fun and flies.</u>

Running before the wind, and sometimes zigzagging just for fun, going NNW up the lake provided a splendid day's sail up the western side of the archipelago. Conditions were ideal for spinnakers. Getting the balloon sail up smartly, and lowering it without letting it billow into the water, or turn into a sea anchor that could pull the bow under, needed skill and co-ordination from helm and crew. Each had an important part to play in the manoeuvres. It was a glorious sight and very exciting when they got everything right with the huge sail drawing properly, lifting the boat and making it rush through white horses at great speed; but it was scary when the spread of nylon material was wallowing about like an unset jelly threatening to collapse and cause chaos.

As *Frolic* and *Percy* bowled along, their bright, multi-coloured spinnakers went up and down more than a dozen times until everyone had enjoyed turns helming and crewing, and could manage to fill the exhilarating curves gracefully.

"Spiffing!" said Kirstin at lunchtime on a tiny crescent-shaped islet with a sandy beach and not much else to it. "Flying a spinnaker's tremendous fun; and it makes the boat feel so light! But it's a bit like Tony doing a wobbly. You have to watch it constantly."

"And concentrate every second," agreed Nick.

Before eating they swam. The goggling was spectacular with scores of fish round each rock.

"There're a whole lot of little volcanoes over here," said Carol surfacing.

"Where?" asked Gerr, flippering across to investigate.

Soon he called to the others:

"Come and see. The fishes are building volcanoes on the sandy bottom of the lake."

"You two are *fruit loops* (idiots)," said Kirsty amiably. "Fish don't make volcanoes!"

"They are! *Dinkum!*" insisted Carol.

"But it's the wrong time of year," said Nick mystified. "In summer, when the water's even warmer than it is now, male Cichlids do make sandy hills with hollows in the tops. Females come along and lay eggs in the cup."

Through goggles they watched a couple of fish, only 10cm long, fanning fins and tails assiduously to enlarge their crater-topped piles. Nearby there was more amazing evidence of hard-working little Cichlids: astonishing hollows up to 2m wide. The swimmers could sit in them. Nicky confirmed:

"Yes. They *are* fish nests; and the water *does* seem to be a good deal warmer round here, doesn't it?"

"Much warmer than elsewhere. That's why I was sticking around," said Carol.

"You're right," agreed her sister. "Maybe there's a hot spring under water that's raising the temp of this little area. Let's see if we can find it."

It was easy to locate the region where the water was warmest. Diving, they spotted lines of bubbles rising from the floor of the lake which, just there, close to the islet, wasn't far down. They put their toes beside the vent holes and smiled at each other.

"You're *grinning like a shot fox*'" Kirstin said to Nick.

57. Mermaid looking for fish cones.

"You Aussies do say odd things," remarked Ella, but didn't press Kirstin to explain. She guessed that she herself might have said 'like a Cheshire cat'. Instead she declared: "It's great where the hot water's coming out. Just like a warm bath."

"That's why I'm wallowing about right over the spring." said Nick with a grin. "You said we needed a good clean up."

Gerald and Kirstin went fishing in the Queen Mary. It was a bit of a squash but they caught enough for supper and, despite Carol's fears, managed not to puncture the plastic dinghy with fishhooks. Nick and Caro nobly helped to gut and clean the catch before they set sail again, heading NNW as before.

"Look!" said Gerr sometime during the afternoon when they were practising 'picking up a man overboard'. He pointed below the spinnaker to the horizon ahead. "Lots of columns of smoke rising straight out of the lake. Maybe there's a bush fire on a very low island that we can't see."

"How very odd!" said Ella who was with him and Kirstin in *Percy*. "Fire can't be coming straight out of the water. Maybe they're waterspouts. And yet the weather's not right for whirly gigs."

"They do look like waterspouts, though," Kirsty studied the phenomenon and added, "but they're a bit too grey... "

"No," persisted Gerald. "It's smoke. I'm certain they're spirals of smoke."

"There must be fires on a shore that we can't see," said Kirstin. "Big ones, too. Maybe there's inter-tribal warfare going on and villages are being razed to the ground."

"Or maybe Bafandoland soldiers have crossed the lake and are devastating villages in Kangalia," suggested Nell soberly. "That's a definite possibility." They remembered the armada.

A few minutes later the mystery was solved when Carol called across to them. She was bobbing about having just been dropped from *Frolic* as a 'man overboard'.

"See the Lake Flies, you lot?"

"Where?" asked Gerald, excited.

"Oh no!" groaned Ella. The last thing she wanted was a dangerous expedition to collect some nasty little insects. She had been hoping they'd never spot even the least sign of the creatures.

"There!" called Nicky, pointing north.

"Can't see anything except smoke from some very large bush fires," Kirstin shouted back.

"That's them, idiot!" laughed Nick.

"What?"

"Those pillars of what you call 'smoke'. Those are the Lake Flies hatching and flying up from just below the surface of the water."

"Wailing Wallabies! Are you sure?" Kirstin was flabbergasted.

"Crikey!" murmured Gerald. "There must be trillions of billions of millions of them!"

"More than that even! Galaxies of them!"

"Thank goodness they're so far away," said Ella. "We'll never reach them today and we're turning back tomorrow," she added thankfully.

"Nick, for Pete's sake stop staring at the flies and get your spinnaker down," shouted Kirstin. "My sister's still waiting to be rescued!"

"Gosh! Sorry!" gulped Nick guiltily. He had completely forgotten his 'man overboard' cousin.

"Coming Caro," he yelled. "Help! Why didn't we lower the spinnaker before you jumped?"

Either Kadenzi Island was further than it seemed from the chart or the wind was not as strong as Kirstin had estimated. They obviously weren't going to get there before sunset.

"Or maybe we took too long over lunch;" suggested Carol.

"Perhaps we can find a suitable island further south – with a beach or cove or something where we can land and camp," said Nick.

Inlets and beaches were rare on the brown and yellow islands further south; and great boulders had encircled them like fortress walls. But now the character of the land had changed. The soil was grey and red. There were few surrounding boulders and the islands ended abruptly in small cliffs that dropped steeply into the lake. Although generally not very high the escarpments were eroded into spectacular pinnacles and spiky gullies. Gerald and the Australians had been busy with their cameras snapping not only the usual Cormorants, Eagles, Pelicans and other birds, but also the rather weird but extremely photogenic scenery.

"Really rugged," was how Nick described it. "There are hardly any bays and even fewer beaches, well – not that I can see here," he added as he pored over the chart, "but maybe we can find a creek that has been eroded enough for us to creep into. I'd like to hide the boats. We were so excited over the spinnakers that we forgot where we were, and stupidly flaunted ourselves out on the water. I hate to think who might have seen us."

"You said we'd be safer as we went north," accused Ella.

"Well, yes – theoretically. But you never know where bandits are going to pop up. I don't suppose they give a toss about where the border actually is."

Lumbo Island, immediately south of Kadenzi, looked promising on the chart, so they pressed on till well after teatime and then made for an inlet on its eastern coast. Of the several crannies that they could choose, this one – according to the chart – looked as if it might be the best place to hide and harbour the boats. Sure enough they found that the east side of Lumbo rose quite steeply out of the water and it had several creeks.

The cleft that they were looking for was barely wider than a boat-length but it cut into the island for at least 30 metres. The sides were so high that the tops of the masts blended with branches of trees on the tall shoulders of red earth on either side. At this time of the evening, with the sun going down on the far (west) side of the island, this cove was a bit spooky; but they were pleased to find a small beach of soft yellow sand at the very end of the inlet where they could land the dinghies and unload. Then they pushed the boats out once more and tied them to rocks at an angle across the channel with a rope from each bow and each stern.

"*Frolic* and *Percy* look really happy resting there side by side in this wonderfully calm water," said Ella.
"Tremendous," said Nick. "They'd weather even a complete cyclone here."
"*Bonza!*" said Kirstin.
"I'm glad we landed here instead of on Kadenzi." Carol sounded strange, but Nick cut in:
"I was hoping to get as far north as possible."
"Same here," said Gerald sadly.
"Well I'm glad. Lumbo Island's super but Kadenzi's horrible" persisted Carol.
"But why?" asked Ella.
"I don't know why? I just *know!* It's got a *feel* about it."
"But," said her sister, "we hardly saw Kadenzi. First it was hidden behind Lumbo. And when it did come into sight it was just a very black lump in the sunset. You've go a *kangaroo loose in the top paddock*, (you're loony) Carol!" Kirstin's words had gone all Aussie because she was worried. Her sister's forebodings so often turned out to be correct.
"Maybe she's like the Kangalians," laughed Ella, "She knows that each island has its own spirits, some are good and some islands have evil spooks."
"Let's *bog in* (eat) anyway," said Kirsty trying to shrug off her sister's fancies.

The cheery meal was accompanied by tunes from Ella's and Gerald's recorders and by songs from the others. The voices, although not invariably in tune were always jolly. Nicky was bullied into trying to dance the Highland Fling but the sand was so soft that he tripped amid a chorus of laughs. Only as they were brushing their teeth did Ella remember Carol's python.
"I hope... no... snakes... here... " she spluttered through a mouthful of toothpaste. "So little... this beach... bushes right... on top of us."

"I don't know about the snakes," said Kirstin, "but there must be heaps of monitor lizards."
Nell looked at her in concern, which increased when Kirsty added: "or crocodiles."
"Why?" asked Gerr.

(Turn the book 90° clock-wise to look at this picture.)
58. Going up the beach: 2 sets of monitor lizard tracks (thin line between claw prints) & 2 different types of crocodile tracks (broad pattern between claw prints). Each claw makes a hand-like mark.

"Didn't you see their prints in the sand when we landed? – before we walked all over them," asked Nick.

"No?"

"Place was criss-crossed all over, with little claw marks on each side of lines that showed where scaly tails got dragged along behind," said Carol. "That's spoor of monitor lizards: huge reptiles, you know, but smaller than crocs."

"You're joking!"

"No, *dinkum*, I'm not. But don't worry. They may try to find our fruit and they eat rotten stuff – flesh and vegetation... but they don't go for living things – well, not usually. You're safe for one more night, El."

"But what if the marks belonged to crocs and not to monitor lizards?"

"Croc tracks are sort-of like tractor marks," said Kirstin." But the tail marks on this beach were too narrow for crocs, I reckon. Or else it was a whole kindergarten of crocs and you're training to look after infants, El, so you'll be alright."

Nell shivered.

"You can sleep in one of the boats," suggested an unsympathetic cousin pointing to the floating dinghies.

"Monitor lizards can swim," put in Caro tactlessly, "so they'd get to the boats."

"Yes," agreed Gerald. "We've seen them sliding off rocks and disappearing into the water."

"But I'm pretty sure even a hungry monitor wouldn't be able to climb over the side and into either boat," said Kirstin.

Ella examined *Percy's* ribs and the ridged duckboards in *Frolic*, then decided that she preferred sand, snakes, and monitor lizards to the cramped quarters between centreboard casing and hard sides. While the others piled all edibles into the boats she placed and lit dozens of mosquito coils strategically all round, and settled very dubiously into her sack.

In the morning birds hopped all round and completely ignored the humans who had *not* been nibbled – not even by tiny, normal-sized lizards – and not even by ants.

"Plovers, Pied Kingfishers, Reed Warblers, Wagtails… " Gerald named only those that he could recognise. There were plenty more…

"As if we were in a Disney film," said his sister, delighted and amazed. "They're not at all scared."

From a nearby bush came a sound as of liquid being poured into a jar.

"Water-bottle bird – Coucal," said Kirsty knowledgeably in hushed tones. "Wouldn't it be wonderful if it came out onto the beach?"

"Coucals only skulk in bushes and keep out of sight," murmured Nick. He was immediately contradicted as a big, supercilious-looking bird hopped out of cover to investigate a piece of pawpaw that someone hadn't yet finished eating. About 16 inches long, he was a handsome specimen with a strong beak, white chest, black tail and russet wings. Entranced and with bated breath the group watched him swagger about as if he owned the beach.

They had agreed to start homewards today but the creek felt so safe and comfortable that no one, not even Nell, wanted to head south. The sun struck rainbows from a world glittering with dew. Baby clouds, propelled by a wind that was just right for carefree sailing, skipped across a brilliant sky, and the water was spread with diamonds.

"If only the cyclone had stayed away," sighed Ella wishing that every day had been like this one.

"It was exciting being blown across the lake," said Carol.

"Hmph!" was Kirsty's comment. If her sister had already forgotten how frightened and how exhausted they'd been, she, Kirstin, could still remember only too well.

"Without the cyclone we'd never have got as far north as this," said Nick. "We'd probably have stayed pottering round the islands in the Double Bay, or south of Baboon Bay."

"Even though we're not meant to be here, so far north," Gerr grinned naughtily, "this is heaps better."

From the top of the knoll just behind their creek they saw nothing moving except cormorants, darters and, of course, waves. Perching Fish Eagles were so still that only the glitter of a beady eye showed that they were alive and alert. Even Carol conceded that Kadenzi didn't glower quite so unpleasantly when surrounded by this scene of unspoilt natural beauty as it had when dramatically lit up by last night's gory sunset.

Gerr gave an electrified yell: "Look! Lake Flies!"

Ella's heart sank. There were still 'smoke' columns like yesterday's, far away to the north; but Gerald was pointing just southeast of Lumbo Island.

"Oh boy!" exclaimed Nick. "We can reach that lot easily. Come on! Lake Flies ahoy!"

"Have we got time? Shouldn't we start straight back as we had planned?" Kirstin was torn between interest in Lake Flies and worry about not reaching Baboon Bay on Thursday, so as to reach Lawara for Tony's birthday on Saturday. The boys, however, wouldn't even listen to such downhearted concerns.

"They're really close! We can tack right up to them."

"It won't take long. Come on! We can't miss a chance like this!"

"There's a little beach on the east of the Dinosaur's snout," said Nick, "but we can't get to that in a day from here. We'll have to risk Midimi for tonight. I don't like that idea but... "

"Well, we don't need a whole day to get to Midimi," said Gerr. "We can get to the Flies and back in no time, and then start south."

Nell was dead set against venturing out to collect samples of the little creatures.

"It's not wise," she said. "Too dangerous! Supposing you were engulfed in the mist of flies?"

"We won't be."

"You might."

"Depends on what the wind does," said Kirstin stopping a potential argument.

"I know!" Nick was at his most persuasive. "We'll take the *Queen Mary* in tow. Then, when we're fairly close to the cloud we'll stop to windward of the spout and two of us will go off in the *Queen*. She's dead easy to move because she's so light. If the wind changes, we can paddle like billy-o and get out of the insects."

"Where're the kil... I mean the preserving jars?" asked Gerald; and that settled the matter.

Nell positively refused to join the expedition. She declared she would stay in the creek and have a washday. Carol, who was not at all sure that she wanted to hobnob with the fearsome Flies, 'nobly' offered to stay to keep Ella company, and also to help her do the scrubbing.

"But we'll probably need four of us: two to catch the flies and manage the *Queen* and two to sail *Frolic*. I can manage *Frolic* alone... but... "

"No. You'd better have a crew in case you need to manoeuvre urgently," said Kirstin. "None of us wants to suddenly find ourselves choking-full of Flies."

They all agreed, so Nell was left, uncomplaining, though she eyed the heap of dirty clothes with distaste. The other four set off in *Frolic*, with the two preserving jars and a towel tied to a couple of long sticks.

"What's that for?" asked Carol as she watched Nick stowing a knife into his boat.

"In case flies stick to the towel: to scrape them off into the jars." So Carol threw in a tea towel.

"To wrap round the knife," she told him. "We don't want it to puncture the *Queen*."

"I don't like it," Ella pointed out. "You'll be sailing straight towards the dangerous border. It's not sensible."

"Aw, El! Can you see a Customs Post? Floating on the water maybe?"

"No rebels are going to rise out of the waves and grab us."

"I just don't like it."

No one noticed how silent Carol had been. She was having one of her foreboding fits.

CHAPTER 43

Filling the preserving jars.
(You might want to refer to the sketch on page 301.)

Four excited sailors in *Frolic* set off towards the weird little Flies. The insects formed a tall grey column that smeared out at the top into low-lying cloud. Even from so close the pillar still looked like a swirling waterspout or a spiral of smoke. The wind was spreading the entire mushroom of hatching mega millions wider and wider, and blowing it slowly across the lake directly towards Kadenzi Island. It was therefore advancing almost straight towards *Frolic* as she approached the insects. So, although the sailors worried in case the wind veered slightly and swept the swarms all over Ella and *Percy* plus their gear on Lumbo, they never realised that the suffocating, opaque pillar was heading their way. They merely noticed that they were approaching it rather faster than anticipated and concluded that they must be sailing particularly brilliantly!

The pile of Flies, which at first had seemed well defined, slow-moving and narrow, swelled incredibly as the GP14 approached it. With slightly fuzzy edges, where insects were less densely packed, it looked first like a tower, then like a wall, and finally like a full-sized cloud floating heavily on the waves. It never became any thinner, but remained dense and black, full of swirling darker regions. The four stared at its churning eddies in amazement. Could all that really consist of miniscule, midge-like creatures? It didn't seem possible. And why did so many hatch? – and why all at once? – why did they materialise *under* the surface? – how did they manage to fly out of the water? – why did they appear in winter? – why...

The questions seemed endless. Of course, Uncle Ken and his research team were trying to answer some of them. The samples that the cousins hoped to collect might help.

But, although the four in *Frolic* had carefully taken the temperature of the water – with a thermometer that Kirstin had luckily remembered at the very last minute, they were not thinking about Uncle Ken's investigations. They were totally overawed by this entire phenomenon. Each of them was secretly wondering how anyone could ever manage to get close enough to collect Flies without actually suffocating. With a sudden shock they noticed that *Frolic* and the cloud were headed for collision.

"Kangas!" cried Nick urgently. "Ready about? Quick now. Lee-O!" He gave the others no time at all to get ready but swung the tiller over immediately.

"Well, this is IT!" he shouted as they completed going about. "Ready to gybe? – NOW" This time he gave them just a moment to reply. To gybe with an unprepared crew could easily turn what should be a controlled manoeuvre into total catastrophe.

The boom came over. Four heads ducked and instead of tacking more or less into the wind, the boat was running before it, bouncing along beside, but fortunately at some distance from, the billowing host of insects. She was moving north-west, long the edge of the mysterious cloud.

"Phew! Well done Nick! Near thing that!" gasped Kirstin.

"Who's going in the *Queen Mary*?" asked Gerald who was always eager for the next step in any action. Everyone except Carol was keen to have the job of collecting specimens. Carol dithered, unsure as to whether or not she actually wanted the thrill of meddling so closely with the Flies. In the end they decided that Nick had better stay in *Frolic* while Gerald should go in the plastic dinghy because he was a strong paddler.

"Carol stays with me," said Nick sensing the youngster's fear; and the girl breathed a sigh of grateful relief. "Kirsty and Gerr had the *Queen* out yesterday when they went fishing and learnt how to manage her eccentricities."

"She takes some getting used to," said Gerald. "She changes shape every time you pull the oars and you sort of bounce up and down as you row."

"And, for some unknown reason she goes round and round in circles like crazy," added Kirstin. "We more or less cottoned on how to deal with that; but, my word! It's not easy!"

Nick worried:

'Would they manage the tricky little rubber bubble well enough not to get caught by the Lake Flies? Should he abandon the whole idea?'

The others weren't thinking of danger. They were too keyed up.

The *Queen Mary* was pulled up alongside and her two crew members climbed cautiously aboard. The little craft wobbled and changed shape and did her best to tip them off into the water.

"We should've called her the *Bucking Bronco,*" said Gerald.

"Do be careful," urged Carol crossing her fingers.

"You bet. We'll take mammoth care not to catch Lake Fly pneumonia," Kirstin assured her relatives seriously.

"Pass the towel please, and the knife. Thank you. You can cast us off now."

The *Queen* was soon in the region where the miniscule creatures were still sparse.

"Let's *give it a burl* here," suggested Kirsty looking with wonder at the huge area of lake surface that was oily and squirming with a coating of emergent Flies. Her cousin paused with the paddles lifted and looked about.

"Crikey!" he said. "The air's like thick soup. Weird isn't it?"

He choked and spat out a mouthful of Flies. Kirstin was sneezing.

"*Holey doley!* (Heavens!) What a stink!" she spluttered.

"If we go a trifle further," suggested her foolhardy cousin, "we'll catch a lot with only one swipe of the towel. Then I'll row straight out while you collect them off the towel into the jars. Hope they enjoy the gin!" He spat again.

"Golly! It's dangerous to even talk!" he muttered through closed lips. Kirsty snuffled an answer with her hands over her nose and mouth.

"Yes. Oke. Go in deeper then. Only a smidgen, mind. That way we can make just one swing and get out quickly. But for heavens' sake don't go too far."

No one quite knew what happened next. Whether the wind changed slightly, or whether Gerald pulled a trifle harder than he had intended, or whether the *Queen* made one of her extraordinary movements, or whether the cloud was simply denser than they had anticipated, was a question later hotly debated. Whatever the cause they both suddenly found themselves coughing and spluttering uncontrollably. They should immediately have given up the scheme and retreated as fast as possible. Instead:

"Quick!" choked Gerald dropping the oars and shutting his mouth with a snap. Kirstin was sneezing as if she was trying to turn herself inside out. Horrified she saw that one of the paddles had slipped out through its loop and was floating in the revolting, greasy surface. With a shiver of horror she understood that with only one paddle they'd never escape the miasma of flies!

However, deciding that there was nothing to be done about that at the moment she hissed through clenched teeth: "Hold your breath!" and passed Gerr one of the sticks. They thrust the towel up like a banner on the end of its poles, and had planned to wave it through the deadly mist. But before they had time to co-ordinate their movements the towel was black on two sides and they were both snorting, wheezing and doing their best not to breathe or to open their mouths to gasp. That would, quite literally have been fatal.

Orders were unnecessary. With one accord the sticks were thrown into the bottom of the *Queen Mary*. The towel fell in a tumbled, blackened heap over them. Gerald seized the remaining oar and started paddling. His forceful swing, performed in a moment of panic had the providential effect of spinning their cockleshell towards the floating oar. In the nick of time Kirstin leant out and grabbed it. Then, trying not to gasp, paddling like fiends escaping from Hell, they made frantically for the edge of the mist.

Luckily the cloud had a deadening effect on the wind so the miasma hadn't advanced too far during their frantic activity. As they worked like mad to escape they were aware of the ominous, black central core of the mist behind the *Queen,* but it was encouraging to see that only a couple of metres of pale grey lay ahead between them and the relatively thin edge of the fog. Yet even that short distance was too far! Both felt that their lungs were on the point of bursting as they shot more or less clear of the spout of flies.

Gerald took a great gulp of air and immediately started to spit and sneeze and cough, all at the same time. Completely helpless, he couldn't paddle. Luckily Kirstin thought of pulling her shirt up over her face. With a desperate tug she wrenched the front and tearing it from under her life jacket she stretched it up over her head. She could barely see through the material but it acted as a sieve, which in this area of fewer insects, did not clog up too rapidly.

"Pull your tee shirt over your face," she gasped to her incapacitated cousin, and went on working her oar frenziedly. The *Queen,* of course, responded by spinning in tight circles!
"PADDLE!" roared Kirstin. Vaguely she knew she had screamed that word in exactly the same terrified tones not so long ago, but she didn't have time to sort out the memory. She plied her instrument furiously, trying to force the tiny bubble to move in a straight line.

Gerald tugged and pulled desperately to free his tee shirt. He was sure his lungs were about to explode. His life jacket was so tight that it was impossible to pull his shirt out and over his mouth and nose. He yanked madly but had to give up. Panic-ridden, he spotted the tea towel that was wrapped round the knife. The cloth was oily black on the outside. He unrolled it from the knife and threw it over his head with the side that was almost clean covering his face. Still spitting, he managed to wield his paddle with a vigour that matched Kirstin's. In a few moments they were in the extreme edge of the flies, their masks already blocked by tiny pitch-like specks. A moment later, tearing off their blinding protection, which was now completely covered, they held their breaths till they reached a place that seemed blessedly *almost* free of insects. They couldn't last out any longer and whether they suffocated or not they both had to gasp huge lungfuls of air. They were lucky! They found that they were able to breathe! It was marvellous; but horrible swallowing some of the stinking insects.

With large, scared eyes they stared at each other. Then they burst out laughing! What a sight they were – covered all over with a mucous-like coating of flies. Their hairs were matted with the malodorous pulp of dead insects. The nauseating creatures spread over eyelashes like thick mascara. Every inch of the paddlers and of the *Queen* was pinkish-black, slimy and stinking of fish.

"Pooh!" exclaimed Kirstin.
"D'you think we've got enough?" laughed Gerr with another cough, waving a hand over the several million creatures on the towel, and the billions of trillions on themselves and the boat. He spat out a few hundred Flies.
"Enough for every single person in Australia to do research for the next ten centuries!" Kirstin cleared her throat of a few more flies.
"Ugh! These things in my gullet make me feel really sick!"

Gerald rowed slowly back to *Frolic* while Kirstin filled the two enormous preserving jars and then rubbed off as much as she could of the remaining gunge from herself and the dinghy. The *Queen* left a messy wake as Kirsty scraped Flies overboard.

Seeing their relatives in trouble the two in the GP had been sorely tempted to change course and sail with all possible speed to their rescue. Luckily they realised how stupid and useless this would be.
"We'd only get into a worse mess, with *all* of us choking," said Nick desperately. "*Frolic*'s not as manoeuvrable as the plastic

whatsit. We'd take ages to pick them up and try to come back out again. It would be sheer suicide. And to try to sail right through would be worse. We'd never get even a tenth of the way."

"Yes," agreed Carol despairingly. They could hear the other two coughing and retching. It was dreadful not to be able to help.

The situation became even worse. *Frolic* was travelling much faster than the pillar of flies, which seemed at times to have become stationary. So as not to outstrip the flies and their embedded companions it became necessary to tack, with the result that they had to actually sail away from Gerr and Kirsty. As soon as feasible they tacked again and sailed back looking anxiously for the *Queen Mary* and her occupants. Dreadfully worried they watched the frenetic battle to escape from the choking mist. Carol didn't know she was muttering: "*Blue! Blue! Blue!*" which, in Aussie language meant: "Fright! Fright! Fright!"

It was not long in fact but it seemed like several aeons before it became evident that the two collectors were out of danger. *Frolic's* crew stared at them incredulously.

"What on earth... " started Nick.

As the toy dinghy drew nearer Carol blurted out: "Pooh! What a *stink*! Don't come near us, for Possum's sake!" The rubber duckling's crew looked at each other yet again. Then, without a word, they rolled over the *Queen's* soft sides and disappeared under water. They scrubbed themselves and their hair. They scraped flies off paddles and off the cockleshell. They scratched insects off the outsides of pickling jars. It was a tough job and not a pleasant one. The mucous was difficult to get rid of and the stench of bad fish remained even after all the sticky muck had been washed away.

Frolic circled for a long time while they scoured; and finally, when they were as clean as they could make themselves they were permitted to approach and hand over the jars full of tiny insects floating in gin. Then they set about cleaning the *Queen Mary* once more. And when that was done they started on themselves again.

"Good thing there's no shortage of water," said Nick.

Even when not a trace of any fly or mucous remained on the tiny bubble or on themselves her crew still had the fishy stink deep in their nostrils and throats.

"Yuk!" said Gerald.

"Ugh! Ugh! Ugh!" croaked Kirstin. "Will you pass me my hat and dark glasses, please? We'll sit in the *Queen* and you can tow us back like lepers. We'll scrape ourselves with Surf and Dettol when we are back in camp."

"Definitely" agreed Carol curtly, holding her nose as she caught their painter. She added heartlessly. "We won't allow you back into the community till you're thoroughly pongless!"

"They'll have to accept us back soon," said Gerr. "They'll be needing us to help pack the boats and as crew for the sail back south."

Although *Frolic* was badly hampered by the weight of the trailing dinghy and her load, the gallant boat began to pick up speed. A chortling wave formed below her bow as she caught the wind efficiently. Soon they would be back on Lumbo Island where Ella was presumably waiting – probably impatiently because the pages of her sodden books were all stuck together and impossible to read. When the washing was done she would have nothing to do and would start getting bored.

"Oh yes!" said Kirsty coming back to reality with a bang. "We'll have to get cracking or we won't get across the lake by tomorrow night to camp somewhere that's safe in the south."

"We *must* get back to Baboon Bay the day after tomorrow and to Lawara the next day," said Carol. "It's Tony's birthday on Saturday and we wouldn't want to disappoint him."

"Catting Kangas!" exclaimed Nick. "We absolutely *must* get back in time."

As he finished speaking they had the most awful shock.

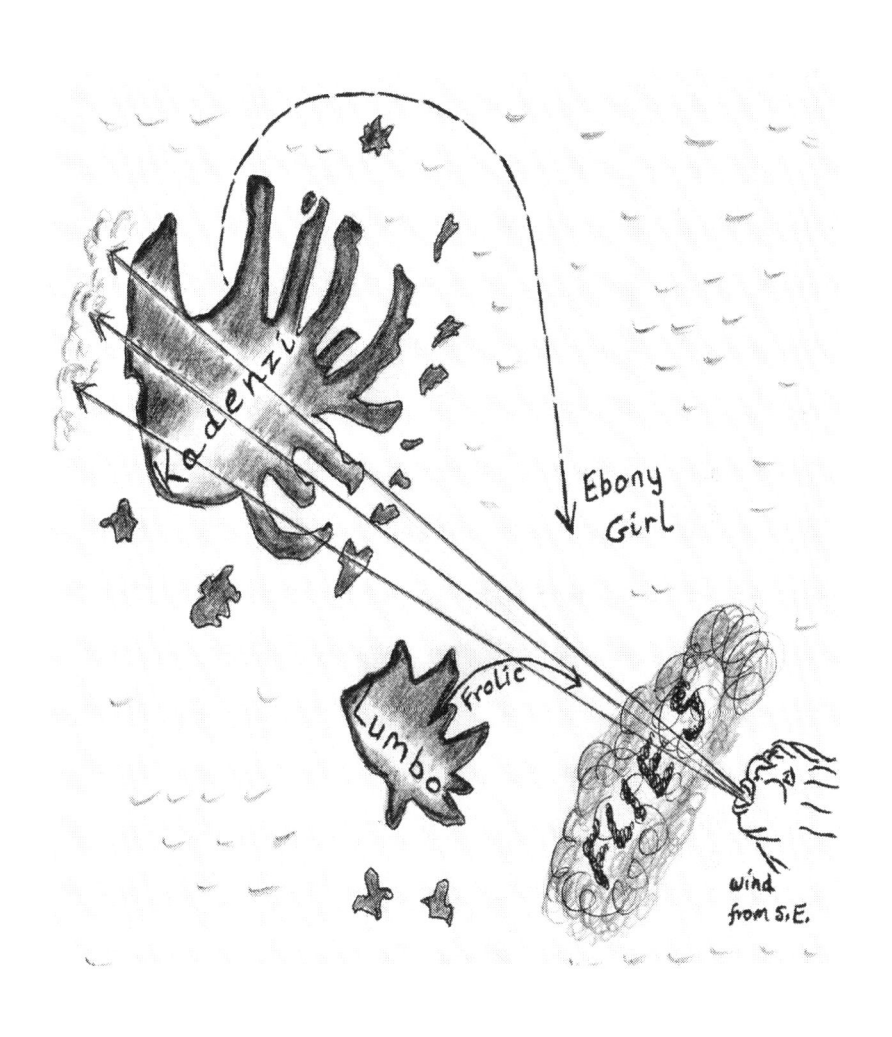

59. *Frolic*'s route towards the Flies, and a strange motor cruiser's course out from Kadenzi Bay.
(At that stage nobody knew that the cruiser was called *Ebony Girl*.)

CHAPTER 44

DOUBLE DISASTER.

Nell was not waiting impatiently. She was standing under a cactus tree absolutely petrified with fear.

When *Frolic* and her crew had gone, Nell took the dirty clothes some distance along the creek to a rock from which she could scrub easily. It also had the advantage of being near to where their inlet opened up to the lake so her rubbing wouldn't pollute the cove with soapsuds. Enjoying the sunshine and glorious surroundings she hummed away as she pounded the clothes against rocks. Eyes of passing Cormorants and Darters seemed to stare with blue curiosity.

Later, when Nell was about to spread clean garments on bushes to dry, she glanced out to 'sea'. There, from the direction of Kadenzi Island a 40ft motorised cabin cruiser, with black hull and white superstructure, was speeding in a lather of spray. It was heading towards *Frolic* and the column of Lake Flies.

Ella nearly had a fit! Abandoning her wet bundle she anxiously puffed up the side of the creek in what, for her, was record time. She looked over the cliff and watched the fast boat with increasing concern. Yes – it was going straight for *Frolic* and the *Queen Mary*.

Whatever should she do? What *could* she do? The brief and only answer was 'Nothing'. Stiff with tension, and stretched to her short maximum height, she instinctively hid behind tall cactus plants. Her eyes remained glued to the three craft. At first *Frolic* seemed oblivious of the newcomer.

A sudden luff and then a change of course indicated that Ella's brother and cousins had become aware of the approaching menace. But the GP, especially with the laden rubber bubble in tow, was no match for the high-powered cruiser. In a very short time the sailing boat was reached.

60. Ella transfixed
as she watches her companions and *Frolic* being captured.

The black hull stopped across *Frolic's* bows. Even from so far away Ella noticed its flaking paint. The horrified watcher also registered that the strange attacker was big enough to sleep about 6 people and, although the enemy boat had two very tall masts she had no sails, and was shaped like a tiny steamer. She even had what the cousins later discovered was a fake funnel that could emit false smoke.

Men on the motorboat appeared to be shouting at Nick and his cousins. Nell could not hear what was going on but negotiations took a long time. Why hadn't she brought binoculars with her? In fact it was lucky that she couldn't see details or hear the verbal fight put up by the crew in *Frolic.* She'd have been frightened silly.

Finally, menaced with guns, the four captives, angry and rebellious, were forced to tie *Frolic* behind the cruiser and to climb on board with their captors, who bashed them roughly. Again it was a good thing that the solitary viewer couldn't see details.

There appeared to be some trouble with the miniature steamer's engine but it finally choked into life and, utterly distraught, Nell watched the big boat, towing *Frolic* and the *Queen,* disappear from sight round one of the distant fingers of Kadenzi Island.

Eventually Ella slowly stopped standing on tiptoe and tottered down the rough side of the inlet. A bundle of sopping items would help no one so automatically she spread the washed clothes on vegetation to dry. That gave her something to do while she tried to force her brain to work. But no inspiration came; and feeling very shaky, she made her way between rocks and trees, back along the side of the creek towards the little beach at its head where they had slept.

Nell noticed tracks on the sands below: a double parallel set of claw marks with a long line between them. Those patterns had not been there when she had left. Suddenly she remembered the previous evening's conversation... snakes? No – monitor lizards... crocodiles...

Whatever they were, this cove was obviously well frequented by scaly creatures. She hesitated above the lapping water.

But it was no use standing forever staring aghast at that awful evidence of nasty visitors. Bravely she stepped down from the rough grass on the side of the gulley and advanced onto the sand. A movement in the creek caught her eye. What *now*? Springing round to face the latest threat, Ella's eyes widened in horror mingled with disbelief. Two large and extraordinary shapes were sliding out of the water. A nauseating mixture of sea-weedy browns and greens, they blended perfectly with the rocks, and were almost invisible in the scarily shadowed water of the cove. A totally irrelevant thought flashed through Nell's panicking mind:
'More ghastly, huge, scaly things! The most terrifying bodies I've ever seen! What sort of tracks do *these* monsters make?'

For some unaccountable reason, the fact that their bodies were matt and not shiny – as they should have been when they slithered out of water – seemed to make the ghastly creatures even more horrifying. Eleanor opened her mouth to scream. But no sound emerged. Could this be an appalling nightmare? Paralysed with terror, she could neither shout nor run. Her legs buckled under her and she fell onto the sand.

The hideous beasts shook themselves and, on four clumsily-flapping webbed feet, they hurried towards her with ungainly steps and great determination.

****

When it became evident that Ebony Girl was bearing down on them Kirstin swore at length. Nick said:
"We can't escape. I'll stay in *Frolic* as long as possible. I may be able to sail off and get help."

He had muddled ideas of 'the captain never leaves his ship' and he was so shocked that he never appreciated that there was absolutely no chance of him escaping, let alone of bringing help. Then he spoke urgently:
"Quick. Take off your life jackets. But do it casually. We don't

want them to notice. Carol stuff them above the bow buoyancy bag and below the front deck."

"Why?" asked Gerald in a petulant tone that hinted at how frightened he was.

"The blighters'll pinch anything they can," said Nick. "They may not notice the life jackets jammed out of sight."

The menacing boat came very close and stopped. Two men on the deck above were cocking guns. *Frolic's* crew had no choice. They had to obey. Kirstin and Carol cringed, and swore again. Gerald growled, but reached for the rope ladder that had been let down. As he climbed over the railing one of the bullies struck him a blow that sent him reeling to the deck. Another man overcame Gerr's struggles, bound his hands behind his back and threw him against a locker.

"I'll go next," croaked Kirstin clutching the bottom of the rope ladder. As she reached the top, her hat and dark glasses were snatched from her head. She shouted in anger; but was soon tied like Gerald. Carol and Nick fared no better.

Bruised, dazzled without sun glasses, and with hands lashed, the four captives, furious and mutinous, were forced to sit back to back on deck. They were scared for themselves and worried about Ella. Had she seen what had happened, or would she wonder why they never came back? In either case what would she do? And what was going to become of them?

Their abductors spoke neither English nor Kangi so communications were difficult. As the cruiser gathered speed and made for Kadenzi Island it became obvious that the fellows were merely obeying orders. Apart from sadistically enjoying their power, they were totally indifferent to their prisoners.

Nick was desperate.

"Slow down. Go slowly!" he screamed. "You will break boat!" The swarthy lout standing nearby holding a revolver in a limp, slipshod manner that the captives considered highly dangerous looked at Nick merely as if a hyena had yodelled in the far distance. The khaki-faced bully was not in the least interested in anything these white people might have to say.

They were just a thorough nuisance. He didn't hold with taking prisoners – unless they came in handy; and how, in the Spirit of Mlungu's name were these youngsters going to be of any use – except, perhaps, in soup?

The camp on Kadenzi was completely out of food. There was no maize flour, no cassava, no rice and, of course, not a vegetable of any kind. Chickens had been finished off some time back and any edible vegetation growing on the island had long since been picked bare. These days the band on Kadenzi existed on such fish as they could catch; but they had not been supplied with adequate or suitable nets. As none of them were lake men they had no idea how to make traps so any catches they achieved were pathetic. In any case, coming from mountain or desert regions, they did not care for fish. They liked to eat porridge made of maize flour and, whenever possible, trapped wild animals for meat. On Kadenzi there was no game left to catch.

The whole situation had been aggravated by a huge influx from mainland gangs. Many visiting petty chiefs with their supporters had arrived for a meeting with the overall boss so the unwelcome visitors had to be tolerated. They made it very clear that they expected at least *some* food. These days in their guerrilla-torn country no one ever hoped for *enough* to eat. The Island's Commandante had promised the intruders rations – but there *was* no food. There had been nothing in any way edible for so long that even the grain stores had rotted and fallen to pieces. So where did the visitors expect those rations to come from? That's what the surly guard wanted to know. And now, instead of providing meals for his starving troops, the Commandante had sent him to capture more mouths to feed!

Passing his gun from one hand to the other in bored frustration, the fellow could not fathom the reason for the Chief's orders, nor why the brutish leader had murmured "Providential" as he had dispatched the cruiser on this mission. This guard had not been on Kadenzi last time prisoners had been eaten to solve the food crisis.

A noise made the warder look at his prisoners. That troublesome youth was talking again. Almost, it seemed, as if he was giving an order! What cheek! The rebel looked vaguely surprised and very annoyed. He pondered whether or not to crash the irritating lad over the head with the butt of his gun. That would shut the nuisance up all right! But his was not a needle brain. As his thoughts rotated slowly he saw that Nick, although restrained by his bonds, was trying to mime something. This was beyond the watchman. He banged on the cabin window. Inside were four men: a fellow of mixed origins managing the boat, and a black giant with two other vicious-looking ruffians idly lolling on seats with torn cushions. At the guard's knock one of the loungers emerged reluctantly on deck.

Nick was relieved to see that he was not the short sallow European who, if possible, seemed to be even more unpleasant than the rest. It was the man who knew a few words of Portuguese. The cousins had picked up a smattering of Spanish from their visits to grandparents in Spain. Would Nick's poorly remembered Castilian be understood?
"Too fast!" he attempted, at the same time trying as best he could to explain with actions. He pointed to *Frolic*. "Too fast… Break in pieces."

The words, or perhaps the movements, made some impression. The fellow raised his head arrogantly and returned to the cabin. Soon they felt the engines being throttled down and the boat settled to a much more sedate pace. The four captives sighed thankfully. For the time being, their immediate worries calmed. They relaxed very slightly.

They were, however, still extremely nervous about what lay ahead.
"Did you see the boat's name?" asked Nick in a voice that oozed despair.
"It's the *Ebony Girl*," said Kirstin.
Gerald looked even more alarmed. 'What was it his mother had told him not so long ago about some newspaper paragraph that his father had read out at breakfast?'

Gerr jumped and exclaimed:

"Oh!" in deeply shocked tones.

"Precisely!" Nick looked thoroughly miserable. "That lot who got blown across the lake last year when the engine of their cruiser failed. They vanished! No-one knows what became of them."

"They got eaten, you said," Gerald chipped in with terrifying accuracy, and total lack of tact.

"I wasn't going to remind you about that," said Nick.

"Well – what about them?" asked Kirstin.

"Their boat was called *Ebony Girl*."

"NO!"

"'Fraid so."

"Was their *Ebony Girl* a cabin cruiser shaped like a miniature steamer?"

"Yes."

"And did it have tall masts even though it worked off an engine?"

"Yes."

"*Blue!*" exclaimed Kirstin.

After that they were all even more terrified and depressed.

It seemed that, like the previous owners of *Ebony Girl*, the four captives were about to vanish in grisly circumstances. No one would ever hear about them again.

Even though their own plight was so appalling the prisoners also worried frantically about Ella – alone on Lumbo Island. She couldn't sail *Percy*. She'd be stuck there until her provisions ran out. They didn't know that Ella was actually in an even more wretched predicament than the one they were imagining.

A double disaster had hit the cousins. Four of them were in the hands of brutal desperadoes and Nell was the prey of foul leviathans that were even now emerging from the deeps and making straight for her.

CHAPTER 45

Captives.

With faulty engines several times juddering painfully and progressing in jerks, *Ebony Girl* skirted round the east and north of Kadenzi so the captives passed the time studying the inlets between the nine 'fingers'. Like the other islands in this part of the lake, Kadenzi rose steeply from the water. Short but steep cliffs were eroded vertically into lumpy pillars and grotesque buttresses.

The cruiser idled into the island's only bay. Surrounded by low cliffs about 6 metres high, it was on the north west coast between the 'thumb' (on the west) and the 'first finger' (on the east.) *(Maps on page 301 and 324.)* The mock-steamer's painter was tied to a floating plastic barrel that was anchored on the east side of the 'harbour'. The prisoners were appalled to see how many scores of men were lying about on shore.

Emerging from the cabin, the surly guerrillas indicated that their victims were to climb down into a large war canoe that was paddled out to meet them. As they were chivvied into it, Nick thought scornfully:
'Lazy blighters! They've not tidied anything on the cruiser or in *Frolic*. But that's good. Perhaps they won't find our life jackets or the preserving jars full of Lake Flies."

It was tricky balancing the enormous hollowed-out log which, like all dugouts, had a pronounced tendency to roll. The bullies followed and two of them picked up pointed, native-style paddles from the water swirling in the bottom of the canoe and helped the original paddler to return to the beach.

A few louts rose from where they were lounging under local scrub trees and ambled over to inspect the newcomers. 'How emaciated they are!' thought Kirstin. 'Like grisly walking skeletons. You can almost hear the bones rattling,' and she was not being funny. The islanders seemed strangely excited and keyed up. One of them prodded Carol and several moved towards her sister. Kirstin edged away and clenched her fists.

"Stop that!" growled Nick. He and Gerald tried to get between the girls and their tormentors, but they would all have been swept away had the guards not shouted something in their uncouth language. The hungry thugs retreated grudgingly but were not cowed. They grinned rudely and made obscene gestures. It was clear that when they got their hands on the captives they would inflict sadistic torture and satisfy lust. Carol repressed sobs with difficulty so Kirstin, just as upset and almost stiff with fear, put a protective arm round her younger sister. All four captives were so traumatised they had trouble forcing their feet to move forward.

The terrified prisoners were pushed roughly up a slope to a dilapidated tent draped with camouflaged netting. It was also hidden under natural branches that had been chopped from trees further inland. The boughs were dead, dry and well on the way to being destroyed by termites. Evidently this camp had been here for a long time. From inside came loud bubbling snores. They sounded as if, in a dark cellar, large putrid puffballs were constantly swelling up and then bursting. The cousins looked at each other in disgust. Their guard stood perplexed. His orders had been primarily to capture the boat and then, as a secondary 'bonus', to bring the crew to the hungry camp's Commandante. No one had expected the sailors to be teenagers! But now, escaping the sultry heat, the commander was asleep. The sentry outside the tent did not dare to rouse his choleric chief.

Nick and his cousins were marched back to the shore and forced along a narrow shelf of rock just above water level on the east of the bay. A number of deep holes had been hacked out of the cliff face for use as storerooms or dwellings. The group was directed to the last cave, the one furthest from the beach. The guard waved his gun but did not force them inside so they sat in a row on the damp ledge with their backs to the smelly, man-made hole and looked over the rebel camp while their watchman perched on a nearby rock and picked between his toes.

The other soldiers, whose skins ranged through all shades from malarial white and bilious yellow, through khaki, to pitch black, had fallen back under the trees. They all looked desperately thin, ragged and tired, but not particularly evil – just brutalised by circumstances. Most lay about spiritlessly.
One group was sluggishly examining the captives' cameras. Others were playing a game with pebbles that they lackadaisically moved between rows of small holes which had been hollowed out of the ground. There was none of the banter and excitement that usually accompanied such games in villages and market places.

The cousins seemed to be the only people on the island with enough energy to use their tongues. In low, desperate voices they discussed their frightful situation till there was nothing left to say. The guards were now so uninterested and lethargic that Gerald suggested that it might be possible to swim out to *Frolic* during the night and steal their boat back. Perhaps they would be able to push or paddle her round the 'thumb' promontory, or even to tow her behind the little *Queen Mary* which could be paddled less conspicuously since she was so much closer to the water than *Frolic*.

"Once out of sight, we'll be able to raise the sails and make headway back to Ella and *Percy*," said Nick optimistically.
"Of course it won't be that easy," said Kirstin accurately.
"And once our absence is noticed *Ebony Girl* will give chase and catch us in no time," added Gerald. "But maybe her temperamental engines won't function," he suggested hopefully; but his tone held no conviction.
"Well, what else can we attempt – cross the island and try to swim back to Lumbo?"
Kirstin had reservations about that:
"I know the lake isn't big enough to have proper tides, but there are definite currents. There's even one round this

tiny bay. See how feathers and dead leaves are swirling towards the western cliffs." She looked thoughtfully at her young sister. "That crossing back to Lumbo's a couple of miles or more and there could well be a rip sweeping sideways between the two islands. We might find it tricky to reach Ella if we swim for it. And our life jackets are in *Frolic*."

Nick also muttered desperately:

"We're not going to swim for it. We'd never make it; and we're not going to desert *Frolic!* We're not going to leave her behind with these savages!"

Gerald and Kirstin had been glad to sit in the sun and dry off after their scrubbing antics in the lake; but no longer wet, they had become dreadfully hot.

"I'm roasting," groaned Gerr.

"We all are," said Nick moving into a small patch of shade cast by a rock. Now that they had finished their desperate discussion there was no longer any need to remain huddled together. They could each find such relief as rocks provided. Or they could go into the unpleasant cave.

"We just have to bear the temperature," said Carol who was almost fainting with fright and heat.

Before them, beyond the narrow opening of the bay, stretched sparkling blue water, fascinating green islands and calm distant mountains. It was all breathtakingly beautiful and such a contrast to the squalor in which these Bafando men were existing. Even distant clouds banking up in tremendous piles did not reduce the splendour of the scenery. If anything the brilliant white cumulous and the mauve and purple shadows that they cast made everything more grandiose and magnificent. The wind was steady and fresh. It would have been a great sail scudding back to Baboon Bay.

"We'll never make it in time for Tony's birthday," sighed Carol.

'We'll probably never make it at all – *ever*!' thought the others, but no one voiced such a doleful opinion.

"I'm hungry," announced Gerald later.

"Yes," agreed the other three in flat voices. Kirstin stated the obvious again:

"No use expecting any food from these bastards. Just look at them. Their ribs are sticking way out."

"They're clearly starving," agreed Nick.

"I can't see a single grain store, or goat or chicken."

"They've nothing edible for themselves and definitely nothing to spare for prisoners." stated Carol pathetically. Again only a huge effort of will stopped her tears.

Kirstin glared at colourful chips of gravel that the waves rolled back and forth. The lads swore. They all scowled, looked defiant, and worried about Ella, wondering what she was doing. They couldn't think what she ought to do, but could only hope that she was being sensible and staying in camp.

Suddenly a fight erupted among the game players. Two men punched and shouted. Their friends took sides. Knives flashed. Screams and shrieks mingled with abuse. Many of the struggling group quickly gave up, bleeding and exhausted. They collapsed onto the sand; but two battled on. Gerald nearly threw up when he noticed that one had a gaping machete wound in his abdomen. Even as the injured fellow tried with one hand to hold his intestines in place, with his other hand he gashed a long knife across the other man's throat. They both fell, screaming; and squirmed in the pebbly sand.

Their companions now stood around watching apathetically. Both fighters would undoubtedly die.

'They must be in terrible agony,' thought Kirstin.

After some time, during which the four captives suffered for the wounded couple, there was a curt order. Each of the writhing victims of their own fury was approached by two men. The bleeding fighters shrieked bestially even louder, and attempted to escape but, incapable of movement, they were picked up and carried roughly, still screeching the only sorts of ghastly sounds that their wounds allowed. Their blood-curdling, anguished howls continued till they reached the 'thumb' peninsular on the far side of the bay from the cousin's cave. There, from the end of the cliffs, the bodies were hurled off onto the rocks below. Then there was silence.

The shock was tremendous! Carol hid her head in her knees and sobbed loudly. Straining backwards, with her hands over her mouth, Kirstin was shaking all over. Nicholas and Gerald, who had risen, were stopped by the guard. They stood with clenched fists and gaping mouths. Nobody could utter a word; but, with an evil leer, the guard grinned.
"Plenty crocodiles," he croaked happily.

Stupor fell over the camp and spread with the sun's midday assault. On Kadenzi there was no attempt to prepare anything to eat. Rats and hyrax had been exterminated. Even snakes had been boiled for rations. Edible plants had been decimated and imported food was finished. Their unsuitable fishing gear had been lost or damaged in the storm and not one of the men knew how to mend it or had the initiative to try. Very soon desperation would drive them to get sustenance *somehow.*

A couple of haggard thugs ambled across to the guard and made remarks which, judging by the gestures deplored the leanness of the four captives. They took hold of Gerald's arm and pinched his flesh. The boy shrugged them off and clenching his fists, prepared to struggle. At least going down fighting might be better than just sitting speculating about sufferings ahead. One of the visitors swung the butt of his rifle and Gerald fell onto the sand below their ledge. He was almost unconscious, but when his cousins tried to run to him they were stopped brutally.

The guard rammed his pistol into Nick's stomach winding him and throwing him against the cliff. Two villains fingered Kirstin's thighs and pawed at Carol's buttocks. They squeezed unmercifully leaving raised purple bruises. The girls kicked and hit out. They tried to bite; but the three bullies just laughed and avoided the blows. Kirstin looked round in panic. There was absolutely nowhere to escape. If they ran they would be deserting the boys and, anyway, they'd only rush slap into scores of other guerrillas lying about under the trees. Appalled, she noticed that some louts were piling wood for a fire – a big one... Surely... Surely... No! It was too ghastly! Cannibals? These days? She fought fiercely, like a civet protecting her kittens, and Carol did her best as well. They were no match for the burly brutes. Others were approaching.

Nick ground his teeth and tried to move. The pistol rammed sadistically again and he doubled up, groaning in agony. Gerald began to struggle up. A cruelly booted foot was brought into action and Gerr lay perfectly still. There was a ragged cheer from some of the bandits. Carol's arm was being twisted beyond endurance. She thought it would soon come right off. She screamed in torment and terror. The rebels laughed and pushed her towards the fire. Would they be satisfied with cooking their victims or would lust take over first? What might they do to the girls before they ate them? – and even to the boys as well? Nick's mind went completely blank with horror.

61. Kangi villages had grain stores like these.
Kadenzi just had nothing to store.

CHAPTER 46

Fateful Flies.

Suddenly a shrill, gurgling cry came from somewhere in the trees above the camp. Lay-abouts lying on the beach roused themselves and looked round. The brutes torturing the girls and those who were preparing the monstrous fire paused. The excitement which had for so long been suppressed, overflowed as the whole company dropped whatever they were doing, picked up an assortment of saucepans, blankets, baskets, mats, and any other gear that came to hand, and stood waiting. An electric tenseness tingled out of each man. They were keyed to some peculiarly high pitch. What was about to happen? The prisoners became extra tense and nervous. What was going to be done to them?

The girls were abandoned. Carol crept back to the cave where the guard was dithering, infected by the same fever that had gripped his companions. Very roughly he shoved the girls and Nick into the cavern and threatened to shoot if they dared to emerge. Glaring at Gerald sprawled on the beach he decided that the boy could stay there and if waves splashed over his face and drowned him – well, who cared? Then he hurried to join his companions round the bay.

Completely winded, Nick couldn't move but the Aussies crept cautiously out of the cave and fetched water in cupped hands to splash on Gerald's face. Slowly he came round. A large bruise was swelling on his temple.

They all knew what had diverted everyone's attention when a nauseating stench of bad fish hit the island and the sun seemed to go in. The wind had slowly moved the source of hatching Flies and now it was sweeping a cloud of insects over Kadenzi. With cries of delight the starved bandits greeted this approaching feast. Meat was meat, and highly desirable; but Lake Flies were a delicacy much sought after even in their mountain villages. So long as the cloud was not suffocatingly thick they would be able to catch the treat of a lifetime. They made ready to run — either to escape death from excess of midges, or to catch as many from the edge of the cloud as they could. When the men realised that the Flies were going to miss the beach they ran up tracks to the tops of the cliffs and hurried to position themselves on the borders of the advancing mist. A few over-enthusiastic catchers turned back choking, having ventured too far into the miasma. The remainder, shrieking and laughing hysterically, with frantic, famished delight, swung their weapons and containers, clothes and even paddles through the stinking insects. It was a scene worthy of an Old Master's vision of Hell.

"Please don't let the Flies come down here," prayed Kirstin watching intently. If the creatures spread all over the island the only way to survive would be to take to the cruiser and she knew that the captives would never be given space on that. Even crammed to the gunwales the forty-foot boat wouldn't hold more than a third of the soldiers anyway. Besides — Gerald, sitting on the sand resting his head on his knees, was groggy and still couldn't stand up. He wouldn't be able to run or swim or fight for a place. They watched events anxiously.

Nick, who was still doubled up, looked dubiously at Gerr.
"Let's make a go for it," he urged with a groan. "They're all so busy. They'll never notice if we swipe *Frolic* and vanish."
"But we wouldn't get far," pointed out Kirstin "They'd come after us in *Ebony Girl* and catch us in next to no time. Then they'll treat us still more viciously than they already have."
"Even if we get as far as Ella and *Percy* it'd be no good," agreed Carol wondering if she'd ever again be able to haul on a jibsheet, let alone a mainsheet. Her arm felt as if it would never recover from that unmerciful twisting. "They'd catch us and they'd find *Percy* and Ella as well."
"Take the cruiser," whispered Gerald holding his head. They looked down at him in amazement. Would they be able to start it? Would they be capable of managing such a big, powerful craft?

Already it was too late. Laden with fish-smelling mucous, the rebels were returning in high spirits, yelling, stamping their feet, chanting and gesticulating violently like Chaka's Zulu Impies returning victorious after a particularly gory battle.

"When we leave we must give ourselves time to get properly clear – before they notice... We'll try as early as possible tonight," said Nick, who was still suffering.

"We'll have to abandon all our stuff on Lumbo," said Kirstin. "There won't be space in *Percy* for *takunda* as well as us five."

The Flies had swept over the south of the island. Now rebels were beating trees and bushes with long sticks to shake down any insects that may have lodged on plants. They returned with baskets full of black mush. Carol was nearly sick at the sight but the ravenous bandits were overjoyed. Shoving handfuls into their mouths, and manipulating the gunge like infants with playdough, they squashed Flies into small round cakes that they spread on rocks or on bamboo mats to dry. These delicacies would be consumed boiled or dry in the days to come. Now that the men had food to eat and plenty to do they cast only occasional glances at the prisoners. The four captives could only be grateful for their neglect.

As hours passed and cake-making came to an end the camp fell back into dazed lethargy. Replete now, in patches of shade and oblivious to the stink, gorged guerrillas lay sleeping in ungainly postures slapping away ordinary flies, hippo flies and bluebottles that had arrived from "nowhere". They buzzed in thousands over the stinking mounds of drying pulp. The only good thing about the stench was that it effectively stopped the cousins from feeling hungry.

The day cooled and the camp slowly came to life. Rifles were cleaned. Some men stripped naked and without any modesty, washed in the lake. Clothes that had been lying on rocks all day were put on and hats torn from the cousins' heads moved amongst yachting caps and other items that appeared incongruous on this emaciated, graceless crowd. They indicated clearly that to supply their needs the bandits stole from prisoners or made use of flotsam from the lake.

Suddenly about two hundred people were wandering about. A general air of spit and polish pervaded though there was pathetically little to polish. Using bundles of twigs a couple of cripples started to sweep a large empty space that was evidently a parade ground and living area.

"That bare patch is the only 'giveaway' that a spotter 'plane could find of the encampment," remarked Nick.

"Yes, except for the boats and canoes," agreed Carol.

"A 'plane might possibly notice the lack of trees which have been torn down for firewood," said Kirstin.

"No. It's indistinguishable from any innocent island," declared Gerald. "All signs of habitation are hidden. No-one would ever suspect Kadenzi as being a bandits' hideout."

With its many inlets, and the man-made caves, far from normal fishing and steamer routes, Kadenzi Island was well positioned for evil powerboat forays to both east and west sides of the lake. It was an ideal place for a rebel camp.

62. Spirals of dangerous Lake Flies on the horizon.
(Spectacular in colour on the website: www.daphne.es)

CHAPTER 47

Pinnacle Prison.

Gerald was still dizzy and had to be supported when the cousins were forced towards the camp Commandante's tent. The gross fellow was sitting in a torn and wobbly canvas chair, observing the approaching prisoners with painful, half-closed, eyes. They were streaming from some infection so he wiped them from time to time with a soiled rag. One leg of his filthy trousers was ripped off unevenly below the knee and there were so many enormous rents in his stained singlet that it was like a collection of rags that had somehow been haphazardly tied together. He slouched heavily, frowning at his thoughts. In front of him, on a primitive and rickety camp table two insignificant pieces of smoked fish were dwarfed by the garish pattern on a chipped enamel plate. His stomach bulged repulsively over a wide, torn-plastic belt which had two revolvers and a knife attached.

When the Comandante glowered at the guard, and growled a remark the man cringed.
"Bah!" The chief spat at their feet, and Kirstin stepped back disdainfully.
"*Bogan!*" (Rude, unkempt, sloven) she muttered. The bulk in the chair threw a rough question at them but none of the captives could understand.
'If the leader is so repulsive,' thought Gerald, 'it's no wonder his men are foul – just hellhounds.'

Carol was staring with loathing at the fellow's bullet head. It had once been shaved but now had sores between untidy, grizzled stubble that stuck up unevenly from a greyish pate. His face was the colour of putty. In contrast to his almost bald scalp, his chest and stomach were covered in a thick mat of wildly curling pepper-and-salt whiskers. They parted to reveal a gruesome sight: wrinkled grey skin in a bald patch round his navel. Nick shivered with disgust and horror.

'This beastly creature will delight in the vilest tortures," he concluded and looked away.

The bettle nuts, which the Commandante chewed constantly, had stained his lips, teeth and tongue a dirty red-brown. He spat often with spittle of the same odious colour so the corner of his tent was smirched with dark splotches that showed he didn't care where his foul shots landed. Again he shouted coarsely at the cousins; but, although very frightened, they could only shake their heads to indicate that it was impossible to make out what he was saying.

"Ha! Kangi!" he yelled disparagingly, making a kicking gesture with one cracked and calloused bare foot.
"No. English," said Nick boldly, "or French if you like… or perhaps Spanish."
"Bah!" It seemed to be the gangster's favourite expression. "Children! No good!" He cursed as he slapped a mosquito off his unshaven face. In fact Gerald and Nick were bigger and stronger than many of the troops on Kadenzi but they hoped that the boss was stating that they were unfit to become part of his army and not that he was saying they were insufficient to provide a decent meal. Perhaps the next explosion explained matters:
"No understand! No understand! No good! Bah!"

Emitting a tremendous spurt of bettle juice, the bully began a long harangue in his own tongue, inserting a word of English, Kangi and Portuguese here and there. His prisoners gathered that he couldn't fathom why they had come interfering; that he was gloating over the capture of a sturdy boat; that there was no food for anyone; and that they were not only useless but also a great trouble. In the same breath he hinted that they would solve part of his food problem, and that, although they were edible, he wished that they had been dropped overboard.
"Charming!" muttered Gerald under his breath.
"Swine!" breathed Kirstin with Australian directness.
"Don't antagonise him" whispered Nick sensibly.
Carol felt the brute's pale blue stare sizing her up and bit her

lip till it bled. She forced herself not to sob. As tears ran down her cheeks in uncontrollable streams another of those inhuman gurgling screeches, like the shrieks that had announced the arrival of Lake Flies, interrupted the Chief's monologue.

The Camp Lookout, a ragged fellow like the rest, but considered very smart because he wore a tea cosy on his head, came clattering down a path from the interior of the island. The tea cosy was impossibly hot in this climate but it concealed a shocking scar where part of his skull had been slashed dreadfully. Another ancient wound – a ghastly gash right across his face – explained his extraordinary, burbling speech. Although healed, it would never close but revealed a damaged tongue and mutilated lips which could not form words correctly. His comrades were used to interpreting his squeals so they seemed to understand what he was saying.

He was unusual. Other bandit camps posted sentries regularly but here on Kadenzi a watch was generally considered unnecessary. Today, however, an important visitor was expected so a lookout had been positioned, and he was having a busy time. It was this watchman who had seen *Frolic*, and later, the approaching Lake Flies. Now he was announcing the sighting of two boats. The big boss was about to arrive.

Immediately preparations, which could have been made long ago, were started. There was frantic activity throughout the camp. The Commandante shouted impatiently at the quaking cousins who were wondering what on earth was happening. The repulsive beast waved pudgy arms and yelled orders to anyone in hearing of his hoarse voice. The prisoners had become a nuisance to be disposed of urgently, hustled away and hurried up a track towards the top of the island.

Four large men, armed with knives, machetes and guns, accompanied them. Two carried a long wooden beam that seemed an unnecessary burden. The captives eyed it askance. Weren't the days of walking the plank over? And if they *were* going to be forced to walk the plank surely that would have been a spectacle to be performed in front of the whole company – not in some private place remote from the camp? However, if they *were* forced to jump into the lake they were all good swimmers... But the rebels would doubtless take pot shots. Did they keep 'pet' crocodiles?

Map of Kadenzi Island, showing: Pinnacle Prison, Frolic & Ebony Girl, Thumb, Index, Second, Third, Fourth, Fifth, Sixth, Seventh, Eighth, Ninth; Camp, Kt Creek, 2nd Creek, 3rd Creek, 4th Creek, 5th Creek, 6th Creek, 7th Creek, 8th Creek; Flotsam Fleet.

KK — Kangi King
M — Maega
D — Dhow
Z — Zodiac
L — Launch

63. Kadenzi at dawn.

They were pushed along a well-trodden but circuitous path where the going was very rough. Carol's ankle was hurting badly and she wondered how the villain with a festering leg wound could keep up such a pace. She was glad to note that her dark glasses were too small for the lout who had stolen them. They obviously pinched his nose and ears terribly. The left lens was already criss-crossed with cracks.

Skirting a rocky hill, they by-passed Kadenzi's index 'finger' and reached the base of the island's second 'finger', which would have been the 'middle' finger of any normal hand. Kadenzi had nine 'fingers' and a thumb. This 'second finger' was by far the highest of any of the promontories and, parallel with the index 'finger', it curved back towards the bay from which they had just come. Wondering, they had to obey their guards and stumbled as fast as possible to the far end of this peninsular.

Then the ghastly truth of their situation hit them. Nearly three metres away from the edge of the cliff reared a tiny outcrop of rock: a sheer spire-like spike. The top of this was almost flat with a few stunted bushes growing in thin soil. The sides were not only vertical and completely bare of vegetation but were surrounded with sharply eroded pinnacles that reached about half way up and pointed skywards like vicious needles. It was a perfect prison from which there could be no hope of unaided escape. Clearly the rock had once been the tip of the 'second finger'. It looked as if some giant had sliced a small chunk off the promontory's extremity and left the amputated section in place. A dark, angled gully separated two sides of the horrifying spit from two walls of the chopped 'finger'.

The cousins could hear lake water far below sucking and oozing as it washed between fearsome rocks that filled the bottom of the chasm. A third side of the prison looked across a narrow creek towards the index 'finger', and the fourth precipitous boundary had the lake as an endless moat. Churning water beat against all sides of the thin, fearsome pillar. Waves smashed cruelly against sharp boulders, and in the confined channel froth seethed backwards and forwards menacingly. A foul odour rose from below.

The prisoners' muscles seized up. Their flesh seemed to shrivel into tiny lumps as they watched two men lower the unsmoothed length of wood across the abyss. It landed with a sullen thud and suddenly, from a portion of the deep, gruesome trench, two repulsive vultures loped into sight, and trying to take off, laboured clumsily over jumbled rocks, then, with difficulty, flapped away in ungainly flight. They had an evil, dirty look. Way below the plank, and dark in shadow, the waters hissed and fussed as if glad to be rid of the unpleasant scavengers. The currents met with a thrash of spray directly below the appalling bridge.

"I can't!" cried Kirstin. Her heart seemed to have stopped beating. Carol went fearfully pale. She started shaking. Nick, who couldn't stand heights, felt dizzy. Gerald, alone, in spite of his throbbing head, was able to say firmly:
"No! We *won't*! We *can't* cross!"

The guerrillas had heard it all before. They knew how to force their victims over. And if the poor wretches did not make it, but tripped and fell into the ravine – well – what difference did it make? That way they merely died sooner and in less agony – that was if they died on impact and did not have to lie, broken, spiked on rocks till they drowned or were picked to pieces by crocs, vultures and other carrion eaters. If prisoners managed to cross the plank and reach the tiny plateau death came by starvation and by thirst. That took longer and was more agonising. The four bandits shrugged. What did it matter anyway? If they were lucky, before they succumbed to tongue-swelling thirst, captives would go mad or have been removed one by one for guerrilla meals.

Of course, on the whole, the men preferred to steal boats and food, or to commit acts of sabotage and atrocities in the heat of action, without, if possible, having to take prisoners. That was easier. But when captives fell into their hands sometimes they came in useful as extra troops and if times were really bad they served as meat. When they were not dumped in the lake, or forced to become saboteurs, or eaten, they were stored on this pinnacle. Sooner or later if men didn't devour them, marabou storks, vultures, ravens, millipedes, ants and other clearers of filth gradually removed all signs of grisly anguish.

The tallest and most emaciated of the bandits – the one with two fingers missing – studied the group briefly. Then he pointed his chin at Gerald and prodded him, making signs that he was to cross the fearsome bridge.

"No!" said Gerald stoutly, resisting as they separated him from his cousins. The tall, skeletal fellow held a machete ready as he stood guard over the girls and Nick. A revolver was brandished in Gerald's face and another poked into his spine.

Backing away from the awful drop Gerald repeated "No!" with a note of panic. Nick and Kirstin tried to dart forward to his aid but were held off by hands that punched, twisted and hurt. The safety catch was clicked off a gun and its muzzle driven hard into Carol's chest.

"Over!" grunted the guard in his own language. One of the others tried to push Gerald onto the plank. For a moment the four prisoners thought of fighting. But for Carol, with the gun in her ribs, movement was impossible, and the others realised that a struggle would do more harm than good. Certainly Gerald and Nick were tall and muscular, and the girls were tough and wiry; but as a group they were no match for these hardened brutes. The outcome would be inevitable: broken bones, smashed heads, and probably much worse.

Shrugging petulantly, Gerald capitulated. Saying:
"All right! All right! Keep your wigs on!" he moved to the brink of the crevasse and looked down. No – that was awful! Mustn't let himself be aware of the bottom so far below. And especially it was hopeless to look at the swirling water sluicing so hypnotically down there. He cleared his head with a typical Geraldish shake, and then as a sharp pain reminded him of the spectacular bruise on his temple, wished violently that he

had kept his head still.

"Oh, Gerald!" sobbed Carol, wringing her hands.

That was all he needed to make up his mind. Must stop the others from getting into a panic. He started to brace himself...

Suddenly... Urgently...

"Wait!" shouted Nick.

There was a sapling nearby. He tried desperately to pull it up. Of course this was completely impossible but the guards were not totally unfeeling, and one of them thought he understood what Nicky wanted. Taking a machete from his neighbour, the thug sliced through the thin trunk with one easy stroke. It was ludicrous, really, how Nick then ordered the bandits to lower the tree across the gap. He made them place it carefully beside the plank, and they obeyed his commands. The chopped end of the trunk was thrust across the chasm to land on the pinnacle. Nick manoeuvred it till the far end was between two rocks. That gave it some sort of stability. With branches now spreading across the void, and shielding the drop a bit, the crossing *seemed* much less formidable. Leaves and small branches gave the sensation, albeit false, of something solid going over beside the board, and this was comforting. Suddenly the piece of wood appeared less narrow and less isolated. Also, it seemed as if the trunk could be grabbed if necessary. Not that such a slender and supple pole would support the slightest weight. Still – it gave the *illusion* of a handrail.

When one of the guards was standing on the nearer end of the tree Nick stepped onto the portion of plank that was resting on the closer edge of the gulf. This would stabilise the narrow beam. Gerald lowered himself gently onto the terrifying bridge. With a leg dangling on each side he sat over the dreadful drop. Then slowly and carefully he inched his way across. Even the callous men held their breaths. How many, and which, of these four would fall? It was seldom that there wasn't at least one casualty when they brought victims up here and forced them across the fearsome chasm. The tormentors considered that probably the girls would slip and crash to their deaths. Neither of them looked tall or strong enough to achieve the crossing.

"Kirstin, you go next," said Nick gruffly. "That way I can make sure that these characters don't do any jiggery pokery with the plank. Besides, I don't want to leave you two girls alone here with these sadists."

Kirstin gulped, and Carol, accepting that it would be her turn next, clasped damp hands.

"Careful, Kirsty," she choked. Her sister needed no urging to proceed gingerly. Like Gerald she sat on the plank, one leg hanging on each side, hands gripping its rough edges in front of her.

"Keep your eyes on the wood," shouted Gerr. "Don't let them stray anywhere else. The tree's a tremendous comfort. It's really not all that bad," he lied.

With Gerald and Nick standing on the ends of the timber to ensure as little vibration as possible Kirstin slowly and safely, if painfully, got over and sobbing, took her cousin's hand to scramble onto the far plateau. Realising that her sister would be next, she quickly pulled herself together. If she could do it, then so could Carol – but only if she was filled with confidence.

"It's really easy," she called back to her sister in a surprisingly firm and happy voice. "Piece o' cake, Caro. Just like the pole in the park at home – only easier because this one isn't round. Just do as Gerr said: watch the plank and don't take your eyes off it."

With a hiccough Carol let Nick help her onto the length of wood. He rested his hand lightly on her shoulder for as far out as he could safely reach. Even leaning over the drop to give Carol that little moral support made his head spin. And then she was on her own. For a moment she hesitated and the others ground their teeth wondering whether to call out encouragement or whether that would distract her from balancing.

Slowly, slowly, wracked by sobs, with tears smudging her vision, but determined not to be beaten, Carol eased forward as the other two had done. All was going as well as could be expected when her eyes slipped past the plank to the whirlpool below. How the waves twisted in that murky passage! How jagged those rocks were! What a stink came up from down there! Suddenly she was dizzy and she felt sick!

"I can't," she shrieked.

The others felt their blood congeal with horror!

Making a desperate effort Caro closed her eyes and clamped her hands even more tightly round the hard corners of the badly-trimmed wood. She groaned and sat frozen. The world was spinning. She didn't know which way was up or which way was down.

'I'm going to be sick!' she thought. The heaving would immediately unbalance her.

"Yes. I expected that his one wouldn't make it," sneered one of the guards. The reply from his friend was a coarse laugh which could well have come from one of the old crones who sat knitting below the knife in the days of the guillotine. Nick, Gerald and Kirstin held their breaths and stood rigid. Would the awful jeers unnerve Carol even more? The grisly chuckle echoed impossibly loudly in the transfixed girl's ears and sounded like her death knell. Again she was certain that she was going to vomit.

Kirstin and Gerald were speaking, trying to encourage her. The words were a blur, and only made her feel worse. If she opened her eyes she saw only a fog. She started to give up... It would be easier to let go, and be killed rapidly. Falling – even the final smash – would be better than this torture. Her spinning head was still unsure which way was up and which was down. The guards approached with the obvious intention of shaking the plank. Nick knew that they wouldn't be patient.

"Buck up, Carol," he said in matter of fact tones. "I want to get across."

What a ridiculous utterance! But it worked! Only Nick knew how much it had cost him to make his voice so very level and calm, the words so commonplace. Carol opened her eyes. She controlled her sobs so her balance became less precarious. Kirsty and Gerr were only a few feet away, smiling at her and holding out their hands. No one could imagine how difficult it was to grin so cheerfully, and not to cry out in fright.

"Come on, Caro. You're nearly here," urged her sister on a confident note. "Hurry up and give us a paw!"

The youngster gulped. With enormous care she moved one hand on the plank. Then she moved the other. Immediately her balance improved. The branches of the tree now hid the blood-curdling view below, so long as she leaned forward and didn't allow herself to catch even a glimpse through them. She willed herself to see the plank and no further. Then she shifted her body to join her hands.

"Well done," breathed Gerald. "Nearly there now."

He had found a small stick. It was only a pliable, dry, reedy thing, dropped onto the plateau by the wind, but he put it gently over her shoulder.

"Come on, Sir Carol," he joked. And this completely useless twig somehow gave the twelve-year-old a little confidence. She shuffled forwards incredibly slowly; but finally she was able to take Kirstin's hand and scramble off the plank... and was violently sick. Then she sat down very abruptly, looking an incredible shade of green.

It was now Nick's turn and they all knew he had no head for heights.

64. One White Headed Vulture and three filthy-looking Marabou Storks beside Pinnacle Prison. All are waiting to pick at carrion. (In colour on www.daphne.es)

CHAPTER 48

No escape.

Very gently, so that the guards would not think that he was trying to escape, Nicholas took hold of the only one who had a small amount of flesh and indicated that this relative 'Fatty' should take his place on the end of the plank. Despite Nick's care, the bony fellow resisted at first, believing that the prisoner was trying to push him over the edge. A fight, which might have ended tragically, nearly erupted. But wriggling to avoid all blows, Nick showed his antagonists that he was merely asking them to steady the bridge. When the penny dropped the thin 'Fatty' was not unwilling to stand stolidly on the end of the beam. After all, he reasoned in a rather woolly way, the more prisoners safely on the jail the more food available.

Nick hated heights. He knew he would be lost if he so much as glanced beyond the narrow plank. Sheer willpower got him across and it was done almost before he "came to" from the state of intense concentration that he had put himself into. He found he was standing beside his cousins, shaky, but – for the time being – safe.

Very rapidly the guerrillas removed the 'bridge'. As they were then about to collect the sapling Gerr quickly grabbed the tree. Nicky and Kirstin instinctively helped. On the other side of the ravine the guards were so starved that their reactions were slow, so the tree was already in the air before they realised what was happening. They lunged at the disappearing branches. But the thin top boughs bent and snapped as the boys backed rapidly away from the brink. One man, who kept hold of a branch, was dragged to the edge so he dropped his end in panic as the gap loomed before him. One of the bandits drew his revolver and shouted. Probably he was ordering the captives to throw their booty off the steeple-like prison.

"Quick!" yelled Kirstin. "Get behind a rock!"

They fell flat. There was scant cover. However, another fellow laughed brutally and in his language he said:

"It's so weak and bendy. It can't possibly be of any service to them. Even if the smallest tries to cross the chasm using that as a bridge – or in any other way – it will break and drop her to crash below."

He waved towards the wicked, rock spikes beneath. With evil grins his companions pictured the fall and shrugged boney shoulders. Then they were suddenly more interested in two boats that they could see splashing fast over the waves from the south east. The Big Boss was arriving so they had more urgent things to do than to fight a senseless battle over a useless tree. Shouldering the long plank that had surprisingly survived the rebels' constant need for firewood, they turned their backs on the pinnacle and hurried away, down the curving spine of Kadenzi's second 'finger', downhill across the base of the index 'finger', and down further into the bay where *Ebony Girl*, *Frolic* and the *Queen* were still bobbing at anchor.

"Possums!" said Kirstin sitting up. They were all shaken and shaking, but thankful to be alive. Their first priority was to extract splinters. That plank had been extremely rough. This painful operation over, as far as it was possible to perform it using thorns and fingers, the next concern was to examine the edge of their prison.

Although it seemed obvious that the spire would not have served as a gaol if there had been any way to escape, they still felt they had to scrutinize every inch round the precipitous edges. Scattered bones below the 'bridge' place told a gruesome tale of fallen prisoners whose dead bodies had been torn apart by vultures – or crocodiles. Normally such a sight would have upset the cousins but now they were completely obsessed with finding a way to escape. The bones seemed to be just one more horror in the terrible landscape.

Wherever they looked it was utterly impossible to climb down. The prospect was simply terrifying. The buttresses up the sides ended so far below the plateau, and

were so skewer-like, that it would be sheer suicide to attempt any form of descent. Even an experienced rock climber (which not one of them was) with ropes and bolts (which they didn't have) would have hesitated to start down those precipices.
"We could abseil, of course," said Nick, "if we had a rope."
"And we could fly if we had wings," said Gerald bitterly.
"Well, we've got no rope. We can't abseil," said Kirsty flatly.

Gerr wandered over to the last side which they had not quite finished examining. The others followed slowly, hopelessly. Nick gazed past Gerald to Kadenzi's third – or middle – 'finger'. It was so close – yet so unattainable. Beyond he could make out Lumbo Island in the far distance but there were dying trees on Kadenzi blocking most of that view. What was Ella doing at the moment? Was she frantic with worry?

In the foreground her brother was looking over the edge into the stinking gulf that separated them from the frightful second 'finger', from freedom, and from Nell. With his hand over his nose he started moving left, searching desperately for any possible scrambling holds. Suddenly he froze, and then stared again. Nick's heart jumped with hope. He started to hurry towards his cousin. Did the statue-like pose mean there was a possible way down? Then Gerr turned away and brought up all the contents of his stomach.
"Don't – " he managed to say as the others, horrified, rushed to sympathise and to try to help. He waved them frenziedly away from the brink, and between paroxysms he choked:
"Don't go there! Don't look!"
Nick and the girls stood paralysed. Whatever had happened?

Gerald recovered, but still panting and yellow-faced, he tottered away and sat down very abruptly.
"Dead man!" he groaned. "Terrible! Must've tried to climb down... Ghastly! Only half body left... Hideous... torn face... One eye... " He couldn't continue but gagged again. After a while, as the others sat in shocked, sympathetic silence, he managed to blurt out:
"Better not look! It's too horrible. Monitor lizards eating... black skin but white fat and scarlet flesh... All mangled up!"

Again he couldn't go on.

"That's really sick. Don't say any more" commanded Kirstin as Nick murmured:

"Those vultures that flew out of the chasm when the plank was dropped across it... "

65. Grisly event.
(Even worse in colour! www.daphne.es)

"Come over here. All of you... " Kirstin ordered leading the way to the furthest corner of the accursed plateau. They sat silently in slight shade of a scrubby bush, trembling and shocked beyond words, and definitely no longer hungry. The awful stench now seemed twice as evil as it had before.

The prisoners heard a large powerboat and a speedboat bouncing round the last seven of Kadenzi's 'fingers' and watched listlessly as the boats drew level with their Prison Pinnacle, passed Kadenzi's index 'finger', slowed down, and nosed carefully into the bay. They could see over the first 'finger', which was comparatively low, so they were able to watch the two vessels idle in, and stop very close to the beach. The newly-arrived speedboat and the powerboat, which dwarfed *Ebony Girl,* barely fitted into the bay. Men were positioned to fend off from the mock steamer. Then, using big canoes, a contingent of scruffy fighters and an incredible load of cargo, most of which looked extremely heavy were set ashore.

"Ammunition, by the looks of it," muttered Nick.

There were also crates of food and large quantities of miscellaneous unidentifiable boxes. It was hard to imagine how so much could have been rammed into two vessels. No wonder they had been fearfully low in the water.

There was no room in the bay to moor the two recent arrivals so, when the lengthy unloading manoeuvre was complete, the massive cruiser and the small speedboat were driven back round the index 'finger' and punted down between it and the second – prison – peninsular. The punters looked up at the captives and jeered at them, making lascivious gestures and shouting coarse remarks. Although the words were so rude that many were incomprehensible the lewd gestures and bawdy intonations were only too frightful to be misinterpreted. The girls cowered out of sight but Nick and Gerald picked up stones with a view to bombarding their tormentors.

"Don't!" yelled Kirstin. "If you hit – or even kill – one of those revolting *hoons,* (louts) that will surely only *come a gutser* (be a terrible mistake) for us."

"They'd probably shoot us for revenge," agreed Carol. "Let's just be glad this rock is so high they can't reach us with their boathooks."

Nick first, and Gerald afterwards, reluctantly dropped their primitive weapons and they all watched silently, but furiously, as the two boats were made fast. There was barely width for the big powerboat in the creek and stupidly, it was punted in first – ahead of the speedboat; so the men had to force it well down the narrow passage to allow room for the smaller craft behind it. The cousins derived some pleasure from the difficulties that this entailed. When both boats were secured, the men climbed up the far end of the creek and scrambled over the index 'finger' back to the main bay.

There a short squat figure was giving orders. He had to be the 'very important person' whom the camp had been expecting. Every one of the guerrillas cow-towed to the little bullying Asiatic in a way that made Gerald snarl with scorn. Even the brutish, sluggish 'Commandante' bowed low and ran to obey screams from the new tyrant.

"I guess some very special new atrocity must be about to be organised," remarked Nick. "Just look at that massive heap of guns!"

Later the ravenous cousins' mouths watered and their stomachs ached with hunger when they saw preparations in full swing for what was evidently going to be a huge feast. They marvelled at the power that the little yellow man must have if he could keep all these rough, starving villains waiting while he spoke to them at enormous length. As the sun went down the captives' awful thirst made them wilt so they noticed less and watched with increasingly hazy attention. As well as desperately longing for water, they were bored, exhausted, famished, shocked and depressed.

Far away to the west the elegant sloop of the Kangalian Lake Police was bustling southwards. A long, straight wake gleamed white. No one on board aimed binoculars at Kadenzi Island. And even if they had, they would not have noticed the prisoners on its north-eastern peninsular. Even the rebels' fire and paraffin lamps were hidden by the high 'thumb' surrounding the bay. As far as the Lake Police were concerned Kadenzi was just another sunset-tinged lump on the eastern horizon. The sloop swept past. No one on her or on Kadenzi was aware that they had been within mortar firing distance of each other.

CHAPTER 49

Horrific news.

As Nell fell in a heap on the beach she saw that her revolting attackers were not weird water monsters, but frogmen whose hideous masks covered dark faces.

'They must be rebels from the neighbouring island,' she thought cringing with horror as she imagined the awful torture that the guerrillas must have inflicted upon her brother and cousins to have forced them to reveal, and in such a short time, where she and *Percy* were hidden! Now a vague hope that she might somehow rescue the others deserted her. This was the final straw to Ella's anguish. She blacked out as the terrifying invaders flopped awkwardly towards her. What ghastly atrocities were they planning?

"She's fainted," said one of them removing his mask. "Poor kid!" replied the other shrugging off a strangely-shaped backpack. "I suppose we may have given her a bit of a shock."

Coming from widely separated tribes, rather than attempt each other's dialects they preferred to communicate in English, which they both spoke fluently. The kindly words, spoken in a language that she understood, must have penetrated Nell's subconscious for she slowly recovered. Lying quietly, she wondered how she could not only overcome these intruders but also somehow perhaps trick them into helping her to rescue her companions. It seemed best to bide her time, hoping that some wonderful opportunity would miraculously present itself.

The frogmen sat on the beach to remove their flippers. "Sorry you got a fright," said one of the men noticing that her eyes were focused on him. Ella didn't reply.

"Sorry your friends have been captured," said the other. The body on the sand gulped but remained silent, determined not to be friendly.

"We're here to help," continued the larger of the two, still in perfect English. "I'm Zak. He's Harry. Kangi Counter Rebels

Special Investigations. Captain," Zak tapped himself on the chest, "and Lieutenant," he added slapping Harry's shoulder.

"Oh!" gasped Nell feeling stunned and inadequate. It was all too utterly confusing. "Er... I'm Ella."

She still didn't understand a thing!

"How... Why... ?" Very slowly she sat up.

"It is our job, together with a few others like ourselves, to patrol these islands and to take action when necessary," Zak explained.

"Our colleagues further south told us about your progress up the lake," put in Harry. "I caught the report over the radio."

"Unfortunately the Kadenzi crowd saw the Lake Flies, and that made them look south, and therefore they spotted your boat. Normally they never notice anything south of their island because all of *its* creeks point north-east, so the men usually look only towards the north. The guerrillas imagine no one knows of their control station on big Kadenzi Island."

'Thank heavens we never made it there last night,' thought Ella. 'If we had, we would *all* have been taken, and *both* boats.' Faint hopes of somehow releasing the others with the help of these friendly frogmen were now starting to creep into her brain.

"We tried to catch up with you before this – to stop you sailing on northwards – but we couldn't get here any sooner."

"Where have you come from?"

"Several islands along the line," said Zak with professional vagueness. "We'd have made it before now but we've been frantically busy with special tasks that we couldn't postpone. We couldn't start out as quickly as we wanted to after hearing about you. I wish to God we'd been able to get here in time to stop your friends from sailing this morning."

Ella was still struggling to take it all in. Suddenly she had an inspiration:

"Er... Would you like a cup of tea? – Something to eat?"

Zak and Harry thought that a spot of lunch with lashings of hot tea would be most welcome so she bustled about to produce a meal for them all. Zak unwrapped one of

the extraordinary bundles and from a load of equipment extracted a radio. He fiddled with this, spreading parts and tools over a rock, until lunch was ready.
Unloading the Enterprise, Harry made a fine pyramid out of *Percy's* cargo and other bundles that had been lying on the sand ready to be tied into *Frolic*.
"If we're going to sail off on a rescue mission in the dinghy we don't want to be heavily laden," he said, adding ominously:
"Let's hope we'll be alive and able to collect it all again later."

As they ate Zak tried to explain the situation to Nell.
"Your friends were lucky – in one way. Sometimes when the Bafando seize a boat they make the owners jump overboard and leave them to drown, or use them for shooting practice, as the ex-owners try to swim. In another way your pals may have been very *un*lucky." He voiced perplexities. "But why did the bounders take your relatives to their lair? Of course they're desperately short of food... Hungry people will stop at nothing – think of survivors in a life raft on the ocean — or survivors of a 'plane crash in high mountains... " Ella wished he hadn't spelled things out so clearly. However, Zak repeated:

"The rebels on that damned island madly want food. At the moment they have no use at all for prisoners. As far as they are concerned the fewer people who know of their hideout the better.

"Those who know of it must be killed – in one way or another – lest they inform Kangi authorities... " Zak's sometimes over-perfect English was the only detail to reveal that he was not a native-born English-speaker. His accent couldn't have been faulted.
"Sometime today," he told Ella, "The Supreme Head of all the Bafando guerrillas is due to arrive to inspect the Kadenzi stronghold and to organise a special assault into Kangalia. We have been watching and waiting for this moment for many months. The head is not a local man. He comes from a far country. His visits are rare and very meaningful."

Harry took over the story:

"In the last few days a great many fighters have arrived on Kadenzi from dozens of sub camps all over Bafandoland. Tonight there will doubtless be feasting and carousing, depending upon how much food the Big Boss is able to bring."

"They may decide to eat it all in one huge binge – if they hope to receive another delivery later," put in Zak. "Or perhaps they'll save a little for the next few days. But they are so starved that we estimate they'll have a blow-out tonight."

"Tonight," Harry took up the tale again, "a great many orders and plans are to be revealed for new attacks and barbarities against our country. We cannot understand why they want to invade us and upset our peaceful, well-run land. They can't even manage their own territory. Why don't they get their own place into order and be satisfied?"

"One wonders," said Zak. He paused. "I do not like to say this to you... you understand... but one wonders what your friends will be forced to do – or what cruelties they'll have to suffer. Why have they been taken to a headquarters from which the rebels usually do everything possible to exclude everyone but themselves? It seems very sinister."

Shivering, Ella whispered urgently. "We must rescue them!"

"We will try," said Zak. "Indeed, we must try hard, because tomorrow, just before dawn, the Kangi Air Force will be dropping a couple of bombs on that little lot. If our spies are correct there is, at the moment on Kadenzi Island, a gathering of leaders of all the guerrilla sections that follow this particular generalissimo. Still more chiefs will soon be arriving with the so-called 'general' himself, bringing a great quantity of arms and ammunition. We believe they are about to start a concerted thrust into our country. They've already got a huge hoard of ammo. Our bombs will set off all that, and the new supplies as well, of course. Altogether it will be quite a show when it all goes up!"

Nell's relatives were on that island which was going to be blown to smithereens before seventeen hours were up!

"No! No! You mustn't destroy Kadenzi!" she cried. "Unfortunately we are unable to alter our plans. Our radio casing has developed a leak and now the wireless will no longer operate. This afternoon we will endeavour to repair it. But even if we manage to make it work... the information I have just given you will make you realise that we cannot cancel the raid. There is too much at stake."

Seeing Ella's stricken face Zak stopped. Harry went on instead:

"We *must* destroy the generalissimo and all his group leaders. This is our one chance to catch them all together. By smashing them we will dislocate the whole rebel organisation. If we manage that, then many ordinary Bafando people – loyal folk who have been terrorised into working for the bandits – will be liberated to return to their normal lives. The villagers – over there," he pointed east, "will be able to start living again. Bafandoland will have an opportunity to re-establish itself, and... "

"And," said Zak, "the menace of raids from the rebels into our country will cease!"

The oratory passed over Nell's head. Only one thing bothered her:

"You mean – " she stuttered, "even if we can't save my brother and cousins, even so – the island will still be bombed?"

Zak nodded sadly. "I am afraid that is correct. Just before dawn tomorrow."

Nell was aghast!

"Then we absolutely *have* to rescue them *now!*"

"No, not now. That would be impossible. Try to sleep while we struggle with this radio. Tonight we will do our utmost to remove them off Kadenzi."

"We *must* get them out of there!"

"Certainly we will try."

The frogmen kindly didn't mention that they never thought their hopes would be achieved. They'd be two against 300 and, as Harry muttered to Zak,

"We have no idea where the captives are hidden. How the devil will we find them, let alone get them off the island?"

CHAPTER 50

A terrible idea.

Carol and Kirstin slumped to the ground. They were hungry, very thirsty and aching all over. There was no escape and the future looked so grim that somehow, enveloped in despair the only thing left was to fall asleep. The boys roamed the tiny, arid area, feeing impotent and furious but eventually, sitting down to make a change, Gerald just keeled over, overcome by pain, physical exhaustion and mental tension.

Nicholas looked at his dozing cousins. 'Might as well do the same,' he decided, dropping to the ground. 'It'll stop me thinking.' He never expected to be able to rest, but, probably delayed shock was taking its toll and his head drooped.

The moon was well risen when the cousins woke, still frightfully hungry and dreadfully thirsty, but revitalized and with cleared brains. What a relief to be out of the blazing sun!

While they slept, down at the guerrillas' camp the visiting 'general' had inspected superciliously, complained excessively, praised not at all, and decreed future policy that was largely impracticable in view of the present state of his troops. Now, on the beach, where a colossal bonfire was burning furiously, food and drink were being consumed in amazing quantities and with absolutely no refinement.

"Makes you feel ill to watch them," said Gerald in disgust. "Just like pigs!"
"Worse – much worse," said Kirstin. "But I could *really* do with some *tucker*, myself."
The other two had already turned away.
"I'm going to have another look round," announced Nick.
"Not that way!" begged Gerald frantically.
"I've got to," replied Nick. "We scrutinized everywhere else very thoroughly but none of us really examined that bit of cliff. You were so horribly overcome by what you saw, that you never studied the place; and the rest of us didn't even

peek there. I've got an idea. I *must* see if it will work *somewhere.*"

"No!" urged Gerald turning a ghastly colour.

"Hell, man!" snapped Nicholas. "It's our one chance. If that poor fellow made an attempt it must be because the spot looked like a possible way down."

Gerald moaned and Kirstin asked crossly:

"Do you *have* to?"

"Yes. Listen! I'm prepared for what I'll see. I won't get a shock as Gerald did. Besides, I'm not as squeamish as he is, so I can stand the sight of blood, mangled limbs and exposed bones. I've *got* to inspect that last bit of precipice. Right? We *have* to get off this pinnacle if we are going to live. I don't want to stay here being grilled by the sun till we're eaten by men, or vultures, or insects... or die off one by one of thirst and starvation. Do *you*?" He finished on a bark.

"You won't see a thing," said Carol shrinking from the abyss beside them. It was in dark shadow. She moaned as she tripped over a dry thigh bone.

"Yes I will. The moon's lighting that bit. I wish there weren't so many clouds flitting about though."

In anxious silence the others watched him cross the tiny plateau. They all jumped and shivered when a night bird gave a sudden piercing shriek.

For a long time Nick stood on the brink staring and thinking; but after the first jolt, he no longer noticed the oozing remains of the bandits' previous victim. Why had the poor wretch not turned guerrilla himself? Why had he preferred such a gruesome death? Had he been so maddened by thirst that he had simply jumped over the edge to try and reach water?

But no! Though the ripped, raw flesh to the left was grisly, the spike immediately below had possibilities. That must have enticed the prisoner to make his desperate attempt. Nick forced his eyes away from the smashed pulp and bones, which had slithered sideways off that spike leaving a trail of intestines. Mercifully they were now in shadow.

66. Simply awful

The waves, vultures and monitor lizards had actually done a reasonable clearing job. He suspected that crocs had also been at work in the interval since Gerald had looked over the edge. There was little left now to sicken anyone who was prepared for the horror. Vaguely Nick wondered why the final remnants had not been carried off. There had to be a reason. Were the crocs, temporarily satisfied, lying about below – ready for the next feast? All this flipped through his mind quickly and superficially. He was really concentrating on the cliff and on that awful upward pointing spear of stone. Slowly, deep in thought, weighing up chances, his face desperately serious, he walked back to his cousins.

"Well?" asked Kirstin.

"Tell us," ordered Carol.

Nick was scared stiff by his own idea so he paused – and prevaricated...

"It would be nothing short of madness to try to even think of climbing down there."

The others shifted, giving way to disappointment. They had been hoping against hope that he might find some solution.

"It'd be a frightful risk. You'll probably be too terrified to try."

"Is there the slightest chance we might succeed?" asked Kirsty impatiently. "No use risking it unless there's at least a smidgen of possible escape in it."

"I *think* so," said Nick sounding anything but confident.

"I'm going to look then."

"Me too," declared Carol. Kirstin turned and stared hard at her sister.

"I'll be all right," declared the younger girl stoutly. Bracing himself, Gerald followed slowly. He could never stand grisly sights. But if the others were taking the bashed-up corpse so matter-of-factly, well – blow it – so would he! Besides, this afternoon – when he'd first seen that appalling, twisted semi-devoured body with the half-eaten head, his wound had been giving him jip. The pain had gone now, though there was still a huge lump and he was developing a magnificent black eye. He stood beside the others and gazed bravely over, forcing his eyes to keep to the cliff immediately below – not allowing them to glance at the bloody bits on the left. In gloom instead of in brilliant sunlight the ghastly remains of shattered human were less devastating; but the horrendous stink was even worse than before.

With hands over their noses, three anxious faces gazed at their Commodore in distressed silence. They could see no way down.

"We've got that tree... " murmured Nick hesitatingly.

"That's no use! It's terribly weak," objected Gerald. "I don't know why I snatched it. I suppose it was just a defiant gesture or something... just to show the blighters that we still had some spirit left in us... "

"I know. Horizontally it won't take any weight to speak of," agreed Nick, "but what I thought... " he wavered, not liking to voice his frightening idea.

"Come on. Out with it," urged Kirstin.

"*Maybe* we can climb *down* it – if we are terribly, terribly careful."

His cousins gasped with horror.

"You're bonkers!"

"We're certain to *come a gutser!*" (Come to grief.)

"*Canaries in your attic!*" (You're mad!)

Nick had expected this reaction but now he pressed his point.

"Look how our prison is surrounded by sharp rock buttresses that come almost half way up. The top of that one down there is broken off – looks as if a boulder has fallen on it in the past and smashed the tip."

"Perhaps a prisoner like us rolled a rock over to bomb it," suggested Kirstin.

"Possibly," said Nick. "Anyway, it's left a miniature flat space on the top of the spike. The sapling might just reach that miniscule, smoothish area. Beyond that, some way further down, see? There's a huge, upstanding boulder... " His voice trailed away. It was an awful thing that he was suggesting.

"The sapling won't reach that far down," Kirstin declared dully.

"It *might* – just," hesitated Carol, "but then – at the start, when we are highest, we'd be climbing down through branches which are dreadfully spindly. They'd just break and we couldn't climb through them."

"I'm absolutely certain the drop to the tiny area is longer than the eucalyptus," said Gerald with conviction.

"Yes. I'm sure you're right; but, if you and I hold onto the bottom of the trunk and let the tree hang upside down," Nick turned to the Australians, "then you girls can climb down the treelet. When you start you'll have the almost firm trunk, and more or less decent boughs, and when you reach the thin top branches – which will be at the bottom – you can simply hang from them and drop down to the ledge."

"Ledge!" choked Kirstin. "*What* ledge? You mean that little ten cent piece on the top of the spike?"

"Yes," said Nick miserably.

"Heck!" exploded Kirstin

"But – it's *minute*!" objected Gerr, shattered by the idea. "They're certain to miss."

They stood petrified .

"No!" exclaimed Kirstin, suddenly summing up the situation. "It's die this way, or die miserably in some other type of agony."

She paused to gather her courage then emphatically she said:

"We jolly well *won't* miss! I'll go first because I'm heavier, and Carol can help you to hold the sapling while I'm on it." Mentally she unconsciously told herself: 'and if anyone is going to be smithereened on those rocks below I'd rather it wasn't my little sister... And anyway, I don't want to see it happen!'

Aloud she said: "Then, when I'm down, I'm sure you two toughies will be able to hold things while Caro follows me. And I'll be there to guide her onto the huge football pitch!" she added sarcastically.

"But what then?" asked Gerald.

"Well – When the girls are on the," Nick hesitated – "on the 'football pitch' we turn the tree round and slither it carefully down to them. Then they can lower it a bit further and wedge the chopped end of the trunk into that cleft between those two boulders near the top of that gully down there. When it's fixed, they climb down the trunk."

The prospect made his listeners gasp with horror. Nick gulped and then added optimistically:

"The drop from the – er – 'football pitch' to the boulders isn't nearly as far as it is from the top here to the ledge. Or at least from up here it doesn't look as far... maybe there's a bit of foreshortening... "

"But what about you two?" asked Carol, recoiling from the impossibility of manipulating the tree and then wedging it. "How will *you* get down?"

"Unfortunately we'll still be stuck up here," said Nick trying to sound comical.

"We'll steal a rope from the powerboat and throw it up to you so you can abseil down," decided Kirstin.

"That's a brainy wheeze – if there's a rope to steal," agreed Nick, sounding pleased. He really hadn't fancied a slow death on top of the prison pinnacle.

"I doubt you'll manage to throw it up so high" added Gerr dolefully facing facts.

In dread silence, cold with fright, they stared at each other with big, worried eyes and sombre thoughts. Then Kirstin rubbed her hands on the seat of her shorts.

"Come on then," she said briskly. "No use hanging about. This is our only chance. Let's do it before we get nervy or weak from lack of food and water."

"You O.K. to try, Carol?" asked Nick gently.

She felt like saying "No! I can't!" Instead her mouth answered: "Yes, sure. Let's go."

Like her sister she rubbed her palms on her shorts. Gerald went to get the sapling.

"If I'd known," he muttered... "If I'd known... I think I'd have let the ruffians take it."

CHAPTER 51

Attempting the impossible.

The young bluegum seemed appallingly flimsy and supple as the boys lowered it upside down over the crag and lay flat on their tummies holding it in position. There was no room for Carol to help so, frightened beyond words, she sat backwards on their legs, her feet braced, and with her hands she desperately forced a foot of each cousin towards the hard ground. Kirstin gave her sister a huge squeeze, then she stepped delicately over the boys' heads and dropped a quick kiss on each forehead.

"It's not exactly easy," she chattered brightly. "You're awfully in the way, you two." They all understood that she was talking just to calm their nerves. "I'm glad the rock isn't the crumbly kind," she added as she edged backwards, feeling for the trunk with her feet. Then her legs were round it. Her arms were holding it.

"Ow!" she exclaimed. "This bark's disgustingly sticky and prickly!"

The boys took the strain and Carol was aware of their legs tensing. She strengthened her hold and begged any good spirits, which might be around, to help them.

"Yow-*ee*!" yelled Kirsty as the tree moved, squeezing her fingers between the trunk and a jutting-out section of cliff. It was sheer anguish, but she didn't let go! Her feet found the first few boughs and after that the going was less tricky. Trying not to let terror overwhelm her, she scrambled carefully down the frail inverted tree as quickly as safety allowed, trying to minimize wrenching the boys' arms by avoiding, as much as was feasible, swinging the trunk about.

When the branches began to feel unsafe she let her feet hang loose, dangled for a moment from her arms, and looked down to try to locate the tiny area on which she had to land. That made her giddy. It looked absolutely impossible. She was sure to miss that tiny spec. But her arms were aching and the boys' muscles must be even more painful. There was no point dangling here becoming more and more terrified... Gathering all her willpower and, shutting her eyes, she released her hold, praying that she had aimed correctly and would find the 'ten cent piece'.

That was the worst part. There was no chance of survival if she missed. She'd end up with her intestines smeared over the spike like the previous victim. Kirstin landed with a thump that winded her. The small thud told the others that she had reached the broken top of the spike. Grabbing for frail, useless twigs that were hardly within her grasp, she teetered, but managed not to topple off her pinpoint landing ground. She couldn't afford to trip and go over the edge.

As Nick had feared, seen from above the drop had been foreshortened. Kirsty had fallen further than any of them had anticipated. Sweating, gasping for breath and panting with reaction she shut her eyes and pressed her forehead against the cliff to balance herself, and to restore her nerve. She was shaking with shock. The boys could relax slightly and let their arms become less tense. Kirstin turned and got her bearings. Then Nick and Gerr heard her quiet: "Caro's turn."

The youngest of the group felt a lump of fear in her throat. But if Kirsty, who was really not *all* that much taller and tougher – was she? – could do it – well, so could she! She blinking well *would*! Carol swallowed the constriction and stepped up to the boys' heads. She couldn't back out now. Kirstin needed her help down the last bit. At least *one* of them had to get down and throw a rope up to the boys – somehow! "Sure you can hold me?" asked the youngest and slightest of the group, trying to make a joke.
"You're such a heavy weight!" growled Gerr, teasing to reassure her. "I don't know if we'll manage, really. Now if you were a featherweight like Ella, we'd have no trouble at all."

The three of them gave a trembling laugh at his weak gag; but it eased the tension and Carol was over the edge like a monkey. Being even more agile than Kirstin she was able to

squirm down the trunk in no time and, lighter than her sister, she could climb somewhat lower through the branches. Kirstin contrived to stretch up and clutch her round the knees. "Step on my shoulders," she said guiding Carol's feet into place, "and acrobat down me." This had been one of their tricks when Caro had been lighter and smaller. Could they still achieve it? Would Carol's twisted, aching shoulder give way?
"No. It'll be easier if I drop. Watch out!"
"NO! Don't drop," commanded Kirstin urgently. "The space here's absolutely zilch. We could easily knock each other off. We *have* to get you down in a very controlled way."
"Cripes!" gasped the suspended girl. "O.K. – Ready?"
"Yes."

Carol trembled, terrified, as Kirsty took her weight. With relief she released the branches and stretched a stabilising hand to the cliff. The older girl thought her back would snap. She released Carol's knees and took her hands. Luckily Kirstin's body and Carol's shoulder both lasted out. Seeking feet slipped down from Kirsty's shoulders to her now clasped hands, and finally found her knee. It had been years since they had performed this trick, and both girls realised only too clearly that not only was there not enough space, but the manoeuvre was much more difficult now than it had been in the past. They grabbed the precipice for support.
"Phew! Made it!"
But that was only the first bit.

The boys' arms were cracking – agonising. They tried to lift the tree in order to turn it over but they simply couldn't manage that; so they were forced to let the tree slide down as soon as the girls had readied themselves, and were prepared to struggle against being thrown off the buttress by falling branches. As the sapling slithered down towards them Kirsty and Caro grabbed, and, with enormous difficulty, prevented it from bouncing on past, out of control, and beyond their reach. Tree and girls nearly crashed down together! They teetered this way and that. The boys gulped and prayed. After some stressful seconds, balance was regained. But next the tree had to be righted – and that was terrible.

Branches waved in their faces and tangled with the rock face. Some, that they hoped would bend, stayed stiffly straight while others, which would have made the process easier had they been rigid, turned out to be willowy and useless. Each girl thought, not once but a dozen times, that she was about to be pushed off the tiny area of safety and that every muscle was about to snap. But miraculously, the trunk eventually hung chopped end down.

Clunk! The lowest section fell onto the boulder below. The girls' trembling limbs forced them to rest. Then it took an immense effort to slide the thin, flexible trunk sideways and fix its end in what they hoped was a secure position in a crevice. The boys uttered not a word for fear of distracting the workers below. They watched with bated breaths, their hearts in their mouths and admired the Aussies' patience and perseverance.

At long last everyone heaved a sigh of surprise and relief, but it was tinged with apprehension of what was yet to be done. After all those long minutes of incredible persistence and exertion, reaction again set in. The girls were amazed to discover that they couldn't stop shivering. They clung to each other and to the cliff, gasping and almost retching with fright. They were so overcome that they never even noticed the reek or the gory chunks further along the abyss. When they were feeling less awful, while her sister held the upper branches Kirsty started to struggle down. But she stopped.

"No," she said, her voice shaking. "It's buckling horribly. You're lighter than I am and will stand a better chance. If the branches break as I go down I'll die and you'll be stuck here on this parapet forever. There'll be no one to go for the rope."

So they reversed roles. Kirstin fought to steady the tree as Carol, heart-in-mouth, somehow managed to slowly scramble lower. Then the youngster tried to balance the sapling from below. Under the heavier weight it bent and sagged alarmingly and very nearly toppled – but it didn't quite break!

Now they had to tackle the very painful matter of negotiating down the jagged boulder.

"These awful prick-y bumps are cutting me to pieces," gasped Kirstin.

Swathed by funereal shadows they reached lake level. Carol immediately bent to take great gulps of water. They were all agonizingly thirsty.

"Don't!" said Kirstin quietly but urgently. "That water's surely polluted!"

Her sister spat out the mouthful and sobbed with frustration. She desperately needed a drink, but remembering what was round the base of the pinnacle she lost all desire for liquid.

Progressing to the right along the gloomy channel between Prison Spike and Second 'Finger' was truly ghastly. Waves buffeted them as they worked their way painfully over sharp rocks and round overhangs. In obscurity they gradually groped along the chasm round the pinnacle. It was from here that those White Headed Vultures had risen like ghouls. Everything felt like a slimy snake – or worse. Footholds seemed to slide away from questing toes. Ghosts waited round every bump in the rocks, and the water wheezed and sucked in every cranny like souls of the departed.

The boys called out encouraging comments even though their cousins below were often out of sight. Disturbing echoes reflected weirdly along the chasm. Though the noise was macabre the Aussies appreciated the boys' intentions.

They had chosen the shorter route – to the right. Going the longer way round would have been less sepulchral, but that would have meant passing over the gruesome bits of stinking corpse at the outset, and neither of them had felt capable of that. Even meeting bats that squeaked and flipped about in the darkness, almost brushing their faces, was less blood-curdling than climbing over those grisly remains.

From above, the boys' straining eyes could barely see movement in the gloom below. Dislodged stones, clattering

down, sometimes splashed into the water. Nick and Gerr winced at exclamations of pain as feet in thin plastic sandals stubbed against sharp rocks. Then they became aware that the Aussies had reached the end of the cut and were now faced with a terrifying prospect: they had to swim across the creek through pitchy dark water that was sucking, swirling and frothing. Who knew what terrors lurked in those murky depths! Suddenly Carol's voice cried out:
"Help! Give us a hand, Kirsty! *Quick!*"

67. Kirstin attempting the impossible!

CHAPTER 52

Night flight.

The watchers on Prison Pinnacle caught muffled words as the girls scrambled aboard the speedboat. Would the uncaring rebels have left anything useful? In the desperate state of Bafandoland probably nobody ever abandoned anything that could be stolen. Kirstin didn't really hope to find a rope. Indeed, in the speedboat there was nothing but some fishing tackle and a lifebuoy. They scrambled over rocks to the mammoth cruiser. There was lots of equipment here but all the rope was terribly heavy.
"That'll be no use for a descent."
"And anyway, we'd never manage to throw it up high enough for the boys to catch it."
They stood on the broad deck in silent despair.
"What about the mooring cables? They're nylon: strong but not too thick or heavy."
"*Good oil*." (Good idea.)

Being well-trained sailors the girls couldn't abandon an unsecured vessel so they took time to re-attach the big craft using the heavy hawsers they'd found inside her.
"Besides," said Kirstin, "If the bandits see things floating off they'll come to find out what's going on. Possums! These whacking ropes are hard to tie up."

Carrying the nylon cords the girls started back along the creek.
"Hang on a sec," said Kirstin. "I'm going to collect the deep-sea fishing rod and line from the speedboat."
"Whatever for?"
"You'll see. Kangas! – Just look at those boys! – outlined against the sky! For Heaven's sake tell them to lie down. We don't want the rebels to look this way and notice movement up there. It might make them wonder what we're up to. I don't know about you but, quite apart from the fear of being

eaten or beaten up, I'm petrified of what they might do to you and me! – and the boys too!" Carol flinched.

Nick and Gerald were waiting for them where the creek passed Prison Pinnacle. Two heads were silhouetted high above, against stars in the temporarily cloudless sky.

"We've got a nice, firm rock here," came Nick's voice. "It's pretty smooth as well, so we should be able to abseil without too much trouble."

"Oke!" answered Kirstin. "Stand back."

Her voice echoed into the abyss and came back garbled. It was creepy. The two blobs vanished as Kirsty took the heavy sinker in her hand, and bounced it up and down a few times to get the feel of its weight, trying to give herself confidence.

"It's going to be horribly difficult to get it right up there," she estimated.

Carol hopped up and down with impatience, till her ankle gave a twinge.

'Get on with it, Kirsty,' she thought. 'We want to get away from this awful place. Those ghastly men might come back to collect us to torture us.'

"Ready?"

"Yes," came two replies, all confused with distorted repetitions and echoes of her own calls.

"Right. Stand well back out of the way. And watch out for the hook."

Her blood froze as booms and gurgles ricocheted about eerily but she swung the rod, oscillated the weight a few times, and sent the lead flying high above her head. Back it clunked, missing Carol by centimetres. That missile could have killed her sister! Angry with shock Kirstin, ordered brusquely:

"Get far away, you *loon* (fool)!"

The next few attempts were equally disastrous, never getting anywhere near to the plateau above. On the fifth throw the line snagged on some of the spiny buttresses. The two still stuck above were becoming more and more jumpy.

"Wish she'd buck up," muttered Gerald. "Who knows when the rebels will take it into their heads to come and get us to do ghastly things to us. I can't bear the thought! Cripes! Those spooky drums are beating really blood-curdling rhythms!"

Nick looked over the index 'finger' and stared at the Bafando men. The wild thrumming and coarse yells made his heart freeze.

"They're really whomping it up! Shooting into the air... The quicker we get away the better. I hate to think what those vandals might do when they're pickled – or even sober!"

"Definitely," agreed Gerald with a shudder.

Kirstin's arms were worn out.

"It's too difficult using the rod," she groaned. "Odd! I thought it would make things easier. But there's not enough room down here to swing it about."

She unreeled a lot of nylon gut and then, ignoring the rod, hurled the weight with all her might. Over the top of the plateau it soared.

"Crikey! Almost went over the other side," exaggerated Gerald. Above the edge his silhouette was no longer clear since a cloud was passing in front of the moon.

"Well done," said Nick. "Hurry now. We want to get well away pronto."

The nylon mooring cord was tied to the fishing line and the boys hauled it up carefully, letting it down a little when the knot caught, and playing it round obstacles. The long rod was useful poking the line out when it stuck in crevices. Once the boys had the rope they were down in no time bringing the cord after them and automatically coiling it neatly.

"Now what? Wish we had our life jackets."

"It's a heck of a long way to swim, so we'd better get started." Nick's cracking voice revealed his tension.

'I hope there're no cross currents between the islands prayed Kirstin inwardly. 'We don't want to be swept sideways and away from the Islands towards the Bafandoland mainland.'

"The water's terribly black," shuddered Carol, "and there're sure to be crocs about, because of the... "

"What about taking the speedboat?"

They all stared at Gerald.

"What a whizzing suggestion!"
"But... "
"Can you drive it?"
"Of course. So can we all. We've all taken over my Dad's speedboat when we've stayed with Granny and Granddad in Mallorca... I bet this one's the same – or very similar."
"Yes, but... "
"It's not as if there were lots of other boats and swimmers to get in the way... "
"Come on. Let's try."
"What about the noise?"
"Just open your ears, will you? Listen to them screaming! Hark at those awful drums! They're making such a racket themselves – they'll never hear a thing."

From the other side of the index promontory came panic-inducing drum rhythms, broken snatches of song, arguments, shouts, shrieks, shots... a regular drunken hubbub. To judge by the din, even if the three hundred or so rebels did hear the speedboat leaving they were in no condition to understand what the engine beat signified.

"We'll punt along the coast a bit, if we can, and start the engine when we're round the other side of the island."
"If we keep the engine ticking very slowly it won't make much noise."

Their promises not to sail or be out on the water after dark were forgotten, and surely did not apply under present circumstances...

"I wish we could collect *Frolic*," said Nick sadly.
"It just wouldn't be sensible to even try."
"No," he acknowledged, sorrow making a huge lump in his throat as he thought of his beloved boat left in the hands of the uncouth crowd. Carol thought miserably of the *Queen Mary* in the same predicament – and the precious Lake Flies.
"At least we've got this speedboat instead. Otherwise it would have been a dreadful squash trying to fit us all and our *takunda* into the poor Enterprise on the way south."
"Yes," agreed Nick, still forlornly

"*Percy*'d have gone under!"

"Or burst at his seams!"

"It would have been downright dangerous too — trying to cross the lake like that. We'd have had to jettison our gear."

"Don't wax too hopeful. The speedboat may not have enough fuel to get us back. Or we may not manage to start her."

That stopped the over-cheerful reaction to their escape off Prison Pinnacle.

They were not able to punt far because the water was deep as soon as they left the creek.

"Double sculling," said Nick quietly in a resigned voice.

Kirstin took the oar that Gerald had been using as a punt pole and went to the stern with Nick. Together they skulled off the transom while Gerald steered and Carol in the bows watched for rocks. All this was tricky but they made it as far as the fifth 'finger' when Gerald groaned:

"I can't last a second longer without a drink."

The others were in the same desperate state. With no bailers the speedboat offered no means of dipping water from the lake and the sides were far too high for bending over to scoop up handfuls of the precious fluid.

"You and Carol go in and wash and drink," said Nick. "Kirstin and I will go on sculling and then help you inboard. Afterwards we'll take our turn."

It was blessed to rub off not only real grime but also the imaginary filth from contact with the foul associations of Kadenzi Island. They drank copiously and felt renewed and brave enough to cautiously start the engine. It fired first go, which surprised them since the rebels' equipment had not appeared well maintained. Keeping the throttle nearly closed they moved slowly off towards Lumbo Island and allowed themselves a smidgen of optimism about the future.

"By the way," said Kirstin who felt sufficiently relaxed now to transmit some news. "This speedboat's name is *Kangi King*. It's painted on her — I mean — *his* bow."

"Gosh! Well spotted. I didn't look for a name."

"And she – I mean *he* – has got the Kangi Lake Police badge on his stern."

"Wow! The Bafando hoodlums must have pinched him. I bet the Lake Police will be glad to have him back!"

Now that they were on the far side of Kadenzi's jagged hill, the noise of boorish revelry was so distant and muted that they could hardly hear it. All round was soft smooth silence of African night. The lake was still, except where it rose and fell in a sort of stroking action; so, although the speedboat was purring quietly, to the anxious four on board it rattled like an amplified machine gun ripping the peace to shreds.

"Can't you tone it down?" snapped Nick. But Gerald was doing his best.

"Spiffy that we've given Prison Pinnacle *the flick*," (left it behind) breathed Kirstin with immense feeling when they had moved some distance. They were still speaking in hushed tones.

"Yes. You said it!" agreed the others.

Carol looked superstitiously round. It didn't do, she felt, to rejoice till they were really safe.

'Who knows what's going to happen?' she thought.

"But we're not even nearly out of danger yet," warned Nick. "It can't be long before dawn and the beasts will probably notice we've gone sometime in the morning – that is, if they don't decide to come to eat us for breakfast."

Gerald consulted his luminous watch face.

"It's only eleven forty two," he said, amazed.

"It feels *very much* later than that," yawned Kirstin. "Are you sure your watch hasn't stopped?"

Caro was almost asleep in the bottom of the boat, her head resting on the coiled nylon mooring ropes that they had brought with them. "For Possum's sakes, let's pick up Ella and get away as fast as we can," she urged.

"But what about *Frolic*? My boat!"

"And the *Queen Mary*!" groaned Carol, remembering her tiny red bubble. "That was going to be Tony's birthday prezzie."

CHAPTER 53

Hazardous undertakings.

"What," asked Gerald tensely, "is that?" His voice trembled as he pointed ahead. The others followed his gaze.
"It's a sail! – I think," gasped Nick in alarm.
"*Percy*!" exclaimed ever-optimistic Kirstin.
"Nonsense! You can't possibly tell from so far away. Besides, Ella couldn't set the sails. Not alone. She's learnt a lot, but... "
"It's probably some rebel dhow or other bandit boat bringing more stores and ammo and fighters to the great carousal."
"Could be. Difficult to tell in this fitful moonlight. And it's so far off. But it does have a bit of the look of old *Percy*."
"Well – It can't be *Percy*. Nell hasn't the first idea of how to rig a boat, let alone of how to sail – and single handed... " said Gerald with a bad case of the jitters.
"She might have absorbed more than she let on during the last few days." Kirstin sounded dubious.

It would really be too bad if they had escaped from Kadenzi only to fall back into the hands of an enemy dhow. The speedboat would leave the mystery vessel standing if it came to a chase but the other craft would report having seen a stranger and sooner or later the powerboat or mock steamer would come out after them. Gerald studied the speedboat's fuel gauge and got no joy. Either it was not working or the tanks were empty.

"Surely Nell wouldn't be so daft as to come out to try and save us all by herself!"
"She doesn't even know where we are!"
"Wailing Wallabies – never mind about Ella. What are *we* going to do, now – this minute? Go and meet that boat and hope it's *Percy* and not a rebel craft – or try to vanish? We've got no sail so they probably haven't spotted us yet."
"But they've probably heard us. Sound travels far over water, especially at night."

"And even if it *is* Percy, maybe he's been captured. Oh Heavens! What's happened to Ella?"

The distant boat must certainly have heard them. The sails came down and the mast, scarcely visible now, began to change course. The four in the speedboat watched in amazement.

Nick broke the incredulous silence.

"That settles it. They can't be guerrillas or they wouldn't be afraid of a speedboat near Kadenzi. After them Gerald! Anyway we can't rush away. We must try to rescue Ella."

"If they're not rebels they may be glad to come in convoy with us to get away from this dangerous region," suggested Kirstin. "The more we have with us the better."

"But I wish we had our life jackets," murmured Carol. "I mean – we don't want to be sailing across the lake without them... "

"We'll get them when we save *Frolic*," said Nick fiercely.

'The louts will have pinched the jackets if we ever *do* rescue her,' thought the others.

'We'll *never* see Nick's boat again,' thought Kirstin. 'If we manage to get away at all – well, we'll just have to sail without life jackets.'

Still going slowly to be as quiet as possible, the speedboat headed towards the pale hull, which was so difficult to see. Clouds would keep floating cross the moon.

"It jolly well *is* Percy," said Carol in awe as they drew closer. *How on earth* had the Enterprise managed to get *here*?

"*Percy* ahoy!" called Nick softly. There was a pause. Then to their utter astonishment they heard Ella's unbelievable, and unbelieving, reply.

"Is that you, Nick?"

"Yes," he called back. His voice held just as much amazement as Nell's had. "We're all here. Hold your course. We're coming to meet you."

As the distance between the two boats gradually dwindled the four escapees held a quick conference so there was no babble of talk as the speedboat drew alongside the dinghy.

"Brilliant effort, El," praised Nick quietly. "Don't talk just now. Kirsty's coming down into *Percy* to help you. We'll give you a tow away from this grisly area and hold an indaba on Lumbo Island. O.K.?"

Carol was already helping Kirstin over the side when they saw that Ella was not alone. There seemed to be two black shapes amidships holding paddles. What on earth was going on?

Zak and Harry were glad to abandon their cramped positions and to transfer, with their backpacks, into *Kangi King*. Kirstin and Ella were left in charge of the now much lighter Enterprise. Then the boats drifted along side by side while two Lake Policemen and five cousins spent several minutes in serious discussion. Low hurried voices exchanged essential news and plans were made – not without some heated disagreement!

"Well! I never thought I'd go back there voluntarily," said Gerald after the arguments ended and they turned back towards Kadenzi, bound for its southernmost inlet (between the eighth and ninth 'fingers'). In response to urgent pleas from ex-prisoners Ella was rummaging in food bundles.

"I don't know why I let you bully me into this," grumbled Zak as the speedboat very slowly towed *Percy* into the creek. "We should all be heading south to safety, not gambling our lives coming back here."

"I'm not leaving without *Frolic*," muttered Nick obstinately.

"And the *Queen Mary*," murmured Carol.

"And the other boats," added Harry who was looking forward to a stack of prize money.

"Are you sure it's safe coming in here?" whispered Ella. She was the only one who had never before been on Kadenzi. They cut the engine and started to paddle.

"Certain," said Nick and Harry together. They had different ulterior motives for not wanting to admit there was any danger.

"We have never, ever, seen this channel in use," Zak assured the worried girl. "We've been studying their habits for two and a half months. They don't know that, of course. We've taken immense pains never to disturb them in any way or to let them guess that they were being watched."

"And as we were taken past – as prisoners – this morning we could easily see that only the first three creeks and the main bay were occupied," added Kirstin. "We spied as much as we could all the time we were captives. Later, on the Pinnacle, we were high up and had a good view of everything."

"Besides," said Gerald. "They're all at the jamboree on the beach. Old Yellow-Face gave them a regular jawing with diagrams held up and even Wobble-Belly, the Commandante, was jumping up and down like a jack-in-the-box saying "Sim!" "Sim!" "Sim!" all the time."

Carol giggled at the picture her cousin had drawn of the obnoxious leader.

"What was Yellow-Face telling them?" asked Zak taking a professional interest.

"Dunno," said Gerr. "Couldn't hear details. Too far away, and the waves were smashing at the bottom of our rock all the time."

"And anyway," Carol pointed out, "they weren't talking any language that we could understand."

"Never mind. We have other means. We'll know all the details tomorrow. Or, at least, *we* won't because our radio's on the blink, but Headquarters will. Tie up to that bush, Harry."

Scarcely inside the creek *Kangi King* was secured with knots that could be rapidly released. *Percy* remained attached behind the speedboat, ready for a quick getaway if necessary. It would be easy to push off and quickly reach deep water well away from the island – so long as *Kangi King* started first go. The four who had starved all day finished the goodies that Ella had excavated from the food packs.

"Mm," said Nick. "I needed that!"

"Jolly good stuff," mumbled Gerald appreciatively through a mouthful of chocolate before crunching into a huge slice of fruitcake.

"Gosh! Was I *hungry*!" agreed Kirstin.

"You're sure you all know what you have to do?" asked Zak wondering why he'd let himself in for this perilous mission? He'd only just met these youngsters. Were they reliable? Was he justified in taking such risks with their lives? He nearly called off the whole exercise, but everyone answered his question with solemn nods.

"Cheerio then. Good luck," he said to Ella and Carol.

Zak and Harry were wearing soft shoes and carrying goggles, snorkels and flippers. Nick, Kirstin and Gerald wore their plastic sandals as usual. They were dressed as they had been when setting off that morning to catch Flies. The men and boys each had a rope over one shoulder looped round his chest and hanging down to his waist on the opposite side.

"I was cursing the clouds earlier – as the girls climbed down that ghastly cliff," said Nick. "But now I'm glad they're there."

"Yes. But it will be tricky crossing the island in the pitchy dark."

"We'll manage."

"Of course. Our eyes'll get used to the gloom."

"Cheerio"

"Good luck!"

"Ripper luck!"

"Push off at the first sign of danger."

Neither Ella nor Carol answered that last order. They would never desert the others. Their job was to stay in the creek with *Percy* and the speedboat, ready to cope with whatever materialised. Everybody else melted into darkness. Neither of them mentioned it but both were glad that the island sloped less precipitously down to the water on this side which meant that the arms of this inlet were not as high and gloomy as those of the other peninsulas. It was less spooky here. In fact the ninth 'finger' was scarcely more than a very low ridge sloping down to a lake-level flattish rock at the tip.

The five on shore crept through bushes and cactus as well as between trees that had been mutilated for firewood.

They could not help making some noise even though they moved as carefully as possible.

"Don't worry," whispered Zak. "They're so certain that this nerve centre of theirs is undetected that they never post sentries. We've been deliberately giving them reason to be grossly overconfident."

Nick thought Zak was too optimistic. He considered telling the Kangalian Captain of the Lake Police about the burbling sentry with the wounded skull and damaged face, who had been on watch earlier in the day.

Zak and Harry led an ultra cautious approach along Kadenzi's stubby fourth 'finger'. (Map on page 324.) From there they reconnoitred both the third and fourth inlets. A sudden rattle made them all jump and fall flat. It turned out to be only a couple of branches rubbing together but Gerald's heart thumped hard for several minutes after that alarm.

"Yoiks! Another boat!" exclaimed Nick in surprise. He pointed to a good-sized fishing launch to their right. "We didn't see round the bend into the fourth creek here, as we came past. We didn't know there was anything more than that rubber duck next door in the third inlet." He indicated a large re-enforced air-filled Zodiac dinghy on their left. It had a plank floor and an outboard motor on the strong wooden transom. The whites of Harry's eyes gleamed in the darkness. They and the palms of his hands were about the only parts of him that showed.

"You'll have to tow," said Nick looking at Kirsty.

"Think you'll manage?" Zak asked the shocked girl who had steeled herself to drive the Zodiac dinghy but not to manage two boats. After a minimal pause she nodded decisively.

"Just help me out of the creek."

They pulled the launch round from the fourth inlet into the third crack where the big, black, rubber dinghy was bobbing quietly. Both boats had been moored with short ropes so Zak unwound the nylon cord that he was carrying. It had done valiant service when the boys had abseiled down from Prison Pinnacle. Now it joined the stern of the launch to the bow of the rubber dinghy. Harry stepped into the Zodiac while Zak and Kirstin climbed into the launch. Zak tried the engine. It was not keen to start. After many attempts they were all jumpy with impatience. They didn't have time to waste like this.

"Shall we reverse the order – use the dinghy to tow the launch?"

At that moment the launch choked and grumbled into life.

"You'll have to be careful not to stall it," Zak told Kirstin. With eyes wide with apprehension she nodded again. What a good thing that her mother's car, on which she was learning to drive, was prone to cutting out on the most meagre of excuses. Even though she couldn't really drive she knew *exactly* how to nurse a temperamental engine.

Slowly the two craft moved out towards the opening between small cliffs that were Kadenzi's third and fifth 'fingers'. Harry and Kirstin fended off with paddles that they'd found in the boats. They were the sort used in native dugouts, with elongated spear-shaped blades and narrow drawn-out tips decorated with carvings of fish and lake animals. Although the beautiful decorations seemed incongruous in the present situation Kirsty was so taken with her paddle that she decided that she would ask to have it as a keepsake – that was, of course, if they made it home... The two boats emerged into open water and crept round the fifth 'finger'.

"All right, now?" asked Zak.

'Have I gone completely mad?' he asked himself – 'expecting this slip of a girl to manage a difficult engine and to tow another boat as well!'

"Yes," said Kirsty taking over. Zak felt that the matter had been swept out of his hands.

An owl hooted but no one paid any attention except for Nick who wondered if watchmen made owl hoots as signals.

"Don't stop till you get there," advised Zak. "If the launch packs up use the dinghy to tow. If it all becomes too difficult abandon the launch."

Blithely he assumed that the rubber duck's engine was in a better state than that of the launch!

"We'll be off then." In his own idiom he added: "May Mlungu be with you!"

He removed his shoes, tied them round his neck, slipped on his flippers and slid overboard. Harry followed suit and they swam gently back round the fifth, fourth and third fingers. There was no point exhausting themselves by racing. They might have to exert a lot of effort in the hours ahead.

Kirstin was on her own! She looked back over her shoulder wondering about crocodiles. Would Zak and Harry be all right? Immediately the launch, as if sensing her lack of concentration, coughed ominously. Hastily she returned all her attention to her awkward charge.

The boys were waiting in the second creek. They had already released the fishing boat, which they had expected to find there, and were pushing it out to the very end of the channel where they planned to re-tie it with slipknots.

"All set," they murmured as the two Kangalian agents joined them. "But… "

The frogmen splashing out of the water didn't hear.

"Well done," they praised as they removed their flippers. "Now for the big one in the first creek, eh?" Then they stared at the boys' prize in amazement.

"By golly! I thought you said it was an ordinary fishing boat."

"This is more of a dhow, I'd say," exclaimed Harry in delight.

"Yes," agreed Nick miserably. "We made a mistake. We only caught a quick glance as we went past this morning and this evening it was too dark to really see it. We thought it was one of those putt-putt things that buzz around the lake from bay to bay – like hippo flies – you know the sort of lake taxi that carries people and their goods from village to village… using a small outboard engine. We couldn't see it from our Prison."

"Well, never mind," comforted Zak. "It's bit big and awkward but… "

"Very fine," grinned Harry. "No complaints! No complaints at all! Good, prize money for us."

"But..." said Gerald for about the fourth time. He'd been trying to get a word in since Zak and Harry had arrived. "As you know we were planning to tow the big powerboat out behind this fishing boat – " He waved at the dhow, " – using this thing's small, quiet engine. But we won't be able to do that. *It hasn't got an engine*! Not even a tiny putt-putt!"

"Oh! My giddy aunt!" groaned Zak. "We'd be demented to start the powerboat's huge thudding machines – not till it's very far away. They'd wake even the drunkest rebel."

"We were depending upon the fishing dhow's small motor to tow the powerboat, but the beast has no engines," repeated Gerald who was furious about the bad luck. He aimed a kick towards the dhow.

"It's got four splendid long oars," said Nick. "Real beauties."

"We can't possibly even hope to row this mammoth round!" moaned Harry. "We'd never make it."

"It'd take a month of Sundays," agreed Zak.

"We *have* to find a way to silently tow the monster that's in the next inlet – the big powerboat." Nick pointed out. "We've *got* to manage somehow... otherwise we can't take it. By the way, the monster's called *Maega*."

"Hm," said Harry into dismayed silence. Then he suggested: "I could walk back and collect the launch from Kirstin, bring it back here and use it to tow the *Maega* round,"

"But you'd have *two* boats to tow: there's the dhow as well as the *Maega*. They're both huge. It'd be almost impossible."

"I'll go with Harry and bring the rubber duck. Then we'll have two tow-ers to pull two boats," offered Nick.

"Why on earth did we send Kirstin off before we had checked this giant?" moaned Harry. He waved a disparaging hand at the dhow as if it was its fault that it had no engine.

"Harry can drag the *Maega* with the rubber duck, and I'll tow the dhow with the launch," Nick enlarged his suggestion tentatively. He dreaded trying to keep the unreliable launch ticking over."

"Bit difficult for the launch," murmured Zak dubiously. "Dhows are such lumbering things unless sailed properly.

They have their own ideas about where they want to go. Better abandon the dhow."

There was another thoughtful pause. Then Zak said:
"Yes – I suppose you'd better fetch the launch, Harry. At least we'll bag the powerboat. H.Q. will be pleased about that. And we don't want to leave the bandits any means with which they might catch us later. But fetching the launch and towing the dhow will take ages. There isn't much time. We *must* be well away before the bombs arrive. I wonder... I still think we should give up the whole exercise and leave with what we've got already... not try to be too greedy..."

Harry was in despair! Leave the big powerboat as well as the dhow!
"And leave *Frolic* to be bombed to bits!" exclaimed Nick in horror.
There was another depressed silence. The owl hooted again and this time they all jumped and looked round, scared.
Nick pulled himself together and stuttered:
"What about... I know it sounds daft – but what about the *Queen Mary*?"
In the moonlight the other three stared at him blankly.
"It'd be quicker than going back through all that undergrowth to fetch one of the other boats – which may not be dependable anyway, and it'd be much quieter too."
Nick outlined the details of his idea.
"Yes," said Zak. "Mm. Yes. It's a good plan. We'll try it."

****

They tied the dhow at the end of the third 'finger' and, getting the horrors as they approached Prison Pinnacle, the boys led a cautious advance on the first creek. That awful spike of rock at the entrance to this inlet conjured ghastly memories, which kept flitting and flashing through their minds. Also – they had to be much more careful here. One or more of the guerrillas could be wandering round to check on the prisoners, or to collect something for Yellow-Face from *Maega*. Stealthily the four crept down towards the big boat.

The stink hit them again. Harry was nearly overcome by the ghastly reek of death.

A nightjar exploded up from under their feet, startling them all badly. On silent wings it zigzagged away, small white squares in its long, trailing tail feathers showed briefly. Then it was gone and Harry heaved a huge sigh.

"Wallabies!" gasped Nick.

"Cripes!" said Gerald.

"Silence!" whispered Zak.

The Aussies' temporary knots holding *Maega* had already worked awry.

"Right," said Zak as he and Harry donned flippers again.

"You're not scared of crocs?" asked Gerald.

"No," snapped Zak tapping an impressive sheath knife on his leg.

"See you soon" said Harry with a flash of white teeth.

Then they vanished into dark waves. Gerald shivered. He didn't like being left in that gruesome gully, and it gave him the creeps to see those dark shapes disappear into gloomy water.

"Mustn't think," said Nick, who felt the same. "Get busy. That's the thing to do." He deliberately avoided noticing the stench.

They studied *Maega*'s controls, and then untied her loose mooring knots and pulled the heavy ropes at bow and stern on board. The boys replaced them with easier-to-manage cords that they had brought. As they punted the powerful machine past Prison Pinnacle the owl hooted again. It was nearer this time. They looked over their shoulders. What an awful eerie wail! Was it a signal? Had they been seen? Or were the hoots blood-curdling howls of dead prisoners?

Bats, which earlier had fluttered round Kirstin and Carol, were still flitting about weirdly. They dropped high-pitched 'clinking' noises that echoed round the dismal chasm.

Moonlight wasn't filtering in here. Sometimes small furry bodies swooped so close to the boys that it was as if the

68. Bats

creatures were curious to investigate human shapes. Gerald remembered horrendous pictures of bat's faces that he'd seen in books. They looked so evil!
"Ugh!" he shivered again.
"They're alright really," said Nick.
"No, they're not! They're ghoulish," declared his cousin in a hollow voice; and then he wished that he hadn't spoken as the words reverberated round the abyss. Was the ghost of that smashed prisoner – and perhaps of others who had crashed on the spikes – were they down here in the channel with the bats? He shuddered yet again and felt hot and cold at the same time.

They reached the limit where their punt poles – the dhow's long paddles in fact – could scarcely touch bottom. Now it was difficult to control the great boat that was being caught by sucking waves. They had to give it all they had to keep the vessel in place: off the rocks but hidden by the index 'finger' and ready to be quickly swung out into open water.

They were very tense. At any moment they expected to hear shots. And if shots were fired they knew what they had to do. They didn't like the idea... but... In the cabin Gerald had found a pistol in its holster. Now he strapped it round his waist.

Fighting the sideways pull of the waves, fending off from spiky cliffs, fearing the sight of a slithering croc, nerves tingling as they anticipated threatening sounds... they waited on tenterhooks.

The pause was particularly painful for Nick. The longer they had to wait the less time there was left in which to rescue *Frolic*. He was frantic to get his beloved dinghy away from Kadenzi Bay where it would be blown out of existence in tomorrow's bombing. It was going to be a desperate attempt and he was all keyed up to fight for his boat – or perhaps die in the effort. If this delay continued, the Kangalian Captain would refuse to have a crack.

'What shall I do then?' he worried. 'Shall I try to elude Zak and creep through the Bafando camp alone, swim out to *Frolic*, cut the line that links her to *Ebony Girl* and try to breast stroke with the rope between my teeth to tow her out of the bay?' He knew he was pipe dreaming. There wasn't a chance of that wild idea succeeding. What *could* he do? His brain was on fire trying to think of how to save his beloved dinghy.

Gerald's fear of what might emerge out of the darkness to attack them kept him silent and on the *qui vive*. Both lads felt that a lifetime had crawled past before Nick thought there was a small object on the water. Was this the attack that they were dreading? He nudged Gerald, and whispered:

"Look!"

CHAPTER 54

A splendid haul.

Scarcely daring to breathe, the boys watched as the shadowy shape approached. Were dangerous rebels creeping up? The 'borrowed' pistol came out of its holster.
"It's a croc!" gasped Gerald.
"May be an otter," whispered less pessimistic Nick.
"It's heading straight for us!" Gerr sounded decidedly scared.
"That's what makes me hope it might be them."
Gerald adjusted his hold on the pistol and looked sceptically at his companion. Nick gazed at the gun with even greater misgivings. He had no faith that his cousin knew how to use it properly.
"It's *got* to be them!" Nick murmured, moving into the bows. He was desperate to get on with their plans. Time was passing.

The mystery object slid into the shadow of cliffs. Suspicious! It vanished, reappeared... bigger now and definitely not looping about like an otter. But what *was* it? Then it was gone again... A submerging croc? Suddenly it was beside the powerboat. Both boys jumped with fright.
"They've got it!" exulted Nick.

There, bobbing merrily beside the tall sides of the once-smart *Maega* was the tiny, ungainly toy, which Carol had snatched from the waves – the little *Queen Mary*. Near it were two dark heads.
"Three cheers!" breathed Nick very quietly but with heartfelt feeling. "Oh! Well done!"
"'Twas easy," said Harry laconically while his superior added:
"They were all so sozzled that they never noticed a thing. Mind you – we didn't exactly advertise our presence. We just cut the rope, and let the little bubble float off as if with the wind. Pulled it fast when we got far out, of course."
"Jolly good!"
"Brilliant!"

Nick didn't waste time. He threw a line from *Maega's* bow down to Harry who attached it to the plastic dinghy. Zak climbed up the powerboat's fixed ladder. Gerald scrambled down into the *Queen* and fitted, as better oars than her own, two paddles, previously taken from the fishing dhow.

"Off you go," Zak urged quietly from *Maega's* deck, and went into the stern with Nick. Gerald rowed as best he could while Harry, using his huge flippers, swam behind *The Queen* and pushed. Zak and Nick sculled from the rear of *Maega*.

The massive craft started slowly – very slowly – to move. Out of the creek she crept. It was a terribly tight fit, especially between two jutting-out boulders! Away from the cliffs and rocks she slid. The two scullers at her stern looked anxiously over their shoulders towards Main Bay. Things there had got out of hand with random shots slapping about among trees, screams and shouts echoing round the cliffs and wild, weird drumming that sent shivers through them all.

The labouring four struggled out of Prison Creek, turned to starboard, and then navigated with difficulty round the second 'finger'. In other circumstances, as they fought to keep their course the antics of the two who were urging on the uncooperative dinghy would have seemed ridiculous, or even comical. The convoy was like a shopping trolley with wonky wheels. At least it didn't have squeaking rowlocks. Apart from a few splashes they were able to press on in silence.

"Harry and I hadn't planned to pinch their boats," panted Zak as he and Nick kept time with their sculling oars. "We couldn't possibly have done it alone." He stopped, temporarily out of breath. But soon he went on:

"With you lot helping we've really got some magnificent prizes. The Kangi government will be pleased – very pleased." Nick grinned happily into the fitful moonlight but felt he had to warn:

"Don't count your chickens, Zak. We're not finished yet. And don't forget *Frolic*. She still has to be saved – and our Flies."

As Nicky saw the Lake Agent make a gesture that seemed to convey hopelessness his heart contracted. No matter what Zak decided he *would* rescue *Frolic*!

They were passing the second creek when Nick thought: 'It's a shame to leave the dhow. It'll waste some time but... '

Aloud he suggested:

"We're just passing the inlet with the dhow. Let's collect it"

"No go," replied the frogman shortly. "Too difficult to tow her."

"We can always try." Nick was at his most persuasive. Although dreadfully torn because he was longing for this section of the manoeuvres to end, so that the attempt to save *Frolic* could begin, nevertheless it seemed wicked not to make any effort to acquire the big fishing vessel.

"Let's tie it to the back of *Maega* and see if we can pull it. After all, we mustn't leave anything on the island for the rebels to get away in... "

There was no reply. Zak was studying the cliffs. 'I should never have let that girl — what's her name? — Christine? Something like that... Kirstin was it? — Such a slip of a thing... ' He was now appreciating the sideways current towards the rocks and was dreading the sight of a pile-up of launch, rubber dinghy and Kirstin (alive perhaps, or maybe dead, mangled on rocks).

"If we find we can't manage the dhow we'll cut her loose," cajoled Nick. "She'll smash on boulders, which will be a pity — but at least she won't be available to the bandits."

That seemed to clinch the matter because Zak gave a non-committal grunt. The boy added a trump to his arguments:

"It will scarcely delay us," he said, trying to persuade himself of this point. "We've already got a rope tied to our stern. Gerald and I can go on, keeping this monster — *Maega* — moving, while you and Harry fetch the dhow."

"Oh — All right," Zak could as yet see no gory accident ahead so he gave in reluctantly. "Mind you don't lose any way. And whatever you do, don't let the powerboat drift inshore. We can't afford to have this damaged, for heavens' sakes!"

"No fear!" agreed Nick.

Zak slipped down the ladder and collected Harry who was as overjoyed to abandon the rubber bubble as he was by the prospect of salvaging the valuable fishing boat after all. The two Kangalians swam towards the cliff where the dhow's massive shape bulked as a darker shadow.

To Nick and Gerald, struggling to keep their huge charge away from the line of breakers as well as floating forwards, it seemed a long time before the dhow appeared almost alongside.
"Throw us the stern sheet," ordered Zak rather crossly. "And pass that oar. It's a nasty, big, cumbersome brute, this thing! Keep sculling!"

Without a word Harry rejoined the *Queen Mary* and resumed pushing. Gerr rowed as well as the toy boat would let him. Nick sculled the *Maega,* and Zak in the stern of the dhow, was wiggling his oar energetically. Surprisingly the convoy got under way without any trouble.
"We'll manage," said Nick to himself.
'What a haul,' thought Harry jubilantly.
"We'll burst!" groaned Gerald. "Why didn't we just leave the stupid old dhow wrecked on the rocks?"
But Zak, working like an automaton was thinking about logistics. Would they be away in time? – Before the bombs were dropped? Had Kirstin managed to get all the way to Kadenzi's pinkie?

It was excruciatingly hard work, and it lasted a painfully long time. But they *had* to get the *Maega* round to congregate with all the rest of their fleet. She was their chief means of escape.

Somewhere off the seventh 'finger', when Gerr and Harry were thinking they'd fallen into a nightmare in which they laboured endlessly and painfully but never got anywhere, as in a daze they became vaguely aware of a shape approaching. It was swathed in a mysterious mist of soft vibrations. Nick had heard something too.

Worried and puffing, he deserted his scull and moved forward along the deck of the powerboat.

He saw a puzzling dark blob moving suspiciously quietly over the water. It was coming towards them! Now what? When at last he recognised the Zodiac, and then Kirstin in its stern, he let out a breath of relief and hurried back to tell Zak what was going on.

"Just thought I'd come to help," said his Australian cousin, putting her vessel's engine into neutral. "Couldn't get the launch started and the speedboat didn't seem a very good idea – too noisy... so I used this."

"Thanks! Thanks a million!" puffed Gerald, gladly passing her the towrope.

"What brought you?" asked Harry.

"Don't lose way," ordered Zak.

"We were worried," explained the brave lass. "You were such ages! We couldn't think what had happened to you."

TOWING ARRANGEMENTS TO ACQUIRE

MAEGA AND THE _DHOW_.

Harry and Gerald with the *QUEEN MARY*

towing

Nick sculling in the back of *MAEGA* (Powerboat)

towing

Zak sculling in the back of the *DHOW*

****

Later they were all towed by Kirstin in the *ZODIAC*.

One cramped sufferer climbed from the plastic bubble into *Maega* and an exhausted swimmer joined Kirstin in the Zodiac. They lifted the source of their tortures – the gallant little *Queen Mary* – up to Nick in the big cruiser.

"I hope the rubber duck's transom can take the strain," said Harry.

Kirsty engaged low gear. Gradually the towrope tightened. Slowly the tandem behind began to move. Nick was at the wheel of *Maega*. Harry and Gerald were stretching arms and legs till it seemed they'd never stop.

"Watch it when we slow down," Zak called to Nick from the bows of the dhow. "Your craft and mine will have lots more momentum than the Zodiac. We don't want either of these monsters to ram into the rubber duck.

"I'll be careful," Nick assured him, and, hoping that the lad would cope, Zak went back to the dhow's enormous tiller.

Up on high, winds were obviously strong because clouds sped across the moon, which was on its way down; but at lake level there was nothing more than a nice breeze. Shadows flitted with the clouds, and the owl still hooted scarily from time to time.

The strange sight that met their eyes as they approached Kadenzi's little 'finger' sent frissons down each of their backs. But each shiver was provoked by their individual ideas about the situation. *Percy* and *Kangi KIng* were in the opening of the creek. Both white hulls gleamed faintly above small splashing waves. The dirty grey launch squatted to one side where Kirstin had tied it between two rocks.

"It's not awfully safe out there," she apologised. "But it's the best I could do. Ella and Carol are standing by with oars to fend off all the boats from the rocks when necessary."

"What a ghastly job!" said Nick.

A meal had been prepared. The girls had even managed to light a fire hidden between boulders, and had boiled up soup and gallons of tea.

"Great!" approved Gerald. Vast quantities of food disappeared in record time. Even remains of 'cobble stone' bread went down with no complaints from anyone.

"Well – Now for the difficult bit. Ready Nick?" said Zak. "Sure you want to come?"

CHAPTER 55

Desperate moves under fire.

"No. I'm scared stiff," Nick admitted. "But I'm jolly well coming just the same."
"Good. I don't think I'll be able to manage on my own; and there'll probably be some firing. If one of us gets shot the other will have to take over."
Zak's ominous words added fuel to Nick's fears. All he could do was nod. The others gazed earnestly at their cousin. Did he *really* have to do this? They wished they could all just go home. But, of course...
"Now, no dilly dallying," Zak told them. "And no noise apart from unavoidable engine sounds."
"Yessir," agreed Harry.
"I rely on you to get this lot of flotsam, and the report, back safely if anything happens to us," went on the senior officer.
"Yessir!"
"Right! Let's get going, Nick."
"See you later – we hope!" said Nick, giving a half wave and half a smile as he and Zak vanished into bushes.

Harry was worried. He couldn't believe that their mad scheme would work. The girls were terrified for Zak and Nick; but Gerald said:
"Aw – they'll be all right!" He was sure that nothing would ever overcome burly Zak, and he didn't appreciate that his cousin and the Kangalian agent would be outnumbered roughly 150 to one by hardened desperadoes.

The group left behind on the rocks strained eyes and ears, but there was nothing to indicate that anyone was moving on the sombre island. Tree frogs were screeching and the owl's ominous hoot echoed hauntingly again.

Used as he was to the African bush, Nick still shivered as fitful moonlight lit Baobabs grotesquely, turning their spiky branches into looming witches with viciously stretching claws.

He pictured the huge python they'd seen on Lumbo

69. Midnight Bush Baby eating a cricket.

Island and wondered how many of its brethren were lying in their way, ready to wind Zak and himself in impossibly muscular coils. But most of all he dreaded a confrontation with the Bafando brutes.

'Strange,' he thought. 'I know I should be quaking – but I'm not. It's terrifying but it's all so exciting.'
He felt, however, that his nerves were stretched to pinging point. Suddenly a blood-curdling shriek, like that of a pig being slaughtered whipped through the trees. The shocking scream made them jump. Zak was jittery. Why had he allowed these youngsters to persuade him into such a harebrained mission? It was fraught with unknowns and blood-drenched possibilities. He looked at the white boy and wondered what he would make of the unearthly howl which had just shattered the night. The murderous screech rebounded horrifically among the trees. But Nick just shuddered.
"That's a lucky one that the bandits didn't get for their cooking pots," he said and went on picking his noiseless way over rough terrain. He always found Bush Babies' dreadful

yells disconcerting, but he knew that it was only cuddly little tree animals that emitted such appalling sounds.

As they approached the index 'finger' the boy dared to breathe a question.

"What's the time?"

Zak opened the cover, which hid the luminous face of his waterproof watch.

"Four thirty-five."

"Gosh! We've done so many scary things all night! I should be exhausted yet I'm not even sleepy!"

"Adrenalin," muttered Zak. "Dawn in about seventy minutes. Get a move on. We don't want to be blasted out of the world when the sun rises."

Although there was a chill in the stinking chasm Nick found he was sweating with revulsion as they climbed down into the grisly creek. They planned to creep from there along to the far end of the 'index finger'. Squeaking bats were even more traumatic now that they were circling to start roosting. The stench of the mutilated human body and eternally grimacing skull engulfed them, making them feel dirty and nauseated. Zak had never seen it but Nick knew all too well what the horror looked like. Thankful to leave that behind, they crept along to the far end of the first promontory, where, bracing themselves, they slipped into the water. My goodness! It was surprisingly cold! Of course, Zak was alright in his wet suit. Nick would have appreciated one himself. He also thought about crocs and wished very much that, like Zak, he had a huge knife on his thigh.

They swam left-about round the end of the pointing finger into Main Bay. Revelry was at last over. The cove was silent in Nature's pre-dawn hush.

'Damn!' thought Zak. 'How maddening that the beasts have stopped carousing. Now one of them may be lying half awake and any movement, however slight, might catch his attention.'

But there was nothing they could do to alter the situation.

As they snorkelled side by side, just under the surface, the experienced frogman watched the boy carefully.

'The youngster's untrained,' he thought. 'He might easily make some mistake that would give us away.'

Man and boy were so tense that it seemed a long swim, but *Frolic* was reached with no one on shore making any sign of having seen them. The dinghy and cruiser were close together with the towing line looping below the water from the stern of the 40-foot vessel to the GP's bow. Then they discovered that *Ebony Girl*'s rope ladder had become twisted round the rail well above their heads. This was a hitch since the deck was very high above them.

"Use *Frolic* as a stepping off platform?" suggested Nick. Zak looked from the dinghy to the closest part of *Ebony Girl*.

"Not high enough to reach that deck," he whispered. "Besides, the less we move about in the boats the less chance that the drunkards will become aware of us. Remember – we don't want to wake the blighters or later they might manage pot shots at the small bomber and kill the pilot."

'And what about the pot shots they might take at *us*?' thought Nick.

"I'll climb the mooring line," decided Zak.

Looking at the slack hawser Nick appreciated how strenuous that would be.

The bows were silhouetted in a position easily visible from the beach so, swimming hard, they slowly pushed the bigger boat till she was pointing away from shore and out towards open water. They hoped it looked as if the boat was swinging in a current. Now the stern was a mere 20m from the beach. Nick held their position as well as he could while the Kangalian officer linked his ankles over the cable and with difficulty hauled himself upwards from the mooring barrel.

Then Nick was in *Frolic,* stealthily making his way past the muddle of lowered mainsail, and Zak was leaning over the dark side of the cruiser murmuring down to him:

"O.K. I've checked the controls. I can start at any time – that is, if she fires first go."

Nick remembered how unreliable the vessel had been when they had been prisoners in her and his heart sank.

Now they had to get the dinghy from the cruiser's stern round to her bows. One end of the towrope was already tied low round the GP's mast. Nick lay on the foredeck hidden below the carelessly dropped jib, and prepared to fend off.

"Ready," he quietly told the man above him. Taking the other end of the rope from *Ebony Girl's* rail Zak gently dragged *Frolic* forwards until he could tie the rope to the cruiser's bow. Then he released the mooring cable and they were set for the dinghy to pull the bigger vessel. Had anyone seen the unaccountable movement of the dinghy? That might raise an alarm. The bay remained quiet.

Still lying flat under loose folds of jib, Nick started careful paddling, and slowly – horribly slowly – the two boats, began to move. He soon felt what a strain this awkward position put upon his back and arm muscles. Without a sound Zak padded aft into the cabin where he opened chests and lockers, searching for something. Finally he picked the lock of a small, narrow wall cupboard and grunted with satisfaction. Meanwhile Nick drove his oar vigorously but quietly. The two boats rippled the water slyly towards the opening of the bay and deep water beyond.

The moon chose this inauspicious moment to blink free from clouds and send a dazzling silver spotlight across the harbour. Nick froze. Caught by a slight breeze the convoy started to swing sideways. Frantically the paddler tried to prevent any veering, but without making obvious and noisy movements he couldn't control the drift, which began to swish the vessels towards the western arm of the bay. They were being swept towards the cliff from which that afternoon the two dreadfully wounded men had been hurled. As they swung further and further round, the zephyr caught greater expanse of boat and had more effect. The sideways slide speeded up. If only the moon were not shining so brightly!

Nick didn't dare to even shift his uncomfortable position. He was now in full view of the beach and movement of any sort would undoubtedly attract attention. Why oh why did the miniature steamer have such high decks? The hull presented such a large area to the wind! Skimming faster and faster she was crabbing rapidly towards rocks and pulling *Frolic* with her.

As he lay, like a fallen statue, dreading the crunch of keel on submerged boulder, longing for a cloud to settle in front of the moon, Nick became aware of a distant throb. In fact it was two vibrations (of Zodiac and speedboat) merging into one pulsing beat. Obeying orders, the fleet on the far side of Kadenzi had managed to get engines going and was moving off. But for the annoying moon, the timing would have been perfect with *Frolic* towing *Ebony Girl* out of danger round the point at precisely the same instant as the flotsam fleet might have disturbed the sozzled louts on the beach by starting to thud away from the rebels' stronghold in the opposite direction.

Unfortunately Zak and Nick were not yet clear of the bay. To the boy's edgy nerves the pounding of remote engines sounded like a school rising bell. The bandits would never sleep through it! Convinced they would all spring up, alert for action, he was glad the others were escaping from this accursed island but, for himself, he felt that the end had come. Either these two boats would smash upon the rocks leaving him and Zak to the merciless rebels or he would be forced to draw attention to himself by paddling.

A couple of shots and all would be over for the two thieves – even, perhaps for the others as well, because, if *Ebony Girl* fell into the guerrillas' hands, the ruffians would be able to rush off after that slowly departing flotilla of extraordinarily assorted craft. With so many small vessels in tow, the flotsam fleet would not be able to speed. Once persuaded to start, the tiny steamer would easily circle round them, picking off his cousins until the bandits had re-captured all the boats.

Nick was simultaneously icy cold, and damp with hot sweat. He longed to act but with a tremendous effort of will he controlled his panic and lay still. He sensed Zak on the deck behind him weighing up conditions.

After what seemed like centuries a large cloud covered the silver disc. Was it still possible for Nick to get the boats out of the bay? They were awfully near the western cliffs. He paddled as hard as he could while trying to make scarcely a sound. A figure rose from the beach. Nick stopped work but the rocks were at hand so he had to resume his efforts. The shape on shore staggered a few metres and stood still. Was the fellow listening to the drumming of the departing fleet? Had he noticed that the boats in the bay had moved and were drifting? ... No – the shadow relieved itself against a tree and collapsed onto painful stones even before it had managed to lurch back to more comfortable sand.

Nick paddled on, opposing the drift with painful muscles. They were almost out of the bay, but close ahead wavelets broke against treacherous rocks. He was fighting an unequal battle. If only he could have sailed *Frolic* out. It would then have been easy – well, less difficult – to tow the cruiser. But they daren't make movements or noise that might wake the men on shore.

Zak was staring over the bows.
"Big jags ahead, under water," he said softly. "You'll never be able to miss them. I'll have to start the motors, damn it!"
They wanted the rebels to be sleeping and unable to take aim at the 'plane when the bomber came over.
"Come aboard, boy."

With mixed feelings Nick back-watered and stopped battling. His arms ached so it was a relief to stow the oar. But now the 'fun and games' would start. Wriggling backwards from under the tumbled jib he tingled with fear of what was to come. Because of his back-paddling *Frolic* had stopped and the cruiser, with more momentum, had overtaken the dinghy. Nick grabbed the rope ladder that Zak threw over the side and climbed quickly to the high deck as the engine fired.

It coughed – and stopped. Zak tried again. The same snorting sound came and then it stalled once more. Nick felt he was suffocating. They *couldn't* have got so far only to be re-captured! 'What did it feel like to be shot?' There were shouts from the beach. Zak swore under his breath, adjusted the diesel-heating coil and, with a desperate yank, attacked the starter for the fourth time.

The choking turned to wheezes. On shore more shouts erupted, but they sounded disorganised. Engine splutters became more regular. It turned over normally. *Ebony Girl* responded. They were under way, weak and shaking with temporarily released tension.

A volley of shots sprayed out from the shore. But the firing was erratic and very wide. Splashes showed white all over the bay. Zak glanced at Nick standing awestruck beside him.

"Get *down*, you fool," he said. "We don't want *both* of us to be hit!" Nick fell to the duckboards and tore cushions from seats to ram them down between himself and the rear starboard side from which the shots were coming. A dreadful heart-stopping crunch wrenched the keel. The rocks! Oh no! Had they holed the cruiser? Would *Ebony Girl* sink? Was *Frolic* damaged? Nick felt the grating slash as if his bones were being scoured and instinctively started to rise.

"Get *down*!" barked Zak.

The little steamer shuddered and went on. Shots spattered like murderous hailstones. Zak looked over his shoulder. A canoe was putting out. Frightened, Nick wondered what was going on as Zak swore again.

"Take over!" he told Nick, and leant over the stern. A more concentrated and exact burst of fire came from the dugout. The Kangalian muttered. Nick's ears popped and his lungs felt as if it they'd done a double somersault as loud explosions from the back of the cruiser told him that, using weapons that he had found in the locked cupboard, Zak was returning the rebels' action. Unlike the enemy who were confused, bleary-eyed and disorientated, Zak took careful aim and each shot told. The canoe swayed unguided. A couple of bodies, draped over its rounded side, upset the balance of the tricky log and it rolled over. Men, who in panic had attempted to stand, were thrown into rocky shallows. Confusion spread as they struggled, tripping and splashing, to escape Zak's lethal shots. A second dugout turned back. Nick rejoiced.

Figures began to run both ways along the beach. Some were heading towards Kadenzi's 'thumb' to cut off the cruiser as she scraped past its tip. But Nick and Zak were almost beyond that now. Shots no longer clattered all round. They splashed into water well behind *Frolic* and *Ebony Girl.* Nick took a second look back. On unsteady feet men were running up the path that led towards the first creek where they expected to find *Maega* and *Kangi King.*

"No good, chums!" he chortled. "The boats are gone. You won't catch us!" Then in a different, alarmed tone he wavered: "Crikey!" as a bullet slammed into the woodwork just beside him.

"Lucky shot from someone who ran faster along the 'thumb' than the others," murmured Zak searching the end of the peninsular with keen eyes. Another shot scratched the top of the cabin.

"Can't see the blighter!" complained Zak; but he fired in the general direction from which the two missiles had come.

They were round the point now, and soon they were out of range of the lone sniper. Zak took the helm so Nick was free to look over the side at *Frolic*. She was bumping along stern first beside the cruiser. It wouldn't do her paint any good but at least they'd rescued her. He exulted that, apart from scraped paint, she'd be all right. But, going backwards, water was spilling over her flat transom. Nick noted frantically that she'd soon be full of water!

Zak steered away from the island. Then he turned south. He switched on the powerful headlamp and beamed it round ahead.

"Can't see them yet." His voice sounded odd. "But I bet they'll spot our light."

As he spoke an answering ray glowed from the southwest. Harry and the others had done their job. They were well clear and waiting hopefully, a strange flotilla of six assorted boats – seven if one included the gallant little *Queen Mary* (who was comfortably aboard the powerboat.)

"You can see to your dinghy now," said Zak, still in that fuzzy voice. Nick looked at him and nearly spoke, but decided that it was urgent to attend to his GP14. He removed the painter from *Ebony Girl's* bow and retied it, as a towrope, to the cruiser's stern. *Frolic* fell behind and turned so that she was progressing forwards. She looked much happier that way round, and with the bows cutting through the water she didn't ship any more liquid. Briefly Nick nipped down to open her self-bailers.

His boat looked bedraggled. Nicky would be glad when he had the chance to stow her sails better; but the main thing now was to join up with the others and to get as far as possible from the doomed island. The sky was lightening and the birds' pre-dawn chorus was well under way. It would not be long before the 'plane arrived with a load of bombs. He had no wish at all to be close to Kadenzi when they dropped!

Briefly Nick felt sorry for the ill-fated men on Kadenzi. Then he remembered all he had heard and read about the appalling atrocities that Bafando bandits had committed. He recalled Prison Pinnacle and the frightful stinking remains of the victim who had died attempting to escape, and the bleached bones of others. He bridled at the foul way the bandits had poked the girls and shuddered to think how that situation would probably have ended had the gurgling sentry not given his inhuman bubbling cry. Nick growled as he recalled the acute pain inflicted on Gerald and Carol. Then he rejoiced that the whole brutish lot were about to be annihilated.

"Can you do something about this?" mumbled Zak switching on the cabin lights. Nick was horrified to see a large sliver of wood sticking out of the dark man's cheek.

"Splinter," remarked the wounded agent briefly, noting Nick's anguished sympathy. "Must've come off the handrail when one of their shots nearly got me. Can you pull it out?"

The prospect of tugging the jagged slice of wood through Zak's cheek turned Nick's stomach. It was all the more frightful because of the way brown skin contrasted with pale raw pink flesh exposed by the jagged wound. A trickle of blood, both running and congealed, fell to Zak's chest. Nick went very white.

"No," he said. "I couldn't. I couldn't possibly. It'd hurt you most dreadfully."

"It'll hurt," agreed the wounded man. "But it has to come out. Has it made a straight cut?" He tried to feel the enormous splinter with one hand and winced.

"Yes. It seems to have gone in more or less cleanly," said Nick.

"Then pull it out," ordered Zak.

Nick shut his eyes, said a quick prayer, and opened them again.

"There's whisky in that gun cupboard," said Zak in his clumsy new voice. "I left it unlocked. Give me a good swig and take a big nip yourself. That's a command."

Nick obeyed, and sneezed. By golly the stuff was fiery!

"Come on now. It must be done. It's damned awkward having a tusk like this getting in the way. Can't even shout at you without the wretched thing digging into my tongue."

That decided the boy. To have that rough chunk of wood constantly lacerating tongue and gums must be agonizing. He studied the splinter, took hold and asked:

"All right?"

"Yes. GET ON WITH IT!"

It came out easily and Nick was almost dizzy with relief. But the wound was really gruesome now and bleeding freely. Zak went back to the wheel and Nick looked round the cabin. A small wall-cabinet marked with a red cross was completely empty. Shocked and furious, Nick's brain could only repeat:

'Not a single bandage, not a drop of antiseptic, no scissors, plaster, gauze, medicines, tablets, drops… or *anything*.' There was not even an empty bottle. Only a spider's web and a dead cockroach with its legs curled upwards in the air, mocked Nick's need.

"No money to keep it stocked," was Zak's laconic comment. "Scissors and everything else swipe-able pinched long since by loyal members of the Bafando Army to buy themselves a blanket or even just a bite to eat. See if you can find a rag or something to mop up the blood. And buck up!"

He surprised Nick by increasing speed. Would *Frolic* stand the buffeting?

"It looks as if our friends are having a spot of trouble in the fleet ahead," said Zak urgently.

TOWING ARRANGEMENTS BEFORE DAWN, WHEN THE FLOTSAM FLEET LEFT THE NINTH FINGER.

Kirstin in *ZODIAC*
    towing
Harry in *MAEGA*

In Kadenzi **Bay**
Nick in *FROLIC*
    towing
Zac in *EBONY GIRL*

Carol and Ella in *PERCY*

Gerald in *KANGI KING*
towing on two separate lines
LAUNCH (no crew)   and   *DHOW* (no crew)

TOWING ARRANGEMENTS LATER, AS EVERYONE LEFT KADENZI

Harry in *MAEGA*
  towing
DHOW (no crew)
  towing
Ella in *LAUNCH*
  towing
Kirstin in *ZODIAC*
  towing
Gerald in *KANGI KING*

Zac in *EBONY GIRL*
  towing
Carol in *PERCY*
  and
Nick in *FROLIC*
  on
separate ropes

CHAPTER 56

Escape into a tsunami.

Harry was out of his comfort zone organising what he thought of as 'a bunch of kids'; but he sent Carol off in *Percy* with Ella crewing. Both of them were yawning prodigiously so he advised them to keep talking – quietly! Gerald, delighted to be in charge of the speedboat, went next with strict instructions to maintain the revs as slow as possible and to make as little noise as he could manage without stalling his energetic machine. He was towing both the engine-less dhow and the temperamental launch, which still refused to start. His instructions were to take his three charges far from the island and then to circle slowly round *Percy* and *Maega*, keeping them in sight. He found it hard watching the Enterprise, which repeatedly disappeared into pre-dawn darkness. Only when the moon emerged and the pale blue sail shone a mysterious azure-silver could the others be sure of Ella and Carol's location. Luckily in spite of her drab grey hull, Gerald could see the big powerboat fairly easily.

Harry was aboard *Maega*, ready to turn on the engines as soon as that became feasible. Her noisy motors would thud into the beautiful African night like kettle drums smashing through singing violins, so Kirstin in the Zodiac towed the giant carefully away from the rebels' island. She felt the responsibility. With the wind broadside on, *Percy* actually made better headway than the rubber dinghy towing such a heavy load.

Although desperate to get shot of the bandits, Ella and Carol were unhappy about leaving Kadenzi. Zak and Nick were still there, engaged upon the most dangerous mission of the whole eventful night. If only Nick had not been so determined to rescue his beloved GP14! They fully understood his love of *Frolic* and would have been heartbroken to know that she had been bombed to smithereens together with the two jars of hard-won Lake Flies, which they hoped were still in her. But it would be the end of the world to lose Nick.

Carol looked over her shoulder. Surely they were well out of rifle shot of Kadenzi now. Couldn't they go head-to-wind and wait for Zak and Nick? Surreptitiously she moved the tiller and sailed further off the wind so that *Percy* would move more slowly. Heading west instead of southwest made her feel she was not moving so far away from her cousin. But she still had the sensation of having deserted companions. It was too terrible when they heard shots. What was going on?

When Harry finally allowed the fleet of assorted boats to pause, they found it difficult to stay head-to-wind and in close proximity so it was a good thing they had only a short time to wait until Zak's headlamp beams told them that the cabin cruiser was on its way. They nearly couldn't believe it. What a relief! Harry replied with a light from *Maega*. They hoped that *Ebony Girl* still had *Frolic* in tow. They prayed that both Nick and Zac were alive.

Jubilantly Gerald, in *Kangi King*, turned and with increased speed, started off to meet the oncoming pair. *Percy* also seemed to veer of his own volition and head the same way! Harry noticed his charges going off 'illegally'. He looked round. All was still shadowy but the sky gave every indication of imminent sunrise. On shore the dawn chorus would be deafening. He appreciated the beauty of his fleet, which appeared to be in a bubble, encompassed within an opal glow that promised colour to come. With daylight at hand his group would not vanish so he shrugged and let Gerald and Carol go. He just hoped they'd stay far enough from the island not to be involved in the bombing. To Kirstin up ahead in the Zodiac Harry called:

"Hold your course. Keep straight on. We're too heavy to play about like them."

So, in fact, was the dhow bumbling along behind *Kangi King*! It was lucky that the speedboat had been going slowly. When he saw the miniature steamer's light and turned towards what he hoped was Zak and Nick, the exultant driver forgot that behind his lively charge, he had two heavy vessels riding more or less side-by-side on adjacent hawsers. He turned to starboard so tightly that their towropes went slack. Launch and dhow lumbered straight on without deviating.

Then, as Gerald continued to circle towards his right, the left hand rope came taut producing a horrid simultaneous jar on the launch and on the *King*. The ebullient steersman was taken aback. What had happened? The launch obediently started to turn in its tower's wake, crossed barely in front of the dhow, missing a collision by mere centimetres, and became horribly entangled in the big fishing vessel's hawser. *Kangi King* shuddered again and coughed as the engine tried to overcome a sudden huge sideways resistance.

Looking back, Gerr was horrified to see a muddle of dhow and launch. Thank goodness he hadn't been speeding – much! He switched off the speedboat's motor with a shaking hand. How much damage had been done by the collision? Were his big charges holed? If they sank would they drag his boat down with them – and him too, if he had to swim for it?

Carol, helming the Enterprise, heard a crunch but noticed nothing until she swivelled round to see what had provoked Nell's starting eyes and dropped jaw. It appeared that Gerald had tangled his three boats into a fine mess!
"Heavens! Oh my goodness!"
Caro went about.
"Hang on, Gerr," she shouted. "We're coming. We'll help unravel things."

Carefully she brought *Percy* alongside the speedboat, but facing in the opposite direction. Gerald untied the launch's painter and handed it to his sister. Carol continued towards the launch. The towrope sank. Luckily it had not jammed anywhere under the dhow and that cumbersome vessel floated free of the jumble.

As *Percy* towed the launch clear, Gerr started his engine with immense caution and the clumsy craft slowly turned and followed. It seemed that no serious damage had been done!

"Phew!" he whistled with a huge sigh of relief. He had been holding his breath ever since the pile-up.

Learning from experience the 'speedboat ace' now took a huge arc and slowed to a gentle halt beside *Percy*. Nell was delighted to hand back the launch's hawser. Sagging below the water it had almost been too heavy for her to keep holding. Her brother was in the process of re-attaching the launch when *Ebony Girl* came within hailing distance.

Zak was cross!

"I told you to get as far away from the island as possible," he shouted across the pre-dawn grey waves. For once Gerald was speechless.

"Yes. Very sorry," he managed. "Just wanted to know if you were both O.K."

"We're fine," answered Zak, holding a gory hand to his wounded cheek and spitting out a gob of blood. "What about you lot?"

"Oh. – We're all O.K. too."

"Thank heaven for that!" exclaimed Nick fervently. Zak's tension eased.

Percy went about and Gerald turned his convoy with incredible care. Then, together, the six boats came up with Kirstin and Harry who were still plugging sedately on in the Zodiac and *Maega*. Both were dying to know details of what had been going on.

"Great work!" Zak called to all his team. "But we must get much further away. The bomb is going to be a biggish horror and there's a stack of ammunition on the island. The blast will be quite something!"

"*And* the waves," said Harry. They'll be huge."

"A tsunami," said Gerr happily, not conscious of what that meant or how colossal the surge would be.

"We must be ready for it," warned Zak.

****

Now that the rebels could do nothing to capture their

fleet, and were unlikely to notice *Maega*'s engines from so far away, the power boat was free to make as much din as she liked. They therefore re-arranged the flotilla. (*Towing diagram on page 392.*) *Maega* towed dhow, launch, rubber dinghy and speedboat, in that order, while *Percy* and *Frolic*, were attached on two lines behind *Ebony Girl*. Nick was glad to be able to sort out the muddle in the GP14. He was delighted to discover the life jackets and Lake Flies still hidden under *Frolic's* bows and then, like Ella and Carol, to lift the boom and two sails into *Maega*. When paddles, whisker pole and preserving jars had followed, the two sailing dinghies were completely empty – except for one navigator apiece to help weather the ordeal soon to come: the expected mammoth waves.

Although without cargo, *Frolic* was carrying something she'd never had before. Nick found a bullet embedded in her mast; and he noticed something was wrong with *Ebony Girl*.
"We'll look into it later," said Zak. "We can't stop now. Got to get clear. At least she's still moving." He asked Ella to hurry into the launch to be ready to fend off when the tsunami came. Kirstin was still in the Zodiac, Gerald in the speedboat, Carol in the Enterprise and Nick in the GP14. Each, looking grim, had an oar or a paddle in readiness. The lack of conversation told its tale of taut nerves and frightened people.

At a gentle pace, so as not to damage the towed dinghies, *Maega* with Harry at her controls, and the mock steamer under Zak's command, moved off through thin greyness that definitely was not night, yet which lacked a few minutes to dawn. Even as Zak chivvied them over tying ropes and hurried them to their posts they knew it was already too late to get far from Kadenzi. The drone of an aeroplane came from the misty-pearl sky. Then, winging up from the southwest, they saw a spec, which turned into a small bomber. By the time it passed – almost overhead – it had lost altitude and was low over the lake, heading straight for

Kadenzi. It veered as if to pass directly over the flotilla.

"Oh no!" exclaimed Nick. "They think we're bandits, getting away!"

"They'll bomb us!" shouted Harry. "Why, for Mlungu's sake, did our radio have to pack up?"

"Show yourselves. Look straight into the cockpit," yelled Zak. In each towed boat the crew was frozen with shock. No one seemed to breathe. But the dreaded bomb wasn't dropped. The pilot had evidently decided to stick strictly to orders.

'There will be time to deal with those boats later,' he thought; so the little aircraft slid away, and resumed its interrupted course.

"Crikey!" whistled Gerald.

"This is IT!" shouted Harry. His voice was high-pitched with the strain of the last few hours. It held fears about the immediate future. Fascinated but frightened, horrified yet triumphant, the seven sailors turned and watched. Would the 'plane save a bomb and come back to blast them – after it had dealt with Kadenzi Island? It was nearly over the island now. Was that the faint sound of shots?

"We woke them! We alerted them! The surprise was not complete," screamed Zak in despair. "Oh my god!"

Two loud 'crumps' burst in quick succession. The aircraft swerved strangely. Then Kadenzi Island rose dramatically out of the lake. It puffed up like a hideous, flaming balloon, getting bigger and bigger every second. A series of vigorous explosions followed swiftly, one after the other, and the rising mass that had been an island disintegrated violently.

Dust and small stones, fragments of trees, huge boulders, and other unidentifiable chunks flew through the air. Here and there a dismembered body was silhouetted against the brilliance of the explosion. Glowing debris scattered and fell from the shining mushroom like misdirected fireworks. Solid rain clattered on and round the boats. Some falling object sliced a great gash in Nick's arm. Ella got an eye full of grit. Glass blew out from several windows on the powerboat. Kirstin's ears were deaf for hours afterwards. The lake lost its pristine clarity and became churned up and muddy. All sorts of flotsam, and weird stuff thrown up from the depths, and debris deposited from the extinguished island, swirled over the surface in unpleasant disorganised eddies. *Maega* and *Ebony Girl* were thrown about madly. The smaller vessels bounced and spun dangerously.

Then came horrendous waves. Huge, monstrous, and overwhelming they rushed down on the little fleet where the cousins, carefully positioned in the various craft, had a hard time balancing their cockleshells and fending each other off. Without the limiting towropes the motion of each individual boat might not have been so alarming. But when one boat was trying to swirl over a crest the vessel behind or ahead, in a gigantic hollow, was dragging it down, tugging it under. And each was twisting its neighbours sideways. The resulting effects were not only dreadful. They were terrifying!

"Puking possums!" shrieked Carol at one stage. Her screech was lost in the all-enveloping din and everyone else was too busy shouting, screaming, and battling to have time to glance her way, or even to hear her! However, the mountainous undulations gradually subsided. They began to stop rushing in all directions at once. Chaos turned into mere disturbance. The fleet had weathered the upheaval but *Percy* and the launch had both capsized. Carol clinging to a rope was half submerged and being dragged, half-laughing and half-crying in relief and shock. Quickly Zak threw a rope ladder over the side of *Ebony Girl* and heaved on the towing cable. As *Percy's* inverted hull bumped alongside, Carol grabbed the ladder and tottered, sopping and bedraggled, onto the cruiser's deck. Zak hawled her over the rail and dashed back to the controls.

'Thank goodness she specialises in grabbing safety lines when she goes into the drink,' thought her relieved sister before immediately turning to yet another urgent matter.

Ella was nowhere to be seen! She had been in the launch behind the dhow, which had no one aboard. Kirstin, who was next in the line, frantically tried to bring the Zodiac close to the upturned boat by hauling desperately on the rope which connected her boat to the launch.

"Oh NO! Oh NO!" she panted repeatedly.

If Nell had been thrown into those waves there was absolutely no telling what might have happened to her.

"Ella!" she screamed. "Ella!"

With incredible bravery Nick leapt off *Frolic* and battled his way through the boiling waters to the inverted launch. Luckily Harry's line of boats was slightly behind Zak's so as Nick battled sideways he had more time to achieve his magnificent effort than if he had only had to swim straight across to the launch. He missed that and ended up near the Zodiac. He was in a bad way when Kirstin yanked him out of the maelstrom and over the side into the rubber duck. She dropped him, choking and puffing tremendously, onto the duckboards and, in a frenzy, went back to pulling her boat up towards Nell. She wasn't helped by Gerald, who, beside himself and in despair, was pulling her backwards as he tried to approach the launch by heaving on the rope that attached *Kangi King* behind Kirstin's bouncing craft.

"Ella!" shrieked Kirstin again as she drew near to the capsized vessel.

"Wait!" yelled Nicky stumbling forward, still panting. "Keep the boats in contact."

All the petrified watchers held their breaths as he managed to crawl onto the launch's barnacled keel. The shells cut his legs but gave him something to grab hold of. Urgently he hammered on the hull. Then he sagged with relief. He had heard a weak response from below.

"She's underneath!" he shouted. Kirstin, being temporarily deaf, understood only because he pointed down and clapped. But how were they to get his cousin out? Was she injured? How much air was trapped below the hull? Was it enough to keep Nell alive?

If he'd realised what he was about to do he would never have mustered the nerve, but, without thinking, Nick ordered Gerald to pass him one of the ropes that had been dropped into *Kangi King*. Telling Kirstin to fasten one end to the Zodiac, he lowered himself into the churning waves and tried to dive under the launch. As he was wearing his life jacket this proved to be impossible so he reappeared, spluttering and gasping terribly, spitting out huge quantities of water. Again he forced himself under, this time clawing his way down the side of the stricken boat. The barnacles tore his hands yet he felt nothing except gratitude for something to latch onto.

Suddenly he bobbed upwards and his face was in darkness BUT IN AIR! He took a huge gulp. It was difficult to see in the obscurity and with water-filled eyes, but after a moment he felt hands clinging to him. Ella! Alive and conscious! Wonderful!

He fastened the rope under her armpits and pushed her under the side of the launch. Her life vest popped her up to the surface where her brother and Kirstin pulled her into the Zodiac. All three were crying and gasping as they turned, hoping to see Nick reappear. But Nicky knew that he might have difficulty reaching help if he burst from under the launch and was swept away from the Zodiac.

Ella had been alright because she had been tied to the rope coming from Kirstin's boat, but he had no such security. He stayed where he was until he felt the Zodiac bumping against the launch's side. Then, hoping for the best, he scrabbled towards the rubber dinghy and was able to catch one of the loops of rope that hung down along its sides. In two ticks he was then in the big 'rubber duck', laughing madly in reaction to his recent terrors.

The waves were still wild echoes of former turmoil. Slowly they ebbed to a mere swell. Now the sailors had time to look back at what had been Kadenzi Island.
"It's gone!" said Carol in a hollow voice. There didn't seem to be anything else to say. The emptiness in her tone reflected the horror and shock that everyone was suffering. Nick thought briefly and sadly about that small, cuddly Bush Baby

with the blood-curdling scream.

"What about the 'plane? Is it coming to bomb us?" yelled Kirstin as the *Queen Mary* was used to collect and ferry them, one by one, from their boats to *Maega* or *Ebony Girl*.

70. The end of Kadenzi

(See it in colour on www.daphne.es)

CHAPTER 57

Airmen in trouble.

"The 'plane's gone down!" bellowed Zak sadly from the cruiser.
"Oh no!"
"Shot, I suppose. If only the blighters on the island had still been asleep they'd never have managed to fire a successful round at all."
"Where did it disappear?"
"Over there." He waved backwards. "A good way beyond Kadenzi."
"We must go and rescue them."
"There won't be anything to save. Not after blasts like those."
"There might be. They may have come down further away than it looks from here."
"Did it crash?" shouted Harry from the powerboat.
"No. It just sort of glided. But it definitely didn't get away. There was smoke streaming from it."
"We *must* go back," urged Nick. "They may be floating about, dreadfully injured... "
"Some of the crocs may have survived," said Carol.
'If so,' thought Kirstin, 'the creatures will be enjoying hundreds of bits of bandit bodies.'

"I'm getting a bit tired of being persuaded into doing things by you lot," grumbled Zak. "And I'm absolutely sick of tying and untying towropes!" he added as he and Gerald set off in the speedboat. Secretly he was glad of a reason to search for the airmen. He'd been about to suggest it himself but he was sure the pilot and navigator must be dead. The rescue mission would fail. Did he have any right to take a youngster into regions where there'd surely be appalling sights?

"How's the petrol?" asked Gerald. After his recent experience he'd for evermore remember to check the fuel.

"The gauge isn't working," he added unhelpfully as Zak peered at the instrument panel.

"Then why ask?" snapped the man. Everybody was tired and reaction was starting to set in. "We'll take a spare can."

He circled to come alongside the dhow. With some difficulty Gerr climbed the primitive fixed 'ladder' on the high side of the empty boat, and handed across a jerry can of fuel.

"I wonder why the dhow – which hasn't got an engine – has a stock of fuel aboard." he said.

"It was probably used as a store," suggested Zak. "Less likely to be accidentally set ablaze than a heap of cans on shore would be."

"Hm," agreed Gerald.

"Isn't it funny?" observed the boy. "The dhow is bowling along behind the powerboat, but because we in *Kangi King* are going at exactly the same speed as all the other boats, I can move from one to the other, and pass things across to you, exactly as if we were both stationary."

"Yes," said Zak, "Relative velocity."

"Ugh?"

"Buck up," said Zak. "If we're going to try to find what's left of those poor devils and then get back to this extraordinary collection of booty that we're taking south we've got to get a move on."

The senior officer was not happy about leaving his command. This 'Flotsam Convoy' was such an unusual set-up. Anything could happen and he wanted to be on hand to cope if necessary. For one thing there were *Percy* and the launch to right and empty. He looked anxiously at the sky. Was bad weather around?

Gerald hopped back into the *King* thinking that it might perhaps have been better if Zak had taken less squeamish Kirstin or Nick with him on this search. He didn't like the sound of Zak's description of what they might find. But it was too late to say anything now. The speedboat's wake made another big curve as this time they turned back towards a few jagged rocks that were all that was left of what had been a large, hand-shaped island. The others waved from the two biggest vessels which were leading the strings of ships.

As Zak and Gerald sped off the sun shot up like a spectacular red gong from behind the range of enormous eastern mountains that were in rebel-held territory. Because they were so far away they showed only as a romantic line of dark silhouettes.

The Flotsam Fleet chugged on but when it was near Lumbo Island it paused. Nick and Kirstin took the Zodiac into the creek where Harry had built the pyramid of *takunda,* and everyone was glad when all their parcels were safely aboard *Maega.* Now they just wanted Gerr and Zak to reappear.

****

In Lawara, the Kangi capital, there was a good deal of concern. The little bomber had reported a strange collection of boats heading south. Were the guerrillas escaping?
"Deal with Kadenzi first," Lawara ordered. "Then go back and investigate that mysterious fleet."
Shortly afterwards the pilot radioed that he was about to go into action. Then had come a surprised exclamation: "They're awake! Much movement on the beach!" His next message was cut short. It might have been a panicky "Bombs away!" or a scream of pain... but Sparks in Lawara couldn't be certain. After that there was nothing. HQ came to the sad conclusion that the rebels had been alerted to expect trouble. It rather looked as if most of them had escaped southwards by water, leaving only a party of crack shots behind. And the marksmen seemed to have scored a bull's eye on the 'plane.

Headquarters were further worried by the lack of contact from Harry and Zak. There had been no response from the Lake Agents for over twenty four hours – nothing in fact since they had reported being about to investigate two extraordinary sailing boats, details of which had seemed incredible enough for their superiors to wonder if, despite their long and efficient service, those two excellent officers had been duped. Whoever heard of *sailing dinghies* venturing up to the islands? And certainly a couple of craft manned only by very young people was a story that top brass considered to be utterly impossible. It all appeared to tie in all too tragically: Zak and Harry had fallen silent; and the bandits had been warned. The extinguishing of the bandit army had failed.

What had the guerrillas been up to? Had they done away with the two agents? Or worse, had the bandits got their hands onto one or both frogmen – and forced information out of them? It was most unlikely that such reliable Kangi agents would speak, but the guerrillas' torture was known to be ghastly. Not only had the two officers recently failed to maintain contact but by now they should have radioed a report on the bombing mission. There was still no news from them or from the bomber's pilot. Lawara decided that the pilot and his navigator were dead, and dreaded what the two frogmen might have suffered.

****

Some time later the five people on the "Flotsam Convoy" were worried. They heard an unexpected drone and saw a distant moving spot in the sky. It was crossing the lake towards the remnants of Kadenzi Island.

"It's not coming from Lawara direction, as the bomber did," said Nick puzzled.

"Possums! Perhaps it's an enemy 'plane!" gasped Kirstin who was with him in *Ebony Girl*. "Kangas! It's scary!"

The machine circled several times over the serrated boulders, which were all that was left of Kadenzi, and then it dipped low over the water.

"Having a look at Zak and Gerald," guessed Ella in the powerboat. "I hope it's not full of enemy soldiers with rifles and bombs at the ready."

"If it's a friendly 'plane the crew may think they're escaping rebels," said Carol. She had been on the point of falling asleep but this new tension shocked her wide-awake.

"The aircraft's got Kangi colours," said Harry in a mystified voice, "but, as you say, it hasn't come from Lawara. Maybe the bandits captured it some time ago."

In the speedboat, at a good distance beyond Kadenzi's remnants, which hid *Kangi King* from the southbound convoy, Zak was also anxious.

"Take the controls," he told Gerald. "I must show my face. If they are our friends they may recognise me and hold their fire. If it's a captured aircraft then we're done for, lad!
Make sure you avoid the big chunks of floating junk."

Giving Gerald no time to panic, he made himself as evident as possible and stared up at the cockpit. Man and boy were very tense as they waited to find out whether the people in the 'plane would attack. The Cesna buzzed round the smashed island and now came directly for them. Zak alternately stood with his arms raised in the "We need help" position and then pointed energetically down into the *King*.

Those in the southbound flotilla, who could not see *Kangi King* or Zak's antics, now observed the dot circle again and finally it changed tactics and came south directly for them.

"At least it didn't shoot up the speedboat," shouted Kirstin from *Ebony Girl* to the others in *Maega*.

Five transfixed people watched the approach with mixed feelings. There was no doubt that the aircraft looked menacing and it was heading straight towards the two large boats, which were leading the convoy. But it had spared *Kangi King* – and that had Kangi colours on its hull...

"I think... Perhaps... " Harry sounded disturbed. There was a tremor in his voice. "Please get onto the cabin roofs and show yourselves," he finished in a rush. So Ella and Carol balanced on the highest spot of the powerboat and Kirstin stood as tall as she could on the top of the cruiser. They all waved with exaggerated enthusiasm and friendliness. Harry took off his hat and glared at the aircraft. He hoped that the pilot was one of his fellow officers and therefore one of his friends, who would recognise him and deduce that the string of boats was not full of escaping bandits. Ella, glancing at him, thought he looked terribly belligerent. Probably that was because he was so scared, but the look wouldn't appease any doubtful pilot.

Evidently the people in the 'plane were not too sure of their own safety. They didn't want a well-directed bullet speeding into their machine. It circled high up beyond rifle range. Finally, either re-assured, or perhaps deciding that they had to investigate closer, the scared airmen, fingers on rifle triggers, came lower and zoomed over the convoy. Nick controlling the cruiser and Harry in charge of the powerboat flinched. Was the fellow going to strafe them? As the girls on the cabin roofs fell flat Ella worried:

'Maybe by lying down we're just giving him bigger targets...' But the 'plane wooshed overhead waggling its flaps. Everyone grasped that it must have friendly intentions and relaxed.

"Phew! They must have recognised me!" Harry let out a deep breath, but the others were stunned speechless. The little aircraft, rose, turned, wiggled its flaps again and headed away towards Lawara.

A long time passed. Muscles ached and eyelids began to droop. But everyone was on the *qui vive* wondering about Gerald and Zak. It wasn't easy but they managed to right *Percy* and the launch, and the sun filled out to a cheery all-pervading gold before *Kangi King* came roaring back to catch up with the fleet. It brought two airmen.

"This is Sammy, the pilot," said Gerald pointing to one of the Kangalians. "And that one's Thomas – the navigator. There they were, bobbing about amongst half the floating island," Gerr exaggerated 'a la Carol'. "Apparently they just glided down to the water, and stepped off a wing into the soup."

"Actually we splashed into almighty waves," corrected Sammy in Kangalian, but Zak translated. "I was sure we'd be overturned. It was totally impossible to launch our inflatable life raft."

The second man's face was red with blood and one ear hung by a thread of skin. He said nothing, and was evidently in much pain. His shoulder had also been shot.

"Our bird was sinking fast. We were terrified that we'd be sucked under with it, and we had to get away from the fire in the engine before the whole thing exploded... so there was nothing for it but to brave the swirling waves and swim away as fast as we could. Thomas had to hold his ear on and he nearly lost it."

Irreverently Gerald wondered whether that meant that Thomas had nearly lost his ear, or had nearly lost his life, or had lost his cool...

"What about all the debris?" asked Kirstin.

"Yes. Well, that was awful! We were constantly very much afraid that sharp pieces would puncture our life jackets and slash us about."

"It was terrifying when we thought the Cesna was going to shoot us up," said Gerr. "Did you see it coming right down very low? Zak thinks that grieving officials in Lawara, having had no message from the bomber, diverted a 'plane that was going from a northern airport to the capital and told it to investigate what had gone wrong."

"You should have seen Zak!" Gerald went on. "He looked as if he had St Vitus' dance, or ants in his pants, or something, as he signalled that we need help for the navigator. Sammy and Thomas stood up to show that they weren't rebels but had just been rescued. We hope HQ will send a helicopter to take them to hospital."

"What about their aircraft?" asked Ella as she and Carol disinfected the airmen's deep cuts and bandaged the lacerated ear into place as well as they could. To everyone's surprise instead of recounting a sad tale of having watched the 'plane sink, Zak and Gerald started to laugh. Even the dark faces of the warplane's erstwhile crew lost their frightened expressions and cracked into smiles.

"What a sight!" chortled Gerr. "You should see it!" He chuckled so much that he had to let Zak finish the story.

"The colossal waves must have extinguished the flames, and then they picked up the 'plane and swept it onto that small rocky lump some distance north of Kadenzi."

"We ourselves were carried right over that islet," said the pilot. "What a fright that gave us! But the bomber got stuck."
"It's sitting there on the rocky lump, like a huge bird on a gi-normous nest," giggled Gerald.
"What will the Fish Eagles make of it," wondered Kirstin.
"They'll think it's drunk," said Zak. "It's squatting there at an awful angle – balancing on a collection of boulders as if they were its eggs." The pair of rescuers laughed again. It really had been a ludicrous sight! They were so relieved to have found the airmen alive and the 'plane salvageable that just now everything and anything seemed a huge joke and perhaps their relief was a little hysterical.

Despite their wounds, bruises and the dangling ear, the pilot and navigator declared themselves to be 'fine' and were very glad of cups of tea. *Ebony Girl,* however, was not in good shape. She was listing dramatically to port.
"Holed one of her buoyancy tanks on those fiendish rocks as we escaped round the 'thumb' promontory, I suppose," said Zak sobering up. Nick remembered the spine-chilling, tearing sounds that had temporarily transfixed him, and shivered.
'If it's only one tank that has been ripped we're lucky,' he thought.

The unpleasant slant to port made the cruiser very uncomfortable but she was still manageable and going reasonably well, though wallowing a lot.
"We'll have to see what develops," said Zak and added optimistically: "I don't expect anything frantic will happen."
However, 'just in case' he positioned Nick and Gerald with a machete and his huge knife so that, should such a dire need arise, they could cut the lines which connected *Frolic* and *Percy* to *Ebony Girl.*
"I'll hate doing it, if it comes to that," said Nick.
"Me too," agreed Gerald, "but it's rather dramatic, isn't it? I wonder how quickly I'll be able to cut through the rope. Do you think we'll be able to jump clear of the sinking steamer in time?"

"What about some *tucker*?" suggested Kirstin.

There was not much food left but they were all hungry. Nick, however, had another idea:
"Let's get everything out of *Ebony Girl* into the powerboat," he said. "We don't want to lose all our stuff and also all that belongs in this tiny steamer if it goes down."
Everyone looked shocked. What an awful thought! But they were all completely exhausted and they really needed breakfast, so *that* was the first priority. They postponed the grand removal till after the meal. Large portions of a strange mixture of foodstuffs were dished out and everyone munched while keeping a cautious eye on the listing boat.

TOWING ARRANGEMENTS BACK TO BABOON BAY on the last day.		
MAEGA towing		EBONY GIRL listing terribly.
DHOW towing	LAUNCH towing	
ZODIAC towing	KANGI KING towing	(*Mentioned on page 420*)
FROLIC	PERCY	

71. Men at Harry's village preparing nets for a fishing trip.

CHAPTER 58

Chugging south.

Half way through breakfast Carol keeled over, fast asleep. Harry picked her up but Kirstin, shuddering over the dirty mattress, wouldn't let him place her on one of the powerboat's bunks till she had covered it with *Percy's* jib. Carol slept so solidly that she never even turned over when, much later, a helicopter rattled noisily past. It circled in the region where Kadenzi Island had been.

"It's probably looking for you and me and the two airmen," said Zak to Gerald. "They don't know that we came over to join this convoy."

Harry operated *Maega*'s light to attract the helicopter pilot's attention and soon the machine was overhead making a hideous din and churning up the water all round. Carol slept on oblivious as it winched up the airmen and then clattered away towards Lawara.

"I wish we could *sail* back," said Nick when the last breakfast crumb and the last drop of tea had vanished. He was still conscientiously clutching his machete.

"Yes, but this is fun too," said Gerald who was sitting beside his potential rope victim. "I think I'll pretend to be chopping off the Wobble-Belly Commandante's head."

"And maybe this way we'll be back in Lawara for Tony's birthday," added Kirsten who was steering *Ebony Girl* while Zak and Harry kindly cleared away the breakfast debris. They said they wanted a change from their usual duties! Ella, rather scared and concentrating hard, was steering the powerboat.

They progressed slowly to avoid straining the towed boats and also because of the condition of the mock steamer. When she had settled to a constant list and they felt that no more water was being shipped Nick and Gerald gave up their vigil. Everyone except for Zak transferred to *Maega* where Harry was in charge. All five cousins then took the chance to sleep soundly all morning.

To everyone's delight, and to Zak and Ella's relief, the convoy was across the lake and some distance due north from Dinosaur Island in time for lunch. Nick and Gerald took over *Maega* and *Ebony Girl* while the others sorted out something to eat. There wasn't much left in the 'larder'.

"Good way of getting out of the commissariat job, eh Nick?" shouted Gerald. His cousin grinned and nodded. After lunch Zak and Harry, who had kept the flotilla on course all morning, took their turn to rest.

"Wake us immediately at the first sign of anything," ordered the senior officer.

"Sure thing," agreed Nick.

It was exciting being in charge of two powerful vessels with various odd boats bobbing along behind. The boys beamed at each other across the intervening stretch of water. Kirstin and Ella were up in *Maega's* bows with the wind blowing through their hair.

"Where will we be tonight?" asked Carol, who was sitting near *Maega's* wheel.

"Dunno," said Nick, holding a straight course. "We'll have to wait and see. If she was alone *Maega* could have been back in Baboon Bay long ago, but we can't go fast with all our 'flotsam' in tow."

"We'd have taken three days in *Percy* and *Frolic*," said Carol.

"Yes. Beating against the wind most of the time."

"Um. It would've been hard work – but good fun."

"I'm glad we got the Lake Flies. They were still safely stowed in *Frolic* when we got her back, you know."

"Yes," said Carol patiently. "That was the first thing you told us when we saw that you'd got *Frolic* all right."

"Oh. Sorry. But I *am* glad we got them; and the life jackets too."

"Yes. We all are. Do you realise, Nick, that it's all because of the Lake Flies that we've had this adventure?"

He looked puzzled so Carol explained:

"In the very first place it was my Dad's joke suggestion that we should catch some Lake Fly specimens for him that made us think of going upon a cruise at all. But for hunting the Flies we'd have happily sailed round close to civilisation – like last year – and never gone very far."

"Yes. That's true," agreed Nick. "After a day or two with the Sampsons' in Baboon Bay, Mother had planned to rent a lake-shore cottage for us all and we'd have made day trips in the boats from there with her and Tony."

Carol pursued her theme: "So – my Dad's idea made us decide to move from cove to cove; and, because you wanted to get into Lake Fly areas, we sailed north out of Baboon Bay instead of going into shallower waters of the south."

"Yes. I suppose that's right."

"Because we saw Lake Flies in the distance we sailed towards them from Lumbo Island instead of turning home."

Nick nodded and said:

"And because we went after that column of insects near Kadenzi Island the rebels saw us and captured us. But at least later that morning the arrival of Lake Fly swarms on Kadenzi saved us from torture or being eaten, or whatever they planned to inflict upon us."

Carol shuddered.

"Yes," she agreed in a tight voice. "The Flies sort of got us into mischief and definitely saved our bacon as well – twice in fact. Gosh! Didn't Gerald and Kirstin pong when they came out of the fog of just-hatched creatures?"

"We all still do rather. Would you like a shower? There's one near the bows. It pumps water up from the lake."

Carol thought it was a splendid idea to get rid of the last vestiges of creepy crawlies and of Pinnacle Prison and of Kadenzi. She reappeared sometime later with clean hair, smelling of soap and wearing clothes that Ella had washed on Lumbo Island.

"Great," she said. "I think I prefer proper sailing on the whole but this sort of luxury is a bit of all right once in a while."

She was not the only person enjoying the motorised voyage. Ella was revelling in it.

"The good thing about night sailing and about having a cabin by day," she told anyone who happened to be listening "is that you don't get sunburnt."

She had taken a bit of a shine to Zak so without any regrets whatsoever, she had abandoned Gerald's pyjamas and was looking very pretty in her own clean shorts and sun top.

After a late tea of miscellaneous leftovers Nell's beam changed to a worried expression.

"Zak," she said anxiously, "we're very short of food. We weren't expecting to feed you big hungry men, you see."

"Hm. And we left our supplies on the island," said Zak.

Kirstin was on the point of asking: "Which island?" but she knew she would get no answer. Zak had made it quite clear that the position of the Lake Security Officers' lair was a secret, which they could not share.

"Harry!" called Zak.

"Sah?" came a happy reply from *Ebony Girl*. For once Harry's impeccable English had lapsed. Like Gerald, Harry exhilarated in the powerful motor vessels. He rejoiced in managing *Maega* and, he even enjoyed persuading *Ebony Girl* along, despite her depressing list. He had been thinking distant thoughts about his home village far away on the northwest coast of the lake and what excitement it would cause if he could arrive up there in the splendid powerboat.

"We need something for supper," Zak told him.

"Aye, aye, Cap'n!" replied the lieutenant grinning broadly. Zak smiled at his enthusiasm. How useful that Harry was a lake man and loved fishing.

"Nick's coming across to relieve you," Zak looked enquiringly at Nick who nodded, and climbed down the ladder on *Maega*'s side.

The *Queen Mary* was coming in useful again. She had ropes connecting her permanently to both leading boats. Now Gerald paid out the line from the *Maega* while Nick and Ella, sitting in the plastic dinghy, pulled themselves across the gap between the two moving vessels. Nick had developed the system because they found that they were always needing to transfer someone or something from one boat to the other. 'It's enormous fun,' he thought, 'sitting in the little *Queen* with the water swooshing past as we move, not only sideways but forwards as well.'

The tiny bubble, looking insignificant beside the high hulls, bounced madly in bow waves from both big boats so Nell clung on as tightly as if she were on a fairground ride. She wasn't sure whether or not she liked this novel but alarming transport. The plastic dinghy bumped against *Ebony Girl*. Nick made the toy fast to the rope ladder, which he then held taut for Ella to climb. He followed. It wasn't an easy manoeuvre with the bottom of the ladder swinging. Sometimes he was far from the ship, hanging over waves. At other moments he was slapped back against the hull with an uncomfortable bump.

Harry handed over the controls and, as Ella paid out rope and Gerald hauled in from *Maega*, he performed Nick's and Ella's journey in reverse and was soon tying the *Queen* to the bottom of *Maega's* rope ladder.

Zak had already established that there was no fishing tackle in the powerboat. The deep-sea rod and line, which had been in the speedboat had been left at the foot of Prison Pinnacle.

"It wouldn't have been of any use to us just now, anyway," consoled Harry. "Not the right type of equipment for the kind of fish we want. Maybe we can use your gear or the other stuff in *Kangi King*."

First, sorting through the cousins' fishing tackle, he shook his head.

"Not very suitable for trolling," he said, but he managed to contrive some sort of line from it. Then he climbed back into the *Queen Mary*.

"Pay out all you've got, Ella," shouted Gerald doing the same with his own line. The *Queen* bobbed further and further back. Holding his rope over the rail Gerald walked to *Maega*'s stern. Kirstin followed as 'backstop.'

"Because," she said, "it would be awful if you let the thing slip and the *Queen*, with Harry in her, got left behind."

Impatiently Gerald pointed out that Harry would not be left behind because Ella was holding the end of the other attachment.

"Anyway," he added, "If we *did* both happen to let go, we'd just tootle round and pick him up again."

"It would be a dreadful palaver and waste of time." declared his cousin still obstinately holding the end of his line.

"Oh well, we're not going to let him loose, so we needn't argue about it. Look! He's already grabbed the *King's* side."

"Oh yes. Good!"

"The *Queen* is going to visit the *King*!" laughed Carol.

Harry worked his way round to the back of the speedboat and climbed aboard with the *Queen Mary's* painter in one hand. Having made this fast he ducked out of sight. When he reappeared he waved happily and let himself down into the plastic dinghy. As Gerald hauled him back to *Maega* Harry's little craft was moving faster than the rest of the fleet and meeting waves caused by the other boats. She bounced about like a ping-pong ball.

"I hope he doesn't make any punctures with the fish hooks," said Caro anxiously.

The fishing expert came aboard with a bundle of gear that he spread on deck. Kirsty and Gerr gave him a hand while Carol was told to "Find something shiny to act as bait."

That was easier said than done, but in the end she had an inspiration. She tied pieces of silver wrapping from their last packet of biscuits round washers "borrowed" from the tool kit. Harry attached these to hooks and soon two adequate lines, and another which was really too short, were streaming out astern.

The lake man showed them the technique and stood by to ensure that catches were landed successfully. Zak, in charge of *Maega,* watched hungrily and soon his hopes were justified. Under his lieutenant's knowledgeable tuition, long before they reached the Dinosaur's snout, the 'fishermen' had hauled out enough silvery treasure for supper.

"That one's *Lyani*," said Harry. "We must have caught him by mistake. Those are *Tamba*. They are usually below the *Lyani*; and most of the rest are *Mchini*. They're rather bony. *Tilapia* – like these – are what people usually eat." The hungry cousins really weren't particular about the names of the fish so, long as they were edible!

Although the Dinosaur's nostrils were again red with the light from impending sunset, the fleet pressed on to reach a cove on the west side of the torso. Inside this tiny bay they had just enough space to secure *Kangi King* and the dhow. The latter already had a huge stone on board for use as an anchor, and the cousins hunted among tumbled boulders to find another for the speedboat. *Ebony Girl* and *Maega* had to be left outside, but were anchored in the lee of a promontory. The remaining four boats (*Frolic, Percy,* Zodiac and launch) were pulled up on the beach.

"Lovely to have so many helpers," said Ella watching as she paused from clattering saucepans. Two men, two boys and two girls more or less lifted the launch, two dinghies and the Zodiac way above the waterline. She remembered how she, Nick and her brother had puffed and strained to haul *Frolic* not nearly so far up the beach at Elephant Island.

Across the water she could see that flat-topped isle where she and the boys had lit the beacon and looked out for Kirsty and Caro. It seemed such a long time ago. She remembered how anxious she'd been and rejoiced that everyone was now all together and, as far as she could foresee, safely on their way home.

'I wish we had some bread for supper and tomorrow's breakfast' she thought. As if by telepathy Kirstin asked Zak:

"Could we whizz off in *Kangi King* to the village and see if we can buy bread and some vegies or fruit?"

"You mean 'cobble stones'" laughed Carol.

Indeed, 'cobble stones' and two pawpaws were all that could be bought, but it was like meeting old friends to bite into those hard lumps of local 'bread'.

72. In 1987 The Rescued Dhow (shown here) was sold to a Kangalian man who made a good living transporting people and *takunda* north and south along the western lakeshore. In this picture it has just unloaded cargo and passengers in a natural harbour. A Kangalian lady is washing her face in the lake.

CHAPTER 59

A strange reunion.

"We must take watches," said Zak. This place isn't big enough for our fleet. We must be prepared to put to 'sea' if bad weather blows up. And anyway – we don't want to be caught unawares as the bandits were."

"Wallabies! No!" Kirstin voiced emphatic agreement for them all. It was difficult to arrange shifts between seven people, but Zak said he'd manage alone so they divided the night into four watches.

In the morning no one had anything more exciting to report on the night's duties than passing hippos, otters, bats, and owls plus various thirsty four-footed visitors. *Ebony Girl* was noticeably lower in the water and her list made it very unpleasant to be in her. They relieved her of towing duties and hoped like mad that she'd make it back to Baboon Bay.

The sailing dinghies were tied behind the Zodiac and *Kangi King,* which were behind the dhow and the launch. With such a long double tail it was advisable to have steersmen in as many of the craft as possible, and for a while, it was amusing to sit in the boats swishing along in the wake of *Maega* without any sails or engines. *(Towing diagram on page 411.)*

When it was their turns to be in *Frolic* and *Percy,* Nicky and Gerr steered close together and, laughing fit to bust, shook hands. It seemed such a strange thing to do because the boys knew that they were being pulled over the water at a good lick, but it was perfectly easy because both dinghies were moving at precisely the same speed. Zak looked back and shook his head.

"Young devils!" he muttered as the boys actually swapped boats. But he said nothing because the towing lines were long enough for such antics to be performed without endangering the convoy.

The Gap was too narrow and bouldery for their assorted fleet and complicated towlines so they had to start by heading back towards the Dinosaur's nostrils. *Ebony Girl* made heavy weather of it but the flotilla managed to get round the snout and turned south towards Baboon Bay. They were all willing the cruiser not to open any more seams and to stay afloat back to harbour; but she was kept away from the rest of the fleet in case she suddenly turned turtle.

"I couldn't bear it if she sank now," said Kirstin, voicing everyone's thought.

"It's very sad being in a craft that's listing so badly," said Zak.

"You'll have to swim very fast to escape if she does go down," said Carol gloomily.

Zak would no longer let anybody except Harry or himself take her helm. They both said the list made him feel as if he had one leg shorter than the other and that being on a slide-y deck was a horrible sensation. They assured the cousins that they were prepared to jump and swim like billy-o if she started to sink. And – if she rolled over... Well – everyone realised that whoever was on her at the time probably wouldn't survive, so that possibility wasn't mentioned, not even when the wind strengthened and conditions became a bit tricky.

In choppy waves it was thrilling passing food or people between the various boats. For a spell, through binoculars, the cousins enjoyed watching Cormorants, Herons, Darters and Fish Eagles, rocks, trees, monkeys and Monitor Lizards. But the sailors were becoming restive. They felt that all this mechanisation made life much too easy. It was a relief to wave madly as the small weekly steamer passed on her way to call at isolated villages further north. Her decks were thickly lined with passengers, goats, bales, bicycles, furniture, bulging sacks, and goodness knew what else.

The Lake Police shot past in their elegant sloop.

"Taking its daily exercise," yelled Nick rather scathingly. "Doesn't achieve much, does it?"

"You'd be surprised," Zak called back darkly from *Ebony Girl*.

They left Dinosaur Island on their starboard quarter just before lunch.

"There's Colander Cove," pointed Ella. Kirstin shivered, remembering how she and Carol had fought against the waves, wind and breakers which had all been determined to smash *Percy* into tiny fragments on those beastly rocks. It had really been a *very* near thing!

Briefly they saw through The Gap into the Double Bay. Looking through binoculars, Gerald spotted the distant village, which was the source of 'cobble stones'. There were the reeds and the patch of water lilies. Presumably the russet Jacana (lily-trotters) on their spindly legs were still stepping delicately from leaf to leaf, with well-spread super-long toes, poking here and there for sustenance. And that Squacco Heron – was that still there, standing superciliously in the shallows, looking so bad tempered? How calm and simple those creatures' lives seemed compared with the adventures and dangers that he had recently been through. Had he enjoyed the exciting events? He thought back over the last few days. Yes. On the whole it had all been hugely stimulating. But he felt hot and cold with fury about some remembered aspects, and shivered with fear at other memories, so he decided to skip recalling less pleasant details.

Then Gerald's binocular view was full of rocks. The Gap vanished and Dinosaur Island again looked like a long peninsular jutting unbroken from the Mainland.

"Nasty currents in and around The Gap," reminisced Nick. The Australian sisters both nodded violently.

In their separate craft they all relaxed over a leisurely lunch dragging hands idly in the water. As they finished, Carol exclaimed:

"Look! There's that funny boulder like an enormous penguin. Wallabies! Do you remember how long it took us to paddle to Colander Cove? I thought we'd never get past that horrid bird-shaped outcrop."

"Goes much quicker this way," shouted Kirstin who was lying back with her feet in the air. When it was his turn to steer

Maega, Gerald was much happier passing the Penguin effortlessly like this than he had been paddling

"But I still prefer sailing," said Nick stoutly. "Shall we cast off and sail on the last bit?"

"*Ripper!*" said Kirstin in delight.

Ella didn't share her cousins' enthusiasm. Looking very attractive and happy, she preferred to stay near Zak and in 'cruise type luxury' as Carol put it; but when the convoy was nearing Baboon Bay the other four climbed into *Frolic* and *Percy,* and cast off the towing lines. For a moment or two it was strange to slow down and watch the bigger boats churn away. Ella and Zak waved from *Maega.*

"See you later," called Harry from *Ebony Girl* who was 'limping' badly.

They waited till the convoy's waves had subsided before raising sails. Then they felt happy to be dependent upon wind again. Although they were beating against it, because it was a feisty breeze they made excellent time, and even felt able to sail round the far side of the island in the mouth of the bay. The baboons barked at them as before.

"This time," decided Caro, "it's a 'welcome back' shout."

Then they were in the shelter of the bluffs and going fast down the long rectangular stretch of water. From the village at the remote end of the western arm, where they had seven evenings previously spotted twinkles of tiny cooking fires, a small one-man dugout emerged and with hard thrusts of the paddle was sent speeding down the shoreline towards the Fisheries Research Depot. Wiston was keeping his promise and hurrying to help them de-rig the dinghies.

But he was not alone on the beach to meet the returning sailors!

"Caramba!" exclaimed Nicky. "There's Mother! What's she doing here?"

"And Tony!" said Carol equally surprised.

"And Dad with Mr Merwamma – and Mr Sampson!" said Kirstin amazed, as three chatting men walked out of the office building. "Whatever's going on?"

"Why on earth are they here?" said Gerald speaking for them all.

"Hello, Uncle Ken. Hello Aunt Maddy," he yelled across the water.

"Hi, Tony! Wotcha, *Ankle biter*!" called Kirsty and Caro.

The grown-ups waved and the small boy's piping

"Hello! Hello! Hurry up!" came to them across the waves.

As they touched the Fishery's beach Aunt Maddy, dreadfully anxious, was asking:

"Where's Ella? *What* have you done with Ella?" She received a barrage of answers:

"Threw her overboard."

"The python ate her because she was peeling better than it was."

"She hitched a lift."

"Got sunburnt to a frazzle and the ashes blew away."

"It was terribly sad," said Carol with a serious face.

Aunt Maddy looked at them very hard.

"She's O.K. – she'll be here in a minute," Nick assured his mother.

Then Gerald went and spoilt it by adding:

"Can't swim as fast as we can sail. Couldn't keep up with us."

"Is Ella al*right?*" persisted his Aunt.

"Yes – yes – she's fine. She'll be here very soon. Don't worry."

The subject was dropped as they greeted Uncle Ken, Mr Sampson, Mr Merwamma and Wiston. Tony didn't wait for niceties. He clambered into *Percy* to join his sisters telling them, all in one breath:

"My friend Mark's got a 'normous HARD plaster on hiz leg and my buffday's coming and I've got *three* cakes. Mrs Sampson made one, and Auntie Maddy made one, and Mummy's going ta make a 'normous whopper. But we've etten all Mrs Sampson's cake - etten it all up - choklet! Commom! Aren't you going to push off and take me for a sail?"

"Let them unload and have a rest first," said his father. Then, as Uncle Ken observed Gerald's magnificent black eye, he added:

"Shouldn't let the boom get you like that, young man! Nasty things booms! Want to watch out for them, you know. Might knock you out!" As he bent to help with the unloading he exclaimed in amazement:

"Where's all your gear?"

Aunt Maddy was just behind.

"What's happened to all your *takunda*?" she asked in spiky tones.

"Etten all up like Tony's cake."

"Gone overboard with Ella."

"Did we *have* any takunda? I don't remember any."

Nicky's mother again looked at them hard and suspiciously. But she knew that they would only be flippant if all was well. She began to ask more questions then decided to keep quiet and not have her leg pulled any more. Events would doubtless provide all the answers in due course.

"I wish I knew why you are all so *clean*," she muttered darkly. "It seems to me there's more to this than meets an egret's eye. Kirstin, how did your forehead get that horrid cut? And why have you got that massive bandage on your arm, Nick? And what are all those *dreadful* scratches on you both?"

"Such a pity you didn't arrive an hour ago," said Mr Sampson. "A most unusual convoy came into harbour."

The cousins exchanged glances. These were not lost on Aunt Maddy.

"Yes. By jingo!" confirmed Uncle Ken. "What a sight! A cabin cruiser, done up like a miniature steamer. Pretty well on her side, she was. Can't think how she managed to make headway."

"You do exaggerate, Dad!" said Carol, herself the greatest of exaggerators.

"What's that? How do you know? Oh – saw it out at 'sea' did you?"

The cousins grinned but said nothing. Aunt Maddy, still suspicious, was staring and trying hard to put two and two together. Nick could almost see her thoughts, like a cloud of Lake Flies, buzzing round inside her head.

Mr Sampson told them how, with the damaged cruiser had come a very large powerboat towing a string of small craft.

"Incredible sight," he finished off. "Never seen anything like it before. All sorts of rumours going round, of course."

"There's more to this than meets the eye," repeated Aunt Maddy noticing the cousins' super-polite reactions to Mr Sampson's story. They didn't seem at all surprised.

"Where *is* Ella. *Where* is your *takunda*? *Why* are you all grinning like Cheshire cats?"

"Why are you here to meet us?" retaliated Kirstin as they pulled the dinghies higher up the beach. "Of course, it's *bonza* (great) to see you, but... "

"There was some American chap, down at the Club in Lawara," said Aunt Maddy, "telling all sorts of dreadful yarns about how he went to rescue a couple of sailing dinghies that had been blown across the lake... "

"Possums! What WHOPPERS!" exploded Kirstin.

"Peeling pythons! When I think how *we* rescued *him*... "

"Just wait till I get my hands on that little red-headed urchin and his stupid questions... "

"So there *was* some truth in the stories!"

"Rubbish!"

"Well – ... "

"Comm*om*," yelled Tony. "Where's my lifejacket?"

Maddy ignored the child and, getting a trifle heated as she remembered how anxious she'd been, she went on, looking at Kirstin and Carol,

"Your mother's sitting by the 'phone in Lawara in case there's an urgent message about you lot. Your dad and I rushed here in my little car to try and get to the truth of the matter. But we needed the Land Rover to get across to the big Double Bay. *Where* have you put the Land Rover keys? We've hunted high and low, but we can't find them *anywhere!* I *told* you not to take them to 'sea' with you." *(Picture of keys on page 36.)*

"You should have looked in the Bolognese sauce."

"In the Bologn... " burst out Uncle Ken.

"Nicholas, will you please be sensible," ordered his mother beginning to be really cross.

"Probably they've sunk to the bottom," said Gerald with a perfectly serious face. "Depends how quickly the stuff froze, of course. But if you unfruz the goo I'm sure we'll be able to fish them out for you."

It was lucky that at that moment a lorry rumbled through the gates and distracted the confused grown-ups from going up in flames of fury. The truck drove almost onto the beach and out tumbled Ella, Harry and Zak. The last was looking fearfully piratical with a splendid dressing over his gashed cheek. It was *much* bigger and more impressive than the bandage that Nell had fixed up for him from the cousins' First Aid kit. A heap of recognisable bundles was in the back of the lorry but Ella had hidden away the *Queen Mary.* That would not appear till Tony's birthday, the day after tomorrow.

"*Ella!*" squealed Aunt Maddy. "Thank *goodness*! Now tell us *exactly* what has been going on."

The eldest of the cousins looked round the group and immediately took in the situation. She was not going to be the one to spoil the fun; so very seriously she changed the subject:

"Aunt Maddy – this is Zak. I can't tell you exactly how it was done but they've just put eleven stitches into his cheek."

Gerald winced. Seeing that Uncle Ken as well as Aunt Maddy was about to go ballistic Ella hurried on.

"Oh – This is Harry.

"Harry, Zak... Perhaps you know Mr Merwamma? This is my Aunt Maddy – Nick's mum – and our uncle Ken, who is Kirstin and Carol's dad. Oh – and Tony... and – er – ..."

"Wiston and Mr Sampson," said Kirstin.

"Aren't you coming for a sail, Caro?" asked the infant tugging at his sister's shorts. "I'm a 'nexcellent sailor, you know. I'm going to catch a *million* Lake Flies for Daddy." He brandished a tiny, toy shrimping net.

Everybody except Nick laughed. He was rummaging in the lorry. The time had come for explanations. His solemn reappearance was a little marred by his mother's squeak:
"My best preserving bottles! How did they get here?"
Ignoring the interruption Nick formally presented his uncle with the two enormous jars.
"Your Lake Flies," he began with a little bow. "You see – It was all because of the Lake Flies… "

73. Lake Flies in Maddy's best preserving jar!

GLOSSARY

Kangi / Middle Eastern / Latin/Greek/ Southern African.	English Version.
Bezan (K)	Watchman.
Brachestegia (L)	A type of bush tree.
Buledi (K)	Bread.
Cichlid (Gr)	Small colourful fish. Each type lives in its own limited area, round one rock say.
Galabiah (ME)	Ankle length gown worn by Arab men.
Hoobrah (ME)	Black garment worn over other clothes by Middle Eastern Muslim women.
Kopje (SA)	Bouldery hillock.
Lyani (K)	A type of lake fish.
Matins (K)	Good Day.
Mchini (K)	A type of lake fish.
Mlungu (K)	A Kangalian deity.
Narchee (SA)	Tangerine.
Putsi (slang)	Easy.
Takunda (K)	Luggage.
Tamba (K)	A type of lake fish.
Tilapia (L)	A type of lake fish.
Voetsak (SA)	Get out of it! GO AWAY!

74. Paddles used on African waters often have pointed ends.
It was one like this (carved with decorative fish and flowers) that Kirstin was able to take home after the adventure.

SAILING TERMS

Bailing	Emptying water out of the boat.
Battens	Thin, strong stiffeners which slide into slots in the sails to keep the sails flat.
Bottle screws	Metal gadgets placed in shrouds. They are twisted to tighten or loosen the shrouds.
Bow	Front of boat.
on a Broad Reach	Sailing when the wind is very much from the side of the boat.
Burgee	Small flag fitted to the top of a mast to show which way the wind is blowing.
Centreboard	Plate which sticks out below the boat. It stops the dinghy going sideways. The plate can be pulled up out of the water to allow the boat to plane (glide) over the waves.
Centreboard casing	Sticks up in the middle of the boat. Holds the centreboard in place.
Cleat	Object that holds the end of a rope.
Daggerboard	Some dinghies have a dagger board instead of a centreboard.
Forestay	Cable from bow to top of mast. Helps to hold the mast in place and provides rig for jib.
Genoa	Large jib, used in light winds.
Going about	Changing direction when tacking.
to Goosewing	Sailing with the jib and mainsail on opposite sides of the boat.
Gunwale	The upper edge of the side of a boat. (Gunwale is pronounced *gunnle.*)
Gybing	Changing direction when wind is coming from behind the boat.
Head to wind	The bow points towards the direction from which the wind is coming.

Heeling	The boat is leaning over sideways.
a Jamming cleat...	holds a rope. It has 'teeth' between which a rope can be 'jammed' – i.e. to stop it running through the cleat.
Jib	Sail in front of the boat. (Usually small.)
Jibsheet	Rope used to control the tightness of the jib.
Mainsail	Sail at the back of the boat (Usually the biggest sail.)
Mainsheet	Rope used to control the tightness of the mainsail.
Rudder	At the stern, controls the way the boat will go.
Self bailers	Valves in the bottom of the boat. When open, if the boat is going fast enough, water in the bottom of the boat is sucked out through them.
Shrouds	Cables that stretch from mast head to deck on each side of the mast. They keep the mast in place.
Spinnaker	Large balloon-like sail that can replace the jib when running, or it's used in addition to the jib.
Stern	Rear of the boat.
Tacking	Sailing in zigzags in order to progress against the wind.
Tender	A small boat, towed behind, or carried in, a bigger craft. Used for transferring crew /items to shore or between boats.
Thwart	Seat or other beam that goes across the boat.
Tiller	A long handle attached to top of the rudder. Used to turn the rudder to port or starboard.
Toe straps	Straps attached to the bottom of the boat. Toes are tucked under them. They enable crew to lean out to balance the boat.
To reach	Sailing with the wind coming partially from the side of the boat.
To run before the wind	Sailing with the wind pushing from astern.
Transom	Back of boat.

Made in the USA
Charleston, SC
21 June 2016